PRAISE FOR BEAR IN THE DRAGON'S SHADOW

"This is a must-read for fans of military thrillers and espionage fiction. Patterson's ability to combine action, strategy, and emotional depth makes this novel a standout in the genre. It's a story that's a movie in the making."
— Carol Thompson, ★★★★★ Readers' Favorite

"Patterson is at home in the shadow world of international espionage and is well versed on our military's tactical response capabilities. Tom Clancy has left us, and Donald E. Patterson has stepped up to take his place as one of America's premier authors."
— K.C. Reinstadler, Author, The Kevin Rhinehardt Mysteries Trilogy

"Donald E. Patterson has a keen sense of timing and tension, and he writes with impressive command of military procedure and international stakes that make for a tightly woven narrative that feels frighteningly possible. *Bear in the Dragon's Shadow* is a smart, edge-of-your-seat thriller that confronts the future of global conflict with chilling clarity."
— K.C. Finn, ★★★★★ Readers' Favorite

"An exciting thriller from start to finish. Patterson does an excellent job weaving suspense, intrigue, and action throughout his first novel. Matt Scales and his team will keep the reader on the edge of their seat. While some may see hints of Jack Carr or Brad Thor, Patterson takes his work to another level."
— Eric Rossler, 21-Year SWAT Veteran

"Donald E. Patterson displays his extensive research on tactical situations and shows a refreshing confidence with technical linguistics, including cybersecurity and the operation of law enforcement organizations. The plot circles constantly, moving fast enough to take your breath away. Patterson knows how to craft an action-packed military thriller that readers will love."
— K.T. Bowes, ★★★★★ Readers' Favorite

"*Bear in the Dragon's Shadow* is a fast-paced and action-packed scenario that pulls back the curtain on international stealth and high-level covert operations that are often masked by feigned diplomatic gestures and media-driven détente."
— Robin Lindsay, Emergency Manager & Author

"Donald E. Patterson's *Bear in the Dragon's Shadow* is a fantastic thriller, with polished writing that brings together a diverse cast of characters and a wild ride around the globe. The integration of multiple agencies—NSA, FBI, even the local sheriff's office—adds realism to the complex and high-stakes mission. Overall, this is a great, action-packed, heart-stopping thriller."
— Asher Syed, ★★★★★ Readers' Favorite

"Patterson hit the mark [ten ring] with this action-packed geopolitical cliffhanger."
— Phil Willis, Sheriff's Lieutenant (Ret.)

BEAR IN THE DRAGON'S SHADOW

Where Deception Meets Strategy

A MATT SCALES THRILLER

By Donald E. Patterson

ISBN (Paperback): 979-8-9986782-0-2
Ebook ISBN (eBook) : 979-8-9986782-1-9

Interior illustrations by Stephanie Patterson
Cover design by Richard Ljoenes
Developmental editing by Matt Henderson-Ellis
Copy and Proof editing by Kenneth Zink
Final manuscript revisions by the author

"The ghosts we carry don't
show up in photographs.
But they shape every mission."

Matt Scales, personal journal

AUTHOR'S NOTE

The events depicted in this novel are fictional, but the threats are not.

As cyberwarfare, misinformation campaigns, and shifting alliances reshape the global balance of power, the line between speculative fiction and strategic forecast grows increasingly thin. This story imagines what might happen if that line is crossed.

Drawing on my background in emergency management and law enforcement, I've built a narrative grounded in realism but carried by imagination. Some locations are based on real places to enhance authenticity, while others, such as secure facilities and staging areas, have been fictionalized for the story. Names and characters are entirely fictional.

Real agencies such as the FBI and DCS appear in this novel; however, their portrayal is fictional and not intended to reflect actual operations, personnel, or internal structures.

Several elements were inspired by conversations with trusted colleagues. Men who have seen the sharp edges of modern conflict and intelligence work. From the credit-card knife to the downing of a drone and the corridors of DCS headquarters, their stories helped shape the fiction.

One early mentor taught me that deception, carefully wielded, can be a weapon as sharp and effective as any blade. That insight, rooted in hard-earned experience, echoes throughout this book.

D. Patterson

CAST OF CHARACTERS

DCS TASK FORCE

- **Matt Scales:** Former DEVGRU operator; now with Defense Clandestine Services (DCS). Tactical lead.
- **April Knight:** Tactical specialist. Recently assigned to the task force.
- **Chin Ho:** Cybersecurity expert and Matt's childhood friend.
- **Chester St. Bernard:** DEVGRU team veteran with a dry sense of humor and strong instincts under fire.
- **Don "Skip" McCoy:** Prior Delta. Irreverent strategist and tech-savvy operative known for sarcasm and precision.
- **Jon Mitchell:** Intelligence analyst with extensive historical knowledge. Assigned to research and support.

ALLIED CONTACTS

- **Dave Johnson:** Western Hemisphere DCS coordinator. Matt Scales's direct supervisor.
- **Ken Jordan:** DCS station chief in Romania. Oversees initial post-operation debriefs.
- **Uncle Ming Ho:** Taiwan-based intelligence contact with personal and professional connections to Chin Ho.
- **Mr. Ho:** Chin's father and a retired intelligence officer. Helps coordinate overseas support.
- **FBI Agent Lucas Decker:** Domestic liaison brought in to assist with the US-based component of the case.

ADVERSARIES

- **Alexei Lebedev:** Ruthless Russian operative. Primary antagonist with deep ties to global chaos.
- **Sergeant Andrei Kuznetsov:** Brutal enforcer working with Lebedev. Ex-military with a shadowy past.
- **Chen Da:** Elusive Chinese strategist.

A glossary of acronyms is included at the end of the book for reference.

PART I

SHADOWS BEFORE DAWN

"The first step in any deception is pretending you have nothing left to hide."

Matt Scales, pre-op briefing note

Chapter 1

Matt Scales's pulse ticked at a steady 120 beats per minute, the optimal rate for combat. He felt no adrenaline. He was focused.

He sat in the front passenger seat of a four-year-old silver Volkswagen transporter van. The duct tape covering the hole in the brown leather barely shielded his left buttock from a spring sticking out of the cushion. The streetlights were too dim to reveal the cracked pavement that made the van jitter as it rolled down the street. As they turned the corner onto Vulytsia Universytetska, they hit a particularly big rut that threw the van into the air and bounced his head into the roof.

Matt gazed out the front window as the apartment complex came into view. The building at 37 University Street wore its years without apology. Its light green facade was faded, and rust-colored streaks crept from beneath the eaves. Paint flaked near the base, blending it into the line of older low-rise structures that ran along both sides of the street. It didn't draw attention, and that was the point.

The location was ideal for a command post. Perched at the corner of a busy intersection, the top floor offered panoramic sight lines in two directions. The wide bay windows gave clear views of both cross streets, perfect for monitoring foot traffic, vehicle movement, and any-one casing the area.

In the driver's seat of the van, Chester Bernard, known simply as "St. Bernard," tapped the steering wheel, his eyes scanning the mirrors. The former DEVGRU operator had a reputation for sensing trouble long before it appeared, and right now, he looked like a man smelling smoke but unable to find the fire.

Behind Matt, Don "Skip" McCoy, a Delta veteran with a keen sense of humor, shifted as his fingers brushed over the .40-caliber MP5SD in his lap.

Next to Skip in the backseat sat Jimmy "One-Shot" Dugan, the Marine Corps sniper who had earned his nickname the hard way, though he rarely spoke about it. "Talking doesn't win wars," he'd say. "Precision shooting does."

Matt adjusted his equipment, giving it one last thorough check be-fore looking around the van at his team. Skip's and St. Bernard's faces were focused and ready. In contrast, One-Shot appeared indifferent, almost bored, his MP5 resting casually across his lap.

"One-Shot, you always look like you're heading to brunch instead of a mission," Matt said. "What's your secret?"

"Less worrying, more doing. You should try it sometime."

Matt shrugged. "One of these days I'm gonna figure out what plan-et you're from."

One-Shot chuckled softly. "Keep dreaming, Scales."

Officially, Matt's team had been labeled "volunteers" by the Ukrainian government, assigned to the Foreign Fighter Unit. Unofficially, they were covert operatives for the US Defense Clandestine Service.

The DCS primarily focused on intelligence gathering, and to-night's mission had emerged from precisely that kind of work. Matt had personally confirmed a crucial lead from an informant: a group of soldiers had arrived at an apartment complex the previous afternoon.

The informant's family lived on the top floor. His father had entered the building to retrieve some belongings and never returned.

Another unit arrived later in the evening.

When Matt showed the informant a binder filled with photographs, the informant immediately pointed to one face, Colonel Alexei Lebedev. Lebedev was among those who'd arrived after dark.

Lebedev was already on DCS's radar as a high-priority target. Matt and his team had been pursuing him for over a year. Intelligence sources indicated Lebedev's superior, Sergei Abdulov, had overseen Russian military operations in Syria years earlier. However, Lebedev himself had been responsible for ordering bombings and chemical weapon attacks on civilians, prompting Interpol to issue a Red Notice for his apprehension. Recent intelligence reports placed Lebedev as a key figure orchestrating the Russian invasion in northern Ukraine.

Lebedev rarely stayed in one place for more than a night. Intelligence suggested he was at the apartment complex for reconnaissance getting firsthand knowledge of the city, learning its rhythms. Based on his past movements, analysts were confident he'd vanish by sunrise.

Protocol dictated waiting for the Ukrainian special forces team to conduct the assault, but the nearest team was at least two hours away. By the time they arrived, Lebedev would be gone.

The right call was to hold and observe.

Matt looked out the van toward the east. The surrounding mountains formed a dark silhouette, just barely visible against the early light. A red-orange glow crept over the peaks. Within minutes, the streets and sidewalks would swell with vehicles and pedestrians. Too many civilians. Too much risk.

He had a window. It was small and risky, but it was there.

His team was professional, each operator bearing a deep history of direct-action missions.

"We're going in," Matt said.

St. Bernard turned and looked at him. "We aren't supposed to—"

Matt cut off St. Bernard. "We're going in fast and quiet."

He laid out the details briefly and efficiently. Each team member nodded silently as he spoke. No further discussion was necessary. They all knew their roles. They were ready.

With the new plan, the Ukrainian special forces team would become a quick response force, although they didn't know that yet.

The van made a right turn onto northbound Cooperative Street, with the apartment building's entrance on the right side. Matt noticed two men standing outside the front door. They were dressed in nondescript clothing, typical of the residents, but the AK-47s they had at their side showed otherwise. The street was empty of pedestrians. A few cars moved up and down the streets. After last night's incident with the informant's father, the residents were avoiding the area.

As the van approached the corner in front of the apartment complex, all humor evaporated. It was showtime.

Matt climbed into the backseat. St Bernard slowed the van and veered right, as if preparing to turn. The team started their tap-up sequence. St. Bernard, who was usually second in the stack, was driving. He would catch up with the team after he parked the van.

One-Shot slid open the side door. The team bolted out before the van stopped. With their second step yet to be taken, Skip fired his MP5, killing the left-hand guard with a single round to the back of the head, and Matt took down the guard to the right of the door before the first guard hit the ground.

As Skip and Matt swept the area outside the front door for other threats, St. Bernard parked the van, jumped out, and slid in behind Skip. The team moved forward with Matt in the number three position and One-Shot taking up the number four position at the rear. Skip saw a guard just inside the front door. As the guard raised a radio to his mouth, Skip double-tapped him on the chest, the subsonic rounds from his MP5 barely audible.

Talking was unnecessary. The team had worked together for four years and could read each other's minds, especially during tactical situations. Dressed in black tactical gear, Matt and One-Shot raced down the hallway to the east stairwell. The plan called for them to reach the top floor within 120 seconds.

They burst into the stairwell. Several lights were broken, making it hard to see clearly. Matt resisted turning on his light, concerned about revealing their position to anyone above. They climbed swiftly yet carefully, weapons ready, their rubber tactical soles scraping softly against the concrete steps. At each landing, they paused for five seconds, listening carefully for any sounds of movement above them. Within two minutes, they reached the top floor. Matt grabbed his radio microphone and double-clicked it twice, signaling their position. He took several deep breaths, slowing his heart rate and preparing for what came next.

Matt knew that back on the ground floor, St. Bernard would have pressed elevator buttons for four floors, including the top one, before slipping quietly into the hallway. Once the elevator doors closed, he'd run swiftly to join Skip, who waited just inside the west stairwell. St. Bernard would tap Skip on the back, signaling readiness, and Skip would double-click his microphone, indicating the start of their ascent to the tenth floor.

After hearing Skip's double clicks, Matt silently counted to fifteen. His hand hovered near the stairwell door. Slowly, carefully, he eased the door open inch by inch, just enough to peer down the hallway. One guard stood near the elevator, perfectly still, his gaze fixed on the closed doors.

One-Shot's single tap on Matt's shoulder signaled his readiness.

The radio crackled in Matt's ear. A triple click. St. Bernard and Skip were at the west stairwell door. Matt clicked his mic three times in reply. Fifteen seconds. The countdown began: fifteen... fourteen... thirteen...

Matt's eyes locked on the guard just as he raised his weapon towards the elevator door. Even under the dim light, Matt could see the serious expression on the guard's face.

Go time. Matt nudged the door open enough to slip through and One-Shot grabbed the edge and held it steady.

Matt slid into the hallway, weapon raised, each step deliberate and smooth. He hugged the right wall. The faint hum of the elevator filled the silence, the sound teasing his nerves as he approached the guard. Around the corner, he trusted St. Bernard and Skip to handle anything that moved.

When Matt was halfway down the hallway, he heard the elevator chime, indicating it had arrived on the tenth floor. He fired two rounds, dropping the guard who was looking at the elevator. Within a second, he heard another body hit the ground.

The four-man team stood outside the entrance of the command post, stacked against the wall. St. Bernard placed a shaped charge on the door. Matt signaled the breach, then averted his gaze from the door to shield his eyes from the explosion. Just before he closed his eyes, he saw a small camera lens mounted above the elevator door, pointing towards the front door of the command post.

The deafening explosion of the door marked the beginning of the assault. Adrenaline surged through Matt's veins. He charged into the room, tucking his MP5 tight against his shoulder, moving to his right, stepping over a broken chair, and sweeping the room for targets in his area of responsibility. Sweat and smoke emanated throughout the room, mingled with the faint odor of scorched fabric from the breaching charge.

He swept right towards the rear bedroom, seeing a guard firing from the doorway. Matt shot him six times before he dropped to the ground. As he was moving towards the rear of the room, Matt saw a man moving towards the bedroom. The man stopped and locked eyes with Matt.

Lebedev. Matt recognized him from the pictures he'd been studying for a year.

Lebedev raised his AK-47 towards Matt and Matt squeezed the trigger of his own firearm just as a guard jumped up between them. Matt's rounds impacted the guard in the chest, but he didn't go down. *Vest*, Matt thought.

Matt aimed at the guard's legs and pelvis and fired. This time, the guard dropped to the floor. Matt put a round in his head. As the guard fell, the bolt on Matt's MP5 locked to the rear. Matt kneeled to reload as One-Shot stood to fire over Matt, but Lebedev fired back. Just as Matt finished his reload, his left shoulder and right leg exploded in pain. He fell backwards, hearing two rounds whistle over his head. He wiggled his left fingers and shifted his left arm. Pain radiated through his shoulder. He willed himself to move as he saw Lebedev disappear into a bedroom.

Matt hobbled to his feet, sweeping the room in front of him for more threats. He heard gunfire to his left but ignored it. St. Bernard and Skip could take of business on their side of the room.

Matt's right leg felt weak, but he pushed through it, moving towards the bedroom door, where he paused. Lebedev had nowhere to go. Matt waited for One-Shot to come up behind him and tap him on the shoulder. But after a few seconds passed without a tap, Matt looked back and saw One-Shot lying on the floor.

Matt pulled a flash-bang from his vest, kicked open the door, and tossed it into the room. Three seconds later, the flash-bang erupted. He felt the familiar concussion rock him, then charged into the room. He swept to his right and then left, expecting to see Lebedev.

But nothing. The room was empty.

Matt moved to the bathroom.

Also empty.

He came out of the bathroom and looked around the empty bedroom, noticing a rope tied to the post of a wooden bed frame, leading out of the window.

Matt ran over to the window and saw Lebedev running down the street. Matt raised his weapon and pointed it at the fleeing man. But just as he was squeezing the trigger, a woman appeared in his sights. He jerked his weapon to the side and looked out the window.

Lebedev was holding the woman in front of his body, blocking Matt's shot. Lebedev pulled the woman around the corner and out of sight.

Then he heard a single shot. The woman's body fell from behind the corner and sprawled on the sidewalk. A small child ran over to the woman.

"Dammit. Bastard," Matt murmured.

"All clear," someone yelled from the other room.

Matt walked back into the main room.

St. Bernard looked at Matt. "Hey Matt, sit down, man, you're hit."

Matt's gaze fixed on Jimmy "One-Shot" Dugan, sprawled on the floor, cradling his MP5 in his right hand. Blood pooling under his head.

"Son of a bitch..." Matt whispered. Then louder. "Radio HQ. Lebedev is westbound on University."

"Sit down, Matt," St. Bernard insisted, placing a hand on his shoulder and guiding him to the ground.

As Matt sat on the floor, he barely registered Skip treating his bullet wounds, patching up his left arm, splinting his leg, and administering a combination of antibiotics and fentanyl. The dose eased his physical pain but did nothing for the anguish gripping him as he stared at One-Shot lying motionless, blood pooling beneath his head.

***

Alexei Lebedev had been reviewing plans for the coordinated attack on Kharkiv, looking at maps on the wall of the area, when his phone rang. The screen displayed no number, just a blank face that made his gut tighten. He answered. The call lasted five seconds. He looked up at the screens monitoring the hallway outside his command post. The guard by the elevator flinched, then crumpled to the ground.

Lebedev swiftly organized his six bodyguards into defensive positions, barking orders with clipped Russian efficiency. They knew the drill. They always knew the drill.

The front door exploded. A shock wave reverberated through the room, plaster dust floating in the air like smoke from an open battlefield.

Lebedev ran toward the rear bedroom. He always had an emergency exit strategy. This time, he had strategically placed a rope anchored to the bed frame near the window and attached a carabiner with a preloaded figure-eight knot to the rope. He had rehearsed every motion in his mind a hundred times. Each knot, each anchor point, was a lifeline, not a detail. To avoid running out of rope and falling, he normally tied a figure-eight knot at the end, but this time, he had measured it to stop two feet above the ground. By doing so, he could pull the rope through the carabiner and free himself, saving a critical five seconds. That could mean the difference between life and death.

A pair of gloves sat on top of the coiled rope, and his belt was already in place. Tactical, always ready. The ten-story drop would hurt his kidneys, but the pain was better than death.

Lebedev turned his head as he walked toward the bedroom and locked eyes with one of the men approaching him. A flash of recognition crossed the attacker's face. Lebedev raised his AK-47. But before he could pull the trigger, one of his bodyguards threw himself into the line of fire. The bodyguard crumpled to the floor. As soon as the path cleared, Lebedev fired a burst of rounds over his shoulder, covering his retreat to the bedroom.

He slammed the door behind him and dropped the rifle. His movements were mechanical, rehearsed. No wasted time, no wasted thought. He connected his belt to the pre-staged figure-eight knot, put on the gloves, and jumped out the window. As soon as he landed, he pulled the rope through the carabiner. He discarded the gloves as he sprinted west towards an alley on University St.

Just before he turned the corner, a mother and child stumbled into his path. As Lebedev moved left to go around her, he glanced back at the open window of the top floor of the apartment complex. A man was up there. His rifle aimed at Lebedev.

Lebedev yanked the woman back, spinning her in front of him as he dragged her around the corner, but she thrashed, slamming her heel down on his instep.

Until he put a single shot in the back of her head.

Her body jolted, then went limp.

He let go. She collapsed onto the pavement with her arm and part of her torso visible just beyond the edge of the alley. It was just enough for the man in the window to see her.

Lebedev ran down the alley. Each step was a countdown, each turned corner a minor victory. He had a car parked two blocks away in a garage for just such an occasion. Contingencies within contingencies. Always the escape artist.

He reached the garage, started the car, and headed out of town. The city blurred into a maze of streets. His primary concern was getting out of Kharkiv and covering the nineteen miles to a remote farmhouse just inside the Russian border. After twenty-five minutes of focused driving, he arrived.

***

Lebedev had never been to the farmhouse, but he had memorized its location from maps. He vividly recalled the satellite image: the road's curve, the cluster of trees on its eastern edge. The farmhouse had been outfitted to serve as a field command post during the "special military exercise." The farmhouse blended perfectly into the landscape. It looked mundane and ordinary to the point of invisibility. One of a thousand scattered across the Russian countryside.

As Lebedev pulled into the driveway, a man stepped onto the porch cradling an AK-47. His stance was casual but alert. Lebedev recognized him as part of a Spetsnaz unit assigned to recon the area for the invasion. The cameras and motion detectors must have warned him of Lebedev's approach.

"Why are you here?" Sergeant Kuznetsov demanded.

Lebedev's voice was steady, controlled. "The Kharkiv location was attacked by a four-man assault team. They were good. They took out the four guards stationed outside and my six bodyguards."

Sergeant Kuznetsov looked suspiciously at Lebedev. "Were they just lucky, or were we betrayed?"

"I don't know. I arrived less than twelve hours ago."

"Come with me," Kuznetsov said. "We must quickly reach the command post. It is unsafe to remain in this building."

Lebedev's brow wrinkled. "I thought this was the command post."

Kuznetsov ignored him and led Lebedev to a trapdoor in the farmhouse's corner. The hinges groaned as he swung it open, revealing a dark, narrow entrance. The smell of damp earth rose to meet them.

"Where does this lead?" Lebedev asked.

"It's an escape tunnel to the command post," Kuznetsov answered as he descended a wooden ladder with a flashlight in hand.

Lebedev hesitated, staring into the darkness. He hated tunnels. Always had. They felt alive and hungry. As he followed Kuznetsov down into the darkness, he gripped the rungs of the ladder as if his life depended on it.

The temperature plummeted within a few steps. Kuznetsov led the way, the flashlight's beam bouncing off the rough walls. After fifty yards, the tunnel took a sharp turn to the left, then another to the right, further on. Lebedev noticed the pattern but dismissed it, focusing instead on the narrow path ahead. The twists felt intentional, as if the tunnel itself were hiding its secrets.

He forced himself to take several deep breaths, exhaling to steady his nerves. His breathing echoed in the confined space. Step-by-step, he moved forward, determined to ignore the creeping tension that tightened his chest.

After five minutes, they entered a large room. The increased space made it easier to breathe, but his heart was still pounding.

"We are here, and safe," Kuznetsov proclaimed. "No prying eyes or eavesdropping devices can detect us."

Kuznetsov started a small generator in the room's corner, which caused a single dim bulb to light up. It cast long shadows across the space. In the middle of the room was a 10'x10' table covered in maps, a computer, and scattered documents.

Lebedev wasn't impressed. "Why wasn't I told about this?"

"We didn't purposely keep it from you," Kuznetsov replied. "We didn't have time to brief you before you left on your current mission. This tunnel has been around for centuries. We reinforced it during the planning stage and added an air vent for the generator. We also added an escape hatch to the surface."

***

Three thousand feet above the city of Kharkiv, a stealthy Bayraktar TB2 drone had been gliding silently in a figure-eight pattern. Equipped with a high-resolution camera and armed with two laser-guided MAM-L missiles, it steadily tracked the movements of Matt's team.

When Lebedev escaped from the apartment complex, the drone followed his movements and tracked him to the farmhouse. The drone's camera recorded the person coming out the front door. The drone operator took still pictures and sent them to an analyst at the Ukrainian Intelligence Command Center.

Within minutes, the analyst confirmed the person who'd gotten out of the car was Alexei Lebedev. The analyst sent the confirmation to Colonel Artem Bondarenko of the Ukrainian Army. Bondarenko was the commander of the flight operations unit that controlled the drone.

Bondarenko gritted his teeth. He knew the face well. Alexei Lebedev. He was one of Russia's most dangerous operatives. The Red Notice issued by Interpol had made his name infamous. Bondarenko didn't need to be told what Lebedev's survival could mean for Kharkiv.

"The farmhouse is just over the border," the analyst said. "Inside Russia."

Bondarenko frowned, his gaze shifting to the map on the table. "How confident are we in this intelligence?"

"One hundred percent, Colonel. He arrived less than ten minutes ago, and he's still there."

Bondarenko's hand hovered over the map. His mind was racing through the implications of what he was going to do next. The farmhouse was well within range of the drone's Hellfire missiles. But an attack inside Russian territory could escalate the conflict in ways nobody could predict.

The room was silent, save for the faint hum of the drone's feed.

Bondarenko straightened. "Prepare to fire."

The drone operator hesitated. "Sir, the border..."

"Do it," Bondarenko snapped. His expression reflected the weight of the decision. "We cannot let him escape again."

The operator's fingers hovered over the controls.

With a click, the missile launched.

Bondarenko watched the feed as the missile descended, the camera fixed on its target.

Seconds later, the farmhouse erupted in a fiery explosion. The structure crumbled in on itself, a plume of smoke rising into the sky.

"Target eliminated," the operator stated.

Bondarenko didn't respond. His gaze stayed fixed on the screen, watching the flames consume the remnants of the farmhouse.

***

The blast echoed through the winding tunnel, its force dissipating with each turn until it faded to silence. At the tunnel entrance to the command post, Sergeant Kuznetsov glanced back, grim satisfaction etched on his face.

"Smart design," Lebedev muttered, His eyes narrowed as he examined the reinforced structure around him.

"Somehow they followed you," Kuznetsov remarked with edged with faint condescension.

Lebedev ignored the jab. "Yes, somehow they did. But now we hold the advantage. They believe I'm dead, and that assumption will hasten their downfall."

While Lebedev was still processing their narrow escape, the frantic evacuation from the apartment, the tense journey through the darkened passageway, and the explosion they'd barely survived, a drone circled silently above the farmhouse. It transmitted real-time images of smoke and rubble to waiting analysts.

***

Matt had just emerged from surgery at the military hospital in Kyiv, Ukraine, now sitting on his bed when Colonel Bondarenko came into his room.

"The surgeons tell me you will make a full recovery."

"Well, I've been in worse shape," Matt said. "But that was when I was a lot younger."

Colonel Bondarenko opened a laptop. "We tracked Lebedev to a farmhouse. I ordered a drone strike. Only ten minutes passed from the time of the criminal Lebedev's arrival, to the missile impact. I will show you that part of the video."

Matt looked at the footage of that started when Lebedev drove up to the farmhouse. He couldn't make out the person Lebedev had met on the front porch, but he carried himself like a military operator.

The video showed the Hellfire missile being launched from the drone. A few seconds later, the farmhouse erupted in a tremendous explosion.

"Our analysts concluded that no one could have survived. Alexei Lebedev is dead," Colonel Bondarenko said.

"Did you get on-the-ground confirmation and DNA samples to confirm the deaths?" Matt asked.

"The video speaks for itself," Colonel Bondarenko said with irritation in his voice.

"What did the team find when they arrived at the location? Did they find any evidence of the bodies?"

"We did not send a team to the location. It is inside Russia. Justifying hitting the target inside Russia will be difficult enough, let alone sending our special operations troops there. We need them on the front lines."

"And how can you be certain of Lebedev's death? Without bodies, there is no way to be certain."

"Alexei Lebedev is dead. We consider this matter closed."

Matt stared at Colonel Bondarenko. He wanted positive confirmation. The responsibility for the mission's outcome rested solely on him. That included One-Shot's death and the escape of Alexei Lebedev. For now, he would have to accept the evidence in the video, but his twenty years in special operations and clandestine services had taught him that until there was visual confirmation and DNA evidence, the matter was anything but settled.

***

After the Hellfire missile hit the farmhouse, Sergeant Kuznetsov looked at Lebedev. "I don't think there will be any ground forces in the area, but we cannot take the chance. Come with me. We need to get out of here now."

Sergeant Kuznetsov led Lebedev to a vertical shaft with a ladder that led to the surface. As they emerged from the tunnel, Lebedev took a deep breath. His heart rate slowed, and the tension in his body lessened as the memory of the tunnel now faded behind him.

They sprinted and stayed under a canopy of trees on a small game path for half a mile. As they emerged from the path into a modest clearing, Lebedev saw a shed, just large enough for a tractor.

Inside the shed was a five-year-old beige Lada Granta sedan. Sergeant Kuznetsov climbed into the driver's seat and Lebedev took the passenger seat.

As the Lada Granta started, a cough of black smoke spurted from the tailpipe, and the engine ran a little rough. It had seen better days, but it was a perfect vehicle to help them blend into the countryside and not call attention to themselves. Sergeant Kuznetsov drove the sedan out of the shed and onto a dirt road. Within ten minutes they were on a paved road and headed towards a field command post where the Russian Army had staged itself for the military exercise.

When they arrived, Lebedev identified himself to the post commander and demanded a helicopter to take him back to Moscow. Once he arrived in Moscow, Lebedev headed straight to the office of the Russian Ministry of Energy.

***

Ken Jordan had been monitoring the radio traffic from Kharkiv when Matt called. As the supervising officer for all DCS operations in Europe, Ken had been waiting for this update.

"Matt, how's your team?"

"We lost One-Shot. The rest of the team is fine, but I'm a little messed up," Matt replied.

There was a moment of silence before Ken spoke. "Yeah, I heard you took a round or two."

"I did. One went through my left shoulder. A through-and-through, just under the clavicle. Another one to my right fibula. Just nicked it and gave me a hairline fracture."

Matt exhaled, letting the words sit there, as if the injuries were the worst of it. But they weren't. Not by a long shot.

"The Ukrainian special forces team arrived about forty-five minutes after we secured the command post. They weren't too happy that we didn't wait for them. Took over the scene and demanded we return to Kyiv. They had a Westland Lynx helo. Fastest in the business. Got us to Kyiv in just over an hour. Medics were waiting when we landed."

A beat passed before Ken responded. "And Lebedev?"

Matt closed his eyes. "I had him in my sights. Finger on the trigger. A woman and her kid came around the corner... He used her as cover."

Silence.

"He killed her. He didn't have to." Matt swallowed. "I saw her body fall. It was like..."

"It wasn't your fault, Matt."

Matt gave a dry chuckle. "Yeah? Try telling her kid that."

The silence stretched before Ken's tone turned firm. "You and your team need to get your asses out of Ukraine. Now."

Matt didn't respond. He knew what was coming.

"You initiated the assault without authorization. That makes this whole thing a goddamn mess. The Ukrainians are pissed, the brass is pissed, and the last thing anyone wants is a firefight between DCS and Russian-backed units on the front page of The Washington Post." Ken sighed. "You're persona non grata, Matt. I've arranged for the spec ops team who flew you to Kyiv to get you down here."

"Down here" meant Mihail Kogălniceanu Air Base, Romania. US forces had been stationed there for years, but it was more than just a military outpost. The CIA had run a black site there since 2005.

Renditions. Interrogations. When Russia invaded Ukraine, DCS needed a discreet base for intel ops. Mihail Kogălniceanu was perfect.

***

Three days blurred together as Matt, St. Bernard, and Skip settled into the DCS office at Mihail Kogălniceanu. Debriefings with Ken Jordan and the intel team dragged on endlessly, punctuated only by hospital visits that weren't much better. After three days of questioning and medical evaluations, all Matt wanted was to leave.

Skip leaned against the doorframe of Matt's hospital room, arms crossed, wearing his usual smirk. "We fly you halfway across the world, and you check yourself into a clinic! That's one way to dodge paperwork."

Matt didn't look up. "Without me, who's going to keep you two from getting arrested?"

St. Bernard pulled up a chair. "Please. Last time you were laid out, we dragged you through three countries."

Skip chuckled. "And we picked up a diplomatic complaint along the way."

St. Bernard nodded. "Honestly, it was quiet and efficient. No one yelling, 'What the hell was that?' every ten minutes."

Matt let out a slow breath, a faint smile breaking through his fatigue. "You're lucky I'm too medicated to respond properly."

Behind them, Ken Jordan stepped into the room, holding a file. "Doc says you're cleared for rehab."

"Thank God," Matt said, finally lifting his gaze. "I'm ready to get out of here."

"Have you picked a facility?"

Matt shook his head firmly. "Not yet. First, I'm escorting One-Shot back to Santa Barbara for burial. That's nonnegotiable. I recruited him. He died on my watch."

Ken started to respond but Matt waved him off. "After the ceremony, I'll figure out the rest. There's a VA clinic in Santa Barbara. Maybe I'll stick around for a bit. People call it the California Riviera. I passed through once. It's beautiful."

Ken nodded. "I'll get it set up. Your team's wrapping debriefs now. They'll join you in time for the funeral."

***

Sergei Abdulov sat in his corner office at the Kremlin, contemplating his future. After his work in Syria, they had rewarded him with the position of Russian Minister of Energy. He had received his appointment to the position just before the planning for the Ukrainian Special Military Operation started. His position made him responsible for the formulation and implementation of state energy policy, including the development of the energy complexes, the electric power industry, and renewable energy sources.

Once Russia invaded Ukraine and sanctions took effect, Abdulov faced immense pressure to find new markets for Russian oil. Increasing revenue was no longer just a goal, it was a matter of national survival. He played a central role in brokering discounted oil deals with the Chinese, securing short-term stability but ceding long-term leverage. In return, China demanded something more than favorable pricing: cooperation in a broader, more audacious plan. One that blurred the lines between energy policy and geopolitical strategy.

Abdulov also orchestrated a complex arrangement that routed Russian oil through Turkey, allowing it to reach Western markets, including the United States. The effort required carefully laundered documentation. Officially, the shipments were legal. Unofficially, they financed something far more dangerous: the incursion into Ukraine.

He had made an appeal to the Russian president for the use of an old colleague from the Russian intelligence community to help him carry out his agreement with China. After he learned of Lebedev's escape from the drone attack, and the West's belief he was dead, the Russian president had approved Lebedev's participation in Abdulov's grandiose scheme.

Abdulov had just received a call that Alexei Lebedev had entered the building and was on his way to his office. A few minutes later, there was a knock at his door, and it opened.

"Welcome back to Moscow, old friend," Abdulov said.

"Thank you, Sergei, and thank you for sending Sergeant Kuznetsov to the forward command post. Without your forethought, I would not be here."

"Yes, yes, yes. They informed me that the farmhouse had been destroyed, but you have returned and are safe."

"Yes, I am, and I'm ready to return to the front and lead our illustrious and dedicated soldiers to victory."

"I know you want to get back to the front as soon as possible, but we have decided you can play a more important role to Mother Russia. We have many who can lead our troops in battle, but you're the only one I trust to carry out our long-range plans in the United States," Abdulov said. "Do you remember what you did for us in Syria?

"You coordinated the delivery of sarin precursors from Iran to Damascus and ordered the dispersal. Ghouta. Over fifteen hundred dead. Civilians. Children. Effective. Uncompromising. A simple message to all who would oppose our allies." Abdulov suppressed a smile as he took a puff from Cuban a cigar and blew a stream of smoke into the air. "You made an impact, Alexei. So much so that the world noticed. Interpol, the Americans... even the UN. That little Red Notice hanging over your head? You earned it."

Lebedev sat still and remained quiet.

"But Syria was nothing," Abdulov continued. "A test. A child's game. What I'm about to give you will cause far greater disorder and misery to our adversaries."

Abdulov stood from his desk and walked over to a world map on the wall. He pointed to the United States.

"It will not start with sirens or explosions. Just a creeping darkness. Video screens failing, electronic payments failing, subway systems stalling mid-tunnel. Brokers scrambling to phones that no longer work, markets freezing as transactions fail. Fear and panic will cause a run on stores, especially for food and essential commodities. Shelves will empty, not by purchase but by force. Riots and looting will follow. And with every passing hour, the thin veneer of social order will crack further."

Abdulov tapped the top of the dossier on his desk and pushed it across the table. Lebedev took the file and opened it. The name *Chen Da* was on the top page.

"Our friends in Beijing have agreed to our plan and will coordinate with you," Abdulov said. "It will be simultaneous, precise, and devastating. Your part is critical. You will coordinate our efforts in the US. Meanwhile, China will handle their end of the operation. You will ensure the Americans are so consumed with chaos that they will not understand the larger plan until it is too late."

Lebedev looked up from the file. "And if I succeed?"

"If you succeed, your country and I will be grateful. We will give you a new identity and enough money to live the rest of your life in peace. You can become a ghost. A man who rewrote history and disappeared."

Then Abdulov added, "But if you fail... you'll wish the Americans had caught you."

"I won't."

Abdulov smiled as he blew another stream of smoke into the air from his cigar.

"See that you don't. Beijing expects results. And Alexei? Remember what you proved in Syria. Precision. Fear. Confusion. Those are your tools. Use them wisely."

As Lebedev left the office, Abdulov remained by the window, watching the snow swirl outside. He didn't need to see the man's face to know what was happening in his mind. Lebedev had always been methodical, disciplined, and dangerous. Abdulov had chosen him for those very reasons. Syria had proven the man's capabilities. Now, the stakes were higher. If Lebedev succeeded, the disruption would be historic. Abdulov took another long pull from his cigar, the smoke curling upward as he stared at the map. The Americans had no idea what was coming.

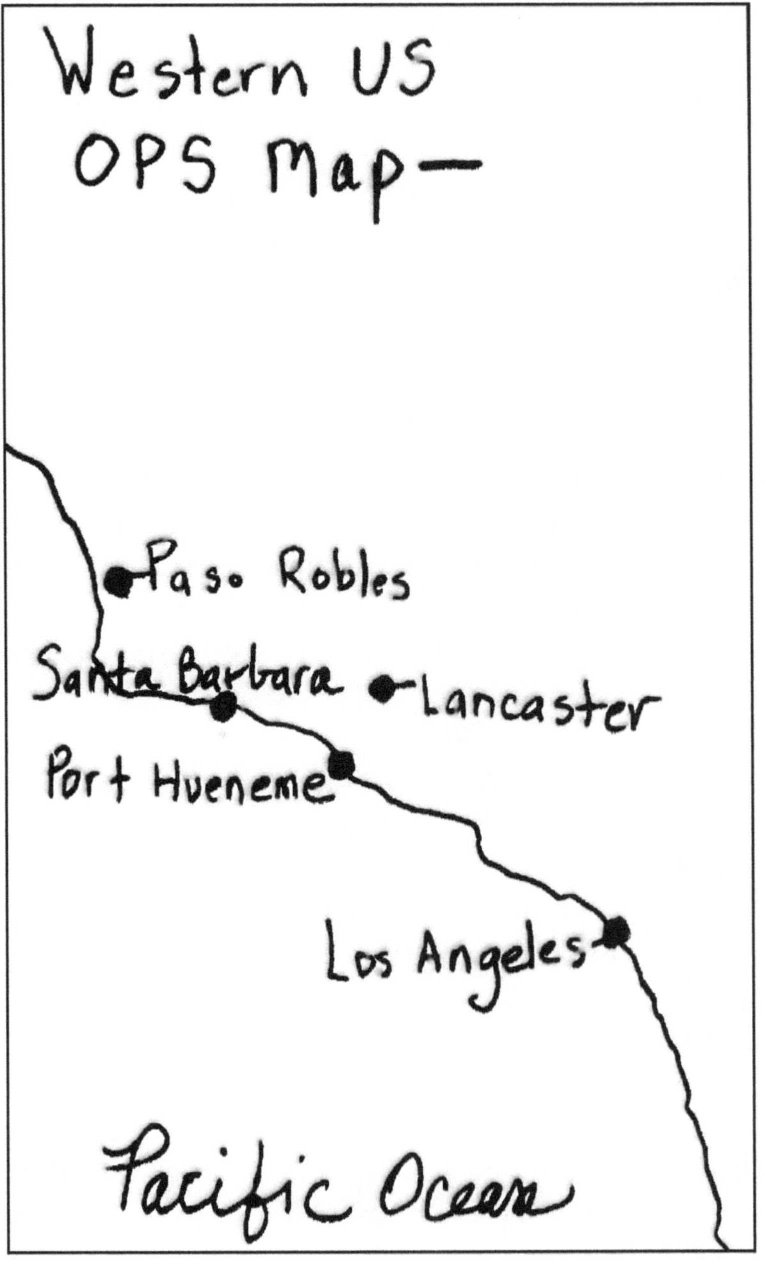
Western US
OPS Map—
Paso Robles
Santa Barbara
Lancaster
Port Hueneme
Los Angeles
Pacific Ocean

Chapter 2

Day 9 - Santa Barbara, California

Matt stood behind the crowd at the Goleta Cemetery just outside Santa Barbara. Beside him were St. Bernard and Skip, the two remaining members of his Kharkiv team. Inside the casket, draped with an American flag, was Jimmy "One-Shot" Dugan. He was another loss in a small brotherhood that felt like it was fading, one funeral at a time.

Matt surveyed the cemetery and its surroundings. A habit, honed over the years, that had been a lifesaver on several occasions. The gravesite was at the top of the hill next to the US flagpole that kept watch over the cemetery. From its perch, it overlooked the Goleta Valley South Little League field where One-Shot had spent the summer days in his youth. The minister's voice became a distant murmur as Matt thought about One-Shot's stories of baseball diamonds and surfing. He'd have liked this place.

As "Taps's played, Matt's mind drifted, not to the sounds of the ceremony, but to the quiet journey that had brought One-Shot home. He'd been there every step of the way, from the extraction from Kharkiv to the base in Romania to the rain-soaked tarmac at Dover, where they boarded their long flight west. The weight of responsibility for One-

Shot's death was more than he could admit, even to himself. At every salute, every nod of acknowledgment from the crew along the way, Matt wondered, *Why wasn't it me?*

Funerals always made him reflect on the fragility of life and the impact of sudden loss. Matt believed that the emotions he felt were not just about the physical death. Funerals meant the loss of the emotional connection you had with the person. They were reminders that friendships were fleeting and could disappear in an instant.

Matt remembered attending his first funeral for his parents when he was only fourteen years old. He'd sat in the front row at their gravesite, watching them both being laid to rest, understanding how one moment could change everything. Overwhelming grief and emptiness followed.

The only time he'd slept since leaving Kharkiv was on the plane. The rest of the time he'd stayed with One-Shot, standing guard in solemn respect. The escort wasn't just a duty. It was a reckoning.

Standing here now, surrounded by mourners, Matt felt the cumulative weight of all the friends he had lost in the last twenty-five years. Jimmy "One-Shot" Dugan had been more than a soldier. He'd been a teammate, a brother-in-arms, a friend.

Am I losing them all, one by one? Or are they losing me? That familiar ache of responsibility crept in, the one that always whispered, *You should've done more. You should've seen it coming.*

After folding the flag, the master sergeant in charge of the funeral detail presented it to Dave Johnson, Matt's direct DCS supervisor. Johnson did an about-face and walked over to Mary Dugan, Jimmy's mother, and kneeled down and presented the flag to her.

"You should be proud of Jimmy. He served his country well and performed at the highest level. On behalf of the president of the United States and a grateful nation, please accept this flag as a symbol of appreciation for Jimmy's honorable and faithful service."

After handing the flag to Mary Dugan, Dave Johnson stood to attention and saluted. He then walked over to Matt and stood next to him. The minister thanked everyone for coming to the funeral and honoring Jimmy Dugan, indicating the funeral service was over.

As he started toward his car, Matt stopped and looked at St. Bernard and Skip.

"How about we head down to the Shoreline Café, grab something to eat, and make a toast to One-Shot?" Matt said.

"Sounds good," St. Bernard said. "Skip and I are in the same car. We'll meet you there."

***

Thirty minutes later, the trio arrived at the Shoreline Café. The café's outdoor seating area, perched on the sand, offered a breathtaking view of the Pacific Ocean and the distant Channel Islands. They each ordered their own food, including a bottle of Pacifico, One-Shot's favorite. Matt led them to the outside seating area with a table in the sand and under an umbrella. They uncapped the bottles and raised them.

"To One-Shot," Matt said, his voice steady, but just barely.

"To One-Shot," St. Bernard echoed.

"Here's to One-Shot," Skip added, his tone reflecting a mix of respect and camaraderie.

The bottles clinked together and then they sipped their beer, their gazes drifting over the ocean. Matt savored the tranquility, the rhythmic sound of the waves providing a soothing backdrop.

"Hey," St. Bernard said. "Remember that time in Kandahar when One-Shot took out that convoy commander? It was 850 meters out!"

"Yeah, and the wind was gusting like crazy," Skip said, laughing. "I still don't know how he calculated that shot. I was calling out adjustments, but he just waved me off."

"And after he made the shot, he just sat back," Matt said. "Acted like it was nothing special and said, 'That's why they call me One-Shot.' And then there was that time in Colombia."

"The helicopter extraction under heavy fire," Skip said. "One-Shot wasn't even supposed to be there, but he volunteered to cover our retreat."

"And when the Huey touched down," St. Bernard chimed in, "he ran across the field like he was jogging in Central Park, waving at the pilot like he had all the time in the world."

"On the helicopter I asked him how he remained so calm," Matt added. "He said, 'It's just another Tuesday, boys.'"

"I really miss that guy," St. Bernard murmured.

"We all do," Skip said.

The crackle of the loudspeaker broke the silence, announcing their food was ready. Matt stood and walked to the pickup window. He returned with their meals and a fresh round of beers, setting them on the table. As the surviving members of DCS Team Alpha 42 ate, the stories flowed, and laughter rose with memories of One-Shot's quirks and their shared missions. In that moment, surrounded by friends and the quiet charm of the café, Matt found a brief, welcome respite from his worries.

But as much as he wanted to sit in the comfort of old memories, reality never stayed away for long.

"We need to discuss our last operation," he said.

"We've completed the formal debrief," Skip replied.

"Yeah, I know, but we need to do another tactical debrief. I keep replaying the mission in my mind, thinking about what we could have done differently. We were rushing and didn't have enough time for proper planning and analysis."

"It was the right call at the time," St. Bernard chimed in. "We've been through plenty of on-the-fly operations over the years. Sometimes, it's necessary."

"Well," Matt continued, "I missed the camera above the elevator that caught us entering the building. They were ready for us when we came through the door. They must have seen us on their surveillance cameras."

"That may be true, but in the end, the mission was a success," St. Bernard reminded him.

"Was it?" Matt said. "Are we sure Lebedev is dead? The images from the drone look conclusive. But absent a body and DNA evidence as proof, there is still a doubt. None of us have survived as long as we have in the clandestine world by taking anything at face value."

"Are you sure you're not angry because you wanted to hunt down Lebedev yourself and put a bullet in his head?" Skip asked.

"I'll admit, I would've preferred it was my bullet that took out Lebedev."

"We've all seen the drone footage. The missile strike happened ten minutes after he went inside. There's no way anyone survived, even if they were in a basement."

"I know," Matt said. "But something's still bothering me. I can't put my finger on it. You know the feeling you get that something isn't right? It's saved my ass many times over the years, and it's there again."

"I know what you're talking about," St. Bernard said. "We've all been there."

"So, when are you going to get back in the game?" Skip asked.

Matt ran a hand over his face, thinking about everything that had led him to this moment. He set his beer down.

"I'm thinking of leaving DCS. Gonna take some time to consider it."

Skip set his beer down too, exchanging glances with St. Bernard.

"Seriously?" Skip asked.

"I've given twenty-five years to this life. Maybe it's time to slow down and see what normal life is about."

Silence stretched between them, only the waves filling the gap.

St. Bernard chuckled, shaking his head. "I give you two months before you go stir-crazy."

"Well, while you're starting a new life, we are returning to Kyiv," Skip said.

As Matt sat there with his teammates, a rare sense of peace settled over him. Whether it stemmed from the serene location, the company, or something less tangible, he couldn't say. In the end, the reason didn't matter. He intended to enjoy the moment for as long as it lasted.

***

After St. Bernard and Skip left, Matt sat alone, nursing his beer. The sky had shifted into hues of orange and gray behind the Channel Islands, the light bleeding away like memory.

The mission was over, but something still bothered him. He tried to shake the feeling and lose it in the waves and salt air, but it lingered like an itch he couldn't scratch.

His teammates, though, seemed ready to move on. He trusted his team. They were some of the best he'd ever worked with. Saint Bernard had twenty years in DEVGRU and never lost his cool, even in the worst of it. Skip, all Delta fire and restless energy, had a knack for seeing threats before they surfaced.

And then there was Jimmy "One-Shot" Dugan.

The memory of One-Shot hit harder than he'd expected. Jimmy was the soul of the unit, the one who found meaning in the quiet moments between the chaos. His voice drifted up from memory. *Every day I wake up, it's a gift. When I see the sun come up, that's the best part of the day.*

Matt didn't know how long he'd been sitting there. His beer had gone warm. The chill had crept in.

He stood and looked out across the ocean.

"Goodbye, Jimmy," he murmured. "It's been an honor."

***

April Knight stepped out of her condo on Meigs Road, sunlight warm on her face. She turned left toward Shoreline Park, falling into a steady rhythm. The breeze picked up as she coasted downhill toward Leadbetter Beach, then past the Dolphin Fountain and onto the palm-lined stretch near East Beach. By the time she reached the Bird Refuge, her Apple Watch buzzed: twenty-seven minutes, just over four miles.

Not bad.

She pivoted and picked up her pace, her legs settling into a comfortable six-minute mile.

Santa Barbara had become home. Not just the place, but the quiet, the ocean, the hills. A long way from Peoria, Illinois.

Peoria was all farmland and modest dreams. Her parents had named her April hoping it would bring light and beauty into a plain world, and maybe offer her a way out. It had. But not the way they'd expected. She'd always had to prove she belonged, especially with two older brothers who treated her like a tagalong. So, she outran them, outplayed them, and earned her place.

Her dad had held on to the family's small fifty-acre corn farm while others sold out to conglomerates. He died behind the wheel of a tractor with country music still playing, just days after her eighteenth birthday. Her brothers were gone. David was working feed contracts and Clayton was in the Army. After the funeral April had joined the Air Force. She scored in the 99th percentile on the ASVAB and picked the hardest job they offered: combat controller.

At five-foot-eight and 145 pounds, April had always been built for endurance. Her brothers used to call her "sturdy," half-teasing, half-jealous. At Combat Controller school, she'd scored a perfect 100 on the male scale of the physical fitness test and still heard whispers from instructors who didn't know what to make of a woman outperforming half the class. But she wasn't just muscle. Back home, the town boys had called her a looker. She knew how to weaponize a smile, but rarely did. Strength was easier to trust than charm.

Thirteen years later, she was done fighting. She'd inherited her mom's Santa Barbara condo and never looked back.

As she passed the Shoreline Café, she caught a figure out of the corner of her eye, a man, late-thirties, fit build, heading toward the tables in the sand. There was something familiar about the way he moved. She noted his height, build, and direction. Just in case.

***

Sergeant Andrei Kuznetsov had been in limbo since dropping Lebedev at the Russian field command post. For more than a week, he waited. When the message finally came, it was brief and direct: "Assigned to special unit. Return to Moscow by the most expeditious means and contact Colonel Alexei Lebedev for further instructions." He knew that the more simplistic the order, the more hazardous and sophisticated the operation. However, as a member of the covert Foreign Intelligence Service Zaslon Unit, he was accustomed to operating in hazardous conditions and frequently executed solo missions. He hadn't known that Lebedev was part of the Foreign Intelligence Service. He'd thought Lebedev was only a colonel in the Army. The orders intrigued him, and he was looking forward to putting his skills to work.

Chapter 3

Day 45 - Santa Barbara, California - Late Morning

Five weeks had passed since One-Shot's burial and Matt had had lunch with his team on the sand at the Shoreline Café. Since then, he had concentrated on his recovery, staying healthy and enjoying his new lifestyle. Officially, he was still on medical leave. He wanted to make sure his recovery was complete before he filed his paperwork for retirement.

His days consisted of waking up, going for a run, and stopping at the Shoreline Café for breakfast. He would then return home, shower, and head to the gym for a workout. He would go to the VA's office once a week for a checkup. On his off days, he would enjoy the sights of Santa Barbara and the plethora of trails in the foothills that gave him panoramic views of downtown Santa Barbara, the ocean, and the Channel Islands.

Matt enjoyed his new routine. He was getting back into shape and healing from his injuries. He would occasionally feel pain, but he could manage it. On this day, he continued his routine of jumping out of bed at 6:30 a.m. and getting a cup of coffee before putting on his black running shorts and favorite T-shirt and stretching for ten minutes. Then he headed out of his apartment complex at 2051

Cliff Drive and turned right. At Meigs Road he turned right again and headed towards Shoreline Park, then through it towards the Santa Barbara wharf, looking to his right to catch the early morning sun hitting the ocean.

Matt sprinted past the familiar barbecue pits at West Beach, the smell of charred wood and salt in the air. The sun glinted off the yachts in the marina, their masts swaying in rhythm with the breeze. He let the pace of his strides and the hint of salt air ease his thoughts.

He slowed his pace to maneuver around some locals who were out walking their dogs. His slower pace allowed him to look up and admire the flight of pelicans flying towards him in a V formation. A serene smile formed on his face as he watched the pelicans gracefully glide over the breakwater. After passing it, they descended to just a foot over the water and floated across the waves in their effortless flight.

Matt took a deep breath and felt the fresh air enter his lungs. On his left was the marina that housed over nine hundred boats, and in front of him was the magnificent Santa Barbara wharf. It was the oldest working wooden wharf in the US, and had been there since 1850, even though it had been rebuilt a few times after fires burned most of it.

As he moved down the breakwater, he looked to his right at the Pacific Ocean. In the distance, he could see the Channel Islands. This view always brought him a sense of awe and appreciation.

Matt and his team had spent four years traveling the world, chasing terrorists. He smiled, reminiscing about the rare moments of downtime during deployment with his team. Back then, One-Shot often regaled the team with fond memories of growing up on the Santa Barbara coast.

He could hear One-Shot say, "Matt, you've got to visit Santa Barbara. Watching the sun rise over the Santa Ynez Mountains from the breaks at Rincon or from the end of the harbor breakwater is an awesome experience. Then you turn around and look towards the Channel Islands and see the perfect wave forming. It's perfection, man!"

Matt came out of the harbor breakwater and turned east on the bike path. When he got to the East Beach volleyball courts, he turned around and started back towards the Mesa. While dashing along the bike path, he avoided the pedestrians who were walking on the bike path and the slower moving bicycles. He adjusted his speed as he passed them and calculated how much time he had to jump back into his lane before colliding with the bicyclists coming from the opposite direction. He came through the S-turn, passing the bathrooms on his right and slowing as he approached the stop sign at the intersection of the bike path and the entrance to the wharf. A vehicle was driving in front of him. He stopped and jogged in place.

Then he glanced to his left and noticed a woman jogging in place beside him. A baseball cap hid her face. Something about her seemed familiar. She looked up at him, and Matt's heart skipped a beat as her striking green eyes triggered a flood of memories. The world around him blurred, and the past came rushing back.

***

Remote Village, Afghanistan - Fifteen Years Ago

The helicopter's rotor blades pounded through the night air, a steady thump that vibrated with Matt's racing heart. Seated beside him sat seven operators. One combat controller. The red lights inside the MH-60 Black Hawk cast an eerie glow over their determined faces.

Matt adjusted his grip on his HK416 rifle, the familiar weight of his gear a reassuring presence. He glanced to his right at Airman Knight, the new Air Force combat controller on her first mission. Her face was all fierce determination, but her eyes gave her away. She was scared. He'd told her to stay right behind him during the assault.

As the Black Hawk descended, Matt's thoughts flashed back to the briefing. He pictured the satellite images, the floor plans, and the labyrinth of narrow streets and buildings. The success of their mission was based on stealth. No easy task in the small city containing two-story buildings and tight alleys. The aerial drone they had deployed provided a live infrared feed of the enemy positions. The risk was high, but the objective was worth it.

The helicopter hovered. Two fast ropes dropped out of each side. Matt's boots hit the ground. He took his place as the third man on the team, with Airman Knight right behind him. The team moved out into the darkness. They covered the two miles to the village in sixty minutes.

At the edge of the compound Matt signaled a halt. Through his night-vision goggles, he studied the guards' patrol patterns, cross-referencing them with the drone's real-time feed.

"Two guards by the main gate, rotating every five minutes. We have a small window to breach the fence," he whispered. "On my mark... Go."

The team crawled up to the fence. The metallic snap of the wire cutter broke the night's stillness for a fraction of a second before silence swallowed them again. They slipped into the compound undetected. The night-vision goggles turned the world into shades of green and black. Matt's pulse quickened as they neared the first row of buildings.

A hidden guard spotted them and shouted an alarm. A burst of gunfire from the rooftops sent the team diving for cover.

"Contact right!" Matt shouted, signaling everyone to spread out and return fire. Bullets ripped through the night as the compound erupted into chaos. Matt and his team returned fire. He ran towards the cover behind a low wall twenty feet away. A muzzle flash flared in his periphery. Suddenly pain exploded in his right leg. A white-hot spike of agony drove into his ribs, knocking the air from his lungs.

His leg buckled, the world tilting sideways. He staggered and fell onto his back, darkness encroaching on his vision, but he fought to stay conscious.

"Six is down! Covering fire!" Airman Knight's commanding voice came over the radio. Matt saw her running towards him. No hesitation. No fear. She reached his side, her rifle still blazing. He forced a breath through his teeth.

She hooked her right arm under his right arm, dragging him towards the wall. She was stronger than she looked. With her left hand, she fired controlled bursts. Bullets whizzed around them as the team provided cover fire.

Knight and Matt collapsed behind a crumbling wall. His breath became ragged as pain radiated through his body. The rounds struck the wall above them, whizzing over their heads.

"Stay with me!" she screamed, tearing at her medical kit. She applied a pressure dressing to the wound on his right side. He fought the darkness as she put a tourniquet on his right leg. He gritted his teeth, blinking hard. He had to stay awake.

As the firefight continued, he heard her calmly reporting their situation and requesting QRF support. Positioned over him, she fired at the attackers between transmissions. He could hear his team pushing back the ambush, but his focus was slipping.

He fumbled for his spare magazines, tapping her shoulder before passing them to her. She took them with a nod.

His vision tunneled, the chaos dissolving into shadows. The last thing he saw was those emerald green eyes, burning into him as the world slipped away.

***

Present Day Santa, Barbara, CA

Matt blinked, the visceral memory fading as the present came back into focus. The woman beside him had stopped jogging and was looking at him with a curious expression. His heart still pounded from the intensity of the flashback.

"Hello, Master Chief Scales," April said.

Matt stared at her.

"Airman Knight. It's been a long time."

She stared back at him. "Yes, it has. Looks like you're running a little slow today. Getting old?"

"Oh no, I'm on a warm-down and heading to the Shoreline Café for breakfast. Care to join me?"

April hesitated. *This is it*, she thought. *Fifteen years*. As she looked at Matt, the old memories surfaced.

She gave a small nod. "Sure, why not? This is my light running day anyway."

At the walk-up window, they checked out the menu. Matt ordered the pancake sandwich with two scrambled eggs and bacon. April ordered off the à la carte menu, asking for two scrambled eggs and fruit.

Matt grabbed the bill and pulled out his credit card.

April gave him a determined look. "We can split the bill, or I'll pay for the whole thing."

"I invited you to breakfast, so I'm paying. Besides, I owe you."

"Okay," April said. "I know better than to argue, but you don't owe me anything."

The clock at the café's order window displayed 8 a.m. The temperature had already reached a pleasant seventy-two degrees. They carried the cup of coffee to Matt's favorite table on the sand under an umbrella.

He picked up his cup of coffee, took a deep breath, and gazed out at the ocean.

***

April sat across from Matt. Watching, studying. He looked different. A little older, a little harder. The years had left their mark, but the quiet calculating way he looked at her and the way he measured people, was the same.

She moved slightly forward, her voice casual but her mind anything but. "Where were you?"

Matt finally pulled his gaze from the ocean and looked at her. "These days, I cherish a few minutes each morning, sitting with my coffee, savoring the start of the day, especially when I'm at the beach. I've learned it's the best time of the day."

She tilted her head. "How do you figure that?"

"It's a reminder you're still alive," he said, his tone lighter than she expected. "Your experiences and knowledge may have shaped you, but the new day remains full of endless possibilities. Before everything starts, before the phone calls, before the day begins its unpredictable journey, I like to pause and appreciate the peace."

She sipped her coffee, considering his words.

"I didn't know you were philosophical."

Matt grinned. "A lot's changed since we worked together overseas."

She wasn't so sure about that.

She took another sip of coffee, letting the warmth chase away a chill that wasn't from the morning breeze. Her grip tightened around the cup as a memory surfaced. One she hadn't thought about in years. One she'd tried not to think about.

***

A few years after the mission with Matt, April had a conversation with a teammate where she'd casually mentioned she'd been on the mission where he'd been injured.

The teammate had raised an eyebrow. "Oh, that one? Yeah, the intel changed last minute. Command thought it might've been a setup, or at least that there was heavier security than they were expecting, but the mission was still a go."

April had frozen. "What?"

Her teammate had shrugged. "You didn't know? Yeah, they got word right before you guys deployed. Higher-ups knew it was riskier than originally thought, but it wasn't enough to pull back."

For years, April had brushed it aside, rationalized it, told herself she had been new and not cleared to know everything. But the older she got and the more experience she accrued, the less that excuse held up. She had risked her life on that op to save Matt.

And he hadn't trusted her with the updated information about the increased threat.

***

April set her cup down. Matt was good at reading people. She didn't see any sign that he noticed the shift in her demeanor, or that he had and was choosing not to acknowledge it.

The loudspeaker announced their order was ready and Matt retrieved their food from the pickup window. As he handed her the plate, he said, "I never knew your first name."

"It's April. And please, no April Fool's jokes."

He pointed to his chest and broke out in a grin. "Matt."

She took a bite of her eggs and glanced at him. Time to test him.

"What are you doing in Santa Barbara that allows you to go running at eight in the morning?"

She listened, waiting for... she wasn't sure what. Hesitation maybe. But there was nothing.

"I'm working for DCS. Got injured on my last mission. Not as bad as the one we were on together, but I'm taking a few months off to recover before going back to work."

She nodded. That much, she believed.

He turned his head towards her. "What about you? Where'd you end up?"

"Did another ten years, then it was time to leave."

He arched a brow. "And now?"

"Sergeant in the sheriff's office."

He gave an approving nod. "Good to see you still put your skills to work. How does that compare to your old job?"

She exhaled. "Well, the hours are better, even though I'm working graveyards. It's just different. There's still some danger and excitement, but it seems like now I have a good normal life. You know what I mean?"

He nodded. "Yeah, I am beginning to."

"I'd like to do some more catching up," she said, "but for right now, I need to get home and get some sleep."

"Can I call you in a few days if I need a breakfast partner?"

I still don't completely trust him. But it doesn't matter now.

"Early mornings or late afternoons are best." April wrote her phone number on a napkin and pushed it across the table to Matt.

"I enjoyed catching up," he said. "Hope you have a great day."

She held up her coffee and moved it towards him for a toast before she left. "Likewise."

***

Matt jumped into the shower as soon as he got home. As he dried off, his phone rang. He realized it was his private phone, not his work phone. Very few people had that number. He looked at the caller ID and recognized the number of his childhood friend, Chin.

"Hey Chin, how's it going up there in northern Washington?"

"The sky is finally blue, and the weather is gorgeous, at least for a few days."

"It's a little early for our six-month check-in. Everything going okay up there? You haven't lost all my money, have you?"

"No, your money's fine. We're on track to hit seventeen-percent returns this year," Chin replied. "Listen, I need to run something by you, but I can't get too specific over an unsecured line. I received a transformer for evaluation that's being installed at Eielson Air Force

Base in Alaska. It was manufactured in China. I don't need to explain why that's worrisome."

"No, you don't," Matt said.

"I found a potential issue in the code. Something I recognize. But it shouldn't be there."

"Now I know why you want to use a secure line. For now, can you give me some general details?"

"Before I get into it, how are things with you?" Chin asked.

"I'm in Santa Barbara for a few more months."

"You're back in the US for a few months," Chin said with a trace of sarcasm. "Last time that happened, it took you four months to recover, and you changed jobs."

"Minor mishap overseas. Just taking some time to heal and make sure I'm in top shape before I jump back in."

Chin hesitated. "You remember back in middle school, when we used to speak Mandarin so the other kids wouldn't understand us?"

"Yeah," Matt said. "Usually while planning something that would get us detention."

Chin chuckled. "Exactly. To everyone else, it just sounded like background noise." He paused. "That's kind of what this feels like. I was reviewing code buried in the transformer's firmware. Most of it looks routine, but there's a section that doesn't sit right. I can follow the structure, recognize the patterns, but the intent? Not sure what it means. It's like hearing a foreign language. You don't know what's being said, but you can tell it means something."

Matt didn't respond right away.

"Look," Chin added, "you're still recovering. I don't want you running around trying to find a secure comms hub. Let me keep digging. If it gets more serious, I'll call you back."

Then Chin switched to Mandarin. "My father asked me to check on you. What should I tell him?"

Matt answered in Mandarin. "Tell him I'm doing just fine and that I still respect and appreciate everything he's done for me."

"I'll let him know," Chin said, shifting back to English.

After Matt hung up, he thought about what Chin had told him. His friend was one of the smartest people he knew. After receiving his master's degree in computer forensics from MIT, the DOD recruited him for some classified programs. Four years later, Chin went back to MIT on a full-ride scholarship and emerged with a PhD in applied physics. At that point, the Department of Energy recruited Chin to work on several highly secret projects. He was working at the Pacific Northwest National Laboratory (PNNL) at the Department of Energy National Laboratory in Richland, Washington.

Matt let out a soft groan as he thought about the phone call. If Chin was worried, there was a reason for it. But he also had faith that Chin could figure it out.

Chapter 4

Alexei Lebedev was standing in the one-thousand-square-foot living room of a Montecito estate. This four-acre estate was typical of the small upper-class community one hundred miles north of Los Angeles where the elite from Hollywood and the top one percent lived.

He was standing facing Zhang Wei. At least, that was the name the man had used when Lebedev met him last year. They had been speaking in English.

They were in the midst of a disagreement about Wei's attack on the power substation on Glen Annie Road. For a moment, Lebedev stopped listening to Wei as he considered how Wei's actions might hinder his plans.

"What did you just say?" Lebedev asked.

"The Americans' electrical grid, especially in Texas, is vulnerable. The catastrophic failure in Texas a few years ago during the ice storm proves that. We merely wanted to probe the local power station to test the local response."

"I agree that the grid failure in Texas shows how vulnerable they are," Lebedev stated, "but attacking the electrical grid now interferes with the plan we carefully developed. We know their electrical power is not resilient. Our plan was designed for a series of coordinated attacks."

"That is your goal!" Wei shouted. "The goal of the People's Republic of China is to move forward. We are ready now!"

"Our original agreement was to coordinate our efforts. Your success is heavily contingent on our successful operation here in the United States. Your shortsightedness has jeopardized everything. You remind me of a spoiled child with impulse control problems."

From the corner of his eye, Lebedev noticed Wei's bodyguard reaching down to his side. As the bodyguard's hand touched the weapon concealed in his waistband, Lebedev pulled his OTs-23 Drotik pistol from his holster. He fired swing-shooting style by putting one shot into the bodyguard's chest and then moved to Wei. After putting two rounds in his chest, Lebedev returned to the bodyguard to put two more shots in the man's chest. Finally, he put a shot to each one's head. The entire effort took less than three seconds.

While shooting, Lebedev instinctively moved two feet to his right behind a couch, After he finished shooting, he snatched up six pieces of brass from the rug. As he put the shell casings in his pocket, Lebedev sprinted through the back door to the waiting Hughes 500 helicopter on the lawn.

***

Greg Saunders was sitting in the right-hand seat of the Hughes 500 in the backyard of the Montecito estate. When he saw Lebedev running towards the helicopter, he started the engine.

"We need to leave now!" Lebedev yelled. "Head towards the New Cuyama Airport!"

Greg Saunders yanked up on the cyclic and added power. The Hughes 500 gingerly lifted off from the field it had been sitting in for the last twenty minutes. Greg spun the aircraft around, heading north towards the Santa Ynez Mountains. As the helicopter gained altitude, he applied full power. In less than a minute, the aircraft was heading towards the mountains at over 170 miles an hour. He ascended to 600 feet, careful to stay above the 500-foot minimums allowed by the US FAA when flying above populated areas. Greg steered them towards the coastal mountains on a line just east of Montecito Peak. He gained altitude and crested the 3000-foot-tall mountains. Once on the north side of the mountains, he stayed at a 500-foot elevation and raced north towards New Cuyama.

Lebedev sat in the left seat of the Hughes 500 helicopter as it skimmed along the north side of the Santa Ynez Mountains. The hills would hide the helicopter from the radar at the Santa Barbara airport.

"Look around," Greg said. "Do you see Cachuma Lake coming up off on our left? The backcountry of Santa Barbara is beautiful."

"Yes, I see it," Lebedev uttered with feigned excitement in his voice.

Every minute he stayed in the helicopter meant a greater chance he would be located.

Lebedev focused on his escape, ensuring his complete disassociation from Greg, the helicopter, and the Montecito estate they had just left. The discovery of the two Chinese bodies would trigger a region-wide alert, and eventually, the authorities would discover he had been on the helicopter. Lebedev needed to be far away before that happened.

"Take me to Santa Ynez Airport," he instructed. "I have a rental car there with some vital equipment I need to retrieve. I'll meet you at New Cuyama Airport. I'll drop the car off with my associate, and we can fly back to Santa Barbara together."

As Greg flared the helicopter for landing, Lebedev's sunglasses slipped from his lap onto the floor. With one hand, he retrieved them. With the other, he removed the handgun from his waistband. After tucking the handgun under the seat, his hand moved to the two twenty-minute pencil timers embedded in the half-pound block of C-4. He had rigged the explosives before they left the airport, while Greg was conducting a final check of the helicopter.

Two detonators ensured reliability. He pulled the wires, activating both. He had a minimum of eighteen minutes before the explosives detonated.

"Where the hell are my glasses?" he muttered, feigning mild frustrating. "Ah, there they are."

***

After dropping Lebedev off at the Santa Ynez Airport, Greg Saunders headed northeast towards New Cuyama. As the Hughes 500 crested a hill, he could see the New Cuyama airstrip three miles ahead. It had only been ten minutes since Alexei had jumped off the helicopter.

Greg maintained the helicopter at fifty feet above the ground. He planned to gain some altitude as he got within a mile of the airstrip and then make a normal approach. Any locals who observed the helicopter touching down would assume it was just another wealthy county resident arriving for a day of hunting in the Los Padres National Forest.

As he was skimming the ground at 130 MPH, the C-4 detonated, engulfing the helicopter and Greg. In the middle of the San Rafael wilderness, about fifteen miles from the New Cuyama airstrip, the helicopter plummeted to the ground. If Lebedev hadn't disconnected it earlier, the crash would have activated the emergency transmitter locator (ELT). Nobody saw the explosion. Eventually the local fire watchers spotted smoke rising into the sky. They made a call to the Santa Barbara County Air Support Unit that was stationed at the Santa Ynez Airport to report the fire.

Chapter 5

Day 60 - Santa Barbara, CA - Early Morning

Matt had called April twice over the past week, inviting her to breakfast, but each time, she was working late and had to take a rain check. He didn't know if she was politely putting him off or if she was telling the truth. She didn't seem like the type to play games.

As he finished his second cup of coffee, his phone rang. April.

"Hey," she said. "I just got off shift. You up for breakfast?"

He glanced at the clock. He'd been planning on a morning run, but he could skip it. "Yeah. Meet you at the Shoreline Café?"

"See you there."

Ten minutes later, April pulled into the lot. They ordered breakfast and carried their coffee to Matt's favorite table in the sand.

Their mission together had left little room for personal conversations. They'd each known how the other handled pressure, how the other moved in a fight, but beyond that, their personal lives before hadn't mattered in the moment. Now, there was space for it.

"So," Matt said, stretching out in his chair. "How'd you end up in Santa Barbara?"

April took a sip of coffee. "Grew up on a farm. Enlisted in the military straight out of high school. Spent thirteen years running around the world. Came here to decompress and figure out what normal life was supposed to look like."

He watched her. Her story had gaps. He knew the move. Keep it simple, keep it clean. He'd done it himself plenty of times.

She set her cup down. "A month after I got here, I took the test for the sheriff's office. My background investigator was a retired Marine master sergeant named John Gordon. He took one look at my DD-214 and told me he understood why years were missing. Said as long as I passed the psych exam and polygraph, the academy would be a breeze."

Matt grinned. "Was it?"

She grinned back. "Boring, but yeah. Allan Hancock Police Academy, 2020. Got assigned to the Santa Maria substation, worked my way up. Physical fitness wasn't an issue, and I had a way of handling rowdy cowboys in the bars on weekends."

He chuckled. He could picture it. "I'd bet on you over them any day."

She tipped her coffee at him. "Smart man."

He smiled.

"What about you? How'd you end up in the Navy?"

Matt let out a breath, watching the foam on the waves dissolve against the shore. "Paso Robles. That's where I grew up."

She waited. No rushing, no prying. Just waiting to see how much he revealed.

"My parents took me and my brother Joshua for a drive one afternoon. Highway 41. A carload of teenagers came around a turn on the wrong side of the road. Head-on collision. Killed both of my parents. Me and Joshua became instant orphans."

April's expression didn't change, but he saw the shift in her posture. The kind that came from understanding.

"The driver?" she asked.

"Drunk. Son of a local politician. Got probation and community service."

She let out a quiet sigh. "That's some bullshit."

Matt gave a tight nod. "We ended up with our aunt and uncle. They had two kids of their own and barely enough money to get by. My cousins didn't like us taking over a bedroom. When Joshua turned seventeen, he enlisted in the Army. I was fifteen then. Without him, things got worse."

Matt took a sip of coffee. "Two years later, I got the news that Joshua was killed in Afghanistan."

April didn't say anything right away. She didn't offer hollow sympathy.

"After that, I had to get out of Paso. My aunt and uncle were more than happy to sign the enlistment papers for me."

April nodded. "So, you ran toward something."

Matt met her eyes. "Or away from something."

A small smile touched her lips. "I get that."

The announcement that their food was ready gave them a moment to shift gears. After a few bites, Matt reignited the conversation. "So, what about you? What did you do after our mission together?"

April stirred her eggs. "Bounced around to different assignments for a few years. After my mom passed, I inherited her place here. Figured it was time to put down roots."

April's phone rang. She glanced at the screen before answering.

"Good morning. Sergeant Knight."

Matt watched as her calm demeanor tightened into something sharp and focused.

"Send out the notifications. I'm on my way."

She ended the call and stood, already reaching for her keys. "Sorry, but I gotta go. Incident in Montecito. A big house with multiple bodies. My team's on point for clearing it."

He nodded. "Stay safe."

She gave him a quick smirk. "Always."

He watched her go, then turned back to his coffee.

***

April and her team entered the house through the back sliding doors. Their boots were silent on the tiled floor. Two bodies lay sprawled in the expansive living room. Blood oozed from their chests and heads as it stained the white Persian rug.

The men appeared to be Asian, perhaps in their thirties. Each had a single gunshot wound to the back of the head. The only sound was the ticktock of a grandfather clock in the corner.

"Two victims," April whispered into her comms. "Execution-style. No visible signs of a struggle. Proceed with caution."

Her team advanced through the house with practiced efficiency, their movements resembling a well-rehearsed ballet. One operator covered the left flank while another swept the right. Each turn of a corner was smooth. Her training kept her focused, yet a nagging feeling tugged at the back of her mind. Something about the scene felt off.

They cleared the fifteen-thousand-square-foot mansion in under an hour. The search revealed no additional threats or victims and no further signs of a struggle.

The team moved to the front door, past the entrance to the living room. April lingered at the living room entrance, scanning the room with her sharp eyes.

Despite understanding the consequences of entering the living room again and disrupting the evidence, her professional curiosity prevailed over her judgment. She walked a few feet into the room. She scrutinized the scene in front of her, moving her eyes from one side to the other, looking for anything unusual.

Her gaze stopped on the couch. She noticed a shell casing wedged between the cushion and back of the couch. She pulled a flashlight from her belt and pointed it at the top of the shell casing.

"Got something," she muttered. The beam illuminated the casing. 5.45x18mm.

April held her breath. She recognized the caliber.

"OTs-23 Drotik," she murmured, but loud enough for Stony Peterson to hear her from the hallway. "Russian special operations and intelligence-issue."

"That's... specific. You sure?"

She nodded. "Yeah. Whoever did this were professionals. But professionals don't leave their brass behind unless they're in a hurry."

The hair on the back of her neck tingled. A sensation she trusted. *This isn't your average homicide.*

Outside, Commander Luther Cornwell was already pacing near the SWAT van, barking orders into his radio. April approached him, her mind still churning over the implications of the scene.

"Sergeant Knight," Cornwell said, turning to face her. "Your team is to secure the scene until we get a Mincey warrant. Could be hours."

April clenched her teeth. "Sir, my team's been on duty all night. They need rest. This isn't standard procedure."

Cornwell's expression hardened. "It is today. I need you to make it happen."

April considered pushing back, but she caught the weary glances of her team and knew better than to let emotions flare.

"Understood, sir," she said curtly.

As Cornwell walked away, April turned to her team. "Alright, circle up. Stony and I will take first watch. The rest of you head back to the station. We'll rotate shifts tonight. Get some rest."

Stony gave her a tired grin. "Guess I'll stick around, Sarge. But only if there's food involved."

April chuckled. "You're impossible, Peterson."

***

Alexei Lebedev had driven to the Santa Barbara Harbor from the Santa Ynez Airport. He was sitting on the upstairs patio of Brophy Brothers, savoring what he knew would be his last clam chowder in Santa Barbara. The salty breeze from the harbor played with the edges of his jacket as he watched the boats bobbing in the marina below.

From his corner table, he could see the entire length of the concrete walkway that led from the parking lot, past the marina, and out to the end of the breakwater. He appeared relaxed, even content. But he was on high alert as he watched for his contact and any unusual activity.

At 11:45, he spotted his contact, Chen Da, a wiry man in his late forties and dressed in casual beachwear. The man's unhurried pace irritated Lebedev. He was thirty minutes late. In Russia, being half an hour late for a meeting could mean losing trust, or worse. In China, such tardiness was equally disrespectful in business dealings. Yet the wiry operative strolled in as if time were of no consequence.

After his contact passed, Lebedev took a deep breath and looked out at the ocean. He took a moment to savor the peaceful sight that he seldom saw in his line of work.

He stood from his table and laid enough cash on the table to cover the bill and a tip big enough to make the waitress happy, but not so big or small as to make her remember him.

After walking down the stairs from the restaurant, he turned right towards the breakwater. He knew his contact would be sitting on the fourth bench.

***

After April received a phone call and left, Matt had breakfast by himself. He had a 9:00 a.m. appointment at the VA clinic and planned to go for a run afterwards. His appointment was uneventful, except that the doctor gave him the green light to go back to work on limited duty if he wanted.

When Matt returned from the VA clinic, he laced up his running shoes and headed out. As he ran through Shoreline Park, he contemplated returning to work or taking advantage of the year of leave he had accumulated and spending a few extra months in Santa Barbara. He was so deep in thought that he barely registered his surroundings until he was passing the yacht club. Taking his usual route, he cut through the alley and turned right toward the breakwater.

As he neared the fourth bench, he noticed two men sitting there, facing each other. When he jogged past, a fragment of their conversation in Mandarin caught his ear. He picked up two words: "Montecito" and "electric."

His pulse kicked up. Instinct more than conscious thought slowed his stride. He glanced toward the ocean, pretending to take in the view while his mind replayed what he had just heard. Then, as if drawn there by some unseen force, he glanced back at the bench.

One man turned just enough for Matt to see a scar along his cheek and a sharp, predatory glint in his eyes.

Lebedev.

It couldn't be. Yet there he was. A ghost from the past, sitting in plain sight.

Matt pulled out his iPhone and acted as though he were taking selfies of himself with the ocean in the background. Amidst the selfies, he snapped multiple pictures of the two men sitting on the bench. A few seconds later, he put the phone back in his pocket and ran another fifty yards down the breakwater until he reached the next bench. He sat down, pulled out his phone, and dialed a number he had memorized years ago.

***

Amy Rodriguez was sitting at her desk in an undisclosed location in Port Hueneme Navy Base. She had two phones on her desk. One had several lines that were connected to the public numbers throughout the base. The second phone served a single purpose. Whenever it rang, she knew it was a DCS agent calling on official business.

The second phone rang. She waited for the third ring and then answered.

"4290 code in."

"Echo 465 Delta Zulu Lincoln Foxtrot," Matt replied.

Amy opened a binder that contained the code names and phrases for all the DCS operatives in the field in the western hemisphere. Even though she recognized the voice, she followed protocol. "Confirmed. State your business," she said matter-of-factly.

"Morning, Amy, this is Matt."

"Matt who?"

"Matt Scales, Amy. Come on, quit joking around. I need to talk to the boss."

"You're still supposed to be recuperating."

"Yeah, something came up," Matt said. "I have to talk to the boss right away."

"You've lost your sense of humor now that you're back in the real world. Okay, wait one sec, it sounds important. Let me track him down for you."

Matt heard a few clicks, indicating Amy was transferring him.

"Matt how is Santa Barbara?" his boss Dave asked.

"Like living in paradise, Dave. Doc told me this morning I'm good to go for light duty, but I was thinking of taking a few months' leave."

"I know you didn't call to ask about taking more time off, or my golf game. So, what's up? I understand you're on an unsecured line."

"That's correct. While I was running at the Santa Barbara break-water, I bumped into an old friend involved in my last business trans-action. The one who was presumed retired."

"What? Are you sure?"

"I saw him and snapped a few pictures. I'm sending them to you for confirmation, but I spent enough time studying this guy and his profile to be sure. He's meeting with a Chinese man. I'm sitting about fifty yards away from him."

"After he retired, the case was archived. If he didn't retire, we have to re-examine the case and make necessary updates. Can you make it to the Ventura office this afternoon?" Dave asked.

"What about taking action now?"

"The Red Notice was canceled, and the case was closed after he retired. We have no authority to act."

"I can be there at two o'clock today. Does that work?"

"That'll work," Dave replied. "See you then."

Chapter 6

Matt arrived at the Pleasant Valley gate to Port Hueneme Navy Base at 1:30 p.m. After flashing his credentials, he drove down Pleasant Valley Road to Dock Road and parked beside a weathered warehouse. His hair now brushed over his ears, and a trimmed goatee framed his jaw. A work crew in the lot glanced at him as he got out, then quickly returned to their tasks when he moved toward a small door on the building's north side.

He approached a nondescript entry in the far-right corner marked only by a plaque that read *Storage Room A*. A faint smile tugged at his lips as he thought someone had clearly enjoyed their Cold War spy flicks. He leaned into the retina scanner, saw the panel flash green, and entered his access code.

Inside was a familiar office. This was where DCS had first recruited him. The modest furnishings included a couch, two chairs, and a pair of worn faux-leather recliners. The décor created the illusion of an ordinary office space.

Decades ago, the room had housed Navy computer technicians who programmed electronics for ships anchored offshore. They'd descend a stairwell at the back, walk through a long underground tunnel, and reach a classified equipment room. From there, a stairwell led to the docks, where a small boat ferried them to the vessels.

Though the original cover story held for years, few now believed it. Too many sharp-eyed operatives with quiet confidence, whose long hair and goatees were a far cry from regulation, had passed through the door. What remained hidden was that the site had become the western-hemisphere coordination office for Defense Clandestine Services.

Matt moved to the rear of the office, scanned his retina again, and entered another code. The door clicked open. As he descended the stairwell, motion sensors lit the path and cameras tracked his progress. At the bottom, a long hallway stretched ahead.

At the final checkpoint, another retina scan and access code granted him entry. The heavy door clicked open, revealing the command center, an entirely different world from the modest office above.

This room was a modern working office with state-of-the-art technology. Six people occupied their individual desks. Eight fifty-two-inch monitors were mounted on the wall in front of the desks. Some of them had several windows open on-screen, showing camera feeds from around the building. Four of the monitors were tracking the major news networks.

As Matt walked through the office, he saw several staff working diligently at their desks. As he continued through the room towards Dave Johnson's office, he heard someone say, "Mr. Scales, I'm Jon Mitchell. I ran logistics for you when you were in Ukraine."

Matt nodded at Mitchell as he walked past him and headed for Dave's office. He stopped at the open door and knocked.

"Come on in, Matt," Dave's booming voice called out from behind the door.

Matt swung the door open and walked into the room. Dave was engrossed in a file on his desk, holding up a finger to indicate he needed a minute.

Thirty seconds later, Dave glanced at Matt. "Let's go to the SCIF."

As he got up, Dave picked up the file he'd been reading on his desk and tucked it under his left arm. They walked to the back of Dave's office and once again had their identity checked with a retina scanner. Dave punched in a door code and Matt heard the familiar click, then they dropped their phones into a tray by the door as they entered the SCIF, a Secure Compartmented Information Facility used for classified discussions.

Once inside, Matt pushed a button that closed the door and activated the electronic jammers. Dave and Matt settled into the large black chairs with high backs and soft cushions.

Dave handed Matt the file he'd carried into the room. Matt took a few minutes to read it. When he was finished, he closed the file and looked at Dave.

"The video from the drone attack shows overwhelming evidence that we killed Lebedev," Dave said. "After analyzing and validating the footage, we closed the file and proceeded to the next project."

"We need to reopen the file!" Matt exclaimed. "He's alive and well, and in the US!"

"I put a rush on analyzing the photos you sent us. I just got the results. The analysts agree with you. It was Lebedev. You need to update the files. Once you do, we can reopen the case and request the re-issuance of the Red Notice."

Matt stared at the ceiling, figuring out how all the pieces fit together, especially considering what he'd overheard. He wasn't sure what everything meant, but his gut told him something big was about to happen.

After a few minutes, he looked at Dave. "I'm more concerned about spending my time figuring out why he's here and tracking him down than spending time writing up statements for some bureaucrat to review."

"I get what you're saying, but unless you're prepared to return to work and pursue leads, that's the best option we have."

"I know, I know," Matt said. "I'll hang out here for a few days and try pulling everything together and write up a report for you. Once we have that information, we can decide our next step."

***

After his meeting with Chen Da, Lebedev left the breakwater and drove to LAX, his mind already many steps ahead. By the time his flight landed in Mexico City, his first identity was discarded. A second passport took him through Europe with minimal scrutiny. In Frankfurt, he used his final alias to board a flight to Moscow, slipping back into the shadows before anyone realized he was gone.

Once he was back in Moscow, Lebedev proceeded straight to Sergei Abdulov's office.

"Alexei, welcome back to Moscow," Abdulov said. "I didn't expect you back so soon. I assume you're here to report on what happened in Santa Barbara?"

"Yes, I am. Zhang Wei recklessly launched an attack at an electrical transfer station in Santa Barbara. He admitted he did it as a probing activity. I tried to explain to him that his actions jeopardized our plans. His behavior was unreasonable. He stated matter-of-factly that he didn't care about our agreement and coordinated attack plans. He was only worried about China's success. At that point, his bodyguard reached for his weapon. He left me no choice but to kill them both. I then met with Chen Da and explained my actions and reasoning. I reiterated that we needed to coordinate our efforts if we wished to succeed."

"Was he agreeable to that?" Sergei asked.

"His government is still committed to the plan. He also said they're running out of patience, and that we need to expedite our part of the operation."

"Are you sure our plan in the US will have the desired impact?"

"Yes," Lebedev said. "We must remain steadfast in our efforts and speed up our plans. I am moving forward with recruiting the required assets. We will be ready to execute within two months."

"You will head back to the United States then?"

"Yes, most of our assets are in place, including the same advanced team we used in Ukraine. I want to personally ensure that everything is ready. Coordination of efforts between us and the Chinese is imperative for a successful operation."

"I trust you implicitly, Alexei. Let me know if there's anything you need," Sergei said.

The blank expression on Lebedev's face betrayed none of his thoughts. He knew that this time, when he left Moscow, he had to succeed, or he would not be returning home.

***

After Dave Johnson confirmed Lebedev was alive, Matt spent the next three days at the Port Hueneme DCS site, reviewing intelligence reports and writing up his observations. He analyzed intelligence reports from DCS, the CIA, and the FBI in an effort to determine why Lebedev might be in the United States.

To Matt, intelligence was like putting a jigsaw puzzle together with all the pieces upside down. But unlike a jigsaw puzzle, with intelligence, the complete picture was unknown to you. You had to concentrate on connecting the pieces based on their shapes. Not only did you not know what crucial pieces you were missing, you were also unaware of the total number of pieces involved. At times, it was incredibly frustrating, but he did the best he could with the information he had, turned in his report, and drove back to Santa Barbara.

Matt sat at his kitchen table, staring at the untouched coffee in front of him. His mind kept drifting back to DCS, to the way he had slipped back into his old rhythm. Hours spent reading intelligence reports, piecing together fragments of global conflicts, had felt natural, like stepping into a comfortable worn pair of boots. He hadn't realized how much he missed it until he was back in the thick of it, his focus sharpening, the familiar mix of anticipation and determination kicking in.

And the anxiety.

That undercurrent of tension had always been there, pushing him to over-prepare, to plan every move, every contingency. He knew better than anyone that no plan survived first contact, but the more time he spent thinking through the angles, the better he performed when the action hit. That was his edge. That was what had always set him apart.

But now he wasn't in the fight. He was sitting at his kitchen table, waiting. The reports he had written would take days to filter through the bureaucratic machine. He had nothing to do but think, and thinking was dangerous.

During the drive back to Santa Barbara, he'd realized how relaxed and almost happy he was now. The most relaxed and happy he'd been since his parents died. That realization should have comforted him, but it left him conflicted. He was pulled between the realization that he might be able to have a good life outside of DCS and unfinished business. The information that Lebedev was still alive made Matt feel like he was on the losing end of a tug-of-war match, slowly being pulled back into the clandestine world.

He exhaled, running a hand over his face. He needed something, or someone, to help break the spiral.

April.

Was he calling her because he needed a distraction? Or because he just wanted someone to talk to? He wasn't sure, and he decided it didn't matter.

He picked up his phone and tapped her number.

She answered on the second ring.

"Well, hello, Mr. Scales," April said.

"Hey April, I'm just calling to check in and see how you're doing."

"I'm doing okay. I'm downtown right now, doing some furniture shopping."

"Well, if you're not busy, I thought it'd be nice to grab lunch," Matt said.

"Sounds good. Shoreline?"

"Absolutely. See you there in a few."

He set the phone down and looked around the quiet kitchen. The stillness didn't feel quite so heavy now. Lunch with April would help.

Chapter 7

Day 63 - Santa Barbara, CA

April pulled her black 2021 Lexus RX 350 into the Leadbetter Beach parking lot, spotting Matt's Adriatic Blue Genesis G80 already tucked into a space near the entrance to the Shoreline Café. Of course he was early. That hadn't changed.

She parked beside him and shut off the engine, taking a quick breath before stepping out. The sea breeze was soft, the smell of salt and grilled food drifting over from the patio. Familiar. Almost comfortable.

She hadn't seen him in a while. She wasn't sure what this was, just lunch, a check-in, or something more. But part of her was glad he'd called.

Matt was waiting by his car, and they fell into step naturally, walking toward the café without needing to fill the silence.

At the counter, she insisted on paying.

They carried their drinks out to his favorite table on the sand, a quiet spot with an unobstructed view of the ocean. She liked it. It made it easier to think.

"It's been a few days, huh?" he said, sliding into the chair opposite her.

"Yep," she replied, managing a small smile. She set down her drink and glanced at the ocean.

"What type of furniture are you looking for?" he asked.

"A new sectional," she said, tucking a strand of hair behind her ear. "Something you can fall asleep on during a movie and not wake up feeling like you need a chiropractor."

He chuckled. "Sounds expensive."

She shrugged. "I'm not settling."

A quiet lull settled between them, broken only by the rhythmic crash of waves and the soft clatter of silverware from other tables. Matt took a sip of his coffee. His posture was relaxed, but not entirely at ease. April noticed that.

"So... I've been off the grid a bit," he said casually. "What's the latest on that Montecito situation that pulled you away from breakfast last week? I haven't really followed the news."

The shift was subtle, but April caught it. His tone was too even. She kept her own voice neutral.

"I'm not directly involved in the investigation," she said. "But I've been getting updates. Two dead Chinese nationals found at a Montecito estate. They've linked a helicopter crash near New Cuyama to the scene. One male dead at the crash site."

Matt didn't flinch. But his fingers closed a little tighter around his cup.

"Any updates on identifying the body?" he asked. "Or anything that's not adding up?"

She watched him carefully before answering, taking a measured sip. "There's not much else. A gardener from a neighboring estate saw the helicopter land. Twenty minutes later, he heard gunshots. He saw two people in the front seat when it took off. That's when he called the sheriff's office. Deputies found the bodies."

She let the next line hang. "I got the call while we were having coffee at your place."

He gave a slow nod, and she watched for another reaction. There wasn't one. But the pause before the nod was just a shade too long. Not enough for anyone else to catch. But she did.

"Forty-five minutes after the helicopter left Montecito," she added, "it crashed just short of New Cuyama."

"Do they know the cause?" he asked. His voice was calm.

She hesitated, just for a breath. "They do, but they're keeping it classified."

His face stayed neutral, but April didn't miss the intensity in his eyes. Not panic. Not guilt. But definitely recognition. She filed it away.

"The chopper was from Island Charters at Santa Barbara Airport. Surveillance footage shows two people boarding. Investigators think the body is the pilot. They're still confirming the identity of the passenger and what happened to him."

Something in that hit him. She didn't say it out loud, but she knew. It meant something.

Still, she let it go.

"What've you been up to?" she asked, shifting the focus.

"Spent a few days down in Port Hueneme," he said. "My old boss needed help wrapping up some old cases."

She nodded, watching him as he spoke.

"How'd it feel being back in that world?"

Matt paused before answering, then smiled faintly. "Made me appreciate the past few months. I didn't realize how much I needed the break, from all the rules and noise. It's been good to focus on myself, my health. Living here."

April offered him a small smile in return, but her thoughts lingered on that pause earlier. The one just a heartbeat too long. She knew when someone was holding back.

And Matt was definitely holding something back.

If he was still playing games, she wasn't sure she had the time, or the patience, to figure out why.

***

After having lunch with April, Matt sat in his car, staring out at the ocean. The gently rolling waves were indifferent to the intense thoughts in his mind. A gull hovered above the shoreline, then dipped low, riding an unseen current. The Montecito murders, the helicopter crash, the missing passenger, and him seeing Lebedev at the breakwater. It all had to be connected.

He tapped his fingers against the steering wheel. He needed to talk to Dave Johnson.

Matt drove to Port Hueneme and laid everything out for Dave, who agreed to reach out to the Santa Barbara Sheriff's Office and pull video and case files. Two days later, Dave called him back.

"Get down here. You'll want to see this."

At the DCS offices, he followed Dave into the SCIF. Dave shut the door behind them, then turned with a look that confirmed Matt's gut feeling.

"Well," Dave started, "I think your hunch paid off. I spoke with Lieutenant Gordon, the supervisor of the Investigation Bureau."

"So, what did you learn?"

"Helicopter pilot was Greg Saunders. Local kid from Goleta. Started part-time with Island Charters at eighteen. The owner took a liking to him, helped him get his license. Three years later, he had enough hours to start running flights."

"April told me they're keeping the cause of the crash confidential," Matt said. "Did they give you anything more?"

Dave's expression darkened. "Preliminary analysis suggests an explosion inside the helicopter."

Matt straightened. "Accidental?"

"Intentional." Dave handed Matt a report. "C-4."

Matt let out a slow breath. Either an execution or getting rid of witnesses.

"They also sent me the video from Island Charters," Dave continued. "After looking at it, I ran it through our analysts. They confirmed the second passenger was Alexei Lebedev. He must have gotten off before the explosion. Most likely, he caused it."

Matt shook his head. "That seals it. Lebedev's alive, and whatever he's doing here isn't clean up. It's preparation."

"Yeah, and now we have another issue," Dave said. "How much do we tell the sheriff's office? And do they have someone with the clearance to handle this?"

Matt considered the questions. "They've got intelligence and Homeland Security guys with at least a Secret clearance. Their bomb techs need Top Secret for certification. And we can invoke the emergency exemption to loop in Gordon."

Dave nodded as he watched Matt closely. "One more thing. Are you going to take that vacation, or are you coming back to work?" He gave a half smile. "You know you're not going to sleep right until you take Lebedev out yourself."

Matt didn't respond. He just turned for the door, raising a hand in a casual wave as he walked out.

Behind him, Dave chuckled. "Yeah. That's what I thought."

Chapter 8

Day 65 - Santa Barbara, CA

Matt sat at what he had come to think of as *his table* at the Shoreline Café, a third cup of coffee cooling in his grip. The morning rush had passed, leaving behind the low murmur of conversation and the steady crash of waves across the sand.

He heard none of it.

His mind was reviewing everything he'd uncovered, especially the Montecito murders and the downed helicopter with its missing passenger. Something kept tugging at him. At the breakwater, Lebedev had mentioned the words "Montecito" and "electric." The words echoed. His thoughts drifted back to his last conversation with Chin. Maybe it was time to call him.

Matt hesitated.

Reaching out would mean more than just reconnecting. It would mean stepping back into the shadows. The clandestine world he had almost walked away from.

But he already knew the truth.

He would never rest. Never find peace. Not until he found Lebedev. And killed him.

***

The drive to Port Hueneme felt like crossing a threshold. By the time Matt walked into Dave Johnson's office at DCS, he was fully committed.

"Hey Dave, I'm ready. What do we need to do to get me officially back in the field?"

"Well, first I need a release from the doctor, and second, I need to recall your team from Europe. They're just finishing up an op and should be available within a week."

"That works for me," Matt said. "Remember, I have a release for light duty. So, I'll do some work in the office today, and then tomorrow I'll talk to the doctor and get him to release me back on full duty."

"Sounds good. Let me get Amy to print out the paperwork so we can officially get you back."

Matt spent the next hour pulling intelligence reports and researching financial records on Lebedev. About an hour later, Dave called him into his office to sign some paperwork.

"Okay," Dave said. "We're all set. You're officially back at work. What are you going to do first?"

"Well, something keeps bothering me. I had a discussion with Chin Ho a few weeks ago about some concerns he had about transformers. Something tells me I need to follow up with him. It may be nothing, but we know how small bits of information can grow into significant intel."

Matt called Chin with his private phone. He did not use the office phone, because he was concerned Chin might not answer a call coming from a restricted line.

"Hey Chin, how's it goin'? I'm calling to check on how you're doing with that minor issue we discussed in our last call."

"My investigation has only heightened my concerns," the man said. "I need to run something by you and might need your help. Can you call me in a secure video link? I have something I want to show you."

"Absolutely, Chin. For you, anything. As a matter of fact, I can make that happen in about five minutes."

Matt walked into the SCIF and made the secure video link call to Chin.

"So, what is it that has you so concerned?" Matt said. "You've got that serious look on your face."

"As I mentioned before, a month ago, I received a power transformer from Eielson Air Force Base in Alaska. It's one of three replacement substation power transformers being installed in the base's electrical substation. There was a delay in getting some parts for the last one. The base commander sent it to the DOE for analysis. It ended up in my lab."

"What's a substation power transformer?"

"Substation power transformers handle substantial power levels and are essential for transmitting electricity over long distances. They regulate entire neighborhoods and critical facilities. The transformers on poles you see on streets are basic. They just step-down voltage with no complex controls. But the substation power transformers? Different ball game. Power transformers have advanced control systems, which include software for monitoring performance, managing load tap changers, and ensuring protection against faults in real time."

"Are you concerned about the Chinese origin of the transformers?"

"Not directly, but I found a sleeper-agent code buried deep in the software of the transformer that was sent to me for analysis. The code looks like it's designed to shut down or overload the transformer. It targets their software. I haven't tracked the source or how it's triggered, but it's genius how they buried the sleeper-agent code so deep."

"Could we be looking at failures across multiple substations?"

"Yep," Chin said. "Substation software in the transformers reroutes power to other substations and stabilizes the grid. If this sleeper agent coordinates a few well-timed overloads of multiple substation transformers, it could cause a cascading failure, resulting in massive power outages. Entire cities could go dark. It could be like the Northeast blackout of 2003. Fifty million people lost their power throughout the Northeast and Canada. The blackout could last for a few hours, a few days, or even weeks."

"How did you find this sleeper agent? Is that what you called it?"

"Yes, it's a sleeper agent, which is basically a virus. I recognized it because I wrote it! Or more correctly, I wrote the first version of it."

"You wrote it? Why? And how the hell did somebody else get it?"

"Do you remember my deployment and assignment during the Afghan war?" Chin asked.

"Yes, you were working on several classified projects."

"Yes, and one was Project Zeno. It was based on Project Socrates."

"Didn't Socrates have something to do with the US stealing intelligence from other countries?"

"Yeah, it was a project established in 1983 under Reagan. The basic premise was that before Project Socrates, the US only concentrated on restricting the export of its technology. Many countries realized it was easier to steal technology from other countries than to develop it on their own. Project Socrates changed our focus from not only developing our own technology, but also importing it, also known as stealing it through espionage."

"So, what does that have to do with our current situation and the transformers?" Matt asked.

"After Project Socrates became an accepted policy, the emphasis on technology control and acquisition took on a new meaning in the US," Chin stated. "The US not only started stealing technology from other nations, but also decided that since other nations were stealing our technology, we might as well take advantage of that. Russia and China have always believed they're masters at stealing secrets from other countries, especially the US. And they are."

"That's interesting," Matt said, "but how does it fit into the code you found in the transformers?"

"One of my assignments was to develop a sleeper agent for the software in the drones that were flying over Afghanistan. The goal back then was to ensure we'd have a back door into anything they reverse engineered from our technology.

"As part of the project, we stripped some of the sophisticated and classified features out of the drones, but we left them able to do basic functions. We programmed a sleeper agent into the software. We then 'crashed' the drone in an area where opposing forces friendly with Russia and/or China could retrieve it. The assumption was that the Russians or Chinese would eventually get the drone and the software. We assumed they would reverse engineer or copy the software and eventually use it in their devices. When that occurred, we could, at the right time, activate the sleeper agent to steal their technology and simultaneously disable any device they installed the software in."

"So, you were actually able to do this?"

"Absolutely. It was a highly compartmentalized project that only a few people know about. When I was digging down through the software in the transformers, I found a variation of the sleeper agent I developed for the drones over Afghanistan."

"Are you telling me that the power transformer from China, and possibly all the others that are being installed in the US, have sleeper agents in them? And that China can cause those transformers to overload and shut down with the push of a button?"

"Yes, that's what it looks like to me," Chin said. "It can also be coded to activate upon certain conditions, or at a certain time in the future. I haven't determine exactly how it's activated, but it's there."

Matt didn't say a word as he thought about the implications of what Chin had told him and how it all might fit into the bigger picture.

Chin pulled up a graph on his laptop. "My concern is that if they activate this virus at the right time, it could cause catastrophic cascading failures across the United States."

He pointed to the screen. "Look at this. There are two ideal times to release the virus. The first is in the evening when people get home from work. It's what the energy industry calls the duck curve. It's a vulnerability window where solar energy production drops off just as electricity demand surges. Traditional power plants can't ramp up fast enough to meet the spike."

"So, it's about timing the attack so the grid can't recover quickly."

"Exactly." Chin tapped the graph. "If they trigger the virus during this window, the system gets overwhelmed. The result? Rolling blackouts that cascade across the country. It's designed to cripple us at our weakest moment and create panic."

"You mean right at sunset?" Matt asked.

"Right. Fossil-fuel plants have to pick up the slack, but it's not instant. The grid struggles to adjust, especially as more homes go electric. That's where the virus comes in."

Matt eyes narrowed. "So, it's designed to hit during that gap? During the duck curve?"

Chin nodded. "That's how I'd do it. Cascading failures across the system. Remember last summer's heat wave in California? The governor asked people not to charge their electric cars in the evening. The grid couldn't handle the demand. He was afraid it would collapse."

Matt shook his head. "So, people had to choose to charge their cars or keep the lights on and make dinner?"

"For the lucky ones," Chin said. "At least they had a choice. But plenty of people rely on medical devices to stay alive, like oxygen and dialysis machines. A few hours without power could be fatal."

Matt exhaled. "This shouldn't happen in a first-world country, especially not here."

Chin gave a grim smile. "There's a worse option. At least psychologically."

Matt frowned. "Worse than blackouts during the evening rush?"

"If they hit in the early morning, just as people wake up and head to work, the psychological impact would be massive. Wall Street shuts down before the opening bell. Automated trading spirals out of control. The market crashes before anyone can react."

Matt's face darkened. "And on the streets?"

Chin tapped his laptop. "Traffic lights, train signals, air-traffic-control systems, all gone. Subways stall underground. Flights are grounded. Emergency services go dark. Gridlock everywhere."

Matt balled his fists. "A coordinated strike that cripples the economy and infrastructure before the day even begins."

"Exactly. And the virus won't just shut things down. It'll delay restarts, corrupt backups, block reboots. Everything will fail again and again."

Matt ran a hand through his hair. "How long would something like this take to plan?"

Chin's expression turned serious. "Years. The shift to an all-electric economy requires doubling our transmission capacity. That means new, sophisticated transformers. We've outsourced most of that manufacturing to China."

"Are the new transformers compromised?"

"I don't know," Chin said. "The real question is what the virus does, and when does it activate. That's why I need to inspect the two units at Eielson Air Force Base. I need to test them and compare their coding."

Matt folded his arms. "And if it has?"

Chin met his eyes. "Then we're already at war. We just don't know it."

Matt gave a slow nod. "All right. Looks like we're going to Eielson. When can you leave?"

"What, me? No!" Chin exclaimed in Mandarin. "I'm giving you this information so you can figure out what to do with it."

"Well, you said yourself you need to inspect the transformers at Eielson Air Force Base to determine the depth of this problem and its potential. What better way than to do it in person?" Matt replied in Mandarin, mimicking his friend's excitement.

***

Three Days Later

After their call ended, Matt had briefed Dave Johnson on his conversation with Chin. Dave agreed that Chin needed to go to Alaska. He authorized Matt to share whatever Chin needed to know to do his job, short of the classified details about their investigation into Lebedev.

Chin's phone buzzed. Matt's voice came through the line.

"I've arranged for you to fly out of Joint Base Lewis-McChord," Matt said. "Military transport. I'll meet you in Alaska."

Now, six hours into the flight, Chin was more than ready to get off the noisy, cramped aircraft. His ears still buzzed from the roar of the engines as the rear ramp of the C-130 lowered with a mechanical whine. Chin grabbed his backpack, stepped toward the opening, and squinted into the rush of frigid air.

At the bottom of the ramp stood a man with long hair and a scruffy beard, a rifle slung casually over one shoulder. Chin immediately recognized the weapon as an M4. He'd seen plenty of those in the video games he used to play.

"Hey, you Ho?" the man called out in a deep, confident voice.

"Yes," Chin replied, clutching the straps of his backpack.

"Gonzo," the man said, pointing to himself. "Grab your gear and weapons. Let's move."

Chin blinked. "I'm a scientist. A researcher. I don't carry weapons."

"What?" Gonzo looked confused. "Thought all you DCS guys were strapped."

Chin hesitated, unsure how much to say. "I don't carry. And even if I did I wouldn't know how to use it."

Gonzo shook his head and gave a crooked grin. "Well, let me help you out. You got a credit card?"

Chin frowned. "Of course."

"Give me one you don't use too often, but always have with you."

Chin pulled out his AMEX Black Diamond card. "Here."

Gonzo took the card and pulled a knife from his belt. He set the card on a piece of wood and sliced it diagonally in one smooth motion. The corner now had a sharp point.

"Now you have a weapon," Gonzo said, handing it back.

Chin turned the two halves over in his hands. "What kind of weapon is this?"

"Homemade credit-card knife. See how sharp the tip is? More than enough to slice a man's throat, or stick him in the neck if you need to."

Chin stared at it, stunned. He slipped the broken card back into his wallet. Two thoughts hit him at once. First, he was way outside his comfort zone. Second, this was the world his best friend, Matt Scales, had lived in for the last twenty-five years.

"Come on, let's go," Gonzo said. "The base commander's waiting. He wants to know what the hell's going on."

***

Chin and Gonzo climbed into a black Ford Expedition that was parked next to the hangar. Chin sat in the passenger seat with his arms around his backpack containing his laptop. For some reason, his wallet in his back pocket felt fatter after he'd put his AMEX card back in it.

As they drove out of the airport, they turned right on Flightline Avenue. After a few more minutes of driving and a couple of turns, they arrived at the base headquarters building.

Chin glanced over at Gonzo. "So, why'd they send you to pick me up? I expected someone in uniform."

"When the call came in from higher up that DCS was sending someone, no one told us much. They figured I might be able to size you up."

Chin gave him a look. "No offense, but you don't exactly scream 'Air Force security.' What's a guy like you doing here, dressed like that and carrying an M4?"

"We're running security assessments across a few sensitive sites. The base commander and I go way back. He asked me to meet you personally." Gonzo gave Chin a lopsided grin. "And now that I know you're a scientist, I'm guessing even if you told me what you're here for, it'd be in a language I'd need a decoder ring to understand."

"Well, I'm not sure what I'm allowed to tell you," Chin said. "I was just brought along as a technical expert to look at some irregularities we found in some software in your equipment. Matt Scales, who works in the field for DCS, should be here anytime. He can give you all the details."

Just then, Gonzo's cell phone rang. He answered the phone and said, "Okay, thanks." Then he looked at Chin. "Did you say Matt Scales? The call was from the tower. There's a flight scheduled to land from Southern California in about twenty minutes. His name is on the manifest. You can come with me to get him if you want, unless you'd rather go sit in the lobby of HQ by yourself."

"No, I'd rather stay with you. Let's go get 'em," Chin said.

Gonzo turned the Expedition around and headed back towards the airport. They sat in the shade next to the hangar. Even with the windows rolled up, Chin could smell the jet fuel. He also thought he knew what cold was, but he had never experienced this type of cold.

"So, you know Matt?" Chin asked.

"Know him? Yeah, you could say that. Scales is one of those guys. You hear about him before you ever meet him. First time I saw him, he was coming out of the ocean like Poseidon himself, dragging a half-dead Russian spy over his shoulder. Didn't even stop to catch his breath. Just dropped the guy at our feet and said, 'You got room in the brig?'"

Chin blinked, not sure if Gonzo was exaggerating. The man had that storyteller's glint in his eye, but the details felt too vivid to be a lie. "That actually happened?"

"Oh yeah. Black Sea operation. Top secret stuff, but you know how spec ops are. Word gets around. 'Scales' was the name on everybody's lips. They say he took down half the crew with nothing but a blade and an attitude."

"Sounds more like a script from a movie."

"Nope. It was real."

Chin frowned. "I've known Matt since he was fifteen. He doesn't talk much about what he's been doing over the last twenty-five years."

"That's because legends don't need to talk about themselves. People like me do it for them."

Absorbing what Gonzo was telling him, Chin looked out across the vast airport. Snow was everywhere. The wind was howling. Chin looked over at Gonzo, who was sipping a cup of coffee.

"You wanna know the truth, Doc? Guys like Scales don't belong in a place like this. He belongs in the field doing what he does best. A ghost. And yet he's here. I don't know what you guys are involved in, but you're lucky to have him in your corner."

Before Chin could respond, the faint hum of an engine broke through the wind. Gonzo straightened as the small military plane taxied into view. Its sleek frame glinted under the hangar lights.

"AC-17," Gonzo muttered. "Those things are monsters. A lot of plane for just one guy."

The aircraft rolled to a halt. Its nose was pointed toward the mountains beyond the runway. They watched the ground crew wave it into position just in front of the hangar. As the engines powered down, the rear cargo ramp began to lower with a hydraulic hiss.

Matt descended the ramp. His silhouette was unmistakable, even in the dim light, as he picked his way across the snow. His boots crunched against the icy tarmac. He adjusted the backpack across his shoulders and zipped up his jacket.

Gonzo got out of the Expedition and walked over to Matt. "Hey old man, you need help carrying that backpack? It looks pretty heavy for you."

"I think I can handle it. Besides, I don't want to see you struggle to carry an M4 and a backpack at the same time. I know coordinating such complex physical movements can be difficult for you."

"Good to see you, Matt, especially since I thought you were dead," Gonzo said.

"Well, as the saying goes, the rumors of my demise have been greatly exaggerated. What the heck are you doing here?"

"Doing a security survey for some of their classified areas."

"Well, appreciate you coming to pick me up, but isn't this an assignment way below your pay grade?"

"Yes it is," Gonzo said. "But, as I told your trustworthy scientist over here, the base commander sent me to find out what you couldn't tell him on a secure line."

"Well, let's just say that I'm here to make the base commander's day a little worse.

***

Matt loaded his equipment into the Expedition and climbed into the backseat, letting Chin keep his spot in the front. Gonzo drove them back to base headquarters. Once inside, they made their way straight to Eielson Air Force Base's command center, a fortress of steel and concrete, a stark contrast to the endless white wilderness surrounding it. Chin's eyes darted around the room, taking in the data streaming across the large monitors. He didn't fully grasp the military-specific operations, but he recognized a highly sophisticated system that required skilled personnel.

He took a steadying breath and forced himself to focus. He was here for a reason.

Matt, clad in Levi's, a T-shirt, and a leather jacket, walked beside him. Chin forced a smile and squared his shoulders, doing his best to mimic Matt's easygoing posture.

At the far end of the bustling room, a man caught Chin's attention. He was over six feet tall, with a muscular build and a chiseled jawline. His sharp eyes scanned the room, his every movement exuding authority and confidence. The man locked his piercing eyes on Chin.

"Dr. Ho. Agent Scales," the man greeted in a deep voice. "I'm Colonel Brown. I trust your journey was uneventful."

"Uneventful, yes," Chin replied, though his insides were a tangle of nerves after his initial interaction with Gonzo.

Colonel Brown motioned for them to follow him into a secure briefing room. The heavy door shut behind them, sealing them off from the rest of the base. A large screen dominated one wall, displaying a complex schematic of the base's electrical grid.

Matt took a seat while Chin remained standing, his eyes drawn to the screen. He recognized the transformers, each a critical node of the base's electrical grid. The diagram mapped connections and pathways.

"So, tell me," Colonel Brown said, with an edge of curiosity, "what brings the infamous Matt Scales to Alaska?"

Matt met Brown's gaze but said nothing.

"Gonzo here has shared some of your exploits. An Air Force base in the middle of nowhere seems a bit mundane for you."

Matt grinned. "Gonzo's got a big mouth, and he drinks too much, so don't believe everything he says. I'm just along for the ride on this one. Dr. Ho here discovered something in the transformer you sent to the Pacific Northwest National Laboratory for analysis."

Colonel Brown's expression darkened. "What did you find?"

Matt gestured to Chin. "Dr. Ho, why don't you explain?"

Chin stepped forward and tapped his laptop's trackpad. The screen came to life, cycling through complex diagrams and maps of the power grid. There were also images of satellite imagery and lines of embedded code.

"The transformer you sent to the DOE ended up in my lab," Chin began. "While reviewing its software, I found a latent virus buried deep in the system."

He paused, letting that sink in.

"The virus gives a remote operator the ability to shut down the transformer. If multiple units are triggered simultaneously, the result could be a massive blackout leading to a cascading failure across the grid."

Colonel Brown's jaw tensed. "Can you remove it? Reverse it?"

"That's what we're here to determine," Chin said. "I need direct access to your transformers. They're the same model as the one I analyzed. If they're compromised, I can compare the variants, isolate the code, and possibly develop an antivirus. Maybe even trace its source."

Matt leaned forward. "What Chin's saying, Colonel, is this isn't some isolated malware. We're looking at a coordinated cyber-attack."

The room fell quiet. As Brown stared at the display, the diagrams reflected in his eyes. His voice, when it came, was low.

"Jesus... You're saying this could be a deliberate strike on our infrastructure?"

Chin nodded. "Yes, sir. And if the right nodes are hit..."

"The failure could spread far beyond this base," Matt finished. "Whoever's behind it is counting on us not seeing it coming."

Brown pounded the table with his fist. The sound cracked through the room like a shot.

"This is a goddamn catastrophe waiting to happen. How the hell did it get this far without anyone catching it?"

Chin cleared his throat. "Because it was built to go unnoticed. Sophisticated code, deep-level obfuscation. This has been years in the making by someone thinking ten steps ahead."

Brown turned back to the screen, then to Matt. "Do you have a plan?"

Matt nodded. "Chin is working on isolating the virus and shutting it down, but there's no guarantee we'll catch it in time. We need full cooperation and unrestricted access to your systems."

Brown's shoulders stiffened. "You'll have it. But I want updates at every stage. If this virus is as dangerous as you say, we don't have time for red tape."

Matt held his gaze, then shifted gears. "If the worst happens and the base loses power, what's your contingency?"

Brown exhaled. "Our cogeneration coal plant pushes electricity through a transfer station before distributing it across the base. If it goes down, emergency generators kick in automatically for critical facilities. They're not built to sustain long-term operations."

Chin leaned forward. "Are the generators wired through the transformers or directly into the buildings?"

"Directly," Brown replied. "The generators bypass the transformers entirely."

"Good," Chin said. "Then we need to disconnect the transformers, before the virus activates. That way, if it triggers, it won't propagate through your system."

Brown studied the schematic on the screen as his fingers drummed against the table.

"Shut down our main power before there's even an attack?" he said slowly. "That's a hell of a gamble."

"It's a calculated risk," Chin replied. "But it's safer than assuming nothing will happen."

The room fell silent.

"Damn it..." Brown muttered. He straightened in his chair. "All right. We disconnect the transformers and switch to backup."

Chin nodded. "I'll keep working on the antivirus. Once it's ready, I'll manually install it in your transformers. If the virus launches after that, the antivirus will auto-activate and neutralize it."

"Get it to us as fast as you can," Brown said. "We'll hold the line until then."

He looked at Matt. "Who else knows about this? If I call someone above me, are they going to know what I'm talking about, or am I going to be the one to break the news that we're staring down a possible national-level infrastructure breach?"

Matt kept his tone steady. "We're early in the investigation. We're not keeping people in the dark, we just don't have the full picture yet. The DOD knows we're tracking malware in certain electrical transformers. That's why we came here first. Not just because the transformer in question came from your base, but because you've got two more from the same batch, already installed. And this is a secure location. Once we start looking in the private sector, we lose control over who finds out."

Brown nodded slowly. "Understood."

He turned to Chin. "I'm assigning Gonzo as your escort. He'll get you into any part of this base. Start immediately. I need something concrete before I make my next call."

Matt exchanged a look with Chin.

Now they just had to confirm their suspicions, and hope Chin could finish an antivirus in time.

***

Chin had been at the base's main substation for six hours when Matt walked in.

"Any progress?"

Chin exhaled, rubbing his temples. "Same sleeper agent I found in the transformer they sent me. It's dormant, waiting for activation."

"Activation from who?"

"That's the million-dollar question," Chin said. "It's triggered under specific conditions or by a remote activation code. Whoever modified it added a layer beyond my original design. Not surprising, since the base code is over a decade old."

Matt folded his arms. "How does it get activated? Don't they need direct access?"

"No. Looks like they're using power line communications or PLCs. Small data packets that ride the electrical current. One of those packets could contain the activation code."

Matt frowned. "You're saying someone in China could send a signal through the grid and trigger the virus?"

"Yes and no," Chin said. "PLCs only work over short distances. If this is a real threat, the activation point is in Moose Creek, just outside the base."

"So, someone's already in place to send the command?"

"Or they've set up a relay," Chin replied. "Could be a rented apartment, internet connection, and a dedicated system. The command gets sent from anywhere in the world, bounces through that relay, and hits the grid locally."

They took the findings straight to Colonel Brown. He stood motionless as Chin walked him through the relay theory and the dormant code buried inside the base's transformers. By the end of the briefing, Colonel Brown was already barking orders to his staff to recheck that the generators were fully functioning and had plenty of fuel. He also ordered them to physically confirm the transformers were disconnected from the entire base.

With nothing more to do at the base, Matt and Chin packed their gear and headed outside. Gonzo was already waiting by the vehicle, engine running, ready to get them to the airport.

***

The crisp Alaskan air hit Chin Ho as he stepped out of the base's main building, the chill biting through his jacket. He pulled the zipper up higher, trying to ward off the cold, but it did little to settle the unease still lingering from what he had found. Beside him, Matt walked with the stride of a man accustomed to military installations and high-stakes situations. Chin, on the other hand, felt like he was navigating a world that was growing stranger by the minute.

Ahead of them, Gonzo waited by a military Humvee with a mischievous glint in his eye.

"So, Doc," Gonzo said, giving Chin a once-over, "how's that new weapon of yours holding up?"

Chin hesitated, his hand unconsciously moving to his pocket where the two halves of the credit card rested. "Uh, it's... fine, I guess, But you know, I'm still not sure how practical it is."

Gonzo chuckled, opening the Humvee's door with a flourish. "Practical? It's got 'tactical innovation' written all over it."

Matt, who had been observing the exchange in silence, grinned. "Gonzo's right, Chin. You're in the big leagues now."

Gonzo grinned, throwing the Humvee into gear. "You know it, Scales. Doc here might surprise us all. You never know what you're capable of until failure is not an option."

Chin chuckled, glancing out the window as the base receded into the distance.

As the Humvee rumbled down the snow-covered road, the banter continued, gradually easing the tension in Chin's chest. Despite the absurdity of the situation, he couldn't help but feel a little more at ease. These were men who lived on the edge, and he was learning they had their own unique ways of dealing with the pressure.

For now, he would focus on what he did best: unraveling the code and stopping the virus.

But somewhere in the back of his mind, he knew this might be the start of something that pulled him far from the safety of his lab.

Chapter 9

Day 68 - Richland, Washington

After leaving the Air Force base in Alaska, Chin returned to his lab in Washington. The place was quiet, except for the hum of fans cooling the computers on his desk. Chin glanced at the clock on the wall. 2:13 a.m. The hours had slipped by as he immersed himself in the analysis of the data from the Air Force base. He was tired, both physically and emotionally. It was the kind of tired where he had to force himself to stand up and walk around. He needed a break.

Chin walked into the break room and opened the drawer next to the refrigerator, pulling out a small, smooth-wrapped package of Iron Goddess of Mercy tea. It was the same tea his mother made at home. He'd found it at Seattle's Best Tea.

Chin's mother taught him at an early age that drinking tea was a ritual to be savored and experienced. That experience included the lesson that brewing and preparing the tea was just as important as drinking it.

He considered heating the water in the microwave, but that would make his ancestors roll over in their graves. Instead, he opted to follow tradition, and he heated the water in the pot on the stove. He ground the tea in a grinder and dropped the leaves into the teapot, then poured the in the boiling water, and let it steep.

As the steam rose out of the teapot, he savored the delicate aroma.

Every part of the process was deliberate. He raised the pot of tea from the table, held it four inches above his cup, and poured. He stopped when the liquid reached just below the rim.

After pouring the tea, he carefully returned the teapot to the counter. He picked up the cup and held it under his nose. The aroma reminded him of his mother. He could almost hear her voice, saying how proud she was of him. A pang of guilt struck him. He wondered how his mother would feel if she knew the damage his work might cause.

He took a slow sip, feeling the warmth and savoring the taste before he lowered the cup.

Is this all my fault?

He held both hands around the teacup. The warmth gave him some comfort.

Sitting in his lab, he noticed the intense silence surrounding him. He had spent countless hours here alone, absorbed in his work. He took solace in not having to justify himself to anyone, but he also realized that this independence contributed to the overpowering loneliness he often felt.

Tonight, the solitude felt suffocating. He didn't have many friends. In fact, Matt was his only true friend. They had shared many experiences, and he longed to call him. Matt would listen without passing judgment and always knew how to lift his spirits.

Chin picked up his phone and opened it to Matt's contact information. He moved his finger over the top of Matt's number, but he stopped. It was 2:30 a.m. Matt had enough on his own plate.

He put the phone back on the table. The silence in the room almost overwhelmed him.

He wrapped his hands around the now-lukewarm cup and took a slow sip of the tea, holding the warm liquid in his mouth for a few seconds, savoring the taste.

He set down the cup. Since he was the one who had created the virus in the first place, his only path to redemption was to develop an antivirus to eliminate it. There was no undoing the past. But he could fix the future.

***

Matt stood at the edge of the conference room in Port Hueneme with his arms crossed, scanning the familiar maps now pinned to the wall. Western US infrastructure grids. Transmission corridors. Substation layouts. It looked like the war room it once had been.

Chin had just arrived, fresh out of three days locked in his lab. His shoulders were tight, his eyes focused, but the dark circles gave him away. Matt gave him a nod as he took a seat. The team was coming together, albeit slowly, but it was happening.

Skip and St. Bernard were already tossing barbs back and forth, their usual rhythm restoring a sense of normalcy. The table was a mess of folders, dossiers on Lebedev's known associates, offshore accounts, airstrip locations, and satellite intel. It felt good to be back in the fight.

Dave Johnson stepped into the room without knocking. Typical.

"Your team has a new member. Jon Mitchell," Dave said. "He'll officially join you in a few days. He's just finishing out a project with another team."

Matt raised an eyebrow. Mitchell was solid, but unexpected.

"Will he be running logistics for us?" he asked.

"Yep," Dave confirmed. "He ran it for you in Kharkiv. Business degree from Harvard."

Matt nodded slowly. Smart. Reliable. Experienced. He should fit right in.

"Hey Matt," Skip said, leaning back in his chair with a smirk that usually meant trouble. "I hear you've got a girlfriend."

Matt let out a low sigh. "She's not my girlfriend, Skip. She's just a friend."

"Okay, Matt. One question. Do you have a picture of her?"

He didn't answer right away. Instead, he pulled out his phone, scrolled to the photo of him and April at the Shoreline Café, sunlight spilling across the table, and handed it over.

"Yeah, I have a picture."

Skip grabbed the phone with both hands like it was evidence. "Yep, just what I thought. She's a girlfriend. If you've got a picture of her having breakfast with you, she's your girlfriend."

Matt rolled his eyes, but he didn't take the phone back.

"Let's see this mystery woman," St. Bernard said, reaching across the table and grabbing the phone from Skip. When he looked at the screen, his entire posture changed.

"Jesus Christ, that's April Knight!"

Matt's head snapped up. "I know! But how do you know her?"

"We worked together in Black Squadron," St. Bernard said. "She's a top-notch operator."

Matt sat with that for a second. "Yeah, I know that. She saved my ass once. But that was a long time ago."

Skip raised an eyebrow. "So, you just bumped into her when you were in Santa Barbara?"

"Yep," Matt said. "Hadn't seen her since that op. I was running along the beach a few weeks ago, looked over, and she was right there beside me. She's a sergeant now in the sheriff's office. She responded to the Montecito double homicide that kicked off this whole investigation."

"Okay, that explains a lot," Skip said, then turned his attention to Chin with a crooked grin. "But I'm curious how *you* became friends with someone as smart as Chin. He seems way out of your league. I mean, he's intelligent and seems to have some class."

Matt chuckled, glancing over at Chin. "I've known him since I was a teenager."

Skip pushed away from the table and walked over to Chin. "Alright, Chin. Let's hear your side of the story. Matt's obviously not going to tell us how a clean-cut genius like you got roped into his knuckle-dragging world."

Chin looked up from his laptop, calm as ever. "It's not my story to tell."

"Well, you can tell us your version," St. Bernard said, leaning in with curiosity.

Matt watched Chin pause. He could see the flicker of memory in his eyes. A moment of reluctance. Then Chin took a breath and began.

"I first met Matt when I was in the eleventh grade at Paso Robles High School. My family had just moved from Seattle, and... well, Paso Robles is about as country as it gets. The only colors there are white and brown."

Matt shifted slightly in his seat. He remembered it all too well.

Chin continued. "Like a lot of rural towns, they worship the football team. Unfortunately, being Chinese made me a target. I stood out."

Matt didn't interrupt. Chin's voice had grown quieter, but steady.

"One day the starting quarterback stepped in front of me and said, 'Hey, math whiz, I need help with my homework. Since you're Chinese, you should be good at this.' I told him no and walked away. He shoved me to the ground."

Chin paused, and Matt felt something twist in his gut. Even now, years later.

"He picked me up and started shaking me. I thought I was done for. Then suddenly... I was on the ground. I looked up and saw the quarterback clutching his eye. And Matt was standing over him, yelling, 'Leave him alone! If I see you touch him again, I'll blacken your other one!'"

Skip let out a low whistle. St. Bernard just nodded slowly.

"I didn't know Matt," Chin added. "Later, I learned about his family and everything he'd been through. He told me he couldn't stand people getting away with things they shouldn't. After that, we started hanging out. At my house mostly. Video games, studying, just talking."

Chin's voice softened. "He gave me a place to belong in a town where I didn't feel like I had one."

Matt looked away for a moment. He'd never thought Chin would tell that story. Not to anyone else.

"Sounds like Matt," St. Bernard said, his voice quieter than usual.

"Yeah," Chin replied. "By the way... what is Black Squadron?"

Matt raised an eyebrow, but it was St. Bernard who leaned forward with a mock-serious tone. "That you even heard the term 'Black Squadron' means I have to kill you."

A pause.

"Black Squadron is a recon unit inside DEVGRU, what the public knows as SEAL Team Six. They specialize in deep recon. No backup, no rescue. Operatives, especially women, go in solo or in pairs. They blend in better. And if they get burned? That's it. There's no cavalry coming."

Chin blinked. "And your new girlfriend was one of them?"

"She's not my girlfriend," Matt repeated. Again. But there was less conviction behind it this time.

"I didn't know she was in Black Squadron. We only worked one op together. I lost touch with her after that."

"Well," St. Bernard said, "I wish she were with us on this one. She could help in a lot of ways."

Matt gave him a pointed look and shook his head.

"Okay, okay," St. Bernard said with a laugh. "Back to work."

Matt glanced around the room. Chin was back at his screen, already scanning data. Skip still wore that smug grin, arms crossed like he'd just won something. St. Bernard had his eyes locked on a map of the West Coast.

They were still one man short.

But this was Team Alpha 42.

And they weren't finished, not by a long shot.

PART II

THE COST OF KNOWING

*"The more you see, the less you sleep.
Awareness isn't clarity. It's weight."*

Matt Scales, situational analysis entry

Chapter 10

The temperature had just crossed triple digits. Jack Roberts had been sitting in his car monitoring a black Chevy Tahoe that was parked in the cafe parking lot. Roberts was waiting for the driver of the black Tahoe to come out of the café.

The cafe was one of a handful of businesses in the small town of New Cuyama that sat along Highway 166 in the northern part of Santa Barbara County. Highway 166 was a highway in name only. In reality, it was a two-lane road connecting northern Santa Barbara County with Kern County and ultimately Bakersfield, California. New Cuyama was so small it didn't have any stop signs or stoplights on the main road. Ranches and agricultural farms dotted the Cuyama Valley.

Jack had recently retired from being a full-time employee with the NSA, although he'd stayed on as a consultant, just in case something came up. He wasn't ready to stop working, but he'd decided he could no longer put up with the bureaucracy and political correctness at the NSA headquarters. When he retired, he bought a small five-acre farm in the Santa Inez Valley, just outside Santa Barbara. A few months after moving to his ranch, he got a call from his old partner at the NSA, who told him they had some suspicious activity in his area and wanted to bring him back as a contract consultant to do some surveillance work.

After agreeing to the contract, Jack was briefed on the situation. The NSA, through its global monitoring system, had flagged a series of cryptic communications between some servers in Russia and an IP address in New Cuyama. The IP address led to a remote farmhouse at the bottom of Wells Canyon two miles north of Highway 166. Roberts's task was straightforward: he was to start surveillance based on the location and identify any persons or potential threats associated with it.

After the first few nights of general surveillance, he made a surreptitious approach to the farmhouse. Being in a remote area, he knew that any vehicle traversing the empty road would attract attention. With his lights out and using night-vision goggles to see the road, he drove to within a mile of the farmhouse, then hiked the last mile along the side of the road. He walked along the fence line, staying as far from the road as possible. While observing the area, he made a mental note of the trees, large rocks, and bushes that could serve as hiding spots if a car approached.

He stopped at the entrance to the hundred-yard lone driveway. His night-vision goggles allowed him to see several infrared light sources crisscrossing the driveway. He also picked up infrared light sources near the farmhouse, indicating night cameras and intrusion alarms. With his Nikon Z9 camera equipped with a telephoto night-vision lens, he took pictures of the farmhouse and the black Tahoe SUV. He took a close-up of the license plate.

After returning home and accessing the encrypted website address provided to him by the NSA, he discovered the Tahoe was a rental out of the Los Angeles International Airport. He collected more information about the rental company, including the credit card information used to pay for the car. He traced the card back to a company registered in the Bahamas.

A few days after he'd sneaked up to the farmhouse, he went to the local cafe for lunch. After enjoying his lunch, he went back to his car. As he was getting into his 2017 green Toyota Highlander, the black Tahoe pulled up and parked right next to him on his left side. He got a good look at the driver but was too close to take a discreet photograph of him.

Once the driver went into the cafe, Roberts got out of his car and kneeled down like he was tying his shoe. As he did, he reached over to the undercarriage of the Tahoe's back tire and placed a GPS tracker behind the wheel well. He then got in his car and drove off.

Over the next three weeks, the tracker showed the Tahoe was driving all over Southern California. Most often, it returned to the farmhouse in the early morning hours. It stayed there for a few days before it started its Southern California loop again.

The Tahoe seemed to follow a pattern when it left the farmhouse for the Southern California loops. It stopped at the local cafe in the mid-morning. Jack assumed the driver was getting a late breakfast.

Today he was sitting in the parking lot of the cafe, parked thirty yards away from the Tahoe. His main goal today was to get a picture of the driver. After sitting in his car for forty-five minutes, he stepped outside and looked up and down the highway. He put his phone up to his ear and started waving his arms around as though he were involved in an intense conversation with someone. He looked at his watch again, moved to the back of his car, and then looked to the west. As he held the phone in his right hand, he threw his left hand up and down as though he were still involved in an intense conversation.

He was fast approaching the one-hour time limit he had given himself before he decided some locals might pay more attention to him than he wanted. After looking at his watch one more time, Jack decided he was pushing his luck. It was time to leave.

Just then, the front door of the cafe opened, and the driver of the Tahoe walked outside.

Jack opened the rear passenger side door of his Highlander and climbed inside. His Nikon was sitting on the seat. He knew the dark tint of the blacked windows of his Highlander would keep the man from seeing him in his backseat.

Jack picked up his camera and started clicking pictures of the man as he came down the stairs. He only had a few seconds before the man got close enough to see him. The man was constantly scanning back and forth as he walked down the stairs of the café towards the Tahoe.

As the black Tahoe pulled away going eastbound on Highway 166, Jack reviewed the pictures he'd taken. He had several photos of the man. He drove back to Santa Ynez and sat himself in front of his computer. After downloading the pictures, he finished his report for the day, logging on to the NSA's encrypted server and uploading the information. With nothing left to do for the rest of the day, he headed outside for a swim in his pool to cool off. After he dried off, he grabbed a beer and some chips, plopping on his couch and turning on the Sunday afternoon football game.

Two hours later, Jack's phone chimed. Someone had uploaded new information to the encrypted website.

He went back to his computer and logged on to the site, opening the file from the NSA. The file identified the driver of the black Tahoe as Andrei Kuznetsov, an ex-Russian Spetsnaz soldier. Authorities believed he had affiliations with Colonel Alexei Lebedev of the Russian Army.

The information revealed that Lebedev, who authorities had assumed was killed in a drone strike, had resurfaced in the US. Authorities spotted him in Santa Barbara a few months ago, and the man was now a suspect in a double homicide. Interpol had just reissued a Red Notice for Lebedev.

The message also said that the NSA had entered Kuznetsov's office name into SAFETNet. They'd learned that another federal agency was engaged in an investigation associated with Lebedev. As part of the deconfliction process, they'd directed Jack to suspend his investigation until contacted by the other federal agency.

But Jack didn't enjoy waiting around. One reason he'd left the NSA was because it took them too long to decide to act. The review process had an excessive number of levels. Even though he'd received the initial information back within a few hours, he didn't have any confidence that the NSA would act swiftly. Unfortunately, there was nothing he could do until the unknown federal agency contacted him.

***

Jack Roberts was sound asleep in his bed when the phone rang at six the next morning. The caller ID was blocked. He decided he needed to answer it.

"Hello, is this Jack Roberts?" a strong, low voice said.

"This is Roberts."

"Jack, Matt Scales. A mutual friend from Maryland said I should call you. Can you make it down to Port Hueneme today or tomorrow?"

"Sure thing. I can be down there in a few hours."

"Excellent," Matt said. "Text me when you get close. I'll meet you at the Pleasant Valley gate."

"Sounds good. My ETA will be around 10 a.m. I'll text you when I get off the freeway."

At 9:50 a.m., Jack Roberts met Matt Scales at the Pleasant Valley gate. After confirming his identity, Matt led Jack to the DCS office. As they entered the office, he introduced Roberts to Skip, St. Bernard, Jon Mitchell, and Dave Johnson. Chin was back at his lab in Washington, running more tests on the data they'd gathered from Alaska.

"Let's head back to the SCIF to start this conversation," Dave said.

Once inside the SCIF, Dave spoke up again. "Okay, Jack, we have the basic background on your assignment and what brought it about.

Can you give us specific information on what you found? We're specifically concerned about the farmhouse and Andrei Kuznetsov."

"Well, you know the NSA tasked me with starting surveillance on a farmhouse at the base of Wells Canyon. The NSA detected some encrypted emails coming from a known intelligence source in Russia that were sent to an IP address at the farmhouse. My assignment was to find out what I could about the farmhouse and identify anyone who was staying there or visiting."

Jack continued to tell them about his initial approach to the farmhouse and the sophisticated security, including night-vision cameras and intrusion devices. He also told them he'd put a tracker on the Tahoe, which meant he could place the Tahoe in various locations throughout Southern California.

"Were any of those locations in the Montecito area?" Matt asked.

"It drove through Montecito a few times. At one point it stopped at the Montecito Village North for five to ten minutes. The Tahoe spent two hours at the Santa Barbara Harbor near the breakwater a few weeks ago. I have the specific routes and times and date in my computer."

Jack pulled out his computer and opened the GPS tracking program. After a minute of searching, he found the day and time for when the black Tahoe had spent some time at the Santa Barbara breakwater.

"Here's the info," Jack said as he spun the computer around to face Matt Scales.

"Jesus Christ..." Matt whispered under his breath. "This is the same day of the Montecito incident, and the day I saw Lebedev at the breakwater."

"This circumstantial evidence suggests a strong connection between the Tahoe and Lebedev," Dave said. "The helicopter that crashed also had New Cuyama listed as the destination for the charter. It's thin, but the info should be enough to get a warrant for the farmhouse. We need to move fast."

"It might be faster, and easier, to get a local warrant than to go to the feds for this one," Matt said. "I'm sure Lieutenant Gordon would appreciate the help with his homicide investigation."

"I agree," Dave said. "Meanwhile, Jack, can you work with the NSA to get a FISA warrant for Kuznetsov's cell phone? I assume you got his number with that sophisticated equipment you carry around with you."

"Yeah, I'll get right on it."

"And I'll head back up to Santa Barbara and brief the Lieutenant Gordon on his new information," Matt said. "I'm sure his detectives will jump right onto getting a warrant."

***

Matt entered the front door of the Santa Barbara Sheriff's headquarters building and asked for Lieutenant Gordon. When Gordon came out to meet Matt, the front desk receptionist asked Matt to sign in. Gordon told him it was unnecessary. Matt followed Gordon through the hallways to the detective bureau. They went into his office and closed the door.

"What can the sheriff's office do for DCS?" Gordon asked.

"It's actually about what I can do for you. We've been able to tie your murder in Montecito to Alexei Lebedev, a Russian. We've also identified a location in New Cuyama where an associate of Lebedev has been receiving encrypted messages from Russia for the last few weeks."

"Sounds interesting. But what do you have that you'll turn over to me, that I can use for my case?"

"We have our team working on all the specifics. It's our belief that we have sufficient grounds to get a warrant and search the farmhouse in New Cuyama for evidence related to the Montecito homicide. We're putting the finishing touches on everything. Since we're asking for your help, I can read you in on some of the intelligence. However, I'm gonna caution you that these are the type of people you don't want to mess around with. You should use your SWAT team to serve the warrant."

"Why don't you bring in a federal team if it's that high-level?" Gordon asked.

"We have to move fast. You can get the local warrant faster than we can get a federal warrant and get a team here. Do you think your SWAT team can handle this?"

Lieutenant Gordon leaned back in his chair. "Yeah, we can make that work. Got a hell of a team. Our sergeant is dynamite. You'd appreciate how she handled selection. Breezed through it like it was a warm-up."

Matt kept his face neutral. *This should be interesting.*

Gordon continued. "Physical test? Crushed it. Shooting quals? Tightest damn groups I've seen in years. But the stress interview, that was something else. Whole team lined up, drilling her, trying to break her and trip her up. One of the guys threw a breaching scenario at her. It had no intel, no layout, nothing. Just to see if she'd take the bait."

Matt smiled, waiting.

"She shut it down. Didn't hesitate. Walked them through POST breaching requirements like she was teaching the damn course. She even broke down the science behind charge-size formulas and structural composition. By the end of it, half the guys were looking at each other like they were the ones being tested." Gordon shook his head, chuckling. "I swear, even I felt like I was getting graded."

Matt exhaled slowly, suppressing a grin. *Yep, that sounds like April.*

"Great. We'll also need a detective with a secret or TS clearance to write the warrant."

"Yes," Gordon said. "I have one deputy who just finished a three-year assignment on an FBI task force. He still has his top-secret clearance and would be perfect for this. He can work on putting the warrant together and you can vet the information he uses to make sure you're okay with it. We can also request to keep the affidavit sealed, at least for a short period."

"Sounds good. We'll separate out all the information we can share as a foundation for the warrant. Can your detective join us at our Port Hueneme office tomorrow?" Matt asked.

"I'll make sure he's there."

"We've only confirmed the name of one person staying at the farmhouse. The bad news is he's extremely dangerous and capable. We also have to assume there's at least one or two more accomplices staying there. By the way, I need the detective's name, and who holds his clearance. I assume it's the FBI."

"His name is Julio Ramirez, and yes, the FBI holds his clearance," Gordon said. "I was wondering if you were going to verify his security clearance. I know you trust me, but I would do the same in your shoes."

***

Jack Roberts and Jon Mitchell had been in the DCS conference room for three hours. Roberts had provided Mitchell with all his photos and digital files on the farmhouse and Kuznetsov.

Mitchell was methodically organizing the material and cross-referencing it with every available source. At the same time, he was developing an assault package for the sheriff's SWAT team, which included detailed aerial photos, diagrams, property blueprints, utility locations and types, as well as an analysis of nearby homes and their residents.

In a separate file, Mitchell compiled the evidence linking the Montecito murder to Lebedev and the New Cuyama farmhouse. The plan was to seek a search warrant based solely on the Montecito case. He would avoid any reference to international or domestic terrorism. The warrant would focus on tying Lebedev to the helicopter seen at the Montecito estate and its subsequent crash in the foothills. It would also reference Matt's sighting of Lebedev at the Santa Barbara breakwater and link him to Kuznetsov and the farmhouse. Based on that connection, they'd request permission to search all the buildings at the farm for evidence related to the murder.

When Detective Julio Ramirez arrived at DCS headquarters at 7:30 a.m. the next morning, Matt immediately realized why he'd been assigned to the FBI task force. Ramirez quickly absorbed the key points and began drafting the warrant. After asking a few clarifying questions, he completed the warrant affidavit in three hours.

By 12:45 p.m., Ramirez and Matt were standing in the chambers of Judge Brannigan.

Brannigan was something of an anomaly in Santa Barbara County. He was a staunch conservative in a jurisdiction largely dominated by progressive politics. Lieutenant Gordon had recommended they bring the warrant to him. The hope was that Brannigan would accept the facts as presented and sign off. If he needed more, they were prepared to brief him on some aspects of the national security concern, though anything beyond a general background would require higher-level approval.

As it turned out, that wasn't necessary. The information related to the Montecito murder and Lebedev's suspected link to the New Cuyama farmhouse was sufficient. After reading the warrant, Judge Brannigan looked up and asked Matt if he was the one who had seen Lebedev at the Santa Barbara breakwater. When Matt answered yes, Brannigan followed up with a simple question: "Do you work for the federal government?"

"Yes," Matt replied.

Brannigan gave a knowing smile and signed the warrant. He agreed to seal it for thirty days, allowing them to continue the investigation quietly. If they needed to keep it sealed longer, they'd have to return with a compelling legal argument.

Chapter 11

Day 75 - Buelton, CA

The Santa Barbara County Sheriff's Department SWAT team, along with Matt, gathered around a large conference table in the SWAT team's main office in Buellton, California. Maps and blueprints of the farmhouse covered the walls and table. The images included overhead shots from Google Earth and long-range photographs taken yesterday from a helicopter landing at the New Cuyama Airport. Surveillance photos taken by Jack Roberts rounded out the material.

April stood off to the side of the table with her arms crossed as her eyes scanned the faces of her team. She had read the warrant earlier. No night service, which meant they were planning a daytime operation. She had learned in the military that the best plans came from open discussion, but she also knew when to listen, and right now, all eyes were on Matt.

Matt stood at the head of the table. His shoulders were squared, and he held his chin high, projecting the confidence of someone entirely at ease in this environment. His eyes swept the room with a steady gaze, acknowledging each person with a nod, as if the surrounding space was a familiar stage.

"We believe Kuznetsov's people have been using this location as a staging ground. Surveillance confirms movement consistent with weapons trafficking and logistical coordination. There's a strong possibility that key players in the operation are on-site, including individuals directly linked to Lebedev." He straightened and looked around the room. "But this isn't a standard raid. They've gone to significant lengths to fortify the property, including infrared cameras, and intrusion sensors with overlapping lines of sight. And that's just what we can see.

"We're assuming high-value assets are inside, which means they may not go down easy. Best case scenario, they walk out and give themselves up and we take them without a firefight. But with these types of people, we have to expect the worst. Expect them to resist and fight. That's why speed and surprise are our best weapons."

April folded her arms. Normally, in a briefing like this she'd expect a breakdown of the threat level and capabilities of the people they were up against. Matt hadn't mentioned it yet. He might get there, but she wasn't going to wait.

"You said these are bad dudes. What's the specific background of the people we're dealing with?" she asked.

Matt gave a slight nod, as if he'd expected the question. "Kuznetsov's people aren't low-level thugs. They're all ex-military. Most are former Russian Spetsnaz and private contractors who've worked in conflict zones from Ukraine to Syria. They've run weapons and fighters for the GRU and Wagner Group under unofficial orders from Moscow. Lebedev was embedded in Syria for nearly a decade, training proxy forces and executing black ops. He's ruthless, calculated, and has a habit of setting traps for anyone hunting him. If he's had a hand in fortifying this place, expect the unexpected."

Matt met her gaze. "That answer your question?"

April held his stare for a fraction longer than necessary, then nodded. "Yeah, that'll do."

Without another word, she turned back to the team.

"Well, this one's going to be interesting," she said, shifting gears. "As Agent Scales said, the farmhouse is wired with infrared cameras and various intrusion devices. That means no standard surround-and-call-out. This is going to be an old-school narcotics-style raid with speed, shock and violence of action. We take the farmhouse and the barn before they know what hit them."

She gestured toward the map. "Our main challenge is approaching the target without setting off any alarms or tipping them off. Ideas?"

The team exchanged looks.

"The situation lends itself to a classic fast rope insertion from the Black Hawk, but the problem is the sound," Deputy Green, one of their most tactical thinkers, chimed in. "That canyon will amplify the noise, especially if we go early in the morning. It'll echo off the walls, and they'll hear us coming long before we're on the ground."

April traced the topography of the canyon on the map. The steep walls would work against them, amplifying any sound.

"That's a valid concern," she said. "A helicopter is loud, and in those canyons, it's practically a bullhorn announcing our arrival. We can't afford to lose the element of surprise."

"What about coming in on foot?" Green asked. "We insert at the top of the canyon and make our way down to the farmhouse. It'll be downhill all the way. The problem is, traveling a couple miles at night while staying invisible and silent in unknown territory is extremely risky. But it might work."

"We'll be carrying a lot of gear," a deputy added. "The chances of someone getting injured are high. We could also come down through the river wash south of the farmhouse. But that doesn't solve the problem with the cameras and intrusion devices. If those cameras have motion sensors and alert the people inside, it could be a problem. We'd need to take them out somehow before we get too close."

April considered this, then turned to a detective from tech services.

"Rivera, what can we do about the cameras? Any way to jam them or disable them without alerting whoever's inside?"

"We just acquired an EMP device," Rivera said. "It should be able to knock out the cameras, but it would have to be done within a few hundred feet of the house. Otherwise, we risk missing some of them. The downside is, if they're monitoring the feeds, they'll know something's wrong the moment the cameras go dark. My bigger concern is that the equipment is new to us. I'm sure it's excellent, but I don't like using untested gear on an op."

"And if they've got backup power or alarms linked to those cameras, the moment they go offline, they could trigger an alert," Stony Peterson added.

April tapped her fingers on the table, thinking through the possibilities. Every option they discussed carried significant risk.

"I have an idea," she said. "It's unconventional, but I need buy-in from a few key people before we can move forward. In the meantime, start planning the details. One team inserted by helicopter, another coming in through the riverbed. If I can make my plan work, I'll brief you when I get back. For now, let's get to work. We have a lot to prepare."

As the team split into small groups, April noted their excitement, smiles, and animated discussions. That energy would soon sharpen into focused determination as the mission took shape.

***

April sat across the desk from Division Chief Mark Navarro at the Santa Barbara County Fire headquarters building. April had become a trusted resource for the fire department when dealing with the many fires that had come to Santa Barbara County. Her main introduction to Chief Navarro had been during the Thomas Fire in 2017.

The fire had threatened communities in Ventura and Santa Barbara County. While authorities had been evacuating several communities, Lieutenant Gordon received a call from a deputy at a roadblock that a resident demanded to get back into his house. When asked why, he refused to tell them. He claimed it was classified and a matter of national security. Normally the deputy at the roadblock would have told the resident to go away, but there was something to the resident's tone that made the deputy take him semi-seriously. The deputy called Lieutenant Gordon to advise him of the situation. Gordon agreed to talk to the resident over the phone.

After the phone call with the resident, Gordon requested that the Dispatch Center send April to the scene to evaluate the situation. At first the resident wouldn't talk to her about why he needed to get to his house. April told him she still carried a top-secret clearance, and if the situation was half as serious as he was intimating, she had a need to know about it. The resident then called someone on the phone and confirmed her clearance. He told her he worked for the Department of Energy and had materials in his house that would make the entire area hazardous if the house burned down.

April contacted Division Chief Navarro, the incident commander, expressing her need to access the resident's house, even though she knew it was in a closed area under threat from the fire.

"It's too dangerous," Chief Navarro replied. "You're not going into the closed area. We don't even have our firefighters in there."

"Well, I'm going with or without your firefighter escort," she stated.

"You need my permission. I can't imagine anything so important that you would risk your safety to get to a house that has already been evacuated."

April stood tall and moved within two feet of Navarro, meeting his gaze. "I do not need your permission. With or without your firefighter escort, I am going. I cannot tell you the specific reasons, but it is that important."

He hadn't liked being challenged, especially without a full picture, and the fact that she'd offered none had grated on him. But she hadn't been bluffing. For a moment, he'd just looked at her, weighing the risk. Then he'd let out a slow breath.

He had approved a plan to include a battalion chief's Expedition and a fully staffed brush truck to escort April and Deputy Stony Peterson to the house to retrieve the materials.

She and another deputy rode with the battalion chief in the BC's Expedition. A brush truck followed them with four firefighters. They drove through the closed area, often driving right through the fire to get to the house. They recovered the hazardous materials and made it back out unscathed. The house ended up succumbing to the flames. Ultimately, the Department of Energy fired the resident from his job.

To this day, Navarro never knew what the materials were or why April had been willing to take such a risk. But after the Department of Energy's follow-up investigation, including him being interviewed by the FBI, he figured April had been telling the truth. He had to admit, he admired her tenacity, her tact, and her ability to make things happen.

Now, as he sat across from her, he noticed she had the same look on her face that she'd had that day during the fire.

She shifted in her seat. "Mark, I need to ask, do you have any controlled burns scheduled in the Cuyama Valley, specifically near Padrones Canyon, in the next few days?"

Navarro frowned and reached for his tablet. He pulled up the current schedule, scrolling through it before shaking his head.

"We don't have any burns planned in the entire Cuyama Valley right now, April. The season's been pretty mild, and we've focused our efforts elsewhere. Why do you ask?"

"We're planning a raid on a farmhouse in Wells Canyon. We need to get in without tipping them off, and a controlled burn nearby could provide cover for a helicopter being in the area."

Navarro studied her. He knew from experience that she didn't ask for favors lightly.

"I'll explore the possibility of adding one to the schedule," he said. "Getting a controlled burn planned and executed in the next few days isn't as easy as it sounds. We need permits, the right conditions, an appropriate location, and permission from the landowner. It's not something we can just do on a whim."

"I know it's not a small ask, Mark, but this operation is crucial. The element of surprise is everything. Without it, we risk the entire mission and dramatically increase the danger to my team."

Navarro drummed his fingers on the desk. Firefighters followed strict procedures for a reason. A last-minute burn wasn't just paperwork, it included safety concerns, pushback from his crews, and explaining himself up the chain. But April wouldn't be here if this wasn't serious.

"Can I assume this is something more than just a general run-of-the-mill drug case?"

"Yes, it is," April replied. "The place has been fortified with infrared cameras, ground sensors, and the works. Let's just say if we don't do this in the next two days, there could be far-reaching consequences. In the grander scheme of things, this is more important than the incident during the Thomas Fire."

"Alright, I'll see what I can do."

April nodded. She could tell he was leaning toward a yes. He just needed a little more reassurance.

"We have to keep this quiet. This is a need-to-know operation. Since the sheriff's office manages the County Aviation Bureau, we'll make sure the helicopter crew is all sheriff's personnel."

"You're putting a lot on the line here, April," Navarro said. "But if it's as important as you say, I'll do what I can. I'll start making the calls tonight, but you need to keep me in the loop every step of the way."

"I will, Mark. And thank you," she said.

He exhaled. "I'll make sure the burn crew knows only what's necessary. The Cuyama station has a captain working in two days who's a terrorism liaison officer. I may have to loop him in, just to make sure he understands the importance of what we're doing. That way, he can handle questions or gripes from his crew. They don't like last-minute operations like this. It'll be a standard operation on the surface, but we'll get the timing and location right for your purposes. Just make sure your team stays safe out there. If anything goes sideways, call me right away."

"I trust your judgment in how to handle this," April said, standing and extending her hand. Navarro took it in a firm shake. "As far as keeping you in the loop. I have your cell phone number. Just make sure you answer when you see a blocked number show up on the caller ID."

As April walked out of Navarro's office, he saw a big smile cross her face.

***

Two days later - Rimfire Ranch, Base of Padrones Canyon

It was a beautiful sunrise in the New Cuyama Valley as Mikkel Hansen stood by the gate leading into his ranch. His face showed the weathered toll of working out in the fields for the last forty years. He broke into a grin as he watched the county fire trucks roll onto his property. The early morning sun was just beginning to peek over the hills, casting long shadows across the dry, dusty ground. For years, Mikkel had worried about the thick brush creeping closer to his cattle grazing lands.

As the fire crew dismounted, Mikkel walked over, tipping his hat in greeting.

"Morning, boys! I can't tell you how glad I am to see you out here. This brush has been a thorn in my side for years. When the local station called and asked if I had any land that needed clearing, I couldn't believe my luck!"

A firefighter stepped forward. He was tall and broad-shouldered, easily six-foot-two and built like a linebacker. He wore a bright yellow fire-retardant jacket and pants, streaked faintly with soot from past burns. His yellow helmet gleamed in the sun, a black *CAPT* stenciled across the top.

He stuck out his hand with a firm grip, his voice confident but easygoing. "Good to meet you, Mr. Hansen. I'm Captain Thompson. We're happy to help. It's a win-win for us. Vegetation management and hands-on training for the crew. You get some of that brush cleared out and we get to sharpen our skills."

He turned and gestured to his team as they began unloading equipment.

"Our plan today starts with a small, controlled burn. We'll monitor the spread and keep it tightly contained. Once we're confident in the perimeter, we'll let it expand, maybe up to ten acres."

"You boys do what you need to do. I'll stay out of your way."

"We've got it under control, Mr. Hansen. You're welcome to stay and watch, but if you've got other things to do, we'll take care of everything from here. Just one thing: this'll start out pretty mellow, but in about thirty minutes there will be a lot of smoke. It may look like it's out of control. It won't be. We plan it this way. We'll have a helicopter coming in about that time to make a pass on it and drop some water. No need to get excited. It's part of the plan."

Mikkel nodded, tipping his hat before stepping back. He watched as the crew set up a line of hoses and laid down controlled ignition points along the perimeter.

Captain Thompson looked back at his crew, then spent the next twenty minutes walking around the perimeter of the planned burn area, ensuring there were no surprises that could sabotage the safe operation.

Once he finished his perimeter walk, he turned to the crew and gave them a nod of approval.

"Alright, let's get this going. Stay sharp, and remember, we've got a narrow window before the winds pick up later today."

As the first flames took hold of the dry brush, lightly colored columns of smoke rose into the air. Mikkel couldn't have been happier with how things were going. The ranch would be safer after today, and he'd even get a front-row seat to the fire crew's work.

He noticed something, though. The captain didn't touch a radio. Instead, he stepped a few yards away and made a call on his cell phone.

Mikkel figured it must be part of their safety protocol, but it struck him as odd. Every fire he'd seen before had someone chattering on a radio.

***

The morning air was crisp and still. From their vantage point four hundred yards above the farmhouse, Deputy Jenkins and his observer lay motionless. They had been in position for almost eight hours.

For most of the night, Jenkins had tracked movement in and around the farmhouse through the ghostly green glow of his night-vision scope. Now that the sun had been up for a few hours, he no longer needed the filter. His powerful scope made the fire crew look much closer than their actual distance of a mile away as he'd watched them arrive and set to work.

Thirty minutes after the fire had started, smoke had begun spreading from the ignition point. It hugged the foothills of Padrones Canyon, rising straight up in the calm air and drifting along the canyon floor in both directions.

During the pre-op briefing, April had emphasized that the farmhouse was part of a highly sophisticated operation. Despite the SWAT team's encrypted radios, she had insisted that communication remain on cell phones until boots were on the ground.

Jenkins dialed her number.

"Smoke's definitely visible to anyone in the valley," he reported. "It's also drifting up toward the farmhouse."

"Copy that," she replied. "We're launching in five."

Jenkins shifted his position forward, careful to keep his rifle steady and his scope trained on the farmhouse. A few minutes later, his phone buzzed again, and April's voice came through, calm and direct.

"Okay, we're flying over the fire into the smoke as if we're going to drop water. We'll keep the smoke between us and the farmhouse for as long as possible. Once we come out of the smoke, we head straight for the house and bank hard, like we're turning back toward the fire. At that point we'll flare out behind the barn, and start our insertion. Keep us updated on any movement around the farmhouse in the barn."

"Roger."

As Jenkins hung up he turned to his observer. "I'll concentrate on the house and the barn. You keep an eye on the perimeter."

Jenkins focused his scope on the farmhouse. He knew Sergeant Green and the ground team were in position at the creek bed, watching the approach. The timing was critical. Green's team would advance on the front of the farmhouse just as the helicopter team hit the ground. Jenkins had already surveyed their planned fields of fire through his scope, ensuring no possibility of crossfire.

***

The helicopter sliced through the rising smoke. Its rotors churned the air into chaos. Below, the fire cast an orange glow through the haze, masking their approach. As they broke through the plume, the outline of the barn emerged. The aircraft banked hard to the left. April leaned out the open door, scanning for the ground and looking for their insertion point.

"Get ready," she said. "We're going in hot."

As a helicopter flared thirty feet above the ground, the crew dropped a fast rope from each side door. She grabbed tightly with both hands and wrapped her feet around the rope. She made a controlled thirty-foot descent. As soon as her boots hit the ground, she raised her MP5 and scanned the area.

A figure bolted from the side door of the barn, He was a tall, muscular man with a cold, calculated expression.

"Suspect exiting the barn," April called over the radio.

She and her partner Rocky Santoro angled to intercept. But instead of running away, the man adjusted his path and sprinted directly toward them.

April raised her MP5 at the man. "Get down on the ground!"

But he didn't slow. His expression was one of sheer determination, each muscle tense and distinct. She calculated that with his closing speed towards her, she had five seconds to decide. If she were still in the military, she'd have dropped him without hesitation. But the rules of engagement here were different. Deadly force wasn't an option.

"He's coming right at us!" April shouted to Santoro. "Cover the rear. I've got this guy."

Slinging her MP5 across her back in one smooth motion, she braced herself. The suspect's intent was clear. He was coming for her.

At the last second, she sidestepped his charge, grabbing his arm and twisting, aiming to lock him in an arm bar. The man spun like a striking snake, breaking free. His right fist shot toward her midsection, hitting her vest with enough force to knock her back a step.

Pain radiated through her ribs, but April absorbed it. This wasn't a random thug. His movements were too sharp, his strikes too precise. Definitely had training. Probably military.

The man grinned, as if he knew exactly what she was thinking, and came at her with a flurry of punches aimed at her head and chest. She ducked, weaving through the strikes. She grabbed his shirt and rolled backward, using her legs to kick him over her head. He landed hard on his back.

But he sprung to his feet in one fluid movement.

The next charge came fast. She dropped low, sweeping his legs out from under him with a roundhouse kick. The man hit the ground hard but rolled and sprang up again. He charged once more, his body coiling for a shoulder throw.

She expected the move. Using his momentum against him, she hooked his leg with her own and drove her weight forward. The man hit the ground with a grunt, and this time, she was on him before he could recover.

April locked him in a tight-guard position, transitioning to side control. Her arms pinned his left arm in a Kimura lock, twisting his shoulder at an unnatural angle.

The man growled and gritted his teeth in defiance. "You think you can take me?" he spat in a thick Russian accent. "I've faced better than you!"

April didn't reply. She applied more pressure, forcing him to arch in pain. But instead of yielding, the man roared, rolled over and yanked on his arm free, He used his momentum to land a glancing blow to her ribs. She twisted with the strike, using her movement to transition into a rear mount.

The man thrashed beneath her, clawing at her arm as she secured a rear-naked choke. Her technique was flawless. She adjusted her position, cutting off the blood flow to his carotid artery.

Four seconds. That was all it took.

His movements slowed, then ceased.

April held the choke for two more seconds, ensuring he was unconscious, then rolled him onto his stomach, her breath steady despite the exertion. She pulled two zip ties from her vest and secured his wrists. Once they were in place, she shifted back on her heels, watching to make sure his chest still rose and fell.

"Nice work, Sarge," Santoro called out, stepping closer. He raised his MP5, scanning the area. "You good?"

April nodded, wiping sweat from her brow. "Yeah, I'm fine. The guy's trained. Wonder what he's trying so hard to protect."

"Nothing good, that's for sure."

She allowed herself a moment to breathe. But as she looked down at the unconscious man, her mind kept turning. Trained. Professional. Russian accent. Just the type of people Matt had said would probably be here.

While April had been busy fighting the unknown suspect, the rest of the SWAT team had cleared the barn and the farmhouse. As Santoro took over control of the suspect, she scanned the area, making sure there were no other threats before she asked for a situation report over the radio.

"All clear," came the reply.

After clearing the barn and the farmhouse, the team gathered in front of the barn. April assigned four team members to complete a perimeter search one hundred yards out from the farmhouse to look for evidence.

Captain Thompson came driving up to the location. "Looks like everything went off without a hitch," he said. "I kind of figured it would when I heard you were involved. A buddy of mine was the driver of the brush truck that escorted you during that Thomas Fire operation."

"Your buddy has a big mouth," April said, then switched her tone. "Your timing was perfect. Thanks for the assist. I hope you got some good training out of it."

"No problem. Glad to help," Thompson replied. "You know, I worked for the sheriff's office before I saw the light and became a firefighter."

She nodded. "Then you know how these things go."

Thompson gave her a knowing look, then nodded before turning back toward his truck. As he walked away, she exhaled.

Chapter 12

Day 75 - Santa Barbara, CA

Detective Ramirez had been interrogating the suspect from the farmhouse for the last three hours in an interview room at the sheriff's headquarters. The interrogation room was hot. The air was thick with sweat and frustration. Before putting him in an interrogation room, they'd taken his fingerprints and determined his name was Victor Markov. The DCS database showed he was former Russian military. They had no record of his activities for the last year.

Ramirez stood from the table, shoving his chair back. The metal legs shrieked against the floor. It had been hours, and Victor Markov hadn't cracked. He'd dodged every question, thrown out every misdirection, or just flat-out refused to answer. It was time to take a different approach.

"You want to keep playing games? Fine," Ramirez said, gathering the scattered photos and documents from the table.

Victor smiled as a drop of blood fell from his lip onto the table. "Do what you have to, Detective."

Ramirez shook his head, turning toward the door. "I will. But remember, it was your idea."

Detective Ramirez walked out the door, and the door clicked shut behind him.

Before the sound had faded, April stepped in.

She didn't rush. She didn't hesitate. Her gaze locked on Markov, cold and unblinking. She was still wearing her SWAT uniform. His eyes widened for only a second before he composed himself. But she saw it. A glimmer of recognition, or was it resentment? A crack in the armor.

She pulled out the chair across from him, the screech of metal echoing through the room as she dragged the chair into place and sat down. She didn't speak right away. Just stared at him.

"Ramirez needs a break," April said quietly. "You don't respect him much, do you?"

Markov sat up, his bravado still clinging on. "He's just a local cop, a nobody, like you."

"You put up a good fight earlier."

Markov looked up at her, studying her face. He shrugged. "You caught me on a bad day."

"Sure. That's what it was."

He didn't reply. She let the silence stretch. People didn't like silence. It made them uncomfortable.

Even though April kept her posture relaxed, she could feel the strong slow pulse in her temples. This wasn't her first interrogation, but this one mattered more than most. Markov wasn't just a thug. He was a trained, disciplined professional. Just like her.

She leaned in closer to him, resting her elbows on the table. "I understand you're tough. You wouldn't have survived Spetsnaz training if you weren't."

His eyes widened. "What do you know about that?"

"You joined the Army at twenty-one. Saw combat in Chechnya."

His silence confirmed it.

"You saw things there. Things you can't unsee. You experienced and did things you can't forget," she said. "Chechnya left scars you never talk about. And now, here you are. Just a pawn in someone else's game. Again."

His body tensed, but he didn't look away from her. She recognized that look, the clash of pride and something heavier. Not shame exactly, but the weight of things done and endured. She'd seen it in the mirror more than once. And she'd seen it in the eyes of men who came back from places that didn't exist on any map.

April kept her posture relaxed, but her gaze stayed sharp. "We know you're just following someone else's orders. You did your best and have dedicated yourself to fighting to the end. Until they just leave you behind."

Markov's eyes narrowed. "What do you know about it?"

He locked eyes with her. She didn't blink. "I've been you," she said. "The difference is, I learned a long time ago that no one's coming to save you. Not your commander, not your government, and definitely not Lebedev."

Markov flinched at the mention of Lebedev, but he tried to hide it, shifting in his seat. April caught the crack in his armor and pressed her advantage.

"Do you think they're coming to save you? They're done with you. Lebedev and Kuznetsov are off to their next adventure, while you're sitting here. You're the one who got caught. They've already forgotten about you."

Markov's expression hardened again. "I don't know who you're talking about."

April moved in closer, her voice just above a whisper. "Don't lie to me. Do you believe that because you were left behind once before and escaped, it'll happen again? Or maybe you think they really will come back for you. Or maybe you're so loyal to them, you want to throw the rest of your life away. Is this plan of theirs so important to you that you're ready to pay the price alone?"

Markov tightened his fists on the table until his knuckles turned white. The tension in his hands betrayed what his face refused to show.

She nodded. "Soldiers like us are the ones who do the work, who get our hands dirty because we believe in the mission. We believe in the ones giving the orders. But we don't survive by being loyal to those who abandon us. We survive by knowing when to look out for ourselves."

His jaw stiffened and his eyes shifted as he struggled to maintain a stoic facade. For the first time, a trace of vulnerability replaced the stubborn defiance in his gaze. It was fleeting, a mere heartbeat, but unmistakably present.

"You fought hard earlier," Victor said.

"So did you. It could've gone either way."

There was a long pause before his shoulders sagged. The bravado slipped, leaving exhaustion in its place. "What's in it for me if I talk?"

April didn't flinch. "You talk and you get a chance to save yourself. Keep holding out and you take the fall for everyone. Lebedev and Kuznetsov will be long gone before you ever get a chance to see daylight."

Victor sat there staring at her. Then he took a deep breath and exhaled with a sigh.

"Kuznetsov got a call. The night before the raid. It was late, probably around 1 a.m. We were in LA."

April's eyes shifted into intense focus. "A call from who?"

Victor shook his head and looked down. He clasped his hands and rested them on the table. "I don't know. He didn't tell me. He looked at the caller ID before he answered it. After listening for a minute, he hung up. He told me to take him to LAX and then come straight back to New Cuyama. That's the last I saw of him."

The only sound in the room was Victor's steady breathing. April let the silence stretch, scrutinizing him. His avoidance of eye contact betrayed his silence.

"And what else?" she demanded. "You weren't just in LA taking in a show, were you? You know more than you're telling me."

He looked up from the table. When he spoke, his voice was quiet. "Colonel Lebedev is planning something big. He always has contingency plans. Your actions will not affect his plan, except to make him speed up its execution."

"What plan?"

Victor shook his head. "All I know is it's got to do with the electrical grid. It's bigger than New Cuyama. I was just a small part of it."

A chill ran through her. but it wasn't based on fear. It came from the confirmation that Lebedev's plan was bigger than they knew. She pushed her chair back and stood and looked at Victor.

"I respect you, Victor. You've fought well for your country."

He took a deep breath, then sat up straight in his chair, fixed his gaze on her, and said, "*Spasibo.*"

***

DCS Team Alpha 42 was gathered around the long conference table inside their Port Hueneme headquarters. The conference table was almost completely swamped with folders, binders, and scattered pieces of paper.

Matt sat at the head of the table. To his right, St. Bernard flipped through a folder with a stoic expression. Across from him, Skip leaned back in his chair, twirling a pen between his fingers. Chin Ho sat at the far end, recently flown in from his lab in Washington at Matt's request. He'd more than earned his seat over the past few weeks.

"You're an associate member now," Skip said.

Chin gave a small shake of his head and cracked a rare smile.

The room shifted as Detective Ramirez entered. He carried a manila folder tucked under his arm. He tapped his fingers on the table.

"We've got solid ties to Lebedev," he said, "no doubt about that, but nothing that proves he pulled the trigger."

Matt studied him. The evidence consisted of GPS hits from Jack Robert's tracker on the Tahoe, surveillance photos of the Montecito victims, and Lebedev's disappearance after the helicopter crash. All circumstantial evidence, but it was not enough to make the case stick.

Chin glanced up from his laptop. "I just decrypted some files from the laptop we recovered from the farmhouse. A file titled 'Western grid operations' has maps of the eastern and western US electrical grids and highlighted locations that have regional substation transformers."

Dave Johnson looked at Ramirez. "Detective Ramirez, thank you for your help, but this case has escalated beyond a homicide. We're now looking at a national security threat. We will make sure that we send you any evidence regarding the homicides we find. But any additional information we have is beyond your need-to-know."

Ramirez gave a slow nod. "Understood. Let me know if anything ties back into my case. I'll do the same." He shook hands with the team and left.

Dave watched him leave. "We're now deep into domestic terrorism and outside our jurisdiction.

Matt knew what was coming. "You're talking about bringing in the FBI."

"We have no choice. If Lebedev is targeting the US electrical grid, the consequences could be catastrophic."

"I know, but bringing in the FBI means losing control of our case."

Dave shook his head. "We're not handing it over. We're bringing in backup. That's different."

Matt nodded. "Fine. But we don't let them push us aside. This is still our fight."

Dave walked out of the conference room and back to his office to call the FBI headquarters in Los Angeles and tell them he and Matt were en route to brief them on a domestic terrorism case.

Matt had been through this before in a different operation and different agency. It always started the same: promises of collaboration, shared priorities. But when things got messy, the scramble to assign blame came fast, and the real work got buried under pissing contests and career-saving cover. He wasn't about to let that happen again.

***

Once they arrived at the FBI headquarters in Los Angeles, Matt and Dave were escorted to a conference room. The room had an oblong table with ten black leather-bound office chairs. It was outfitted with the latest technology, including a large screen displaying a digital map of the United States with key locations highlighted.

As Matt looked around the room, the door opened and two figures entered, a female and a male. They each gave a polite nod and took a seat across from Matt and Dave.

As the female set a manila folder on the table, she flipped it open. Matt caught a glimpse of his DCS badge photo, clipped beside another photo, probably Dave's. Nothing about it surprised him. She'd done her homework.

"Thank you for coming in, gentlemen. I am Special Agent in Charge Karen Lawson. This is Agent Lucas Decker."

Her tone was measured but respectful.

"I've been briefed on your case. Agent Decker has been tracking overlapping chatter on a related threat stream and expressed strong interest in taking over the case. Given the information you provided, and the Bureau's jurisdiction, I've asked him to sit in on this meeting.

"But, since you came here in person, I assume you want something more than just turning over the case to us. Mr. Scales, why don't you start by walking us through the events leading up to and following the raid on the New Cuyama farmhouse?"

"Absolutely," Matt said. "Over the past few months, we've been tracking a series of anomalies linked to potential cyber threats against the US electrical grid. Our suspicions led us to a network of operatives with ties to both domestic and international actors. The chief operative is also the prime suspect in a double murder in Montecito. With the help of the Santa Barbara County Sheriff's Office, we secured a warrant for a farmhouse in New Cuyama to search for evidence pertaining to the murder. We hoped to find evidence of a broader conspiracy as well. But what we found exceeded our expectations. We uncovered substantial evidence, including a laptop that, once decrypted, revealed connections to a secure communication server used by our prime suspect, Alexei Lebedev.

"The evidence from the farmhouse points to a sophisticated plot. This has the hallmarks of a coordinated attack by a foreign state that could have catastrophic implications."

"After evaluating the evidence," Dave Johnson added, "we realized this is a domestic terrorism issue. That's when we decided we needed to turn the investigation over to the FBI."

Agent Lawson's tone remained serious. "We're stretched thin with numerous ongoing operations, but considering the severity of what you've uncovered, the FBI will take over. The case will be assigned to Agent Decker."

"We understand, and we're ready to cooperate fully," Dave said. "We'd like to propose the formation of a joint task force. Our team has the historical knowledge of the suspect and the on-the-ground experience, but we need the FBI's resources and authority to keep going.

"If we go the task force route, the task force members would include at least four of our team members, including Matt and myself. This will ensure seamless collaboration and allow us to act with the full authority needed while operating in the United States."

"I agree. Given the evidence you've presented, this clearly requires a multi-agency response," Lawson said. "We'll move forward with forming the task force. I'll have the MOU drafted and make sure it gets signed by both agencies. We'll get your team sworn in as special federal officers with cross-designation as FBI agents. That will give you all the authority you need to continue the investigation. Agent Lucas Decker here will be the official task force leader."

"I'll work closely with you to ensure that we coordinate resources," Agent Decker said. "While I'll be officially leading the task force from the FBI's side, I want this to be a collaborative effort. I'll rely on your expertise and insights as we move forward."

"Understood," Matt said with a nod. "We appreciate the Bureau's support. We're committed to seeing this through. The sooner we get started, the better."

"We'll handle the paperwork for the swearing-in immediately," Agent Lawson said. "I'll also have our cyber and domestic terrorism units briefed on the situation so they can start coordinating with your team."

"That's exactly what we need," Dave Johnson said with a smile. "We've got a lot of ground to cover, and time isn't on our side."

"Then let's get this show on the road," Agent Lawson replied.

"Thank you," Dave Johnson said as he stood. "We're looking forward to working together on this."

Everyone in the room shook hands and exchanged contact information.

As Matt and Dave stepped out of the room, Matt glanced back at Decker. The agent had barely said a word until being assigned as lead. Now he seemed completely at ease. Matt tucked the thought away.

***

After they left the FBI office, Matt and Dave started the drive back to Port Hueneme. They got caught in the normal stop-and-go traffic on

Highway 101 as they headed north. Once they passed Calabasas, the freeway opened up, and they were up to speed.

"They always want control," Matt said, breaking the silence. "Until it goes bad. Then they blame everybody but themselves."

Dave gave him a half smile. "Yeah, if this goes south, there'll be plenty of blame to go around."

They drove a few more miles in silence.

"Hey Dave," Matt said in a serious tone. "I've been thinking about this a lot. I want to bring April Knight in on the task force. She has the connections in Santa Barbara County, and once we expand beyond the county, she has the background and expertise to make a significant contribution to the team."

Dave didn't answer. Matt was beginning to wonder whether Dave had heard him, when the man finally responded. "You're scaring me, Matt!"

"Why is that?"

"I was thinking the same thing. I would hate to think you and I are thinking alike," Dave chuckled.

Dave picked up his cell phone and dialed Lieutenant Gordon's number. He asked Gordon if they could meet that afternoon on an urgent matter. Gordon said he was happy to meet with them, and was also hoping they could update him on any part of the investigation that was not classified.

***

Dave Johnson and Matt Scales walked into the Santa Barbara County Sheriff's Office headquarters building at 3:05 p.m. Lieutenant Gordon met them at the front counter and escorted them back to his office.

Dave started the conversation. "Lieutenant Gordon, by this time, I'm sure you've heard rumors of how extensive the evidence is from the farmhouse. It goes way beyond your homicide investigation. We just received authorization to start a joint task force with the FBI, as this is now classified as a domestic terrorism case."

"Detective Ramirez gave me an overview of the case without any specifics."

"We'd like Sergeant Knight to join our team as the local member," Dave said. "She's already been critical to our operation, and she has the required security clearance. She also has some unique skills from her time in the military that would assist us during this investigation."

Gordon sat quietly for a moment, weighing the request. He knew April had experience with special operations and clandestine assignments in the military. He assumed Dave Johnson and Matt Scales knew the details of those operations, which was why they wanted her as part of the JTF.

After a long pause, he nodded. "I'll approve the request. She's on her days off right now. I'll call her and proofread your request. But remember, it's her decision whether she wants to join."

Chapter 13

Day 78 - Santa Barbara, CA

After they left Lieutenant Gordon's office, Matt asked Dave to drop him off at his condo. Matt wanted to get a change of clothes and pick up his car to drive back to DCS headquarters in Port Hueneme.

A few minutes after Matt walked into his condo, his phone rang. It was April. She asked him to meet her at the Shoreline Café so they could talk about her joining the task force.

Matt was sitting at his favorite table out on the sand at the Shoreline Café, looking out over the ocean, contemplating the unfolding events, when he saw April round the corner of the café and head for his table.

"The view here never gets old," she said as she walked up and took a seat.

"Yeah, it's the one place where things still feel normal. Sometimes I want to sit here all day and wait for the sun to rise the next morning. Here, I got you coffee."

"Thanks. So, as I mentioned on the phone, Lieutenant Gordon called me about joining your task force."

"I figured he would. What did he say?"

"He said you're in the middle of something big that has grown out of the raid at the farmhouse, and that you could use my help. But I wanted to hear from you. What exactly would I be getting into?"

"First, thanks again for you and your team helping us out with the farmhouse raid and making Markov talk," Matt said. "It means a lot. More than I can explain in a quick conversation. The evidence is pointing at something way bigger than we expected, something with real homeland security implications. We've only just touched the tip of the iceberg. I need people I can trust."

April took a sip of coffee and looked at Matt. "And you trust me?"

He held her gaze. "You know I do. What makes you think I don't?"

She took another sip of her coffee, letting the question hang in the air before answering. "Because you didn't tell me everything during the Afghanistan raid. You kept me on the outside when you already knew more than you let on."

He exhaled, looking out toward the water. "You were new to the operation. I needed you to stay focused, not worry about how dangerous things had become."

She scoffed. "So, you were protecting me?"

He looked back at her. "Yeah. I was."

From her side of the table, she studied him for a long second. Part of her wanted to believe him. That it had been about protection, not doubt. But another part remembered exactly how it felt back then to be kept in the dark, sidelined. Not because she was inexperienced, but because he hadn't trusted her to handle the truth.

April opened her mouth, ready to fire back, but paused. She had spent years assuming Matt hadn't trusted her, that he saw her as a new soldier to be used, not a member of his team.

But now, hearing his explanation, it kind of made sense. Maybe it hadn't been mistrust. Maybe he was just shielding her from information she didn't really need to know. Not because she wasn't cleared for the information, but because he was concerned it might be overwhelming on her first op.

She studied him for a moment, before saying, "You always protect your team."

He didn't hesitate. "Yes. I always take care of them."

April nodded, the realization settling in. This was who Matt was. He made the hard calls and carried the weight alone. If she had understood it back then, she wouldn't have carried this chip on her shoulder for so long.

She took a deep breath and moved her gaze to the ocean. She took a few sips of coffee as she thought about the decision facing her.

"You don't need to convince me, Matt. I just need to know one thing: what's your endgame?"

"To take down Lebedev. For good. And to stop whatever he's planning. There's not a lot of time to get ahead of this."

April let out a slow breath. "Alright. I'm in."

Matt nodded, but she could see something lingering behind his eyes.

"But before we get to work," she added, "I want to know something."

"What's that?"

"How much of this is about Dugan?"

Matt gripped his coffee cup, his knuckles turning white. He looked away.

"I'm not gonna lie, it has a lot to do with Jimmy. He died on my watch during my mission. It's personal. But it's also about making sure no one else pays the same price."

April stared at Matt. "Want to go visit him?"

Matt exhaled and nodded. "Yeah, I do," he said. "And I would appreciate it if you came with me."

***

The sun was setting as they pulled into the small cemetery. The golden light cast long shadows over the rows of headstones, the air still and quiet. Matt led the way, walking respectfully around the other gravesites until they reached One-Shot's marker.

Matt stopped in front of the headstone. His shoulders tensed as the memory of losing his friend surfaced.

The air around him felt heavy. Like the ground itself remembered.

He stared at the headstone. "We should've been celebrating his promotion right about now." Matt exhaled slowly. "Instead, I'm here. Looking at his grave."

April stood beside Matt. "He didn't die alone. He was with his team. Your team. Don't carry this weight alone, Matt. One-Shot knew the risks, just like all of us who've been downrange."

Matt nodded. "I know."

He said it, but the words felt hollow. Knowing the risks wasn't the same as being ready to accept them.

What he kept to himself was that One-Shot's voice still found him sometimes late at night. The biting humor, his big grin and easygoing attitude. Those weren't things you forgot. Not if you knew Jimmy the way Matt had.

"But it doesn't change the fact that he's gone," Matt added. "It was my op. I was responsible for him."

April placed a hand on his shoulder. Her touch was firm, grounding. "We'll get Lebedev."

Matt reached into his pocket and pulled out a quarter. He kneeled before the headstone and placed the coin on top. A token of shared service. Of being there in the final moment. But for Matt, it was something more.

"I'm sorry, Jimmy," he murmured. "It should have been me."

The breeze rustled through the trees, but Matt barely noticed. The world had gone still.

He stood and came to attention, executing a textbook salute. The motion was crisp, precise, muscle memory ingrained through years of service.

April reached into her pocket and pulled out a penny. She placed it beside the quarter. A small gesture from a soldier who came to pay her respects.

Different coin. Same weight.

She straightened, came to attention, and saluted.

For a long moment, neither of them spoke. The wind stirred the trees and rustled through the grass. A silent reminder that time kept moving, even when some things felt frozen in place.

Matt finally broke the silence. "Ready to get back into the fight?"

April glanced at the headstone one last time, then turned to him. "Yeah. I am."

They walked back to the car without saying another word.

After they left One-Shot's grave, Matt took her back to the Shoreline Cafe so she could pick up her car. They agreed Matt would pick her up the next morning, and together, they would head down to DCS headquarters in Port Hueneme.

Chapter 14

Day 79 - DCS Headquarters - Port Hueneme, CA

St. Bernard and Skip were sitting at the conference table in the DCS conference room, discussing the shortcomings of each other's tactical firearms proficiency.

"I'm telling you, your grip's all wrong," St. Bernard said. "That low-left drift on your last string? Classic sign."

Skip didn't look up as he adjusted the sling on his rifle. "Funny, I spent two straight weeks doing nothing but mag changes, malfunction drills, and dry fires before I was even allowed to send a round down-range."

"Let me guess, Delta hazing ritual?" St. Bernard said, glancing over.

"Tradition," Skip corrected. "Intense training in handgun manipulation. Meanwhile, SEALs think a gunfight's just pulling the trigger and looking cool doing it."

St. Bernard laughed. "Well, we do look exceptionally cool."

"That part's true. But it's the fundamentals that tend to be fuzzy."

The door opened mid-sentence, and April stepped in with Matt behind her, catching the tail end of the exchange.

"Sounds like some deep-seated trust issues going on here," April said dryly. She wore khaki Crye Precision pants and a fitted black T-shirt, her hair tied back in a no-nonsense knot, and a black duffel hung from her shoulder like it belonged there.

St. Bernard didn't miss a beat. "Took you long enough, Knight. I figured once you heard where the real action was, you'd come running. Or maybe you just missed me."

She gave a mock sigh. "Oh Bernard... I'll never forget the day we met." She paused. "Doesn't mean I won't keep trying."

The room chuckled.

"Figured I'd better step in before you boys trying to out-peacock each other get out of control and forget which end of the rifle goes bang," she said.

Matt shook his head with a smile. "I told them to expect professionalism from you."

April raised an eyebrow. "Guess you forgot to give me the memo."

"I'm just here to make sure you don't mess things up. Someone's gotta keep these boys on track, right?"

St. Bernard got up and went over to April and picked her up in a bear hug. After he put her down, he said, "Great to see you, Knight. If there's one person I would add to the team, it's you. Remember that mission in the sandbox when we had to disappear behind enemy lines for a recon? You're the reason we got out clean."

"She probably did all the work," Skip said. "Most likely came out of that mission with a sore back from carrying you, and then you took the credit."

"Well, since she didn't technically exist, I had no choice but to take the credit," St. Bernard said.

"You boys know how it goes," April said as she rolled her eyes at St. Bernard and Skip. "Black Squadron missions are about proper recon and someone willing and able to blend in. We all know St. Bernard here couldn't blend into a thirty-thousand-person crowd at a football stadium, much less a small village in the mountains of Afghanistan."

"Yeah, but with you watching my back, I knew I was in good hands. With you on the team now, it'll be just like old times."

Skip nodded. "Black Squadron makes sense. You've got that quiet ghost vibe."

"She also went through Combat Controller selection," Matt, still flipping through the op packet, added without looking up. "One of the few women to make it all the way through."

April raised an eyebrow. "I appreciate the trip down memory lane, Matt."

"Just facts," he said, flipping to the next page.

Skip gave her a glance. "Great, another overachiever. Just what this room needed."

She shot him a smirk as she walked past. "Don't worry. I've learned to tone it down for you Delta guys."

She dropped her duffel by the chair and took a seat at the table, already scanning the documents in front of her.

***

It had been three days since the raid at the farmhouse, and the team had spent every waking hour going through the reports and evidence, figuring out what it all meant.

Dave Johnson sat at his desk, reviewing reports from other DCS operations in the western US, but his mind kept slipping back to the op going on in the next room.

His phone rang. He glanced down and saw Amy Johnson's line.

"Hey Amy, what's up?" Dave asked.

"I have Jack Roberts at the outer office. He says he has some new intel from NSA."

"Thanks, Amy. I'll send someone out to get him."

Dave got up from his desk and stuck his head into the other room. "Hey, Mitchell, head out to the main entrance and escort Jack Roberts back here. He has some intel from NSA."

"Sure thing, boss," Jon Mitchell said as he stood.

Mitchell made his way through the office and into the underground tunnel that led to the main building entrance of the DCS office. Before opening the door to allow Roberts in, he checked the monitor to make sure he was alone. Satisfied, he opened the door.

"Hey Jack, I hear you got some info for us," Mitchell said.

"I think the team will find this interesting," Roberts said. "Kind of throws some new light on what we're looking at."

"Care to give me the *Reader's Digest* version?"

"Nope, sorry, not 'til we get in the SCIF. This info is from the NSA intercepts based on the FISA warrant. We need to follow strict protocol on this one."

"You sure you can't just give me a hint?"

"Sorry, Mitchell. You should know better. Discussing this level of classified info outside of the SCIF is not possible."

Without another word, both men walked back down the tunnel and into the main DCS office.

***

Matt, April, St. Bernard, and Skip were sitting around the long table in the DCS conference room, studying the maps and folders in front of them. Chin was at the far end of the table working on his laptop.

The door creaked open, and St. Bernard looked up.

"Well look what the cat dragged in."

"Hey, St. Bernard, good to see you again," Roberts said. "I thought you DEVGRU guys are all about being in the field and kicking down doors. Never took you for the analyst type."

"It's getting harder and harder," St. Bernard admitted. "I'm not cut out for this intelligence analysis stuff. I need to get back in the field and into some action."

"What I have here might help make that happen," Roberts said. "Not sure what it means, but I'm sure it's important in the big picture."

He placed a folder on the table. "As you know, the FISA warrant went active on what we believe is Kuznetsov's phone." He paused, letting that sink in before continuing.

"We got a FISA intercept from the warrant at one a.m. the night before the raid and traced the incoming call back to an unknown number in Taiwan. The caller spoke Mandarin and lasted only five seconds. The only one who talked was the one in Taiwan, saying, 'Cuyama location compromised. Activate secondary location.' There's been no further activity on either phone."

"What the hell!" Matt yelled as he pushed back from the table. "This doesn't just confirm Markov's info that Kuznetsov got a call the night before the raid, it confirms someone leaked the location."

"Yep, someone leaked it," St. Bernard said matter-of-factly. "The question is, who?"

Matt's gaze swept over the team. "St. Bernard, Skip, your job now is to figure out how this got leaked and who did it. It's a short list. Follow the evidence no matter where it goes and who it implicates."

"Will do, boss," St. Bernard said. "Once we find out who it was, do I get to take care of the problem?"

Matt just looked at St. Bernard and shook his head. "We'll deal with that when the time comes."

***

Chin Ho had fallen asleep at the table, surrounded by reports from the farmhouse raid. He didn't know how long he had been out, but when he sat up suddenly, the pieces of the puzzle clicked together in his mind.

"Holy shit…" he muttered. "It all makes sense now."

He had always trusted his subconscious to work through problems while he slept, and this time was no different. Rubbing his temples, he pushed back from the table and headed straight for the main conference room.

Inside, the rest of the team was deep in their own investigations, each struggling to fit the latest intel into the bigger picture. The NSA intercept and the FISA warrant linking Kuznetsov to a call from Taiwan had plunged everyone into uncertainty.

St. Bernard glanced up. "Chin, you look pensive, man. What's going on?"

Chin took a breath. "I think we're being played."

"By whom? Lebedev?"

Chin nodded. "Yeah, partially. But I think there's something else going on here." He glanced around the room, making sure he had everyone's attention. "What if this isn't just about us? What if we're looking at this all wrong?"

Matt folded his arms. "Explain."

Chin stepped forward. "It's like this. America plays checkers. Straightforward moves, direct attacks. Russia? Chess—calculated, patient, sets up traps." He let that sink in before delivering the punch line. "But China? China plays Go."

"And what does that mean?" April asked.

"Go isn't like chess. You don't win by taking pieces. You win by shaping the board. Every stone matters, even the ones that don't look important at first. You play it slow. Quiet. You build influence. You make the other side feel like they still have control. Force your opponent into bad decisions without them realizing it. The trap doesn't look like a trap until you're already inside it. By then, it's too late. You lose."

Chin looked around the room. Everyone was watching him.

"What if that's what's happening to us? Lebedev, the cyber hits, the power grid. They're real, but what if they're meant to keep us busy in the corners, while the center of the board, wherever that is, gets taken right out from under us?"

St. Bernard blew out a breath. "Damn. That makes sense."

Skip looked up. "So, what's the move?"

Chin met his eyes. "If we're playing Go, we stop reacting. We start shaping the board. We look for what's not obvious yet. And we lay our own stones where they won't see them coming."

***

After Chin's insight about Go, Matt said nothing. He just sat there and let everything sink in, then quietly pushed back from the table and slipped out the side door.

He took the back stairs, bypassing the main hallway, and stepped out onto the docks behind the building. The chill hit him, but he welcomed it. Moving to a weathered pillar near the harbor's edge, he leaned against it and stared into the distance.

A lukewarm cup of coffee rested in his hands. The gray, flat, and unmoving Pacific stretched out beyond the marina.

He tried to clear his mind. A virus targeting the US grid. Two Chinese nationals dead in Montecito. A cryptic call from Taiwan to Kuznetsov. Lebedev, always just out of reach.

Too much precision. Too much misdirection.

He stared out at the water. If this was chess, they were thinking in moves. But if this was Go, like Chin had said, then it wasn't about pieces. It was about territory. About shape. About the long game.

Matt closed his eyes.

What if this wasn't really just about crippling America? What if the actual goal was to keep us distracted and so focused on the chaos here that we'd miss what was coming next?

"Son of a bitch..."

***

Everyone in the room looked up as Matt ran in. He headed straight to the conference table, grabbed a stack of reports, and flipped through them, faster and faster.

There it was.

Increased Chinese naval activity around Taiwan, much more than in the past. A spike in encrypted chatter. Cyber intrusions targeting Taiwan's infrastructure, flagged but never prioritized. All of it had been right in front of them.

He slammed a fist on the table. "We thought they were coming after us. But what if it was never just about us? Taking down our grid isn't just an attempt to incapacitate us. It's meant to keep us busy, putting out fires while the Chinese make their real move: an invasion of Taiwan."

"Yes!" April exclaimed. "If Taiwan's transformers and grid are infected with the virus, it'll make an invasion easy."

Matt planted his hands on the table. "It's not about our electrical grid, or even the chaos. Those are just tools. This has always been about Taiwan."

Silence settled over the room.

Chin gave a slow nod. "Taiwan is the center of the board."

Matt looked over at him. "You've always said they'd never stop trying. Why now?"

Chin leaned back in his chair. "Semiconductors run everything. Phones, satellites, missiles, infrastructure. Whoever controls them controls the future. Taiwan makes sixty percent of the world's supply. China wants control of that production. But that's not the core of it. For China, this goes way deeper."

No one spoke.

"In 1949, when the Nationalists fled to Taiwan, the Communist Party considered it a temporary loss. They've been waiting ever since.

Reunification isn't just a political goal. It's a national obsession. The Party's legitimacy is tied to that outcome."

Matt's gaze stayed fixed on him.

"And from Taiwan's side?" Chin continued. "It's about survival. They've built their own identity, their own government. The Taiwanese don't see themselves as Chinese anymore. So, when Beijing talks about 'one nation,' Taiwan hears conquest and control. That's why they resist."

Matt blew out a breath. They'd been so focused on Lebedev and so convinced he was the mastermind behind everything that they hadn't seen the whole board.

"We need to go back. Reexamine everything. From the beginning. Mitchell, call Decker. Get him down here for a full briefing. I want everything we have categorized and analyzed for inconsistencies."

He turned to St. Bernard. "Get in touch with your DEVGRU contacts. Find out if anyone is training Taiwan's Special Forces."

Then he looked at April. "I want you in a room, alone with the raw intel. You weren't here for the early investigation. That gives you a fresh perspective. Look at the data like it's a recon mission. Find what's missing."

"And what are you doing while we're working?" St. Bernard asked.

Matt glanced at Chin. "We're going to see Chin's dad."

Chapter 15

Day 80 - Paso Robles, CA

As the Genesis G80 eased down the gravel driveway, Mr. Ho stood on the porch, his sharp eyes tracking the vehicle as its tires stirred a cloud of dust behind it. Mr. Ho had designed the house to look like any other property in rural Paso Robles. But Mr. Ho had designed the house and surrounding property as a barrier, a calculated buffer against prying eyes. Cameras, sensors, and silent alarms ensured nothing came near his home without him knowing.

As Chin and Matt stepped out of the car, the changes in their appearance since he had last seen them were clear in the way they carried themselves. Chin, his son by blood, and Matt, his son by bond.

Chin climbed the stairs in front of Matt. Mr. Ho reached out and embraced him. Mr. Ho held the embrace for just a moment longer than usual. After releasing Chin, Mr. Ho turned his attention to Matt and reached out and pulled him in for a warm embrace. Matt was tense. Mr. Ho could feel this wasn't a normal visit.

The comforting aroma of jasmine tea filled the air as they came into the living room. Mrs. Ho appeared from the kitchen carrying a tray with four cups and a teapot. She placed the tray down on the table.

"You both look thinner. Are you eating properly?"

Chin chuckled nervously as Mr. Ho poured the tea into the cups. Mr. Ho tried to steady his hands, but they were not as steady as they once were. He could feel Matt watching him. He knew the young man could see it. He also knew Matt would not mention it out of respect for him.

As he poured the tea, Mr. Ho asked, "What brings my sons back home?"

Chin spoke. "Ba, we need your help. China is preparing to attack Taiwan. Within the next week or two."

The teapot hovered over the last cup. A single drop fell, echoing in the stillness. Mr. Ho carefully set the pot on the table. His eyes locked onto Chin. The words weren't unexpected, but hearing them aloud, here in his home, made them real.

He turned his gaze to Matt, taking a deep breath. "We knew this day would come. The day China would reclaim what they believe is rightfully theirs."

Mr. Ho continued looking at Matt. He had come to the Ho household when he was struggling as a child. Matt had been to war, more than once. He knew about sacrifice. Mr. Ho understood Matt's experiences and the lessons of life more than Matt realized.

"You have always understood the importance of fighting for something greater than yourself," Mr. Ho said. "Our family shares that understanding with you."

Matt clasped his hands together and put his elbows on the table.

"Ba, we wouldn't be here if we had any other choice," Matt said. "Time is slipping away. We need your help. This isn't just about Taiwan. This is about family."

Matt's words sunk into Mr. Ho's body with the force of a sledgehammer.

He closed his eyes for a moment. Images flooded his mind. The streets of China, the whispers of resistance, the knock at the door that could mean life or death. He had smuggled his wife and children out of China in the dead of night. Uncle Ming had stayed in Taiwan, risking everything to ensure their escape.

And now, the past had come knocking once more.

When he opened his eyes, Matt was watching him. Waiting.

Mr. Ho studied Matt's face. For all his strength, all his resolve, there was something beneath it. Doubt? No. It was something deeper.

"Ba, I've fought for strangers my entire life. But now, I'm asking you to help me fight for those in Taiwan who can't protect themselves. If Taiwan falls, we won't just lose a country. The people we love will suffer."

Mr. Ho knew this moment would come. For years, he had prepared himself, although he'd wanted to deny the real possibility that it would happen. But now it was here.

He looked toward the window. The peaceful and untouched countryside stretched for miles. Just the way he had designed it. But lifelong peace was an illusion. A temporary sanctuary. Nothing more.

He looked at Chin and then Matt with a serious yet understanding look. As he gazed at them, he realized their true nature. They were no longer boys. They had become men.

His fingers tightened into fists, and then he slowly exhaled.

"I will reach out to Uncle Ming," he said. "I know he will help. But once we go down this road, there is no turning back.

"This will put all of us, the entire family, both here and in Taiwan, at risk," Mr. Ho continued. "If the Chinese find out Uncle Ming is involved, he will be their first target. And if they trace this back to me, there will be no place that is safe. Not here, not anywhere."

His voice softened. He looked at Matt. "Are you sure?"

Matt met his gaze. "As sure as the sun will rise tomorrow."

Mr. Ho held his eyes for a long moment. He had always been proud of Matt. But this was different. This was a moment of reckoning.

"We will do what we must," he said finally. "I will make sure Uncle Ming knows what's at stake."

Matt rose. He hesitated, then bowed. "Thank you, Ba."

"Now is the time to fulfill our destiny," Mr. Ho whispered in Mandarin.

He had spent thirty years preparing for this moment, and now, the moment had arrived.

***

April pulled into the driveway of her place in Santa Barbara, killing the engine, but not moving right away. Her Lexus NX 350 was still covered in a thin layer of dust caused by being parked too long in a spot where things were supposed to be temporary. A teammate from her SWAT team had dropped it off at DCS a few days ago, no questions asked.

The late afternoon sun had warmed the roof tiles, casting long slants of golden light across the small lawn. It looked the same, with the same cracked walkway, but something about it felt distant now.

She sat for a minute, watching a kid ride by on a skateboard on the sidewalk, trying to land a kickflip. He missed it twice, then tried again, spinning the board under his feet. For a moment, she found herself rooting for him to land it.

Inside, she dropped her go-bag by the door and peeled off her jacket. She kicked off her boots and walked barefoot across the hardwood floor, feeling the familiar creak of the second board near the kitchen.

It was supposed to feel like home, but her body still moved like she was clearing corners.

She took a long hot shower, letting the water scald her shoulders. As she dried off, her eyes caught the corner of a photo she'd stuck on the fridge a few days earlier and hadn't taken down. It showed her in a desert village, dressed in a loose black abaya and headscarf, sitting cross-legged on a woven mat, sipping tea beside a group of local women. Only someone who knew her well would recognize her. She remembered the heat, the nerves, the way the SEAL team had waited three klicks outside the village in case the op went sideways. She hadn't meant to keep the photo up. But somehow, it had stayed.

For a moment, her chest tightened.

She needed air.

Ten minutes later, she was jogging through Shoreline Park with the Pacific on her right. The sun was out, and the breeze was just enough to help cool her sweaty skin.

She wasn't running to stay sharp. She was running to feel *anything* that wasn't tactical.

By the time she hit the four-mile turnaround point at the Bird Refuge, her breath had settled, and her mind had cleared just enough.

She glanced at her phone. One new message. Matt.

Meeting at DCS 1900. Hope you got your run in.

She smiled. Just barely.

She headed home, finishing the last mile in under five minutes. After another shower, she grabbed a protein from the refrigerator. She drank it as she pulled on jeans and an old UCSB sweatshirt. She tied her hair back in a loose braid and holstered her Sig under the sweatshirt on her right side. She stepped outside and headed for the Lexus.

***

After leaving Paso Robles, Matt and Chin drove straight back to DCS headquarters and Port Hueneme. The trip took them just under three hours. Matt admitted to himself that he had broken a few speed limits on the way.

As Matt and Chin walked through the bullpen, they could feel the energy in the room. The team hustled between desks, phone conversations buzzed in the background, and the steady clack of fingers on keyboards filled the air. Matt sensed the heightened pace as the team prepared for whatever came next. He raised a hand, signaling for the team to gather in the SCIF for a debrief.

Inside the conference room, a large digital map of Asia dominated the wall. Taiwan was at its center. The conference table was a mess of papers, open files, and half-empty coffee cups. Crumpled napkins and crumbs from late-night snacks were near the chairs. Matt moved to the head of the table, scanning the room before his eyes fell back on the map.

"All right, let's settle in. We've got some updates to run through."

St. Bernard, Skip, and April sat on one side of the long conference table. Agent Decker, Jon Mitchell, and Dave Johnson sat opposite. Matt had given Decker a heads-up on the way back that an important briefing was about to go down.

As Matt was looking over at his team, he saw St. Bernard grinning back at him. "So, how was the big reunion in the thriving metropolis of Paso Robles? Let me guess, you guys spent the whole time chasing tumbleweeds or checking out the county fair?"

"Yeah, we swung by the fairgrounds for old times' sake," said Chin. "Still smells like funnel cakes and cow pastures." The laughter that followed felt genuine and served as a brief break in the tension. But Matt's mind was already wandering back to the mission. Even in moments like this, his brain had a way of splitting in two. One half was still in Paso Robles, reminiscing with Chin, while the other half was reviewing the upcoming op and the challenges they would encounter.

Matt knew the banter grounded the team. It was necessary, but the clock was ticking. He knew in a few minutes the easygoing vibe would fade. Cold calculation and determination would replace it. This was a team of professionals in every sense of the word. They knew the situation could flip from light to dark in the blink of an eye.

And in their world, it often did.

Matt's mind came back and focused on the banter still going on.

"Tumbleweeds would've been the highlight," Chin chuckled. "I swear, that wind's gotten worse since we were kids. We were practically dodging debris like we were in some action movie."

St. Bernard laughed. "Please tell me you didn't waste time trying to win one of those giant stuffed animals at the ring toss."

Chin adjusted his glasses. "I was never one for mindless feats of physical coordination. While others wasted time on carnival games, I was perfecting the art of returning library books two weeks late without a single late fee. A true intellectual heist."

Skip chuckled. "Book smuggling, huh? That's wild. Never heard of anyone smuggling books *into* a library."

Matt grinned and pointed at Chin. "Don't let him fool you. Chin's a master of deception."

St. Bernard shook his head, laughing. "Well, I'm just glad you two didn't get swept up by the high winds or try to relive your high-school adventures. Paso Robles probably hasn't changed much. Still have that one gas station?"

Chin raised an eyebrow. "Two now. And if you're really feeling fancy, they even have an artisan coffee shop."

April giggled. "Look at you, moving up in the world."

Matt nodded with mock seriousness. "Yep, it's practically the next Silicon Valley."

The laughter settled. Matt's tone shifted, signaling the transition to business. "All right, jokes aside, we've got some critical updates, and it's time to get everyone caught up on our meeting with Mr. Ho."

The humor drained from the room, and the weight of the mission pressed in again.

"Mr. Ho has agreed to help us establish secure communication with his brother, Uncle Ming Ho, in Taiwan. For those of you who don't know, Mr. Ho was a Chinese intelligence officer. His brother, Ming Ho, stayed in Taiwan after Mr. Ho smuggled most of the family into the US. Uncle Ming is now a high-ranking intelligence officer for the

Taiwanese government. He's well connected and will provide us with on-the-ground intel regarding our concerns about the electrical grid and a potential invasion."

"My uncle has been in intelligence for many years," Chin added. "He keeps a low profile but is deeply embedded in the Taiwanese underground movement for independence. His network is solid, with several reliable informants."

Matt noticed Decker sitting rigid in his chair, arms crossed, his focus sharpening at the mention of Taiwanese intelligence.

"Wait, so we're focusing on Taiwan now?" Decker asked. "I thought we were tracking this virus as a domestic threat. Last I checked, this JTF's jurisdiction doesn't stretch across the Pacific."

"The virus is global," Matt said. "It's connected to China's larger strategy, and that includes Taiwan."

"Our priority should be the continental US," Decker argued. "That's why the FBI agreed to a joint task force. My superiors expect domestic results, not detours to Asia."

April and St. Bernard exchanged knowing glances. She raised her eyebrows and tilted her head toward Decker. St. Bernard looked like he was suppressing a grin.

"I've been monitoring encrypted chatter from known Chinese military channels," St. Bernard said, rising to address the room. "Look at the satellite imagery. Chinese naval warships are maneuvering around Taiwan."

"Looks like their standard military training to me," Skip commented. "They do this every couple of years. Although this does look a bit larger than in the past."

"That's why we need to get in contact with Uncle Ming immediately," Matt said. "He can help us determine if this is just a drill or something more."

"I spoke with an old teammate, Commander Harris. He said they know eventually China's going to make a move to take Taiwan back.

Every few years DEVGRU sends a team to Taiwan to help them work on invasion preparedness," St. Bernard added. "He and his team were deployed to Taiwan a few weeks ago. Officially, they're there to assist with joint training and advise on coastal defense. But unofficially? They're getting jumpy."

April, who had been listening quietly, finally spoke. "I've reached out to my contacts. There's chatter about increased surveillance on Taiwanese government officials. Some intel analysts think the virus is only the beginning. They're planning something else. Whether it's another hit on the US or something specific to Taiwan, we need to figure out their endgame, and fast."

"This is all well and good," Decker stated, "but how does it help us here? We don't have much time left. We don't even know for sure if, how, and when the virus is going to hit the US. Before worrying about solving an issue in another country, we should concentrate on our own problem."

Matt looked over at Decker and took a breath before he answered. "It becomes our problem if China invades Taiwan and destabilizes the region. We can't afford to be reactive. We're concentrating on the domestic angle, but we need to collect information about the potential invasion for Taiwan, in case our concerns prove to be true."

"We know the virus is in the transformers in the United States," Decker said firmly. "Our job is to protect the United States and stop this from happening or mitigate any impact if it does. That is the reason for this task force, and that is what we're going to do. We can take the information about Taiwan and pass it off to DOD. They can handle the international implications."

"I'm still figuring out how the virus will be triggered, and when it will hit the US grid," Chin said. "I'm close to being able to shut it down within hours of it being activated. As much as I want to focus on Taiwan right now, I need another day or two to finish up my analysis of the impact in the United States and figure out how to shut it down. We have a lot of data on the domestic side. If I can figure out how to shut down or control the virus in the US, then the same method should work in Taiwan if it gets hit."

"There you have it," Decker said. "Even Chin wants to concentrate on the domestic aspect of this investigation."

Jon Mitchell had been keeping quiet during this entire discussion, but had been looking at Decker all the while. "Funny thing about this virus, Decker," Mitchell said. "You'd think someone working so close to this case would be interested in following all the leads and getting as much information as they can, no matter where it takes them. Why is it that you're so concerned about just protecting the United States, to the detriment of Taiwan?"

Mitchell's gaze fixed on Decker. "If this case is purely domestic, then how did Lebedev and Kuznetsov get involved? They're clearly Russian intelligence officers," Mitchell challenged. "And let's not forget the murders in Montecito that also involved two Chinese intelligence officers. Our priority should be solving the problem, not worrying about FBI jurisdiction."

The room fell quiet as Mitchell's words hung in the air, his eyes fixed on Agent Decker.

"We don't have time to debate," Matt said sternly. "Chin, get to work on figuring out how to stop the virus and where it's being triggered from. Meanwhile, I'll follow up on establishing secure communications with Ming Ho and start analyzing some of his intel. St. Bernard, continue tracking encrypted traffic from China. Skip, dig into the recent media releases and news coverage out of Beijing. Compare this so-called exercise to past ones. Look for changes in language, scope, deployment patterns. Anything that doesn't line up. April, see if you can pull more from your contacts about targets in Taiwan. Decker..."

"Yeah, yeah," Decker said. "I hear what you're saying. But I need to report this up the chain of command. You guys are stretching your jurisdiction and yourselves awful thin on this one."

Matt stared at Decker. "We're a team, Decker. We don't get the luxury of whining about jurisdiction when it comes to international security. Keep pressing on the domestic angle. Start pulling in more FBI assets on this to help us out. I agree we need to prioritize the domestic investigation, but we can't afford to ignore what's happening abroad. Alright, everybody else, get to work."

As soon as Matt signaled the meeting was over, Decker got up and started for the door. Matt noticed he was muttering something to himself as he walked up the stairway to the exit leading to the dock area. As he disappeared through the doorway, Matt saw Decker pull out his phone.

Then Mitchell came up behind Matt and whispered, "Something's off with him. Don't know what yet, but he's not giving us the full picture."

Matt nodded, unsure about whether Decker was on board with the direction of the team or not.

***

The team had worked through the night and into the morning. Everyone was tired and operating on a minimal amount of sleep.

Chin walked out of the DCS conference room. He had a dull ache in the back of his neck and shoulders. As he walked down the hallway towards the break room, he swung his arm back and forth, stretching and relieving the tension.

The break room was empty. Chin reached into his pocket and pulled out a package of the Iron Goddess of Mercy tea. Somehow, just holding the tea in his hand made him feel a little better.

He was glad he was alone in the break room, because he could go through the ritual of filling the kettle, tearing open a tea bag, watching the steam rise, and savoring the aroma with no one bothering him. As he watched the steam rise from the teacup, guilt settled over him.

He reached down with both hands to pick up the teacup and take his first sip but heard footsteps behind him. April walked in. She gave him a slight nod as she moved toward the coffeemaker. After pouring a cup of coffee, she looked over at Chin, who was still sitting at the table, looking down at the cup of tea in his hands.

"You look like you've been hit by a truck," she said.

"Just a long day," he replied without looking up.

"Looks like something more than just working long hours. Want to talk about it?"

He hesitated. He was pretty sure no one else on the team, other than Matt, knew he was the original author of the virus. For months, he'd held it in. But the guilt was becoming overwhelming. He was anxious about his work and constantly second-guessing himself. But there was something about April's calm, no-nonsense presence that made him feel like he could talk to her.

Chin took a deep breath and looked at her. "What would you say if I told you I was responsible for all of this?"

She set her coffee down on the table and looked directly at him. "Responsible? What do you mean?"

He continued looking intently at his tea, unable to make eye contact with her. "The virus. The one we're fighting now. I created the original version of it." He let the words hang in the air, waiting for the weight of judgment he thought would follow. "I was working for the DOD at the time on a classified project. My assignment was to create the virus that we're now dealing with. It's been changed a bit, but the foundation is still my creation. Soon after I finished that project, they moved me to another one. I never knew what happened to it."

April didn't seem shocked or angry. "You were working for DOD, and they assigned you a project. You successfully completed the project, turned it in, and moved on. I don't think that makes you responsible for what's happening now."

Chin shook his head. "But it's my fault it exists at all!"

She crossed her arms and looked at him. "Do you remember why you got into this field in the first place?"

Her question caught him off guard. "I wanted to be involved in advancing the technology and helping to keep everyone safe."

"Look, Chin, you created something intended to help and protect the United States. That was your job. You should not feel guilty for doing it."

He looked at her, surprised by the clarity in her words. "You really believe that?"

She smiled. "I do. You're still trying to save people. You have the entire team behind you."

Chin looked intently at April. Emotionally, he still felt some guilt about his role in the situation. But he knew in his mind that she was right.

"Thanks, April. I didn't realize how much I needed to hear that."

She picked up her coffee again, pausing for a moment before raising it in a small toast. "You're not the only one who's had to carry stuff like this. You'll get through it."

Chin raised an eyebrow. "You?"

"First op I ever ran was in Afghanistan with Matt. We got ambushed. He was nearly killed. I didn't find out until later that he'd been sitting on intel."

She glanced down at her cup.

"He told me later it wasn't about trust. It was that I was new and hadn't been tested under fire. He wasn't sure I could handle the truth about the rising threat. Part of it, I think, was that he didn't want me distracted, worrying about how bad it might get. After that, I never knew if he was telling me what I needed to know, or just what he thought I could handle. I still don't like what he did. But working with him now... I'm starting to see why he did it."

Chin said nothing. He just listened.

"Anyway," she added, straightening up, "you're doing good work, Chin. Just remember that."

He nodded. "Thanks. That actually helps. A lot."

She raised her coffee towards him. "Anytime. Now go get some rest. We've got a long way to go before this is over, and we need you in top form."

He watched her walk out of the break room.

As he sat there with his tea, he found himself thinking about what she'd said, not just about him, but about Matt. Matt wasn't easy to understand. But the more you saw him in action, the more the pieces started to fit.

Chin exhaled slowly. For the first time since coming back from Alaska, he felt like he could face the work ahead without the crushing weight of guilt. He had a team. People who believed in him. And a purpose worth fighting for.

When he went back to the conference room, he mentioned to the group that it would be great to just get off the base for a few minutes and get some fast food and coffee.

"Sounds like an excellent idea," Skip said. "I call shotgun."

"I have to finish up some work here, but you could bring me back a vanilla latte," St. Bernard added. "This office coffee is eating a hole in my stomach."

"All right," Matt said, "I'll drive. April, you in?"

"I can't let you guys venture out alone," she replied. "Remember, I joined the team to make sure I keep you guys out of trouble."

Matt, Skip, Chin, and April went out to the main parking lot and piled into Matt's blue Genesis, starting up the car and heading towards the Pleasant Valley gate for a two-mile drive to the local McDonald's.

***

Carlos "Cuchillo" Ríos had been part of the Los Sangre Negra gang since he was eight years old. Known as "the Black Bloods," the gang had built a fearsome reputation in Southern California through drug trafficking, extortion, and ruthless enforcement of their territory. They prided themselves on their connections to various underground operations throughout the region, and especially for carrying out paid hits.

The previous evening, Cuchillo had been relaxing at the gang's clubhouse in Oxnard when he received a call from Marco "El Veneno" Ortiz, one of the top shot callers for Southern California gangs. El Veneno told Cuchillo that orders had come for a hit. They were to eliminate or severely injure an Asian federal agent named Chin, who was currently operating out of an office in Port Hueneme. While they didn't know exactly when Chin would leave the base, they were told to look for a blue Genesis G80 that he would likely be riding in.

Cuchillo, a lifelong Oxnard resident, knew the area inside and out, including the ebb and flow of military personnel and contractors coming in and out of the Port Hueneme base. He instructed his crew to stake out the main roads leading out of the base, hoping to spot the car. El Veneno told Cuchillo he could afford to wait a few days, but if they couldn't catch Chin outside the base, they were to get access to the base and to go in and find him. Cuchillo's crew stationed themselves at the key exits of the base, ready to move as soon as they spotted the target.

His crew had been watching the gates all night and into the morning, rotating cars every couple of hours to avoid suspicion from the locals or the police. At that moment, Cuchillo and three other gang members sat in a stolen three-year-old gray Ford Explorer with darkened windows. They had parked the car near the Pleasant Valley gate and had been there for three hours, looking for any sign of their target.

Cuchillo sat in the front passenger seat while Miguel "Tormenta" Herrera was behind the wheel. Sitting in the back were Luis "Chacal" Mendoza and Javier "Relámpago" Soto, who were still going through the initiation process.

"There it is," Cuchillo said. "Looks like four people inside. Let's go," he ordered. "But keep your distance. We follow, not chase."

Tormenta merged into the light traffic, tailing the blue Genesis. After two miles, it made its way into a McDonald's parking lot. Tormenta maneuvered the Explorer into a spot five spaces away from the Genesis. The crew kept the windows rolled up as Tormenta turned the engine off.

As the Genesis parked, three men and a woman got out. "See the guy who just got out of the backseat?" Cuchillo asked. "He's Asian. Matches the description."

Tormenta squinted as he focused on the people getting out of the Genesis. "Yeah, that's him. But there are four of them, and we're only cleared to deal with the Asian. No one else."

"Chill, man," Cuchillo snapped. "Boss said to handle the Asian guy, not the entire group. We just need the right moment."

In the back, Relámpago and Chacal exchanged uneasy looks. Chacal fiddled with a small switchblade. "What if they all come out together? We ain't got the numbers for that. Boss didn't tell us there'd be four. This isn't what we agreed to."

***

The four federal agents approached the McDonald's counter. As Chin reached into his pocket, he realized his wallet wasn't there.

"I left something in the car. Be right back," Chin said casually, turning on his heel before anyone could respond.

Matt stared at the menu with tired eyes. "No rush, man. We'll be here."

Chin grabbed the keys from Matt's outstretched hand with a quick nod and slipped out before anyone could offer to cover him. He had always paid for himself and always would.

As he stepped outside, the late morning sun hit him in the eyes. He headed toward Matt's car, opened the driver's door, and leaned in, spotting his wallet wedged between the seat and center console. With a quick tug, Chin retrieved it and slipped it into his back pocket. He stood upright and pushed the door closed with a thunk. As he turned to head back, movement caught his eye. Four men were stepping out of the gray Explorer, fanning out around him.

"Yo, got a second, man?" Tormenta asked, a predatory grin spreading across his face as he blocked Chin's path. Relámpago and Chacal circled behind the car.

"You're in the wrong place, man. You gotta pay the toll," Tormenta said.

Chin looked around and realized he had nowhere to run. He raised his hands in front of him. "I'm just here for food, same as you. Don't want any trouble."

"Well, you got trouble, chink," Tormenta sneered as he pushed Chin against the Genesis.

Chin understood that there was no way to talk his way out of this situation. The gang members' eyes were icy and predatory. They reminded him of the relentless bullying he'd endured as a child. The taunts and the bruises that left deep unseen scars.

Chin felt a surge of anger rising within him, fueled by the determination not to be a victim. He was no longer the kid who passively accepted the beatings. Adrenaline coursed through his veins. Gonzo's words flashed through his mind.

You never know what you're capable of until failure is not an option.

With his back against Matt's car, Chin felt his mind sharpen, focusing on the immediate threat.

No more running. No more taking it.

He reached into his back pocket and calmly pulled out his wallet. He moved slowly, not wanting to startle the gang members who had surrounded him. He held his wallet in front of Tormenta and opened it as if preparing to hand it over. But as he held his wallet in his left hand, his right hand moved subtly, reaching for his concealed, cut-up American Express card. His heart pounded, but he knew this distraction might be his only chance to survive the first few seconds of the confrontation.

Just hold on. Matt's inside. He'll notice. I just need to keep them off me until then. The thought gave him a strange sense of calm. He didn't need to win. He just needed to buy time.

Tormenta reached for the wallet. In one swift motion, Chin pulled his credit card out of the wallet as he tossed the wallet at Tormenta. Chin slashed downward, across Tormenta's face. The sharp end connected just below Tormenta's ear, cutting a deep three-inch gash along his cheek. Tormenta screamed, stumbling backward, blood pouring from the wound.

As Tormenta stepped backwards, cussing, the other gang members froze for a split second.

The sensation of the blade hitting its mark surprised Chin. But he didn't stop to think. Chin's heart raced. He realized he would be in control only for a few seconds. He felt a calm determination settle over him. Chin started wildly swinging his arm around with the credit-card knife in his hand, slashing and jabbing and yelling at the other gang members. He appeared out of control, but inside he knew exactly what he was doing.

He glanced toward the McDonald's. *Just a little longer. Just survive.*

***

Inside McDonald's, Matt's attention was pulled away from the menu by the sound of distant yelling. It was from the parking lot.

His eyes scanned the lot. His expression darkened when he spotted Chin surrounded by a group of men. His friend was wildly swinging his arms around as though he was trying to hit them. The scene unfolded like a slow-motion nightmare. One of the gang members lunged at Chin while another circled around behind him. Chin continued to flail his arms around as his attackers came towards him.

"Damn it," Matt muttered under his breath, every muscle in his body tensing.

He bolted for the door, shouting, "Lock and load!" as he pushed through the crowd of customers.

Skip and April, who had been chatting by the counter, immediately reacted to Matt's call. Without hesitation, they turned and sprinted after him, the sudden shift from casual conversation to full alert making it clear this was no drill.

Matt burst through the door, focusing on Chin. As he was running toward Chin and the four gang members, he did a tactical evaluation of the scene. His friend was outnumbered but was holding his own. He saw one of the men hit Chin in the head with his fist, and Chin stumbled backwards while he continued to wave his arms around, screaming like a banshee. Matt made the decision to scream at the top of his lungs. He knew yelling would probably chase the attackers away and limit their ability to catch them, but he also knew that the priority was stopping their attack on Chin.

"Hey motherfuckers!"

****

Cuchillo had been watching his crew take down the China guy. It should've been quick, not a full-on street brawl. But the guy had fought back, and now it was getting messy. Just as Cuchillo decided to step in and end it, a voice cut through the night.

He looked up. Three very serious-looking individuals were charging out of McDonald's. They were coming fast, and looking like they were ready to fight.

Then he heard the sirens. Not close but coming fast.

Shit. They had thirty seconds to disappear or risk getting hemmed in.

"Let's go, let's go!" Cuchillo barked. "Split up! Meet back at the clubhouse!"

No hesitation. His crew scattered in different directions, blending into the night. Cuchillo took off, slipping between parked cars before disappearing down a side street.

***

As the gang scattered. Skip locked onto the straggler, heading for the exit.

Cutting a diagonal path across the parking lot, he vaulted a low wall and landed smoothly on the sidewalk behind the guy. The gang-banger slowed to a walk, playing it casual as sirens wailed past, turning into the McDonald's lot. He tilted his head, feigning curiosity at the scene behind him.

After the last patrol car disappeared, Skip struck. He drove into the gangbanger's back, sending him face-first into the pavement with a sharp thud.

April caught up just as Skip grabbed a fistful of the kid's jacket and yanked him toward a hole in a wooden fence. He hauled him through the whole into an abandoned lot and dropped him on his stomach. Skip planted his knee on the gangbanger's back.

"All right, tough guy, what the hell was that all about?"

The gangbanger coughed, blood pooling from his broken nose. "F-Fuck you, *cabrón,*" he spat. "You pigs think you scare me?"

Skip chuckled. "Pigs? Oh, buddy, I have never been so insulted." He pressed harder. "Here's the deal. You're gonna talk. The only question is how much pain do you want first?"

"You can't do shit to me. I want my lawyer."

Skip sighed. "That's adorable. You still think this is a police matter."

The gangbanger hesitated. Good. He was scared now. But not scared enough.

Skip glanced at April. "Keep a lookout."

"You got it." She stepped outside the fence, scanning the street.

Skip rolled the kid onto his back and straddled his chest. "Why were you picking on our friend?"

"I told you, I ain't saying shi..."

Skip's fist hammered into his left clavicle. A sickening snap rang out.

The gangbanger screamed.

Skip stuffed napkins in his mouth, muffling the noise. He let him thrash, riding out the pain. Then, slowly, he pressed down on the shattered bone.

The body jerked, another muffled scream tearing from his throat.

"Talk. This is just the beginning."

The kid nodded frantically, and Skip yanked the napkins out. Blood dribbled from his mouth as he turned his head and spit.

"Hey man, come on, I don't know shit!" he gasped. "I was just along for the ride. All I know is, we were told to mess up the Chinaman."

"Who told you?"

The kid gritted his teeth. "Cuchillo got a call last night. Gave us a description. Said he might come out of the Pleasant Valley gate in a blue Genesis G80 in the next few days. We were up all night waiting for him. Finally saw the car come out a little while ago. We followed it here. They don't tell me why. We just do what we're told."

Skip flipped him onto his stomach and yanked his wallet from his back pocket.

Luis Mendoza.

Skip laughed. "Okay, Luis, now we're getting somewhere." He crouched lower. "Here's how this works. You walk away, tell your friends whatever the hell you want. But if I see you, or any of your homies again, tonight will feel like a birthday party compared to what happens next. Understand?"

Chacal nodded quickly. "Yeah, yeah, man, I got it."

Skip held his gaze. "Tell me. What happens if I see you again?"

Chacal's breath came in short gasps. "You'll make today seem like a birthday party."

"That's right."

Skip stood, wiped his hands on his jeans, and stepped back through the fence. April fell in beside him.

She shot him a look. "That was quick."

He exhaled. "Yeah. But now we've got bigger problems."

They picked up the pace, heading toward the flashing lights.

***

The flashing lights of two squad cars reflected off the McDonald's windows as a pair of Oxnard police officers finished taking statements from Matt and Chin. One officer obviously had years of street patrol behind him. He sighed as he flipped his notepad closed.

"Looks like you two were just in the wrong place at the wrong time," the officer said, eyeing Matt and Chin with a mix of sympathy and boredom. "Classic gang initiation. Steal a car, pick a random target, start a fight, show the new recruits how to handle themselves." He gave a nonchalant shrug. "Nothing personal. Just bad luck."

Matt stood with his arms crossed and nodded as the cop talked to Chin.

"Yeah, I guess so," Matt said. Chin rubbed the back of his neck, the tension in his posture still evident.

The younger officer looked at Chin and raised an eyebrow as his eyes landed on the small, bloodied credit card Chin had in his hand. "That's pretty clever," he said. "American Express. Don't leave home without it. Just be careful with that thing, alright?"

Chin gave a nervous chuckle, still gripping the credit card a little too tightly. "Yeah, I'll be careful," he said, appreciating the officer's unexpected compliment.

As Matt and Chin finished talking to the police in the McDonald's parking lot, the officer handed Matt a business card before walking off. Matt pocketed it and gave Chin a reassuring nod. The two officers got back in the patrol car and left.

Just then, Skip and April jogged up. Skip's usual cocky grin was gone.

"Everything cool here?" Skip asked, masking the underlying tension that only Matt could sense.

"Yeah," Matt replied, his tone equally steady. "Cops think it's just a gang initiation. Wrong place, wrong time."

Skip raised an eyebrow but didn't say anything.

Chin exhaled slowly, his grip finally easing on the bloodied credit card. "Can we get breakfast now?" he asked, eager to leave the scene behind.

Matt clapped him on the shoulder. "Yeah, let's get back inside. I can almost taste that greasy fast food and weak coffee."

Chapter 16

Day 85 - DCS Headquarters - Port Hueneme, CA

Matt walked through the door of the DCS conference room and shut it behind him. He crossed his arms while surveying the room. Skip was lounging on the edge of the table, and St. Bernard had steadied himself against the wall, silent as ever. April had taken a seat directly across from Skip.

Matt broke the silence first. "Alright, let's get to it. I don't for a second believe the attack on Chin was random, regardless of what the cops are calling it. Skip, you have something?"

"Yeah," Skip said with a nod, briefly glancing at St. Bernard before looking back at Matt. "The gang member we interrogated dropped a little nugget of info. Said they got a call last night. It wasn't some random street initiation. They were told to find someone matching Chin's description and severely injure him. And here's the kicker: they were told Chin would probably be in a blue Genesis."

"There's gotta be a leak somewhere," Skip said.

"Yeah, but who?" St. Bernard asked. "The circle of those who know about this investigation is pretty small."

Matt nodded as his mind worked through the possibilities.

"You know, I saw Decker grab his phone when he walked out of the briefing last night. He was talking to someone as he headed up the exit towards the dock area."

"Suspicious, but not a smoking gun," Skip said.

"If he is dirty, we have a big problem on our hands," St. Bernard added.

Matt didn't respond right away. He knew the team disliked Decker, but he had given them no reason to mistrust him. Yet there was evidence that someone was leaking information about their investigation. Matt wasn't about to jump to conclusions. He needed proof.

He stepped toward the table and rubbed his chin. "We need to play this smart. We keep the circle tight. If Decker's involved, we can't confront him head-on without proof."

April's gaze fixed on Matt. "What's the play then?"

Matt looked at her, then at the rest of the team. "We keep Decker in the loop for now. But from this point forward, we will control every piece of intel we feed him. If he's a mole, he'll make a move soon. We'll give him just enough rope to hang himself."

Skip grinned. "And if it's not him?"

Matt's eyes darkened. "Then we find out who's pulling the strings, but either way, we don't tip anyone off."

St. Bernard uncrossed his arms and pushed himself forward from his spot by the wall. "We still have time before the virus launches. Chin's close to finalizing the antivirus, and we know the grid attack is their first step. We need to lock down communications tighter than ever. No loose ends."

"Agreed," Matt said, looking at April. "You're running point on this. Keep digging into the phone records and trace it as far as you can. I don't care if we have to call in every favor we've got. We need to know."

With a final glance around the room, Matt addressed the group. "This is a dangerous game we're playing. Decker might be innocent, or he might be our leak. Either way, we can't afford any more mistakes. We lock this down, we stay alert, and we take control of the situation. Understood?"

A series of nods followed.

As the team dispersed, Matt lingered at the door, watching as Skip headed to his station and April moved toward the central conference table. If Decker was the mole, they'd have to act fast. If he wasn't, someone else was pulling the strings, and the attack on Chin meant they knew about the task force's progress and suspicions about Taiwan.

St. Bernard stepped up beside him, his voice low. "You think this is all tied to Taiwan?"

Matt nodded. "I do, and if we don't stop it, a lot more people are going to get hurt."

Chapter 17

Day 85 - DCS Headquarters - Port Hueneme, CA

Matt sat back in what he thought of as his office. It had been a storage closet, but now it held a desk, a chair, and a cot with just enough space left to close the door. It gave him somewhere to focus without interruption.

Matt wasn't sure how many hours, or days, he'd been awake. His eyes drifted toward the cot in the corner.

A knock interrupted his thought of getting some sleep. Chin stepped in, carrying his laptop.

"I've finished a preliminary version of the antivirus for the US," Chin said, setting it down. "It's built around a lightweight AI module with just enough autonomy to move through the grid. Once it finds an infected transformer, it goes dormant."

Matt looked up. "Dormant?"

Chin nodded. "Normally I'd program it to wipe the virus as soon as it's detected, but I think the Chinese may be pinging the virus, checking to see if it's still live. If we kill it too early, we could tip our hand."

"So, it just sits there?"

"It finds the virus, confirms it, and waits. Once the virus launches, the antivirus triggers and begins the counteraction."

Matt exhaled. "Clever. How soon can we roll it out?"

"The US version is ready. But Taiwan's infrastructure is different. I'll need to adapt the antivirus for their grid. That's going to take time."

"How much?"

"Forty-eight hours, maybe more."

Over the next twenty minutes, Chin explained the AI antivirus's functionality to Matt, emphasizing the need to upload it to the individual power companies' grids across the US for the most efficient deployment.

***

After the meeting with Chin, Matt laid down. Before falling asleep, he had called Decker, asking him to come to DCS headquarters for an updated briefing. He wanted Decker's input. At least, that was what Matt told him.

He had just woken from a five-hour nap when he heard a knock at the door. He looked up as Decker stepped inside.

"Did I do something wrong, Matt?" Decker asked, crossing the threshold. "I've noticed I've been out of the loop lately."

Matt nodded slightly. "You're not wrong. We've been careful. Wouldn't want to waste your time with briefings until we were sure about a few things."

"What do you mean, 'being careful'?"

Matt kept his tone neutral. "A lot of moving parts, Decker. We wanted to organize the intel and make sure we understood what we had before we updated you. The last thing we need is to brief you on something as fact, only to find out days later we were incorrect. This case is too big for us to make those kinds of mistakes."

Decker studied him. "I guess that makes sense," he said. "For a second there, I thought you were saying you didn't trust me."

"The AI antivirus is ready for the US. For the most efficient distribution, it needs to be manually installed at every major energy provider, like PG&E, SoCal Edison, ERCOT in Texas, Duke Energy. If we don't manually distribute it across the national grid, it could take days to permeate the entire US grid. That delay could be catastrophic."

Decker frowned. "Why not just launch it from a central point?"

Matt exhaled. "Because the grid isn't one seamless system."

Decker nodded. "Does it attack the virus as it spreads through the grid?"

Matt hesitated. "Not exactly. It embeds itself and waits until the virus activates. Until then there's no way to confirm if it's working."

"No way to confirm it? I thought Chin was supposed to be some kind of genius. I shouldn't really expect too much from a physicist from Washington state. Those credentials don't inspire much confidence."

Matt didn't rise to the bait. He leaned forward, voice calm but sharp. "Chin's the reason we're even having this conversation. He's the one who discovered the virus. He's one of the top cyber-defense minds in the country. After a master's degree from MIT, he was pulled into classified DOD programs. After that he earned his PhD in applied physics and got recruited by the Department of Energy to work on infrastructure protection. Places like PNNL don't hire hobbyists, Decker."

Decker looked like he wanted to fire back, but Matt didn't give him the chance.

"He's already cracked several encrypted files tying Lebedev to the Montecito hits, and he's working directly with DOE analysts to map a deeper vulnerability in the grid. Does that sound like amateur hour to you?"

"Then what are we waiting for? Why aren't we launching it now? Sitting on this doesn't make sense. We should take the shot while we've got the advantage."

Matt had expected this. He kept his tone even. "The antivirus is AI-driven and customized for US systems. But Taiwan's grid architecture is different. Chin needs more time to study and adapt to it."

"Then let's release the US version immediately," Decker said. "Why wait?"

"Because if we act too soon, China will adapt. They wouldn't launch something of this scale without safeguards. Chin's confident they're running intermittent burst checks and silent transmissions into the transformers to confirm the virus is still intact. Right now, we're invisible. If we launch too early, we tip our hand."

Decker paused, chewing on the implication. "So, you're suggesting we wait. But what if something goes wrong while we're stalling? The virus could spiral out of control before we respond."

"Timing is everything," Matt said. "Chin's antivirus is our trump card. But it only works once. If we show it too soon, we lose the element of surprise, and maybe Taiwan."

Decker's face flushed red. "It's not your call. It's not mine either."

Matt met his gaze without blinking. "It may not be my call, but I'm making it. I trust Chin. We hold off a few hours, maybe a few days. If that's the price of stopping a war, I'll pay it. In the field, we make tough calls, and live with the consequences."

Decker shook his head. "This is beyond any risk I'm willing to take."

Matt didn't let it drop. "Lately, too much has gone sideways. Compromised ops. Missed intel. Gaps that shouldn't exist. It's not paranoia. it's patterns. And patterns mean something."

He studied Decker, searching his face.

Decker frowned. "You think someone's feeding intel to the other side?"

"A lot of things aren't adding up."

Matt wasn't sure how Decker would take it. Either he would feel cornered, or the honesty would disarm him. But the bait was there. Now it was Decker's move.

Decker sighed. "Okay, I get where you're coming from. It's just hard to sit back when we've got something that could stop this thing. But I get it. We can't risk giving China a chance to counter. I don't have the authority to risk the entire US electrical grid going down just because China might change tactics."

Then he asked, "What about Taiwan? How long until the antivirus is operational there?"

The question caught Matt off guard. "It'll take at least a few more days. We've prioritized the U.S."

Decker nodded. "I have to run this up the chain. This is way above my pay grade."

"I understand. Remember, once it's out there, we can't take it back." His voice stayed calm. "That's why we want to hold off deploying it in the United States."

Decker looked unconvinced. "It still feels like we're rolling the dice here."

"Well, that's the game we're playing," Matt said. "I'm a field operative. Making risky decisions is what I do. With high risk comes high reward. Granted, most of the risky decisions I make don't involve millions of lives."

Decker held his gaze for a long moment. Then, after what felt like an eternity, he extended his hand. "I appreciate your confidence in me."

Matt shook it.

As Decker turned to leave, Matt spoke again, keeping his tone neutral.

"By the way, I noticed you made a phone call right after the meeting last night. Who did you call?"

Decker answered immediately. "My old partner. I felt like I was getting in over my head and needed to run a few things by him. I gave him general info, but no details. He talked me down. Helped me get my head straight."

Matt nodded, saying nothing. He didn't press further.

As Decker left, Matt turned over the answer in his mind. Decker had explained the call without hesitation. Either the call was exactly as Decker had said, a call to his old partner, or he was very good at deception. The call could be a coincidence.

But Matt didn't believe in coincidences.

***

Lucas Decker felt conflicted. At his request, Supervising Agent Karen Lawson had given him the case from DCS. She had warned him to keep it within FBI jurisdiction. Easier said than done.

Stepping into Lawson's office, he found her typing away. "Decker, sit. What's the latest?"

He took a breath. "The task force has an antivirus ready. DCS wants to hold off on releasing it."

"Why? Never mind why. Get it to cyber. As soon as they configure it, push it out."

Decker hesitated. "There's more at stake. Matt Scales and Chin Ho believe this virus is part of a larger attack. One tied to Taiwan. If we neutralize it here first, we could tip off the people behind it. We'll lose our shot at stopping them."

Lawson looked back, unimpressed. "And you're basing this on what? A theory?"

Decker met her gaze. "Hard evidence. Chinese and Russian operatives are working together to weaken us ahead of an operation in Taiwan. If we roll out the antivirus now, there's a good chance they'll know we're on to them. They'll disappear."

Lawson tapped her pen on the desk. "So, you're asking me to delay protecting the US power grid... based on a gamble?"

"I'm asking for time. Chin is finalizing the counterpart antivirus for Taiwan. If we coordinate both releases, we cripple their operation. But if we jump too soon, they scatter. Next time, we won't see them coming."

"Henshaw won't sign off on this."

"We need to convince him."

She studied him for a moment before nodding. "Fine. But if this backfires, you're taking the fall."

Decker stood. "I understand."

As he left, the weight of the decision settled on his shoulders. It was up to him to convince Henshaw.

***

Decker and Special Agent in Charge Karen Lawson sat in chairs in a secure conference room at the FBI headquarters in Los Angeles. They were waiting for the secure link to go through to Assistant Director Henshaw in Washington, DC.

As Assistant Director Henshaw's face popped up on the monitor, Decker had the urge to jump to attention. He took a deep breath and tried to compose himself as he started briefing Henshaw.

Decker laid out the details of the investigation, the status of the virus in the United States and the US antivirus. He told Henshaw of their suspicions about the connection to Taiwan, and that another virus was being readied to be released in Taiwan as a precursor to an invasion by China. He'd made the case for caution, explaining the strategic risks of launching too early. But Henshaw, ever the pragmatist, wasn't interested in delays. After listening in silence, he gave a single definitive command.

"Release the antivirus in the US immediately."

Decker had no room to argue. The order was final, and he knew better than to push back. "I'll call Cyber and hook up them up with Chin. He can walk them through loading the antivirus onto our servers."

As he walked out, Decker knew exactly what had to be done.

Matt's going to be pissed.

***

Outside, the late afternoon sun cast long shadows across the Port Hueneme docks. Inside the windowless DCS headquarters, Matt sat at his desk, reviewing the logistics for Taiwan that included flight schedules, insertion routes, gear manifests, and fallback sites in case the virus attack escalated before they touched down. He cross-checked the team's weapons loadout with DEVGRU's inventory in-country and flagged a note about encrypted comms, firearms and a safe house. It wasn't just a matter of getting there, it was everything that came after.

A sharp knock at the door pulled his focus. It opened before he could answer. Decker stepped inside. He had tension written all over his face.

Matt leaned back in his chair, laced his fingers behind his head, and watched the FBI agent shut the door behind him.

"Let me guess," Matt said. "Henshaw wants it released."

"Yeah." Decker's voice was tight. "He's ordered me to launch the antivirus immediately. I agreed... but I came here first."

Matt stood and came around the desk. "Go on."

"I've been thinking about what you said. Chin's concern that China might be pinging the virus, checking to see if it's still live. How neutralizing it too early could tip them off."

Matt gave a single nod. "If that happens, Lebedev disappears. Taiwan has no defense against the virus and ultimately the invasion. A lot of people will die, and China takes over Taiwan."

Decker shifted his weight. "Cyber Division wants to go live by tomorrow."

"Then let them launch it," Matt said flatly.

Decker blinked. "What?"

"Tell them to contact Chin. He'll walk them through the deployment." Matt said. "Chin built in a safeguard. The antivirus won't activate until he gives the go-code. Until then, it searches, finds, and waits."

"So, it doesn't really work?"

"It works," Matt said. "Once it finds an infected transformer it stays dormant until Chin gives the activation signal. This way we don't show our hand until Chin completes the AI antivirus for the Taiwanese grid."

Decker's shoulders eased. "Henshaw thinks I'm following orders, but we're still holding the line."

Matt nodded. "We're buying time. And when time's short, deception is a weapon."

Decker let out a slow exhale, feeling the weight lift from his shoulders. A lingering unease remained. "That's... brilliant," he muttered.

***

Decker could see how Matt was balancing several layers of deception in a larger strategy. Henshaw would think Decker followed orders. The antivirus would be "released" but wouldn't be active. Chin held the key. Matt and his team would maintain control, and once Taiwan was ready, they could execute their plan.

"So, when they release the virus, and the electrical grid in the US goes down and the antivirus appears not to be working, what do I do?"

Matt shrugged. "You point the finger at us. DCS screwed up. They'll believe it. After all, it's not like we haven't run fast and loose before."

Decker's stomach twisted. He felt the adrenaline as his heart rate increased. He had been thrust into a much larger game than he had bargained for. And to think, Matt had planned this all along.

Decker nodded, seeing the broader picture. "So, we're only delaying by a day or two. Just long enough to make sure everything's in place."

"Exactly," Matt said. "We'll make our move when we're ready. But for now, we let Henshaw think you're following his orders."

Decker had never experienced such a conflict between his obligation to the FBI and his personal loyalty to his team. A hint of uncertainty crossed his mind. Was he making the right decision?

"Was this your plan from the start?"

Matt looked at Decker with a hint of amusement. "Chin's been teaching me the strategy behind Go," he said, with a nod to the Go game board sitting on a coffee table in front of his desk. "It's not just about capturing territory, it's about controlling the flow of the game, making moves that distract your opponent and force them into a corner before they even realize it."

Decker hesitated and looked at the board. "And this is one of those moves?"

Matt smiled. "Exactly. We let the enemy think they're safe, unaware we have all the power to stop them. Chin's strategy is about patience and seeing the long game. We're just waiting for the perfect moment to act when everything's lined up."

Decker exhaled, finally seeing the brilliance behind it. "So, we wait. And when the time's right, we strike..."

"And when we do, they won't even see it coming," Matt said, finishing Decker's sentence.

***

Matt sat at his desk, the dim light of his office casting long shadows on the walls. He was thinking about how intelligence was like an upside-down jigsaw puzzle. Several pieces had finally been turned over, and now he was starting to see the bigger picture. The problem was, he didn't know yet what was missing.

Across from him, St. Bernard and Skip sat in the office's two chairs, engaged in yet another debate—this time about the finer points of controlled demolitions.

"Delta treats breaching as a science," Skip said, shaking his head. "We calculate the exact charge needed. Precise, clean, controlled. SEALs? You clowns just slap on whatever's in the truck and hope it doesn't bring the whole building down."

St. Bernard gave him a look, unimpressed. "That's because SEALs get the job done. You wanna dance around with micro-measured C-4 charges? Be my guest. Me? If two blocks does the trick, four blocks will do it better. Hell, why stop there? Let's make the wall just disappear."

Skip waved his hand through the air. "That's not how precision works, Bernard."

"Precision's not about being gentle. It's about making sure the wall goes boom exactly when and where you want. Bigger just means you don't have to wonder if it is going to work."

Matt laughed as he shook his head. Same argument, different day.

"You two ever consider debating something important?" he said.

Skip opened his mouth to fire back, but a knock at the door cut him off.

"Come in," Matt called.

April entered and closed the door behind her. Her expression told him she was all business. The atmosphere in the room shifted.

"Got a minute?" she asked.

"For you, always," Matt replied.

Skip and St. Bernard quieted and gave April their full attention.

She propped herself against the wall.

"Remember a few days ago when you asked me to go over everything on the case?"

"You found something, didn't you?"

She tapped her tablet and slid it across the desk. "There's a pattern."

Matt frowned, taking the tablet and glancing at the screen. He couldn't understand the data, although he was sure it made sense to April. He noticed that the phone calls were time-stamped with the locations.

"I don't see it," he admitted.

"Well, based on a hunch, I had our friend Jack Roberts use his contacts at the NSA to download some data.

"Remember the phone call Kuznetsov got the night before the raid at the New Cuyama farmhouse? That same number called a phone in Oxnard the night before they attacked Chin. Here's the kicker: both calls originated in Taiwan."

Matt's eyes widened as the pieces started to connect. Someone in Taiwan was coordinating operatives here in Oxnard.

"Looks like someone overseas is calling the shots," he said.

"Yeah," April agreed. "We have to assume Kuznetsov ditched his old phone after the New Cuyama raid, but I'd bet the Oxnard one belongs to him."

Matt exhaled sharply. "And?"

She tapped the screen in front of her. "That Oxnard phone pinged off a tower in Lancaster last night."

Matt's eyes perked up. "Lancaster."

"Exactly. Ranch country. And we both know how Kuznetsov likes rural areas to coordinate his operations."

Matt thought fast. "Who else knows about this?"

"No one that I know of," April said. "Roberts could have figured it out from the data, but I don't think he did."

Matt nodded. "Alright. We may have an edge here. We need to move on that phone in Lancaster."

April hesitated. "There's more. The Taiwan number received a call from a blocked number the night before Chin was attacked. It pinged off a cell tower on this base."

Matt's mind worked fast. Too many coincidences.

St. Bernard frowned. "Who do we trust now that we know there's a problem?"

"Trust in this job is built under pressure, through combat, and watching each other's backs," Matt exhaled. "Not everyone on the team has been tested like that yet."

St. Bernard, who had been quietly observing, finally spoke. "Decker's the newest member of the team. He's the one we know the least about."

April crossed her arms. "To be safe, we keep this tight. Just between us in the room for now?"

Matt looked around at the team. "Yes. Just us in the room."

"And of course you have a plan," St. Bernard stated.

"You know my mantra—if you don't have a plan, you're counting on luck."

***

The next morning, Matt stood at the front of the table in the SCIF. April, St. Bernard, Skip, and Dave Johnson were seated. Matt had scheduled the meeting to bring Dave up to speed on their investigation and to prep for the next phase.

He had asked Mitchell to stay focused on the Taiwan logistics. It was nothing unusual, just keeping him out of the more sensitive discussion for now. Matt planned to loop him in after the meeting, once decisions were made.

"Dave, I've kept this meeting limited to us for a reason," Matt said. "We've got a problem. Someone has been feeding Lebedev information."

April summarized the metadata trail, the cell tower logs, and the call linked to Chin's attackers.

"We don't have proof yet," Matt continued, "but someone's been getting information to Lebedev. Outside of this room, there are only two people with enough access to piece it all together."

Matt allowed the corner of his mouth to twitch before continuing the briefing. "A burner phone tied to Chin's attack pinged in Lancaster two days ago. We've traced it to a general location that may link back to Kuznetsov."

"I see a road trip in our future," St. Bernard said, still grinning.

"Exactly," Matt said. "We're heading to Lancaster. I'm bringing Decker. If he's clean, he'll help us pin down the target. If he's not, we may walk into a ghost site."

Skip folded his arms. "And if it's a setup?"

"Then we regroup. But exposing the leak takes priority."

April tapped her fingers on the table. "What's our cover?"

"Electrical contractors doing utility inspections. Decker will help us get the surveillance vans."

St. Bernard nodded. "If Kuznetsov shows, we move?"

"Yes," Matt said. "No hesitation. If he's not there, we sweep for evidence and fall back."

He turned to April. "You're handling drones, long lenses, and remote mics. We may not need them but be prepared just in case."

"Already started running gear checks," she said.

Skip glanced at Matt. "What about Mitchell?"

"He's staying here," Matt said. "I've got him locked in on prepping the logistics for Taiwan. It's what he does. Checking gear manifests, comms links, getting the handoff with DEVGRU tight. I don't want him distracted with the field stuff. That's our job."

Matt sat down at the head of the table. "Questions? Anything we've missed?"

He knew the team was satisfied with the plan because no one asked questions. He stood, signaling that the meeting was over. "Everyone, gear up. We're heading out in an hour for Lancaster."

As the team dispersed, Matt saw the resolve on their faces. They knew the stakes were high and the danger higher. But he also knew this was where his team excelled.

***

After the meeting, Dave asked Matt to join him in his office.

"You've got a lot of moving parts, Matt," Dave said. "But it looks like you thought this through pretty well."

"As best I can. Lancaster is the test for Decker."

"What happens if Decker passes the test?"

"Right now, we're focusing on Decker, but we're also keeping Mitchell at arm's length until we figure out who the leak is."

After the meeting, Matt went to Mitchell's office. He knocked on the door and stepped inside. "Mitchell, we're close to launching for Taiwan, but there are a few things that we need to take care of here. We need to head to LA to give the FBI an update on our investigation. For now, I need you to stay here and concentrate on the logistics for Taiwan, including infiltrating into the country and access to the safe house you mentioned. Once we head out to Taiwan, things are going to move fast."

"I'm on it," Mitchell said.

Chapter 18

Matt called Decker and asked him to meet him at the FBI headquarters. He also told him to clear his calendar for the rest of the day and evening. He would explain when he got there.

They met in Decker's office. Matt laid out how the phone logs led to a farmhouse in Lancaster. He didn't tell him they suspected the phone belonged to Kuznetsov. He said he wanted to set up surveillance and find the phone's owner.

Decker sold the plan to Lawson. Agent Lawson gave them permission to use the FBI's utility trucks for the surveillance. The surveillance vehicles came equipped with a StingRay device.

The StingRay device mimicked a cell phone tower and intercepted cell phones that came within its proximity. Once a cell phone connected to the StingRay, it identified the number. Once locked on the number, the StingRay could triangulate the cell phone's position and allow the operator to follow at a safe distance.

***

Matt's team parked near the cell phone tower where their target phone had pinged days earlier. The trucks displayed the logo of a local electrical line contractor. It provided them the perfect cover for a rural area that always had work being done on the utility lines.

The team had been in position since 6 a.m. The sun was setting soon, and they had to decide how long they would stay in the area without drawing undue attention. On the surface, they were just workers going about their day. In reality, the StingRay device hidden inside one of the vehicles was doing its work, searching for the cellular signal. One they assumed belonged to Kuznetsov.

St. Bernard sat in the passenger seat of the lead truck with the StingRay monitor on his lap.

"Got something," he muttered. "Tracking our target number. It's moving towards us."

Matt looked at the readout. "That's our guy."

The blip grew stronger as it moved toward them.

"Okay everyone, start packing up and look like we're ending work for the day. We'll stay about half a mile behind him and see where he goes."

They saw a pickup truck approaching. As it passed them, Matt recognized the driver. Kuznetsov.

"Let him pass," Matt said calmly.

Kuznetsov's truck rumbled by.

The convoy of electric company trucks started rolling slowly down the road behind the truck, careful to maintain their distance, not rushing the moment. They kept the truck just inside the range of the StingRay device.

"It's turning off the road. According to the overhead maps, it's heading into a ranch," St. Bernard said over the comms.

The two utility trucks approached the area where the truck had turned onto a dirt road.

"No signs and no gate. We can legally drive down the road," April said. "It's just like walking up to someone's front door from the sidewalk. If there are no barriers or signs, there's an implied consent for anyone to use it."

"Okay," Matt said. "We turn onto the road and follow it. Keep your heads on a swivel."

After a half mile down the road, they came around a bend. Matt could see a few scattered structures up ahead, including a house, a barn, and several outbuildings. Trees and small hills surrounded them. The barn had Kuznetsov's truck parked in front of it. Matt's team slowed, each truck taking strategic positions along the driveway, keeping a low profile.

As they pulled up, they saw Kuznetsov get out of his truck. He turned around and looked at the utility trucks, but only for a second. He then started walking toward the barn.

Matt knew the next sixty seconds were crucial. Kuznetsov was a seasoned tactical operator and would not believe in the coincidence of the utility trucks following him into the ranch.

As Kuznetsov walked into the barn, another man came out and started walking towards Matt.

Matt stepped out of the truck, clipboard in hand. "Hey there," he called, forcing a friendly smile. "We're with the electric company. Just checking the lines. Got a report about some interference in the area."

"You're on private property," the man said. "You need to leave."

"Sorry man, thought this road was public easement. We are getting some strange energy fluctuations in the lines around here. We're concerned they may fail during high winds and start a fire. We'll be quick."

The man's hand twitched near his side. Matt's grip on his clipboard tightened, but he kept his stance relaxed. "Mind if we check the lines by the barn? It'll only take five minutes."

"You're not going anywhere near that barn," the man snapped.

***

After Kuznetsov stepped into the barn, he shut the heavy door behind him. He moved to the window. He stood four feet from the window to make sure no one outside could see him.

The utility trucks had parked fifty yards from the barn. He pulled out a pair of compact binoculars. From the shadows inside the barn, he scanned the scene outside.

When his eyes landed on the man standing outside one of the trucks, clipboard in hand, his stomach dropped.

Matt Scales.

Kuznetsov's lips tightened into a thin line. He had studied this man and his team for months. The dossiers stashed in the barn had detailed their investigation. He recognized the sharpness in Scales's gaze, even from a distance. Somehow, they had found him.

Without hesitation, Kuznetsov shoved the binoculars into his pocket and looked around the dimly lit barn. Every operation demanded an exit strategy, and he always had one. Basic survival in his line of work. He hadn't planned to use it, not yet, but Scales's sudden appearance outside the farmhouse forced his hand. No more waiting.

Kuznetsov grabbed a small device from a hidden compartment beneath the table along the back wall. He slipped out through the back door, where an ATV sat. He had started the ATV every day and let it run for five minutes each time to make sure it worked. He started up the ATV and gunned the engine. When he was fifty yards from the barn, he pushed down on the detonator. He'd rigged the explosives to destroy the barn and eliminate any evidence of the plan and his involvement.

***

Outside, Matt started walking toward the barn, but the man he'd been talking to stepped in front of him, blocking his path.

Matt sidestepped. The man mirrored him.

Without hesitation, Matt shoved past him.

A sudden tremor. *Boom.*

The shock wave tore through the air.

Matt barely had time to register the meaning of the sound before the blast slammed him off his feet.

He hit the ground hard; his breath ripped from his lungs. Before he could move, a burning chunk of wood smashed into the dirt inches from his head. Hot embers hit his face.

Flames roared skyward. The heat blasted against his skin.

His lungs burned. As he pushed himself off the ground, someone hit him from the side, slamming him back down.

Matt took a punch to the jaw but used the momentum to twist himself, getting his legs under him.

He threw an elbow back and caught the man in the temple.

He wrenched the attacker's wrist sideways, spun him around, and forced his arm into a punishing arm lock.

The man screamed. Matt drove him face-first into the dirt.

He snapped flex cuffs onto his wrists.

Smoke billowed, flames chewing through the remains of the barn. Matt looked up, scanning the fire, searching for movement, but the smoke was too thick.

He cursed. Whoever had been inside was already gone.

"Flanking movement to the right!" Matt barked. "April, control the perp!"

As St. Bernard and Skip rushed toward the side of the barn, Matt's radio crackled with Decker's voice. "What the hell's going on?!"

"Target escaped..." Matt growled as he fought to get some clean air in his lungs. "He blew up the barn as cover. Stay at the entrance by the main road and intercept local law enforcement."

"Will do," Decker said. "I'll keep them off this scene as long as I can, but I doubt it'll be more than a few minutes. They're gonna want to evaluate the scene for themselves."

Matt took a deep breath, shaking off the frustration. "Buy us time."

Through the thickening smoke, Matt spotted Decker's vehicle parked near the entrance, where they had planned for him to block unauthorized access. Now, with the explosion drawing law enforcement, his role had shifted. Decker would have to stall the LA County Sheriff's Office long enough for Matt and his team to grab any evidence they could and clear out.

Matt turned back toward the burning barn, then back to his team.

"Okay, everybody, listen up. We have five, maybe ten minutes. Gather what you can and load up."

They spent the next five minutes battling the blistering heat as they tried to get into the burning barn. Smoke billowed from the structure, thick and acrid, stinging their eyes and clogging their throats. The flames roared, consuming the wooden beams with crackling snaps, sending embers swirling through the air like fireflies. The searing heat radiated outward, forcing them to shield their faces. Their boots crunched against debris scattered across the dirt.

After five minutes, Matt surveyed the scene. They were running out of time.

"Pull back!" he ordered, his voice hoarse from the smoke.

They retreated to the trucks, slamming doors shut as the scent of burning wood clung to the air and their clothes. The convoy rumbled down the dirt road. Their tires kicked up dust that disappeared as it was absorbed in the smoke.

Just before they reached the main road, headlights pierced the haze ahead. Decker's vehicle emerged from the dust, followed by two LA Sheriff's vehicles, closing in fast.

Matt eased off the gas and pulled to the side. The team exchanged tense glances as the sheriff's units roared past, red-and-blue lights flashing. Decker followed close behind them and waved as he sped by.

As soon as they had a clear path, Matt pressed forward, steering them toward the highway. There was no time to dwell on their losses.

Kuznetsov was gone. Any evidence they could have pulled from the barn was ash.

But the mission didn't stop.

They would go to Los Angeles first to drop the trucks, pick up their vehicles, then straight back to DCS headquarters. Taiwan was coming fast, and they had to be ready.

***

While the team cleared the Lancaster location and headed back to the FBI office in Los Angeles, DCS headquarters continued with business as usual.

The soft hum of the computers and portable fans filled the office as Amy Rodriguez clicked through emails. She was about to step away for a coffee refill when the public line rang.

"DCS Headquarters, this is Amy."

A male voice came through. "This is Special Agent Tom Reiner with the FBI's Santa Maria office. I need to speak with Matt Scales regarding a Mr. Ho in Paso Robles."

Amy's fingers tightened on the handset. The name was familiar. Chin's father.

"Matt's not at his desk at the moment, but I can take a message."

As she spoke, Jon Mitchell walked by, flipping through a case file. He paused at the sound of Matt's name.

Amy glanced at him. "Hey Jon, do you know where Matt is? The FBI's calling about some issue with Chin's dad in Paso."

"What kind of issue?" Jon's voice was casual, but his eyes sharpened with interest.

Amy cupped the phone. "Didn't say. Just that they need to talk to Matt."

Mitchell nodded. "The team went down to the LA FBI headquarters to brief them. I haven't heard from them in several hours."

Amy turned back to the line. "The last we heard, they were at the FBI office in Los Angeles. What office did you say you're from?"

"I'm assigned out of the Santa Maria office," Reiner said. "This isn't urgent. Mr. Scales is the courtesy contact anytime the Sentinel Program issues an alert for Mr. Ho. Can you pass the message along?"

"Understood. I'll have Matt call you back shortly." Amy jotted down the details, ending the call.

As she hung up. Mitchell came walking past her desk. "What's going on?"

Amy shrugged. "No idea. Something about the Sentinel Program sending an alert to the FBI about Mr. Ho."

Mitchell gave a slow nod. "Interesting." He tapped the folder against his palm and walked off.

Chapter 19

Decker stepped into DCS headquarters. His mind was reviewing the details of the scene he'd left at the farmhouse. The FBI response team was still processing the scene, cataloging evidence, securing statements, but he had done everything he could on-site.

Then, over the radio, he'd heard the last thing he wanted to.

Larson was en route to the farmhouse.

Sticking around would have meant one thing: explaining this mess to her before he and Matt had a chance to compare notes.

And he wasn't ready for that.

If she got the details first, she'd have enough leverage to pull him off the task force. Even dissolve it. Kuznetsov had slipped through their fingers, and as far as Larson was concerned, that was all she needed to bury him.

Decker marched down the hallway towards Matt's office. He wasn't here to argue. He needed answers.

***

Matt exhaled as he sank into his desk chair, rolling his shoulders. The farmhouse raid had been a mess, but at least it had confirmed one thing—Decker wasn't the leak.

As Matt had expected, Kuznetsov had been there. He'd only escaped at the last second. He must have spotted Matt. If Decker had been feeding the man information, Kuznetsov would have cleared out long before they arrived.

Matt reached for his coffee mug, then noticed the yellow sticky note placed on his keyboard.

FBI Santa Maria office, Special Agent Reiner. Nonurgent call re: Mr. Ho in Paso Robles. Wants to speak with you.

Matt frowned, rubbing his temple. Why the hell would the FBI be calling about Mr. Ho?

He picked up the note, reading it again.

As he reached for his phone, the door swung open without a knock.

Decker stepped inside, looking like he'd just walked off a battlefield. His tie was loose, sleeves rolled up, tension coiled in his shoulders. He shut the door behind him.

Matt smiled and crossed his arms. "Long day?"

Decker scoffed. "It's about to get worse." He ran a hand through his hair. "We need to talk before I report to Larson. If we don't get ahead of this, we're screwed."

Matt studied him. "How bad?"

Decker let out a dry chuckle. "How's 'career-ending disaster' sound?"

Matt's expression didn't change. "Alright. Talk."

Decker dropped into the seat across from Matt, who could see the frustration burning just beneath the surface.

"What the hell happened at the farmhouse? It was never about surveillance, was it?"

Matt let that sit for a moment before answering. "No, it wasn't. We thought Kuznetsov was there, and we were going to get him."

Decker tensed. "But you didn't trust me with that information?"

Matt met his gaze. "Compartmentalization."

Decker shook his head. "What?"

Matt slid a printout from the NSA across the table. The highlighted numbers traced calls to Taiwan, then back to a burner phone in the local area. As Decker skimmed the document, Matt tossed another set of papers toward him.

"See the number that traced back to the Lancaster farmhouse?" Matt asked. "The StingRay device logged that phone in the same vehicle Kuznetsov was in when he passed us on the road."

Decker's eyes scanned the data.

Matt continued. "Now look at the time and location of the cell towers routing these calls."

Decker's face darkened. "They're near the base."

Matt nodded. "And one of them was made the night before Chin was attacked."

Decker tightened his grip on the papers. "Jesus Christ." He looked up at Matt. "That's why you asked me about the phone call that night."

Matt didn't blink. "What do you think?"

"Fuck you, Scales." Decker tossed the papers onto the table. "You really thought I was a traitor? The whole damn farmhouse op was just a setup to see if I'd warn Kuznetsov?"

Matt didn't flinch. "Yep."

Decker stared at Matt, challenging him. Matt held his gaze, unflinching, a mad-dog stare meeting Decker's challenge.

Neither blinked.

Suddenly, Decker let out a bitter laugh, shaking his head. "That's pretty ballsy. What if I didn't take the bait?"

"Then we'd still be looking at you as a suspect."

Silence stretched between them for a long moment before Decker sighed. "Shit." His voice was quieter now. "So, who's been playing us?"

"The only suspect we have left is Mitchell."

As soon as he said Mitchell's name, Matt's thoughts shifted to a past conversation. He had been focused on the antivirus, on Decker, on keeping things locked down. But now, that moment stood out.

"Mitchell mentioned a safe house he was preparing in Taiwan."

Decker frowned. "And?"

"The way he said it, he was... casual. Too casual."

Decker exhaled, shaking his head. "So now what?"

Matt met his gaze. "We set a trap for a traitor."

***

Matt stood at the head of the conference room in DCS headquarters. He realized how tired he was. Every sound seemed a little louder and sharper. The lights a little too bright. The scent of strong coffee hung in the air. Candy wrappers and snack debris littered the table. Around him sat St. Bernard, Skip, April, Chin, and Mitchell.

Matt had invited Mitchell to sit in on the first part of the meeting to maintain the illusion he was deeply involved in the Taiwan operation.

"Man, you guys look beat. Where have you been for the last twenty-four hours? I couldn't find you anywhere," Mitchell said.

"FBI pulled us into a last-minute surveillance op," Matt replied. "Phones off, GPS off. You know the drill."

St. Bernard flipped open his tablet and tapped the screen. Skip stood off to the side, arms crossed, a piece of beef jerky dangling from his lips. Chin, still bruised from the recent attack, hunched over a set of maps. April scanned her tablet, reviewing the Taiwan logistics.

"We've got everything locked down," Chin muttered, not looking up. "While you guys were out playing last night, I was polishing the AI antivirus. It's technically ready, but I keep finding ways to make it better. Call it insurance."

Matt glanced at him. Chin's tone was steady, but the tightness in his voice and shoulders told a different story. Across the table, April looked up from her tablet and looked at Chin. Her lips parted slightly, like she might say something, but she stopped herself and looked back down. Matt noticed. He didn't press. Not now.

"Travel plans are solid," April said, shifting gears. "Ming Ho is expecting us. We've got less than three hours before wheels up from LAX. Direct to Taipei."

Matt gave a slow nod, his thoughts drifting to the farmhouse. The charred remains of their last lead sat as a reminder of how close they'd come. Only for Kuznetsov to vanish in the smoke. The explosion had been a middle finger to their operation, a deliberate message that this wasn't over.

No time to dwell. He turned his focus back to the task ahead.

"Mitchell, run us through the Taiwan logistics one more time." Mitchell nodded and talked for nearly twenty minutes about gear manifests, comms routing, and transport coordination.

When he wrapped up, Matt nodded. "Solid work. Looks like you've done your usual masterful planning. I want you to start running exit scenarios just in case we need to pull out fast if the invasion gets traction."

"I'll get right on it," Mitchell said. He stood, gathered his notes, and offered a quick smile.

"Also," Matt added casually, "I'll be sticking around a bit longer. The FBI asked for someone to coordinate with their cyber unit on the antivirus rollout. Doesn't make sense for all of us to go if they've still got questions."

"Copy that," Mitchell said, and left the room.

Matt watched him leave. As the door clicked shut, St. Bernard leaned back. "You sure about staying behind?"

"It's better if I stay for now," Matt said. "I need you to have eyes on that safe house. If Lebedev's team shows, we'll know Mitchell's the leak. If so, I need to be here to deal with that directly."

Chin gave a quiet nod. "We'll keep you updated on our end, but if we don't get to Taiwan soon..."

Matt raised a hand. "I know. You go to Taiwan, shut down the virus, and protect Uncle Ming. I'll handle things here. As soon as we get confirmation, I'm on the way."

He scanned the room, reading the fatigue on each of their faces. They were running on fumes, but they had ten hours in the air to sleep before hitting Taiwan.

Skip gave him a look. "Don't worry, Matt. We'll get it done."

The door opened, and Decker stepped in. His suit was rumpled, and shadows ringed his eyes, but there was a sign of energy behind them. Excitement, maybe. Or news.

"Looks like you're getting ready to head out. Tight turnaround."

"Yes, we're on a tight time schedule," Matt said, leading Decker down the hall to his small office. He shut the door. "Mitchell's still in play. The team has to get to Taiwan to carry out the next part of the plan."

Decker dropped into a chair, his posture slumping. The tiredness was finally showing through.

"How's the FBI side?"

"Bad," Decker said. "ATF's digging through the rubble. They're calling it a pro job. FBI's talking about leads, but let's be honest. Kuznetsov's long gone."

"We can't chase him right now. Our focus is Taiwan. Once we confirm Mitchell's the leak, I'll confront him and get a confession."

Decker gave a skeptical look. "You say that like it'll be easy."

Matt shrugged. "If he's dirty, it won't take long to break him. I've dealt with guys like him before."

"And if it's not Mitchell? Or he doesn't bite?"

Matt turned to face him. "The pieces fit too well. He had access to everything. The timing lines up. But yeah... if I'm wrong, we'll know soon."

Decker nodded slowly. "Once we pull the trigger on this, there's no walking it back."

"I know. That's why the team's going to stage near the safe house. We'll tell Mitchell they're inside waiting for Ming Ho's intel. We're betting Lebedev's people will show up fast. They won't risk us slipping away."

Decker gave a dry chuckle. "So, we sit back, wait for the trap to spring, and hope the right rat walks in."

Matt checked the wall clock. "Yep. I've got to talk to the team before they leave."

He walked into the conference room. The team was finishing their gear checks, prepping for departure.

"LAX is waiting," Matt said. "Get over there and don't look back. I'll join you as soon as I can."

St. Bernard clapped a hand on his shoulder. "We'll keep you posted the moment anything happens."

Matt watched as his team filed out, one by one. He knew how many things could still go sideways. Murphy's Law, *whatever can go wrong, will*, was always lurking. And tonight, it had plenty of opportunities.

***

Mitchell leaned against the doorway, watching the last of the team disappear down the hall.

"Everything okay with Mr. Ho?" he asked Matt casually.

Matt glanced up, keeping his expression neutral. "Not sure yet." He tapped the yellow slip he was holding in his hand that Amy had left on his desk. "I just got off the phone with the FBI. Something about a suspicious vehicle and a drone on his property."

Mitchell frowned. "That serious?"

Matt exhaled, leaning back in his chair. "Don't know. The FBI got a Sentinel notification incident and sent an agent to check it out. I figured I'd go up there myself, see what's what."

"Sentinel? What's that?"

Matt looked at him and smiled. "It's above your pay grade."

Mitchell gave a dry chuckle. "Everything around here is."

Matt relented. "It's a covert protection program for foreign intelligence assets who've worked with the US Mr. Ho's a high-value defector. He helped smuggle intelligence out of China. Sentinel keeps an eye on guys like him."

Mitchell nodded. "So, if Ho sees something suspicious, he contacts Sentinel, and they send the FBI?"

"Depends on the situation. This time, they had a field agent in the area, so they passed it off."

Mitchell studied him. "So, you're heading up there now?"

Matt nodded. "Yeah. Since I'm still here coordinating with the FBI anyway, I figured I'd take the opportunity to check on Mr. Ho before the team lands in Taiwan."

Mitchell seemed satisfied with the answer. "Alright. Safe travels."

Matt stepped into his office to grab his jacket and backpack. On the desk, he spotted the tablet Chin had given him as part of his cover for staying behind to coordinate the antivirus rollout with the FBI. He opened it.

The screen lit up with the latest cyber intel packet pushed from FBI headquarters: projected attack timelines, potential impact scenarios, and Chin's proposed firewall countermeasures. Matt scrolled through simulated breach maps, noting how cleanly the data was organized. It wasn't just Chin's genius on display. This was a full joint effort now. FBI analysts had woven in predictive modeling, coordinated updates from DHS, and the latest specs on the AI-driven antivirus Chin had embedded in the code.

It felt strange, seeing Chin's work laid out so precisely on-screen, knowing he was headed into the heart of the threat. Matt could feel the shape of it, the way each puzzle piece snapped into place. Chin had built something that just might hold the line.

And yet, here Matt was, still in California. For the first time in a long while, Matt wasn't charging ahead with the team. He was holding the rear, playing the long game. It didn't sit comfortably, but he knew it had to be this way. Sometimes leading meant staying behind, watching the door no one else could.

He shut the tablet, grabbed his jacket, and headed out to his car.

***

The drive north was uneventful. Early morning fog clung to the hills along Highway 101, softening the landscape in pale gray until it gave way to bright sunshine near Santa Maria. Vineyards rolled past in golden-green rows as Matt cruised toward San Luis Obispo. Just past the Cuesta Grade, he took a call from Agent Reiner. The FBI agent had requested increased patrols from the San Luis Obispo County Sheriff's Office. Matt thanked him and continued the drive, his thoughts already shifting to what Mr. Ho might reveal in person.

Thirty minutes later, Matt turned onto the familiar dirt driveway. Mr. Ho was standing on the porch waiting for him, arms crossed, unreadable as ever.

"You made good time," Mr. Ho said as Matt stepped out.

They moved inside to the living room. Mrs. Ho arrived right on time with tea. As the tea steeped, Matt told Mr. Ho about his conversation with Agent Reiner. "I still want to look at everything for myself. Walk me through it."

"A week ago. At the market. I was in the aisle near the international section. Soy sauce, dried noodles, that area."

Mr. Ho paused, gathering the details.

"An Asian male, early thirties, stood at the end of the aisle. Nothing overt. Just... too much attention. Not watching the shelves. Watching me."

"Someone from the community?" Matt asked.

Mr. Ho shook his head. "No. And that's what caught my attention. I've been here twenty-three years. I know every Asian family in Paso

Robles. This man wasn't part of any of them. Possibly a visitor, but he didn't behave like one."

Matt sipped the tea. "How so?"

"He greeted me in English, but it wasn't natural. The tone was off, like he'd learned from a language school. He used a lot of contractions. It was almost too perfect."

"You sure he was tailing you?"

"I don't know," Mr. Ho said, "but it was different enough to make me pay attention."

Matt gave a nod.

"Three nights later," Mr. Ho continued, "my perimeter cameras picked up headlights out on the side trail, off the old fire road behind the eucalyptus. The vehicle was there for just under an hour. No reason to be out there."

"No plates?"

"Too far. Low light. The next night around two in the morning my monitors picked up a drone. Low pass. Silent. Just outside my eastern boundary. It looked like a compact reconnaissance drone. Definitely not recreational."

"So, you logged in to Sentinel," Matt said.

"Yes," Mr. Ho replied. "A week before my monthly check-in. I included a note on the drone, the vehicle, and the man in the store. It must have been what triggered a soft flag."

Matt nodded. "Enough to get a Level III push from Sentinel to the FBI."

"Agent Reiner visited yesterday," Mr. Ho said. "Polite. Discreet. He asked if I'd seen any unusual vehicle patterns or unfamiliar faces. I gave them the details and showed him the video surveillance. He said he'd follow up."

"He did," Matt replied. "He contacted the San Luis Obispo Sheriff's Homeland Security Unit. He asked them to look for anything strange:

drone complaints, traffic stops near your area, or trespass calls. Kept it vague but serious."

Mr. Ho poured another round of tea. "He handled it well."

"Anything since then?"

"No, but I did receive a message from Taiwan. From Ming."

Matt looked up. "What'd it say?"

Mr. Ho paused. "Just this, 'If your birds seem restless, it's because the hawk is near.'"

Matt exhaled. "Uncle Ming doesn't get poetic unless something's in motion."

"No," Mr. Ho agreed, "he doesn't."

Matt stood. "Let's walk the trail."

Mr. Ho led him through the garden and toward the outer edge of the property. The eucalyptus trees stood in rows, casting long shadows over the sloped fire road. They stopped near the boundary fence.

"There," Mr. Ho said, gesturing to a faint depression in the dirt.

Matt crouched. A single boot print, partially worn. Something with structure. Tactical. Definitely not someone out for a walk in their tennis shoes. He glanced toward the road, then back to the house.

"You think he was on foot looking around?" Mr. Ho asked.

"Possibly. Checking for gaps in coverage. Or looking for a blind spot. He was good. He didn't trip any of the ground sensors."

"After Ming's warning, I'm sure this is connected to Taiwan."

"If someone is suddenly watching you after all these years, something triggered it. It's definitely related to Taiwan."

They turned and started back towards the main house. They walked in silence, taking in the sound of the wind blowing through the eucalyptus trees. The sun had set, and the air was turning crisp.

As they reached the patio, Matt's phone buzzed. A message from Reiner. Matt read it out loud to Mr. Ho.

"'Local traffic stop four days ago, driver matched the man from the store. Tourist visa. No ticket issued, warning only.'"

Matt pocketed his phone.

"What now?" Mr. Ho asked.

"Now," Matt said, "we act like nothing's wrong. And we wait for them to make their move."

Mr. Ho nodded. "I will be ready."

"I know you will, Ba. Nothing left to do now but have another cup of tea before I head south."

***

By the time Matt rolled back into DCS, the stars had been out for three hours. He parked and checked his phone. The team was still en route to Taiwan.

Inside, the office felt quieter than usual. He moved through the hall, Mitchell looked up from his desk as Matt walked past his office.

"That was a quick trip."

Matt shrugged. "Nothing there. Just being thorough."

Mitchell nodded. "Good to know."

As Matt walked away, he could almost feel Mitchell watching him.

Chapter 20

Day 92 - Barstow, CA

Sergeant Andrei Kuznetsov of the Russian army, assigned to the Foreign Intelligence Service Zaslon Unit, was sitting in the dimly lit corner of a run-down motel room on the outskirts of Barstow. It was three in the morning, but even at this hour, with the shades closed, he could see the light from the flashing neon sign outside.

Kuznetsov unwrapped a new burner phone. He was sure Matt Scales had discovered the number of his last one. That explained how they'd found them. Reluctantly, Kuznetsov acknowledged the necessity of his upcoming conversation. He dialed the number from memory, knowing that once the person on the other end of the line answered, his mission, and probably his life, would take a dramatic turn.

"Kuznetsov. What happened?" Lebedev asked. "I did not expect to hear from you until tomorrow."

Kuznetsov was tired, and a little frustrated, but he tried his best to hide his mood. "We've got a problem. Matt Scales and his team hit the farmhouse. The building's gone. I had to blow it. I escaped, but they captured one of our men."

Kuznetsov waited for the fury of Lebedev to come over the phone line. There was a short silence.

"How much does the captured man know? If he cracks, what can he tell them about our plans?"

"He was a local hire known for his muscle and poor attitude. There's nothing he can tell them that will compromise our plans."

"Well at least that is some good news," Lebedev said. "Scales. He's more persistent than I gave him credit for.

"Then we move now," Lebedev stated. "I will request authorization to launch the virus in the US first thing tomorrow morning. Once the power grids go down, it'll give you cover to escape. You will become an afterthought."

"And what about Taiwan? When will you release the virus there?"

"We may advance the timeline, but for now, we will wait for two days after the virus hits the US."

Kuznetsov took a moment to think about what he would say next. "And what about me? Do you need me in Taiwan to assist?"

"Yes Sergeant, the reality is I need you in Taiwan, but you won't make it in time to be of any real help. Get yourself out of the US and back to Russia immediately. Moscow will be safe for you. You will live to fight another day."

Kuznetsov felt a surge of resentment and anger at Lebedev's words. He appreciated the nod to his usefulness in Taiwan, but it stung not to be given the chance thumb his nose in Matt Scales's face. Then a flash of clarity cut through the emotion. Maybe Lebedev was right. By the time he arrived, it'd be too late for him to make a difference. Returning to Moscow gave him the opportunity to shape the narrative, cast himself in a favorable light, and secure another high-level assignment. "Understood. I'll head to Moscow. But with Scales on the hunt, it won't be easy to disappear."

"Disappearing is your specialty," Lebedev said with a bit of amusement in his voice. "Don't forget your training. You're one of the best. Once the virus hits, Scales's world will fall apart. As his world is crumbling, Taiwan will also fall. By the time he realizes the sheer magnitude of our plan, it'll be too late."

"Okay, I'll head to Moscow. I look forward to congratulating you on your success when you return."

"Our success will allow us to control the playing field. The old rules won't apply anymore. Stay alive, Kuznetsov. We'll need you when the new world begins."

Before leaving the motel, Kuznetsov paused. One last call remained. He dialed a burner number and waited to hear the deep voice on the other end.

"I'm leaving the country. Make sure you finish your part."

The reply came. "It'll be done. No loose ends."

Kuznetsov ended the call without another word. Popping open the back of the phone, he removed the SIM card, intending to discard each piece in separate locations on the way to the airport. After wiping down every surface in the room, he stood at the doorway, scanning the space one last time. Then he pulled the door shut behind him and walked toward the car.

Within hours, he had crossed the border into Mexico, slipping past watch lists and checkpoints. A series of flights through Europe covered his tracks before he finally boarded a plane to Moscow under a clean alias.

***

The dim light of a tungsten desk lamp cast long shadows across the granite surface of the underground command room. Lebedev sat alone. The recycled air was thick and stale. With every breath, he felt it settling into his chest like dust in a sealed crypt. A reminder of how deep below ground he was.

A secure laptop rested open in front of him, its uplink encrypted through a narrow satellite corridor bouncing off nodes in Southeast Asia.

The screen came to life.

Chen Da appeared, seated beneath the overhang of a tea pavilion. Behind him, a still lake reflected overcast skies. No wind. No movement. He wore a plain black windbreaker.

For a moment, Lebedev was back on the Santa Barbara breakwater. The memory of the smell of the ocean air brought a small sense of relief. Chen Da had worn the same windbreaker then. He always looked the same.

Now, Chen Da sipped his tea as if time didn't exist.

"Mr. Lebedev," he said evenly. "Is something amiss?"

"The Americans struck earlier than expected," Lebedev replied. "They found the farmhouse. We had to detonate it. We lost one man. Scales is closing in."

Chen Da showed no sign of concern. Only a shallow nod. "What do you require?"

"Authorization to start the US phase," Lebedev said. "The digital payload is staged. Sector profiles are complete. If I launch at 0800 Eastern, we'll still have a full two days to complete preparing for Taiwan."

"It is not Taiwan," Chen Da said, his voice low but firm. "It is China. And it will be returned. The Party sees this as inevitable."

He leaned slightly closer to the camera. "This isn't just about cultural reunification—that's the façade. Underneath, it's economic reclamation. The West has siphoned off our most valuable strategic asset: semiconductors. That $500-billion chip facility currently being moved to Arizona? In Beijing's eyes, that's theft. They believe the island's economic success was built on China's stolen labor and innovation. And we want it back.

"Whoever controls advanced chip production controls the global economy. And we will not let the United States dominate that sector while we sit across the Strait, watching our people sink under the weight of Western control. That's why we must act before the island fully turns west."

"Of course," Lebedev said. "It will be returned. But we must initiate a plan now to ensure success."

"If you believe acceleration is necessary."

"It is," Lebedev emphasized. "Scales is rapidly putting the pieces together. He doesn't know everything, but he knows enough. Waiting risks exposure."

"Very well," Chen Da said. "Proceed. When their lights go out, we will not be the ones groping in the dark."

Lebedev did not respond, giving deference to Chen Da.

"I trust your American teams are in position?"

"They are," Lebedev confirmed. "Kuznetsov is exfilling. He'll be out of the US before the launch."

"Good," Chen Da said, setting his tea down. "Then let the curtain rise, and let the Americans see the immense power of the People's Republic of China."

The screen went dark.

Lebedev sat in silence, then turned to the folder on his desk that contained his final checklist before detonation.

Tomorrow the United States would descend into darkness.

And by the time they reached for the light switch, it would be too late.

Chapter 21

Day 93 - DCS Headquarters - Port Hueneme, CA

The four big-screen monitors cast a cold glow over the dim confer-ence room. Matt and Decker each sat in a chair with their feet up on the table, waiting for any news about the virus.

Decker's phone buzzed again. The vibrations sent it skidding an inch across the table. Decker let it ring out, rubbing a hand through his hair. It started up again.

Matt noticed the tension in Decker's shoulders. After another round of calls, Decker finally checked his voicemail. His expression didn't change, but there was something in the way he exhaled that told Matt all he needed to know.

A second later, Decker did something Matt had never seen him do before—he shut off his phone.

Matt looked back at the screens. Waiting wasn't his strong suit. Without a word, he stood and walked out, heading for the under-ground corridor that connected the office to the main entrance. He needed to burn off the tension before it got the best of him.

He broke into a sprint. His boots pounded against concrete as he breathed in the cool damp air. The long, dim corridor echoed with each stride. He ran it back and forth, again and again, until the motion dulled the edge of his frustration. After what felt like a mile, he veered into the restroom, twisted the faucet, and splashed cold water on his face.

I should be out there.

Gripping the sink, water dripping from his chin, he stared into the mirror. He was a field operative. His place was with his team, not pacing behind a screen while the real fight was happening 6,800 miles away. But this wasn't about what he wanted.

One last move before I can join them.

He had to be sure, absolutely sure, that Mitchell was the mole. Without that, everything could fall apart.

He took a breath, steadying himself, then left for the restroom.

By the time he got back to his office, exhaustion was clawing at him. It had been twelve hours since his team had left for Taiwan. He looked at the cot in the corner before lowering himself onto it. A few hours. That was all he needed.

Then footsteps.

Matt sat up as Decker stepped inside, closing the door behind him.

"I listened to the voicemails," Decker said. "Lawson's furious. Wants both of us in her office at 0800 to explain what the hell happened in Lancaster."

Matt exhaled slowly, pushing himself to his feet. He met Decker's gaze. "They're going to be disappointed. The plan's in motion. We're past the point of no return."

Decker didn't look away.

Matt took a step closer. "So, decide now. Are you with us? Or are you going back to LA to try and salvage what's left of your career?"

"I'm already in deep. Staying with the team is the right move. But Lawson said if we don't show, they're coming here with a team to drag us back."

Matt barely hesitated. "Let them come. They won't get in here without our say-so. And by tomorrow, the world might look a hell of a lot different. They'll have bigger problems than us."

Decker held his stare for a long second, then gave a slow nod. "All right. But we're on borrowed time, Matt. We need to be ready."

Matt watched as Decker left.

His body screamed for sleep, but his mind was already spinning through the next steps. He lay back and pulled the blanket over him. Before he could think about what came next, the exhaustion finally won.

***

Matt woke to someone pounding on his door. His eyes shot open. His body was sluggish as he struggled to pull himself from sleep.

"Matt! Matt! It's happening!" Mitchell was frantic, practically kicking the door open.

"What? What's happening?" Matt mumbled, wiping his face and clearing the fog in his brain. "What time is it?"

"It's 5:15."

"Day or night?"

"Morning. Matt, they released the virus. It's hitting the East Coast. It's 8:15 there."

"All right, it's showtime." He jumped to his feet and grabbed his jacket. "Go find Decker and Dave and let them know. I'll meet you at the conference room in five."

Mitchell nodded and darted out of the room.

Matt walked down the hallway towards the conference center, anticipating what the next few hours would bring. As he entered the room, he saw Decker, Mitchell, and Dave Johnson sitting around the central table.

"The team and Chin are somewhere over the Pacific Ocean, but we have to get Chin looped in. How do we do that?"

"The team is on an EVA Air Boeing 777 out of LAX," Mitchell said. "It has encrypted in-flight Wi-Fi strong enough for Chin to monitor the antivirus deployment."

Matt stared at the four large monitors mounted across the room. Each one scrolled the same urgent message across the bottom of the screen: power systems were failing across the Eastern US. The president had already suspended trading on Wall Street.

He watched as the country unraveled in real time.

"The virus has been active for about an hour," Mitchell continued. "So far, it's concentrated along the Eastern Seaboard. The grid is collapsing in several major cities including New York, DC, and Boston."

Decker shifted forward and whispered to Matt. "What's the backup plan if we don't activate the antivirus before this spirals out of control?"

Matt didn't take his eyes off the screens. "We don't have a backup plan."

Decker's hands closed into fists. "So, we sit and wait."

Matt nodded and quietly said, "Yes. Can't move until China commits."

***

The cabin lights were dim and the faint hum of the Boeing 777's engines filled the air as Chin adjusted his laptop on the foldout tray. The glow from his screen cast shadows across his face. His fingers danced across the keyboard, navigating the encrypted dashboard he'd built during the long hours leading up to this flight.

Data streams from servers on the East Coast lagged, then spiked erratically. A series of red alerts lit up the screen. The virus in the US had been released.

Chin glanced up at April, who was sitting a row ahead of him. She seemed relaxed and looked like she was reading a magazine. He tapped the seat in front of him. "April, we've got a situation."

She twisted around. "What kind of situation?"

"The virus is live. The East Coast power grids are dropping in sequence."

Chin opened the secure messaging app he'd preinstalled, one that mimicked routine web browsing activity to evade in-flight Wi-Fi restrictions. Matt had insisted Chin set up the prearranged protocol. Chin marveled at Matt's continued ability to foresee specific situations and plan for them ahead of time. The plan was if Chin saw the virus go live, he'd send a specific phrase, *blackout*.

Chin typed the phrase and hit send. His fingers hovered over the keyboard as he watched the status indicator spin. A soft ping confirmed that the message had been delivered.

Seconds later, Matt's reply appeared.

Can you call?

Flipping to another tab, Chin activated a lightweight VoIP protocol he'd embedded into his laptop's secure network. The program used the plane's in-flight Wi-Fi as a relay, tunneling the connection through a series of encrypted proxies to obscure its true nature. The plan was risky and against regulations, but Chin didn't care.

He tested the connection by calling his phone first, then switched to Matt's secure number.

The call rang twice before Matt picked up. "Chin, talk to me."

"The virus is spreading faster than we expected. Early data shows an adaptive element. They've refined it since our last analysis," Chin said, keeping his voice low. "The East Coast grids are dropping in sequence. New York, DC, Philly."

Matt swore under his breath. "Do we have any control?"

Chin glanced at the window that displayed a series of commands sent to servers across the East Coast. "They're hitting the systems we expected. The AI code has identified several transformers and the critical nodes across the United States that the virus has infected. Once I activate the antivirus, it should work pretty quickly to restore energy in those nodes. But remember, after neutralizing the virus, each location has specific startup protocols. If they don't do it right, they will overload the system and crash it again."

The flight attendant walking past Chin stopped and looked at him. "Sir, are you talking on your phone?"

Chin raised a hand. "Of course not. I'm creating dialogue for a video I'm making." As she walked away, he resumed the call in a whisper. "Matt, I can't keep this open for long. Tell Decker the antivirus is ready, but it's not going live unless you tell me to launch it."

"Understood."

As the call ended, the cabin felt smaller, almost cramped, claustrophobic. Reclining his seat did nothing to ease the pressure. Maybe it was the altitude. Or maybe it was the weight of reality sinking in. This was no longer a theoretical exercise. Chin gripped the armrest as the turbulence rattled the fuselage. A grim echo of the chaos unfolding thousands of miles away.

***

The screens inside the DCS operations center updated in bursts as raw data streams, grid diagnostics, and camera feeds, all came in at once. Matt stood behind the central console watching a map of the US power infrastructure. Red zones began to spread across the East Coast.

"It's happening," Decker said, his voice low.

Mitchell leaned toward a terminal, eyes scanning the numbers. "LA just started going offline. Phoenix is dropping fast. Five substations in Colorado just tripped offline."

Matt stood at the conference table, scanning the damage across the US. The virus was spreading like a wildfire, crippling infrastructure in numerous major cities. Hospitals were running on emergency power, airports were frozen, and entire regions were without electricity. But one report caught his attention.

Eielson Air Force Base: fully operational.

Matt allowed himself the briefest hint of satisfaction. Chin had fulfilled his promise to Colonel Brown. After Chin developed the antivirus, he'd installed it on the two transformers at the base, removing the manual activation component, so when the virus activated, the antivirus activated automatically. Power had returned to Eielson after only a few minutes of darkness.

Decker looked over his shoulder. "No way the Chinese didn't notice that."

Matt nodded. "The virus is wreaking havoc on the rest of the country. They may suspect something at Eielson, but they won't be sure what. The military had its own protocols, its own cybersecurity layers. They'll chalk it up to better readiness."

They all stared at the monitors illustrating the scenario playing out in front of them. Now, there was nothing to do but wait until the virus was launched in Taiwan.

***

Mitchell had been standing at the back of the room listening to Matt and Decker. He waited for a few minutes, looking at the information and data being flashed across the screen in front of them.

"What about Taiwan? How long until the team lands?"

"Our team should land in an hour. If the virus hits Taiwan, we're expecting an invasion to follow within twenty-four hours," Matt answered.

Decker was sitting at the table taking everything in. The four monitors showed the cascading effect of the virus. Decker was worried. He wanted to trust everything would work, but he had never been involved in this type of high-risk situation before. He was having second thoughts and worrying about losing control. "Matt, what if all this goes wrong? If we wait too long, it could become more than just a short-term power outage. People could die. And you know that eventually they'll find out that we could have stopped it."

Matt looked at Decker. "Chin is keeping a close eye on the virus. He's also monitoring the Taiwan systems. Call Lawson. Tell her the antivirus is working. It's just taking time as it works its way through all the different substations to find the virus."

Decker hesitated, then gave a nod.

Chapter 22

St. Bernard, Chin, April, and Skip had been sitting in different parts of the airplane during the trip. They didn't want to call attention to themselves by sitting together. Once they got out of the plane, they made their way through the busy terminal to baggage claim.

The terminal buzzed with a soft hum along with rolling luggage, overlapping languages, and announcements in Mandarin echoing from overhead speakers. The scent of roasted chestnuts and brewed oolong tea drifted from a nearby kiosk. Outside the windows, Taipei's skyline rose like a jagged silhouette beyond a veil of humidity. Neon signs hung along the streets, displaying a vertical script.

St. Bernard was the first to see Lieutenant Commander Benjamin Harris, the DEVGRU team leader.

St. Bernard walked over to Commander Harris to greet him, but before St. Bernard could say anything, Harris said in a low voice, "You're a little late to the party."

"You know me, I let the eager beavers get there first. I arrive when the actual work needs to be done."

"Damn good to see you, Bernard. When I got your call a few days ago about this op, I had doubts whether you could pull it off. But, when you told me Matt Scales was the team leader, all my doubts vanished. I came to DEVGRU after he left, but they still tell stories about him."

"Yep, we appreciate your help. This thing has a lot of moving pieces. Matt had to stay in CONUS to finish up something. He'll be joining us soon."

The five of them walked outside to a black Toyota Land Cruiser Prado. The windows were tinted, and the body showed just enough wear to look local, not leased. St. Bernard climbed into the front passenger seat while Commander Harris took the wheel and April, Skip, and Chin slid into the back.

"We've had eyes on the safe house since last night," Harris said. "My guys rigged it with a few surprises in case Lebedev's people show up early."

"Can't thank you enough for your help on this, Ben," St. Bernard said. "Can you guys hang out until we get oriented and get over there and take over?"

Harris nodded. "Yeah, no problem. We have about a two-hour window before we need to move to our next operation. Right now, I've got two four-man teams pulling surveillance on the place. They'll stay in until you guys relieve them."

Commander Harrison looked over at April. "Oh, sorry, ma'am, didn't mean to exclude you by saying 'guys.'"

"Relax, Commander. I've been operating in a boy's club so long, I thought 'ma'am' was a code word for 'troublemaker.'"

St. Bernard chuckled and crossed his arms. "Let's just say half the guys in Black Squadron won't bet against her anymore. Harris, she doesn't just hang, she usually leads."

April raised an eyebrow. "If we're done with the introductions, can we get to work?"

"You have some weapons and other nice toys for us to pick up somewhere?" St. Bernard asked. "Once we have them, we'll head straight over and relieve your guys at the safe house. While we're getting ready and picking up the gear, can you escort Chin to the cyber-security headquarters?"

"Sure, no problem," Commander Harris said.

As the Land Cruiser wove through Taipei's narrow streets, the city revealed its evening rhythm. Scooters were darting between cars, shopkeepers were rolling down metal gates, and paper lanterns strung above side alleys shed light, like low-hanging stars. The scent of night market food hung in the air.

St. Bernard checked his phone. 9:45 a.m. back in Port Hueneme. He could practically picture Matt pacing the office, going stir-crazy while the team rolled deeper into the mission.

The SUV pushed west, leaving the city lights behind. Concrete sidewalks and parking lots gave way to winding two-lane roads flanked by forested hills and scattered farmland. The scent of rain still hung in the air, clinging to the windows as clouds pressed low overhead. A sharp turn took them off the main route and onto a gravel path lined with camphor trees.

Just ahead, the DEVGRU command post came into view, an unremarkable compound half-hidden behind a ridge. The structure was low-slung and built like a bunker, with dark green paint and minimal lighting. A chain-link fence surrounded the property, broken only by a single steel gate guarded by two operators in local camo.

Harris glanced at them in the rearview mirror. "We outfitted this place as our forward command post. Weapons, comms, shortwave backups, and drone feeds. We'll get you geared up and rolling to the farmhouse. My team's been holding the perimeter all night. You'll take over from here."

Inside the command post, the air was cool and dry. The interior had been stripped down to the bare essentials. It included maps, gear racks, and hardened comms equipment lining the walls. April moved first, making a beeline for the weapons locker.

"Grab what you need," Harris said, popping open the secure cage. "You're rolling out in ten."

***

DCS HQ -10:00 a.m. Local/7:00 p.m. Taiwan

Matt's phone buzzed on the table in front of him. He glanced down and saw it was a blocked number. But the time was about right. At first he thought it may be Agent Lawson calling him. But then he remembered he'd had his team switch out all their phones after Lancaster. Only his team members had this phone number. It had to be St. Bernard. Things were about to get better, or a lot worse.

"St. Bernard, talk to me. You on the ground?"

"We've landed. DEVGRU's got the safe house rigged and under surveillance. We're moving in now to relieve them after we drop Chin at the cybersecurity headquarters building. I'll text you again when we're in place. It should be about sixty minutes."

"Good. Keep me posted. Once you're set, I'll brief the others."

"Roger that. We're on it."

As Matt hung up, he realized that Decker and Mitchell had only been able to hear his end of the conversation.

"They're on the ground. Bernard will let me know when they're at the safe house."

***

DCS Headquarters - 11:15 a.m. Local/8:15 p.m. Taiwan

The last twenty-five minutes had crawled by. Matt tried to distract himself by staring at the four screens that were spewing forth information about how the virus was spreading across the US. *Come on, Bernard, you said sixty minutes. It's been seventy-five.* Finally, Matt's phone buzzed.

All set. Tally Ho.

Matt broke into a grin. Trust St. Bernard to slip in a pun. *Tally Ho* wasn't just an old-school hunting phrase. It was a nod to Chin Ho, whose code had just gone live. Matt could almost hear Bernard laughing as he sent it.

"Classic Bernard," Matt muttered.

"All right," Matt said, with Decker and Mitchell listening in. "The team is in the safe house, waiting for contact from Uncle Ming. Until then, we're in a holding pattern."

Matt, Mitchell, and Decker sat in the conference room for five more minutes, watching the screens and the information about the virus unfold, until a new headline appeared.

The electrical grid in Northern California has shut down. The concern is a monumental cascading effect that could collapse the entire Western US electrical grid.

"I'm going to step out for a minute," Mitchell said. "Going to grab some stuff from my office."

Matt gave a small nod without looking up. "Go ahead."

Matt tracked the sound of the closing door, then turned back to the data.

He wanted to believe Mitchell was just grabbing paper. He really did. But in the back of his mind, a darker possibility uncoiled.

If they show up at the safe house... we'll know.

Chapter 23

On a hill overlooking the safe house, the team lay prone in a cold nest of moss and flattened grass. The fog clung to the treetops, veiling the valley below in a silver haze. The forest smelled of wet stone and pine sap. Crickets chirped in the brush. In the distance, temple bells rang faintly, echoing through the mountain ridges like distant war drums.

The safe house was a shadow in the thick forest. Uncle Ming had identified it as a safe place to lie low once Matt and the rest of the team arrived in Taiwan. But everything had changed when they'd found evidence Mitchell might have betrayed them.

Now, instead of using it as a safe haven, it had become a trap.

St. Bernard glanced at the ridge to their left, the one they had used to circle around the safe house without hitting the main road. There was no way they were going to take a direct route to the location. Any professionals Lebedev would use would have recon teams along the road.

St. Bernard glanced over at April. She sat hunched over her tablet, wearing a poncho. He could barely see the soft blue glow from the drone feed on the ground by her feet. "Any movement by the main body?" he whispered.

"Nothing so far," she replied. "Lebedev's men haven't moved from their staging point. They're still about three miles down the road, waiting."

"They're waiting for the green light from Lebedev," Skip muttered under his breath, lying prone beside them with his rifle trained on the safe house. "They won't move until he gives them the go-ahead."

St. Bernard nodded. "Makes sense. They wouldn't risk spooking us by getting too close before they're sure."

It all fit. The only way Lebedev could have known about this safe house was through Mitchell's communication. They'd confirmed that. The betrayal was fresh in their minds, but now it was time to use that information to their advantage.

April stared intently at the tablet as she guided the drone from the staging area back to the safe house. She had started an elliptical flight pattern between the two locations just to make sure she would track anyone who was approaching on foot.

"I've got movement," April said. "Looks like a three-man recon team at the tree line behind the house."

Then her eyes dialed in even further to the drone feed, and she whispered, "They're scanning the house."

St. Bernard's heart quickened. "What kind of scan?"

"Infrared." She adjusted the settings on her tablet. "They've got a handheld scanner pointed at the windows. I can see the beam heading out from it. Could be a FLIR. Definitely military grade."

"Professionals," St. Bernard commented. "Can they see the charges?"

April shook her head. "No, no way. DEVGRU showed me the floor plans. They put them in the same place I would've. Their scanner can't pick them up."

The three men in the tree line crept to the side of the house. After scanning the house for a few more minutes, they went back to the tree line. Five minutes later they emerged from the opposite side of the house. After a moment, one of them looked at the other two, then gave a small nod. It never ceased to amaze April how good the technology was in these small drones.

"I think they're convinced the place is empty," she said, watching the infrared signatures on her screen. "They're heading inside."

St. Bernard pulled an infrared scope to his eyes and looked for the operatives. He saw them approaching the house.

"They're coming in the back door," April said. "These guys are good. They know what they're doing."

"We wait for them to get inside," St. Bernard whispered. "Once they're inside, we detonate."

Skip held the detonator in his right hand. It was a feeling he knew well. Each time he'd hit the button on one of these detonators, he had the satisfaction of ending the life of a terrorist.

The seconds stretched into a minute. Then, April whispered, "They're inside. Heat signatures just went stationary."

April, St. Bernard, and Skip closed their eyes and looked away from the house.

Skip pressed the detonator.

A powerful explosion tore apart the night. The house disintegrated. The shock wave hit St. Bernard's team even from their distant vantage point, shaking the ground beneath them as the inferno consumed the structure.

"Well, those DEVGRU guys haven't changed. They don't skimp on explosives," Skip mentioned.

"Told you SEALs make sure they use enough to make sure the job gets done," St. Bernard said.

As they moved out, April monitored the feed from the drone that she'd moved back over the staging area for the primary team. "Main team's still three miles down the road. They're moving now."

As the fire raged behind them, they pulled back into the trees, disappearing into the shadows. They moved quickly, sticking to the side paths they had scouted earlier, staying well clear of the main road. The fire from the explosion lit up the night behind them. They didn't look back.

This mission was over. They would now get to the real safe house and regroup, rest, and get ready for Matt to arrive. The next twenty-four hours were going to be busy.

Once they were safely out of range, St. Bernard pulled out his phone. "Matt, we sprung the trap. Lebedev's men showed up. More details when you get here."

***

DCS HQ -6:30 p.m. Local/3:30 a.m. Taiwan

Matt had been sitting at his desk when the call came in from St. Bernard. He looked at the caller ID and unconsciously stood before answering.

"They showed," Bernard said. "Advanced team came in first. We had to take them down before the main element arrived."

Matt didn't speak.

"They wouldn't have come unless they believed we were inside that safe house," Bernard continued.

Matt closed his eyes and took a deep breath. The final piece had snapped into place.

"Copy that," he said.

He ended the call and stared at the wall for a moment before turning slowly toward the hallway.

Mitchell.

He'd given them everything.

Gotten Chin beat up.

Tipped off the New Cuyama farmhouse.

Set up Matt's team to get killed in Taiwan.

Matt stepped into the hallway. The compound felt colder now, quieter. Each step carried weight. No fury. Just clarity.

He reached Mitchell's door and opened it without knocking.

Mitchell looked up, startled. When their eyes met, the color drained from Mitchell's face.

Matt slammed the door behind him.

Mitchell looked down, shaking his head. "Matt, I didn't want to. They forced me. You don't understand."

"Then explain it," Matt demanded.

Mitchell glanced away, licking his lips. "I had to. They had leverage. It started with my sister. She disappeared in Poland. I didn't know if she was alive. Lebedev said he could help... or make sure I never saw her again."

"You should've come to us. We could've helped you."

"I thought about it," Mitchell cried. "But they must've figured it out. That's when he sent the picture. It was my sister. Just her head. A message. Told me my wife would be next if I didn't cooperate."

His breath came in shallow, panicked bursts. "I only gave them just enough, enough to make them think I was fully on board."

Matt didn't blink. "How long have you been doing this?"

"I... I tipped him off about Kharkiv. But it wasn't supposed to go like that. He was just supposed to escape."

A dead silence hung between them.

Matt's mind locked onto one word.

Kharkiv.

The memory of the mission, One-Shot lying dead on the floor, hit him like a fist to the gut. His hand dropped to his side.

Mitchell's eyes locked onto Matt's hand, hovering over his sidearm. "Matt, please! I swear, I had no choice!"

Matt drew his weapon, leveling it at Mitchell's head.

His finger hovered over the trigger.

One round. That's all it would take.

No one would blame me.

Mitchell's voice shook. "I swear, I didn't want to."

Taiwan.

If he pulled the trigger now, he'd never make it.

Matt exhaled, forcing the rage down.

He holstered the weapon.

"You're not worth it. Not now. We've got bigger problems."

Matt turned toward the door.

"Come in, Decker."

Decker stepped inside. "I expected to hear a gunshot. I'll take it from here."

Matt didn't look back as he walked out, Mitchell's voice trailing behind him in a desperate plea.

"Matt, wait! You don't understand."

I understand enough.

***

Lebedev was pleased. Reports confirmed the virus was active across the United States. It was like a slow-moving digital wildfire spreading through the electrical system. Power grids had failed, leaving entire cities in darkness. Traffic lights froze mid-cycle, snarling intersections with wrecks. Airports ground to a halt, their monitors flashing *ERROR* while stranded passengers argued with helpless staff. On live broadcasts, news anchors struggled to keep their composure, their voices edged with barely concealed panic.

The next phase was Taiwan. Some final steps remained, but the overall picture showed an operation unfolding as planned.

Lebedev had just finished inspecting the farmhouse's main floor. The wooden planks creaked under his boots. The air was thick with mildew and the scent of old timber. He needed to confirm his escape plan.

Lebedev moved through the building while checking each room, looking for anything out of place.

After a final sweep of the main floor, he stopped at the basement door. The handle was rusted from years of neglect. He turned the handle and pushed the door open. The hinges groaned, and the open door revealed a steep staircase descending into darkness.

The smell hit him first. Earthy. Damp. Stale. Dust swirled in the beam of his flashlight.

He hesitated, then muttered, "Nothing I haven't seen before."

The creaking stairs echoed in the still air as he descended. The further down he went, the thicker the air felt. His flashlight's beam flickered over damp brick walls, catching glints of rusted tools and shattered glass on the floor among the debris.

At the far end of the room loomed a six-foot-wide tunnel. The tunnel was designed for drainage, not escape. The passage narrowed to three feet before reaching the lake.

As he took a step closer, the scent of wet earth and stale air hit him.

Then came the memory.

Trapped. Dust choking his lungs. Darkness pressing in. Groaning beams. Distant cries. The silence that followed.

Lebedev exhaled sharply and pressed his palm against the cold wall.

I'm not a child anymore. No danger exists here. Deal with it and move on.

The tunnel sloped downward. Gravel shifted under his boots. The air felt tighter. He moved forward, his flashlight beam bouncing along the uneven walls.

After a hundred yards, he had to crouch as his shoulders scraped both sides of the tunnel. Tighter. Tighter. His breathing came in short, shallow breaths. He forced himself to inhale through his nose, but it wasn't enough. The stale air sat heavy in his lungs. His ability to assess the situation wavered beneath the creeping sensation of suffocation.

He stopped.

The logical move was to press forward, confirm the tunnel's end. But the darkness, the smell, the way the space wrapped around him. This was far enough.

He turned and made his way back, slamming the door shut behind him as he reentered the main floor.

A slow smile crossed his lips.

Soon, we will be victorious.

***

Wulai District - 4:45 a.m. Local/1:45 p.m. DCQ HQ

The van's tires crunched on the gravel road as the van rolled to a stop. Captain Demitri Kozlov and his assault team jumped out with their weapons drawn, ready for a fight. The safe house was a smoldering ruin. Ash swirled in the air, carried by a breeze that did little to mask the stench of burning flesh and melted plastic. Kozlov pulled off his balaclava. The heat radiating from the wreckage was warm despite the bitter cold of the night.

Kozlov's boots crunched over shattered glass and debris as he moved closer to the burned building. The blackened beams of the farmhouse sagged as if they were bowing in defeat. His team fanned out, scanning the area in tense silence. No one needed to speak.

"Spread out," he growled, his voice tight, barely above a whisper. His team obeyed without hesitation, boots scraping against the blackened ground as they checked the perimeter.

Kozlov watched his team perform a search of the exterior around the burning building. There was no sign of his advance team. They must have been inside when it exploded.

Kozlov walked around the exterior of the safe house. He looked at the scene through the eyes of a seasoned soldier. *A trap.* The realization settled in his mind like poison, slow and deadly.

Whoever did this knew exactly when and how to hit. Someone was watching us, waiting for their moment to strike. But how could this be? The intelligence is only an hour old. This wasn't supposed to happen. I planned for contingencies. I did everything right. I followed orders to the letter.

Kozlov stood next to the van as he scanned the wreckage. He pulled out a phone and hit number one on the speed dial.

"Colonel Lebedev, the safe house exploded. Took out three of my men. It was a setup. We walked right into a trap."

There was a long silence on the line before Lebedev's voice crackled through. "What? You walked into a trap? You were supposed to be the ones to set the trap. What happened?"

"The farmhouse exploded. Someone knew we were coming. The explosion killed my three advance team members."

Lebedev shrieked. "You're telling me they got wiped out before you even got there?"

"Yes, sir. The enemy knew we were coming."

"Get your team out of there and back to base immediately."

Captain Kozlov didn't respond. Stepping away from the wreckage, he signaled his remaining team members to get back in the van.

***

Chen Da was sitting at his desk when the text arrived. It was from Lebedev, requesting an immediate secure video call.

The screen blinked to life, casting a pale wash of light across his face. On the other end, Lebedev appeared stressed, or was it anxious? It was hard to see the details of his face in the dim glow of a remote terminal.

"The ambush failed," Lebedev said. "My operatives are dead. Scales and his team walked away. They know we're here. The element of surprise is gone. If we delay any longer, they'll regroup and harden their defenses."

Chen Da didn't speak right away. Stillness was its own form of leverage.

"The window has narrowed," he said finally. "Not closed."

Lebedev leaned in. "The Americans are stretched thin. Taiwan's cyber defenses are exposed. If you don't launch now, we risk losing everything we've built."

Chen Da studied the man on the screen, noting the tone behind the words. Panic. Ego. A man mistaking speed for strategy.

After a moment, he gave a slow nod. "I will issue the order."

The screen went dark.

Chen remained seated. The situation had shifted, but that was expected. Plans rarely survived first contact. What mattered was adjusting without hesitation and remembering the ultimate goal.

***

Taiwan - 5:00 a.m. Local/DCS HQ 2:00 p.m.

When Captain Kozlov walked into the command post, Lebedev was on his phone talking. Kozlov waited until Lebedev ended his conversation. Kozlov saw the anger and frustration on Lebedev's face as he turned towards Kozlov. Lebedev motioned for Kozlov to step outside.

Kozlov walked outside and stood in front of his team. The team members fidgeted upon seeing Lebedev. Their breath was visible in the freezing air. Lebedev's leather gloves squeaked as he flexed his fingers and walked up to Kozlov.

"Do you know what I hate, Demitri?"

"Failure?"

"Failure and incompetence. You had one job. Kill the team at the farmhouse. You failed. Tell me, do you think this is redeemable?"

Kozlov opened his mouth to speak, but Lebedev's pistol was already in his hand. The shot cracked the silence of the frosty night air. The back of Koslov's head exploded as his body crumpled to the ground, blood pooling beneath him. No one flinched except Kozlov's second-in-command, who had been standing next to him.

Lebedev locked eyes with him. "Congratulations. You are now the team leader. Do not fail me."

***

Taiwan Cyber Command Center - 5:15 a.m. Local/DCS HQ 2:15 p.m.

Inside the command center, LED light strips lined the walls in cool blue, illuminating rows of low-profile workstations. Holographic data feeds hovered above each console, displaying shifting power-grid diagrams, cyberattack signatures, and satellite telemetry in real time. Servers hummed beneath the floor grates. The air carried the sharp scent of ozone and coolant.

"This digital signature is unmistakable," Chin said as he stared at the cascading data on his monitor. "It belongs to Unit 61398, China's elite cyber warfare division. They've just sent the activation code for the virus. Critical infrastructure is going offline across Taiwan."

The room fell silent for a fraction of a second before everyone sprang into action. Analysts called out updates, fingers racing over keyboards as screens filled with incoming data.

"Power grids are collapsing!" one technician shouted.

"Transportation networks are down. Trains, highways, everything automated," another added. "Civil aviation systems are unresponsive."

Chin leaned in. "The virus is bypassing military installations," he muttered, piecing it together. "They must plan to hit those separately, maybe via remote access once the grid is disabled."

From the far side of the room, Ming Ho stepped closer. He studied the scrolling code. "Chinese destroyers have been sitting offshore for weeks. Fighters have been flying overhead every few days. Pretty common. But more than in the past. And, they've never tried to blind us." He glanced toward Chin. "This isn't routine. It's preparation."

Chin hesitated, then reached for his phone and dialed a secure number. It rang once before connecting.

"Matt," he said, his voice steady despite the surrounding storm. "They launched the virus. Taiwan's falling apart."

"Release the antivirus in the US and Taiwan."

Chin nodded, though Matt couldn't see him. "Understood."

He had put the finishing touches on the AI antivirus for Taiwan just yesterday. He took a deep breath as he held his hands poised over the keyboard. Then, quickly, he flipped both systems from passive to active, first the US, then Taiwan.

***

DCS HQ - 2:45 p.m. Local/Taiwan 5:45 a.m.

After talking to Chin and authorizing the release of the antivirus, Matt went back to his office. He clutched his phone in his hand. Somehow, it made him feel a little more connected to his team in Taiwan.

But now he needed to get there.

As Matt was arranging commercial flights, he received another call from St. Bernard. The entire infrastructure in Taiwan was shutting down, including all commercial airports and even military bases.

Matt reached out to his contacts, seeking information on any military transports headed for Guam and then Taiwan. The result of each phone call was a resounding, "No." He'd been making calls for hours, each one bringing the same frustrating result. There was no military transportation available. After his last phone call, he slammed the phone down on the table. It bounced across the table onto the floor.

He sat down in his chair and looked up at the ceiling. *There has to be another way.*

Dave Johnson had also spent the last few hours calling his contacts and making arrangements for Matt to get to Taiwan. After his last phone call, Dave looked over at Matt and gave him a shake of his head.

"That was the last one. No dice," Dave said. "The airlift coordinators and my other contacts are all tied up with other ops. Even the private contractors say they can't do anything on such short notice."

"I don't have time for this, Dave," Matt said, frustrated. "My team is already in Taiwan. I need to be there with them. Every minute I'm stuck here, the situation in Taiwan gets worse. I can't help them from there."

Dave Johnson rubbed his temples. "We've tried everything, Matt. I really don't know what else to do."

Matt stood and started walking around the conference table. He always thought better when he was moving.

"I should not have stayed here to confront Mitchell. It would have been better if I had let Decker do it on his own. That way, I could've been with my team and not stuck here like this."

Matt stopped and turned to look at Dave on the other side of the conference table. "What if I don't get there in time, Dave? What if they need me, and I'm here spinning my wheels, just sitting on my ass? I can't help them from here."

"You made the right call with Mitchell. It was your plan. You had to see it through. You're the one who needed to confront Mitchell, so you would know without a doubt he was guilty."

Matt looked over at the monitors on the wall. *I didn't see this problem coming. I should have but I didn't.*

"Your team is good," Dave said, as though he were reading Matt's mind. "They'll hold things down until you can get there. We'll figure this out. We always do."

"That's not good enough," Matt said, shaking his head. "The plan. We shut down Lebedev's team, but we're still missing pieces. Lebedev and Kuznetsov have some more surprises for us. I can't stay here and watch it happen. I have to get there."

Dave looked at Matt. He had known Matt for a long time. Dave was the one who'd recruited Matt into DCS. He wasn't sure what to say. They had tried everything they could think of. There was just no way to get Matt to Taiwan.

Matt looked back at Dave. "I hate this, Dave. I just fucking hate it."

They sat in their chairs looking at the news feeds coming over the monitors. The situation in the United States was getting a bit better every minute, obvious signs that Chin's antivirus was slowly regaining control of the electrical grid. Information about the situation in Taiwan was sporadic, but the reports still showed that Taiwan was being severely impacted by the virus. He knew Chin's antivirus would soon have the same positive effect in Taiwan as it was having in the United States. But Matt also knew Lebedev always had a contingency plan. He had to get to Taiwan. He had to get there to help his team shut this down.

But most of all, he had to get there and find Lebedev.

Matt didn't know how long he was staring at the screen. His phone buzzed as it started sliding across the table. Matt looked at the caller ID. The call came from an unidentified blocked number. He answered the phone, realizing it took incredible effort to sound calm.

"Scales."

The voice on the other end was firm but unfamiliar. "Matt Scales, Commander Harris here."

"Harris?" The name didn't immediately click. "Do I know you?"

There was a pause, then the voice became slightly more cryptic. "Not personally, but I'm currently working with some of your people. Saint's been keeping things interesting."

Matt blinked. "Saint…" he repeated, piecing it together. St. Bernard was with the DEVGRU team in Taiwan. Matt suddenly remembered the briefing about a "Harris" who was running point for DEVGRU ops in the region.

"Your team and I've had some fun," Harris continued. "But that's not why I called. At St. Bernard's urging, and after telling key people that your presence is essential for the success of my mission, I was able to get you a ride over here.

"There's a squadron of F-18s moving out from Miramar to Guam in an hour. One of them has an open backseat. It can detour to Point Mugu to pick you up. Can you be there within ninety minutes?"

Matt felt a big smile break out on his face as he recalled how much pull a DEVGRU team commander had in the field, especially when the commander said his request was essential to his mission's success. "Got it, Commander. I'll be there."

"Don't be late, Scales. The op's heating up." And with that, the line went dead.

"You get what you needed?" Dave asked.

"Yeah. My day just got a whole lot better."

PART III

ASHES AND ECHOES

*"The mission ends, but it doesn't leave you.
It echoes in quiet moments, especially the ones
that were supposed to bring peace."*

Matt Scales, logbook entry

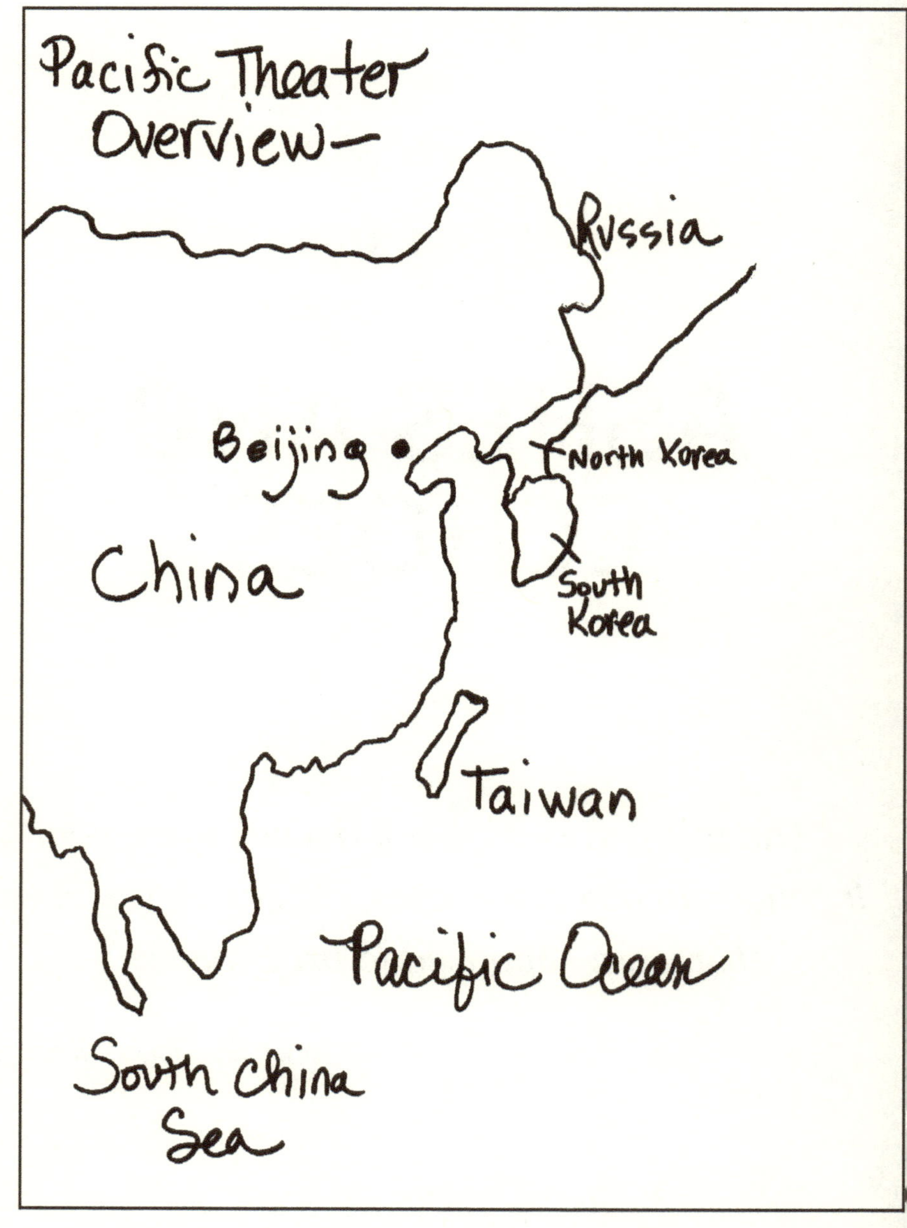
Pacific Theater Overview—
Russia
Beijing
North Korea
China
South Korea
Taiwan
Pacific Ocean
South China Sea

Chapter 24

Day 94 - Camarillo, CA

Matt kept a steady grip on the wheel. His eyes moved between the road ahead and the rearview mirror. The sun was dipping low, casting long shadows over the 101.

Traffic was light, with a semi-truck lumbering along in the right lane. Matt drove with the traffic. His mind was already in Taiwan, running through variables, contingencies, what-ifs. The farmhouse raid had solidified one thing: Lebedev wasn't just playing defense anymore.

Then something felt off.

Two cars had been tailing him for the last two miles. They'd been maintaining a consistent distance, always keeping at least two cars between him and them. Standard surveillance techniques. Another sedan had entered the freeway at the last exit and merged ahead of him. They were approaching the Rancho Conejo Boulevard exit.

Matt recognized the classic box formation. If these guys were professional, they wouldn't attack in heavy traffic. Too much of a chance of collateral damage and too many witnesses. He just needed an opening.

The lead car braked.

Matt cut the wheel left just as the car to his left surged forward. The SUV behind him closed in, attempting to lock him in a tight kill box.

Then the right-side sedan's window rolled down and a muzzle flash exploded from the dark.

Nothing professional about this. Or they're desperate.

Matt yanked the wheel to the right, slamming his foot on the gas. His front fender clipped the lead car's rear bumper, sending it skidding into the right shoulder. He burst free from the trap. The flanking vehicle swerved towards him, but Matt had already cut across the exit ramp onto Rancho Conejo Boulevard.

***

Matt took the off-ramp hard, tires screeching as he exited the 101 onto Rancho Conejo Boulevard. The road curved toward a stretch of light industrial buildings and trailhead parking lots tucked along the northern edge of Newbury Park. Up ahead was the Conejo Canyons Open Space. The terrain opened into dry hills and chaparral. Classic California foothill country. He spotted a narrow access road breaking away from the main boulevard, just beyond a faded trail marker. Probably maintenance for the Western Plateau trail system. It was barely more than a dirt path, but it would have to do.

He accelerated, creating a cloud of dust between him and the cars behind him. At the intersection, he yanked the wheel to the left, sending his car into a controlled skid. He pushed the engine into neutral and then dove out onto the ground. The vehicle continued rolling down a small incline. The two pursuing vehicles followed Matt's car as it slowed to a stop.

The two chasing cars braked, stopping between him and his car.

Four men stepped out, silhouetted against the dimming sky.

Two were holding suppressed submachine guns.

Matt, still crouched in the brush, counted their steps. Seven yards. Six. Close enough.

He whipped out his pistol, popped up, and fired. Two rapid shots. His first shot hit a gunman's chest, spinning him back. The second shot slammed into a second gunman's leg, sending him sprawling to the ground. The other two returned fire. Bullets chewed through the brush where Matt had been.

He was already moving left, circling wide, using the terrain as cover. The shooter with the injured leg was crawling towards a large tumbleweed. Matt put two rounds in his chest, then rolled right to avoid another burst of fire.

The last two were spreading out. Smart.

Matt waited, controlled his breathing, then popped up again and fired. His first two shots caught a man in the chest. He fired two more shots. The first shot missed, but the second clipped the last attacker's left knee. The man collapsed, screaming.

Silence settled over the canyon, except for the labored breath of the lone surviving shooter.

***

Matt closed the distance, kicking the attacker's gun away before grabbing him by the collar and slamming him onto the dirt.

"Who sent you?" Matt growled.

The man spat blood and glared at him.

Matt pressed his knee onto the man's wounded left leg, grinding down. The man let out a strangled scream, his body tensing in agony.

"I want a name."

The attacker's face contorted as he fought the pain. He was trained, that was clear. Not some street-level thug. He was a professional.

But his eyes betrayed him: fear.

Matt eased up slightly, giving him a second to reconsider.

The man panted, swallowing hard. Then...

"My boss." His voice was hoarse. "I don't know who he works for. I just do what I'm told."

"Who's your boss?"

The man hesitated, then exhaled. "Kuznetsov."

Matt's stomach tensed.

The guy coughed, blood speckling his lips. His face twisted. "Doesn't matter." His voice was fading. "You're already dead."

Matt held his gaze for a moment, then stepped back.

***

Matt wiped the blood from his knuckles and took a breath. He pulled out his phone and called Dave Johnson.

Dave answered immediately. "Talk to me."

"Three dead, one wounded. Conejo Canyons Open Space, off Western Plateau Trail."

Dave swore. "You need medical?"

"No. But I need this cleaned up fast. Call Decker at the Ventura Field Office."

"Decker?" Dave asked.

"He's stopping there to get help transporting Mitchell to headquarters in LA. He knows what's going on and the necessity to keep this investigation at the federal level."

Dave exhaled sharply. "Copy. I'll make the call."

"Make it fast.

***

The office had jumped to life with activity as soon as Decker and Mitchell came through the door of the FBI's Ventura Field Office. The agents knew Decker had apprehended a real-life traitor, and went out of their way to get involved.

Decker stood in the operations room, watching through the one-way glass into the holding room. Mitchell sat motionless. He was cuffed to the table. His eyes were closed.

Decker's phone buzzed.

He answered immediately. "Decker."

"Matt just got hit," Dave said.

"Where?"

"Conejo Canyons Open Space, off Western Plateau Trail."

Decker pulled up a mental map. Twenty-five minutes away.

"How bad?"

"Three dead, one wounded. Locals are already inbound."

Decker exhaled. Of course they were. A gunfight in the hills outside Newbury Park? No way it went unnoticed.

"Shit," Decker muttered. "Matt still on-site?"

"Yeah, but we need this cleaned up now. He's on his way to catch a plane to Taiwan."

Decker was already moving to the middle of the room. He held up his hand, motioning everyone in the room to stop what they were doing.

"Ventura County Sheriff's Office?" he asked.

"Yeah. They'll be first on the scene. They'll need a reason to step aside. That's where you come in."

Decker sighed. *Again.*

"He just dropped Mitchell on my lap and now he's throwing me a murder scene?"

"You asked to stay on the team, Decker. Consider this still being part of the team," Dave said.

Decker didn't argue.

He turned toward the nearest field agents. "Gear up. Three vehicles. We're rolling out."

Within five minutes, they were in the SUVs, headed south.

***

Decker's convoy of three black SUVs swung onto the dirt access road, dust kicking up as they neared the site.

He saw flashing red-and-blue lights. Ventura County sheriff's deputies were on scene.

Two patrol units sat angled across the dirt road, emergency lights pulsing. A supervisor's Tahoe was parked near the bodies, and three deputies stood near Matt, talking. One of them, a sergeant, had his arms crossed.

As soon as Decker's convoy rolled to a stop, one of his agents stepped out first, flashing a badge. "Federal jurisdiction. We'll take it from here."

The sergeant turned, clearly unimpressed.

"Like hell you will," he muttered. "We respond to a shooting, find three bodies, and the feds just show up to snatch it from us?"

Decker climbed out, walking straight for the sergeant as he pulled out his credentials. "Special Agent Decker, FBI. This case is part of a highly classified ongoing federal investigation."

The sergeant exchanged glances with his deputies. "We're gonna need more than that."

Decker lowered his voice. "Look, I get it. But these guys"—he motioned toward the bodies—"aren't local gangbangers, This is foreign-intelligence shit. You call this in and suddenly you've got DHS, counter intel, and every three-letter agency you ever heard of on your ass asking why you're poking around in it."

The sergeant exhaled sharply. "Fine. You feds can run the scene for now. But I'm staying until my lieutenant gets here, and we're gonna work out the specifics. You good with that?"

Decker nodded. "Fair enough. Just know this: once your lieutenant calls it in to FBI HQ in LA, this won't be your case anymore. But you can stick around."

The sergeant studied Decker for another second, then nodded to his deputies. "Alright, boys, pack it up and get back to your beats. I'm staying here. The lieutenant and I will handle this."

One by one, the local patrol units rolled out, leaving the scene to the FBI and one still-unhappy sheriff's sergeant.

Matt watched the whole exchange, standing near a rock.

Decker shook his head. "Jesus, Scales, you always leave a mess?"

Matt wiped his knuckles on his jeans. "Only when someone tries to kill me."

Decker turned toward the bodies.

Three dead. One barely clinging to life. A burner phone on the ground.

Matt nudged the wounded guy with his boot. "One left."

Decker crouched, studying the injured hit man. Looked Russian. Just like he expected.

"Let me guess," Decker muttered. "Kuznetsov?"

Matt tossed Decker the burner phone.

"Last call came in twelve hours ago," Matt said. "They got the order before we even confronted Mitchell at DCS."

Decker gave him his "no shit" look.

Decker then looked at the other agents. "Secure the wounded guy. Get the bodies tagged, photos taken, and evidence collected. The coroner still has to process the bodies, so we'll hold the scene until he gets here."

As the agents got to work, Matt stretched, rolling his shoulders to shake off the last of the adrenaline.

Decker sighed. "Get out of here, Scales. We'll handle it."

"Hey, Decker."

Decker glanced up.

Matt broke into a wide smile. "Looks like you're still part of the team."

Decker rolled his eyes, but he had no comeback.

Because Matt was right.

***

Matt walked toward the road as one of the black SUVs pulled up beside him.

The driver, a stone-faced FBI agent, reached over and opened the passenger door.

Matt exhaled as he settled in the leather seat. His hands still ached from the fight.

Through the tinted glass, he could see Decker overseeing the collection of evidence and cleanup.

Matt's eyes locked onto Decker as he stared at the burner phone in his hand.

Matt grinned.

Yeah, Decker. You're still in this.

The SUV pulled away, the dirt road kicking up dust behind them.

The driver glanced at him in the mirror.

"You were never here?" the agent muttered.

Matt grinned faintly. "That's the idea."

They sped toward Point Mugu and the waiting F-18.

Chapter 25

Matt had never been in the back seat of an F-18 Super Hornet. The space proved tighter than expected. Eight hours in an airplane, without being able to get up and move around or use the restroom, presented its own challenges. But the in-air refueling experience made up for the cramped quarters. It wasn't exactly first-class, but speed meant more than convenience and comfort. The jet screamed across the Pacific, cutting his travel time to Guam to just under eight hours.

As soon as he landed at Andersen Air Force Base, Matt leaped out of the F-18 cockpit and scanned the tarmac. Parked near one of the hangars was his next ride, a squat, rugged MC-130 Combat Talon II, already idling. He turned back and thanked the pilot with a quick handshake before jogging toward the Talon.

Waiting near the open ramp was the man in charge: Lieutenant Commander Blake "Razor" Callahan, tall, lean, and wearing a flight helmet tucked under one arm. "Scales?" he asked, offering a hand. "I'm Razor. We'll get you where you need to go."

As they climbed into the plane, Razor gave him a brief rundown. "Officially, we're running recon flights near Taiwan. Chinese Navy's been getting more aggressive. Unofficially? My crew's been waiting for something like this. Sneaking you in under the radar sounds like fun."

Once aboard, Razor led Matt toward the cargo bay, where the gear had already been secured. Standing over it, clipboard in hand and a flashlight clipped to his vest, was the crew chief: Chief Petty Officer Kyle "Brick" Thompson, built like a wrecking ball and twice as solid.

"I checked it all myself," Brick said without looking up. "Jump gear's good to go. Packer's one of ours. The best in the squadron."

Matt gave a curt nod as his eyes landed on the rig. Full HALO set-up. This was going to be a rough one.

***

The trip to Taiwan took just under two hours. But somewhere over the Philippine Sea, a weak tropical depression had flared into a full-blown storm. They skirted the worst of it, threading the Combat Talon through dark skies, jagged lightning flashing like strobes across the cabin walls.

"It's getting rough out here," Brick muttered from his seat near the gear rack. "We're zigzagging like crazy to stay out of the punch zone."

Matt felt the plane yaw left, then right, the turbulence kicking harder now as Razor worked the controls from the cockpit.

The original plan had been to drop Matt on a beach near the coast. That was looking less likely by the minute.

"We're trying to find you a pocket with calmer winds," Razor's voice came over the comms. "But it's shifting fast. Be ready to go with just a few seconds' notice."

Matt checked his harness again. Brick moved over and gave it a second look, his hands moving with the calm precision of someone who'd done this a hundred times.

Matt had seen the updated imagery of gusting winds, lightning bursts behind the ridgeline, and a jagged coastal approach that looked more like a meat grinder than a landing zone. Black volcanic rock.

Sheer drops. Narrow ledges lined with pine and scrub. Any one of them could break a man in half.

The water drop had been the backup plan. He'd made the call himself when the satellite feed showed the land corridor collapsing under the squall line. Matt didn't like it, but there was no alternative. St. Bernard and the rest of the team were in position offshore.

Originally, the jump had been planned at thirty thousand feet with oxygen masks, long free fall, and maximum cover. But not in this storm. Not with this terrain.

"Drop altitude to fifteen thousand," Matt told Brick. "I want less time in the air."

He adjusted his gear, checked his altimeter, toggled the backup nav HUD, and double-tapped the clasp on his chest harness, then dumped the oxygen mask and bottle. Simpler this way. Less gear to fight with if things went sideways.

He stepped into the wind.

He was out and falling. Wind tore past his body, sleet slapping his visor. His suit vibrated with the turbulence. For a few seconds, it was all angles and instincts, body tight, arms tucked, tracking clean.

A violent gust rolled him sideways, He fought back into a box position and looked at his altitude indicator. Ten thousand feet. Lightning flashed through the clouds off to his right. He angled down, increasing his speed to terminal velocity. The less time in the air the better.

At three thousand feet, he pulled the rip cord, feeling the familiar jolt, especially in his left shoulder, before he saw lightning flash in the distance.

Below, the Taiwanese coastline was an invisible threat, a black saw of cliffs and ridgelines cutting into the sea. Lightning flashed to his right. The strong winds jostled him.

He adjusted his direction and steered away from the coastline.

His GPS showed a negative ground speed. The cliffs were getting closer. He fought it, pulling against the drift. He spiraled, trying to gain forward momentum.

But it wasn't enough.

"Shit," he hissed.

He yanked down hard on the risers, dumping altitude by dropping almost vertically. The ocean rushed up at him in a black roar. No time to cut the chute. He slammed into the water feetfirst.

The chute dragged him down, its cords wrapped tight around his legs.

Down he went, ten, fifteen, twenty, thirty feet. Pressure built in his ears as his lungs tightened. Salt water surged into his nose. His limbs felt heavy as the weight of the chute tugged him toward the seafloor.

No time for panic. He reached for the harness. Found the release. Pulled. The chute slid free.

Matt grabbed his knife off of his waist and cut the cords from his legs.

He hung in the water for a moment, weightless. A stream of bubbles slid past his face. He followed them.

When he broke the surface and felt the crash of waves on his face, the mist was relentless in the heavy wind. He pulled the cord of his LPU-10/P. He'd grabbed the small compact military-grade flotation device at the last minute. Now he was glad he had.

The rain beat down on him like needles. Salt water burned his eyes as he surfaced. He controlled his breathing and concentrated on getting into the rhythm of the waves.

He activated his infrared diode and held it above his head, rotating in a circle. Lightning flashed in the distance, illuminating the churning sea for just a moment.

He knew his team was out there cutting through the waves, tracking his GPS. The locator strapped to his wrist showed he was a half mile offshore. He fought the instinct to swim. In calm seas, it would've been a relaxed swim. But in these conditions it would be easy to get disoriented, and making headway through ten-foot waves was tough.

He'd been in the water for fifteen minutes when he heard the faint but unmistakable low hum of a motor cutting through the storm. They were close.

Moments later, an inflatable Zodiac with a rigid hull took shape in the darkness. Matt raised the infrared diode higher, and saw the boat adjust its course toward him.

***

"Got him," April said, pointing towards Matt as she scanned ahead of the boat with night-vision goggles.

As the Zodiac got closer to him, Matt saw that St. Bernard was at the helm. Of course he was, being a master boatswain's mate.

St. Bernard maneuvered the boat alongside Matt and April tossed a rope into the water. Matt grabbed it, feeling her pull him up and into the boat.

"Nice night for a swim, eh?" St. Bernard grinned.

Even with the wind and rain, Matt could hear St. Bernard's Southern drawl. "Yeah, I needed to cool off, plus I'd been on planes for ten hours and needed a bath, not to mention needing to pee."

Skip, who'd been sitting in the back of the boat watching everything unfold, gave Matt a thumbs-up.

"Let's get out of here before this weather gets any worse," Matt said.

St. Bernard pushed the throttle forward and the Zodiac surged ahead. Rain lashed the sides of the boat as he adjusted course towards a remote dock. They had a vehicle waiting there for them that they could take to the cybersecurity command post.

Tactical Operations Overlay : Taiwan Area of Interest

Compiled for DCS Task Force Use: Taipei Region, Cybersecurity HQ, Safe Houses, and Key Targets

Pacific Theater Overview—
Russia
Beijing
North Korea
China
South Korea
Taiwan
Pacific Ocean
South China Sea

Chapter 26

Day 96 - Taipei, Taiwan

The black van navigated the winding road ascending Toad Mountain, dense foliage pressing in from both sides. The urban sprawl of Taipei lay below, softened by a light haze. As they climbed higher, the air grew cooler, and the persistent hum of the city faded into silence.

Near the summit, the van slowed at a discreet checkpoint guarded by two armed soldiers in digital camouflage. One stepped forward, scanning the license plate, while the other approached the driver's window with a handheld biometric reader. St. Bernard, who was driving, lowered all four of the car's windows.

The soldier held out a palm reader. The light turned green after St. Bernard, April, and Skip placed their hands on the palm reader.

The soldier then approached Matt.

"My first time here, soldier," Matt said, handing over his ID. The guard scrutinized it, then lit Matt's face with a flashlight. After ten seconds he handed the ID back to Matt and told him to place his hand on the palm reader.

Once the machine cycled and saved Matt's information, a green icon appeared at the top of the tablet. The soldier gave a curt nod and tapped his comms. The steel blast doors ahead of them shuddered, then groaned open, revealing a tunnel that plunged into the heart of the mountain.

St. Bernard steered their vehicle into the cool, sterile tunnel that led to the Taiwan Cybersecurity Command Center. Inside the tunnel, the air was crisp and dry, a stark contrast to the tropical forest outside. The tunnel opened into a vast chamber, its walls hewn from solid rock and reinforced with steel. Fluorescent lights cast a bluish hue over rows of advanced computer terminals. A technician dressed in a dark blue uniform sat at each terminal.

On one wall, a faded emblem hinted at the site's military origins, a silent testament to its transformation from a wartime bunker to a modern cyber-defense hub.

Matt stepped out of the van, taking in the sheer scale of the operation, but April was already moving, nodding to a technician she recognized. Skip and St. Bernard peeled off and headed down a corridor and then turned right out of sight.

Chin noticed Matt's gaze and walked up beside him. "Good to see you, Matt. I assume your trip over wasn't as comfortable as ours?"

"Let's just say it epitomized the saying that 'half the fun is getting there.'"

"You look like you could use a hot shower and some dry clothes. After that, I'll introduce you to Uncle Ming."

***

Chin glanced up as Matt stepped into the control room. His hair was still damp from the shower. He was now dressed in fresh tactical gear.

"Matt, this is Uncle Ming."

The older man extended his hand. "I've heard much about you. Welcome."

Matt took his hand. "An honor, sir. Thank you for everything you're doing."

Uncle Ming nodded, studying him. "Family stands together when the storm comes. I'm glad you're here."

Matt offered a respectful bow, aware of the weight behind those words.

After introductions, Chin walked back to his desk and looked up at the screens. Outwardly, he projected confidence, but inside, doubt lingered. He had tested every string of code, simulated hundreds of failure points, scrubbed each logic tree until his vision blurred, and still, he couldn't shake the feeling that he might've missed something. The AI antivirus had been rushed to fit Taiwan's outdated infrastructure. A malformed packet, a buried OS quirk, one overlooked logic flaw... that was all it would take.

If a core sector failed, power wouldn't return.

Water systems would stall, hospitals would remain dark, and Taiwan would fall.

Chin knew, though no one said it aloud, that the fate of two nations rested on his shoulders.

Matt, April, St. Bernard, and Skip stood behind Chin as he sat at the desk.

"The antivirus AI is slowly pushing back the virus attack, both here and in the US," Chin said. "But here in Taiwan, hackers manually compromised our military systems. That's where the real threat is now."

Skip let out a frustrated sigh, shaking his head. "So even though civilian infrastructure is coming back online, the main military targets are still locked down, and you're saying there's nothing we can do from here?"

"Not for the airports, military sites, and key defense systems," Chin said. "Each location requires an on-site reconfiguration to override their changes. The antivirus has no effect on these individual hacks. We have to be physically present at each site to reverse the breach and lock them out one by one."

St. Bernard stepped forward. "Sounds like they planned this pretty well. They knew we'd have to choose to protect civilians or maintain military readiness."

"Exactly," Chin said as his fingers drummed against the keyboard. "Civilian systems are stabilizing. Grid sectors are recovering. Water treatment facilities are coming back online."

He paused, watching another cluster of red indicators fade to green.

He didn't celebrate, he didn't cheer, but for the first time in hours, he let himself breathe.

A full, deep breath.

Not the shallow air he'd rationed while pretending everything was fine, but the kind that started at the bottom of the lungs and reached all the way to his spine.

***

Commander Benjamin Harris's eight operators were biding their time in a safe house just south of Yangmingshan National Forest. After the release of the virus, their mission had shifted to a quick reaction force protecting the northern part of the island from a ground attack coming through the forest.

A burst of static crackled through the radio.

"Ranger Six, Eagle One."

Commander Harris knew Eagle One was an AWACS that the military had activated to watch the airspace around Taiwan. He also knew they wouldn't be calling him unless they had something important to tell him.

"Go ahead, Eagle One."

"Eagle One. We're tracking a slow-moving, unidentified aircraft entering Taiwanese airspace from the east. It's just above radar detection height, approximately ten thousand feet. It's not on any civilian or military flight path."

"Is it one of ours?"

"Negative. No transponder codes. The flight path has been skirting monitored airspace. The aircraft had been traveling at three hundred knots, but it just slowed down to just over a hundred knots. It is currently twenty-five miles northwest of your location."

"If I didn't know better I'd say they're getting ready to drop some parachutists into our region," Commander Harris said.

"That's a roger, Ranger Six. We're picking up ten infrared blips dropping below the plane. Looks like they'll be landing northwest of you in the Yangmingshan National Forest."

"Roger that, Eagle One. Give me a bearing from our location to where they might be landing."

"They are at 310 degrees from your location. Will send you the projected coordinates of the landing zone."

"Roger that, Eagle One. Will take care of it from here. Thanks for the heads-up." Commander Harris turned to his team members. "Looks like ten paratroopers landing northwest of us, most likely heading for the cybersecurity headquarters."

Commander Harris then turned around and looked at Carson "Spade" McGraw. Spade was a skilled remote surveillant and UAV operator. "Spade, get our drone up and get me surveillance on these paratroopers."

"Roger that," Spade said. "Wind has calmed down quite a bit. It'll be dicey, but the drone should be okay."

Harris turned around and looked at CPO Rollie Mendoza. "Work with Spade and figure out the best ambush site for these guys. Need to make sure we hustle over there and take them out before they get close to the cybersecurity headquarters."

***

Matt didn't enjoy sitting around waiting for something to happen, but he wasn't sure what else to do. The current situation called for computer technicians, not a team specializing in developing intelligence, surveillance, and direct action. Without a mission or other task, he lay down and closed his eyes.

Then his phone rang. When he answered it, he recognized Commander Harris's voice.

"Scales, a Chinese aircraft just dropped ten paratroopers northwest of our location. We're moving to intercept them and keep you informed. Meanwhile, keep your head on a swivel. The Chinese always attack on multiple fronts at once."

"Will do. Thanks for the heads-up. Let us know when you've broken contact."

Matt decided rest and sleep would have to wait. He got up and walked back to the main control room. Just as he walked into the room, Ming Ho came over.

"I just got word that President Fang is coming here," Ming Ho said. "With all the other military installations under attack and nonfunctional, her security team decided to come here. She'll be here in sixty minutes."

"Isn't that a little risky?" St. Bernard asked. "There's no real military presence to protect her here."

"That may be true, but this facility has a fully functioning backup command post, and it's the only one the virus hasn't infiltrated or taken down," Ming Ho replied. "She travels with a full security contingent. The military is sending troops to protect the building. They're about fifteen minutes behind her."

Uncle Ming turned and looked at Matt. "Matt, I need your team to set up a protective perimeter and coordinate with the president's security team until the military gets here."

"Consider it done, but we have another problem. Commander Harris told me there's a team of ten paratroopers who just landed in the Yangmingshan National Forest. But the good news is his team is moving to intercept, and they should be more than able to take care of the problem."

"Well, if that's true, then what's the problem?" Uncle Ming asked.

"The problem is that the Chinese never put all their apples in one basket," Matt said. "You can bet the paratroopers are part of a bigger plan."

Chin looked up at Matt with a smile. "Go philosophy."

"Absolutely." Matt then looked at his team. "Let's start planning our defense in depth."

***

Lying flat on his stomach in the thick underbrush, Commander Harris steadied his suppressed Noveske N4 rifle, the matte-black Dead Air suppressor threaded to the barrel barely visible in the dim light. Through the faint green glow of his GPNVG-18 panoramic night vision goggles, he locked onto the tree line ahead, scanning for movement through the EOTech EXPS3 holographic sight.

His team lay silent and motionless around him, each man shrouded by ferns and moss, the eerie hum of their goggles the only sound in the darkness. Harris had reminded them during the briefing to kill their infrared lasers and assume the enemy had NVGs.

Humidity clung to their skin. The distant crack of a branch echoed softly through the trees, close enough to tighten Harris's grip on the rifle.

To his left, the point man raised a gloved hand in a subtle movement ahead. The overhead drone had tracked ten white thermal blips fanning out after their drop. Spade's route prediction had been dead-on, guiding the team into a textbook L-shaped ambush.

Just behind Harris, a shooter nestled an SPR with a 77-grain load, steadying it against a backpack. To the right, someone checked the claymore clacker once more, fingers brushing against the webbing of a MultiCam plate carrier bristling with breaching charges and flex cuffs.

"Three... two..." Harris counted silently.

The first Chinese commando broke through the foliage. The suppressed *pop* of the point man's round cracked the tension wide open. Harris squeezed his trigger, the Noveske bucking gently against his shoulder as he dropped his target. Around him, controlled fire stitched through the underbrush, and seven paratroopers collapsed before they even realized they were in the kill zone.

The final three scattered for cover, but they didn't get far. The demolitions expert had wired the claymores for directional kill zones. The dual *click-pop* of the detonator was followed by a harsh *thump* as the ground trembled and shrapnel tore through the foliage.

Thirty seconds later, silence returned. Ten bodies lay still.

Harris gave the hand signal. Three team members fanned out to confirm the kills, gliding through the terrain like shadows. No unnecessary chatter. No wasted movement.

Once they returned with wordless nods, Harris gave a curt signal. The team swept the bodies quickly, checking for comms gear, map fragments, or unit patches, anything that might hint at what these commandos were after. One of them yanked a small tablet from a chest rig and stuffed it into his pack.

Satisfied, Harris tapped twice on his comms mic and gestured forward.

Time to move.

The op had gone as planned. Tight, clean, and efficient, but Harris knew better than to relax. This was just the opening act.

***

Commander Harris's call came through just as Matt was running down worst-case scenarios at the cybersecurity headquarters.

"Ambush successful. Paratroopers eliminated. We're heading back to the safe house."

Matt acknowledged the report and hung up, turning back to the conference table, where his team and the cybersecurity center's guard detail were locked in a debate over defensive positions.

Then the door opened, and Ming Ho stepped in.

"Matt, I need you and Chin for a moment."

Something in his tone cut through the room's noise. Matt pushed back his chair and Chin exhaled sharply and stood.

Ming Ho led them down the hallway to a small conference room and shut the door. He didn't ease into the conversation.

"President Fang is coming," he said. "But before she arrives, you need to know she's not just the president of Taiwan. She's family."

Matt frowned. "What do you mean?"

Ming Ho turned to Chin. "She's your aunt. Fang Xiu-ying."

Chin's mouth opened, but no sound came out. He blinked, gripping the back of a chair to steady himself.

Matt studied his friend. Aunt? His mind raced, recalculating everything he knew about Chin's family history.

"Why am I just now hearing this?" Chin finally managed.

Ming Ho's expression softened, but his voice remained firm. "Because it wasn't relevant until now."

Chin exhaled, dragging his hand down. Matt recognized the look. His friend was compartmentalizing, forcing emotions down so he could keep moving.

Chin straightened. "I need to get back to work. If we don't stop this virus, it won't matter who my family is."

Ming Ho nodded. "When she arrives, I'll come get you."

Chin hesitated, then gave a nod before heading back to the command center.

Matt lingered a second longer. "You really think now's the time to drop this on him?"

Ming Ho met his eyes. "Would there ever be a right time?"

Matt had no answer to that.

***

On the outskirts of Taipei, the president's convoy sped down the dark, deserted road, its headlights slicing through the thick night air. The urgency of the last-minute diversion to the cybersecurity headquarters weighed heavily on Officer Lin's mind. His duty was to protect the president. Route changes like this were always a red flag. There were too many variables, too many unknowns.

Lin sat in the front passenger seat of the rear vehicle of the three-car convoy, an armored Toyota Land Cruiser 300. His eyes shifted between the road and the GPS tracker mounted on the dashboard.

Directly ahead, President Fang rode with Captain Wei in the middle SUV. Lin couldn't see them, but he knew Wei. He was calculating, disciplined, and always alert. Wei had sounded tense when he announced their diversion to the cyber command center. If Wei was concerned, there had to be a reason.

Then, without warning, the lead SUV erupted into a fireball. The explosion shook the earth, sending a shock wave through the convoy. A deafening roar followed, and the vehicle disappeared in a column of fire, flinging shrapnel across the road.

Lin's vehicle lifted off the ground slightly before slamming back down. The tires screeched as the Toyota skidded sideways.

Lin's heart pounded. Before he could react, five gunmen burst from the tree line on the right. Muzzle flashes strobed through the night. A barrage of bullets tore into Lin's SUV, spider-webbing the bulletproof glass.

"Ambush!" Lin shouted, ducking instinctively.

Rounds slammed into the vehicle. He climbed out of the driver's door and rolled onto the ground. Three other security officers met him on the ground.

"Controlled fire! Ready to maneuver!" Lin shouted.

Another burst cracked through the air. Lin dove beneath the Toyota, a sudden searing pain lancing through his shoulder as he hit the ground. His vision blurred. Where were the others?

Officer Wu lay beside him, unmoving. Blood pooled beneath his body. Lin flinched as fresh rounds slammed into Wu's back. The horror settled in. Wu was gone. But in death, he had shielded Lin with his body.

Lin crawled further under the vehicle, steadying his breathing.

Then he saw it.

Through the smoke and chaos, the rear door of the president's vehicle swung open. Captain Wei stood motionless beside it.

Lin blinked, disbelieving.

Wei reached in and yanked President Fang out by her hair, throwing her to the ground.

Two men rushed forward and grabbed her, dragging her toward a waiting vehicle.

Then Wei climbed in with them.

The SUV sped off toward the Yangmingshan National Forest before the door was closed.

Lin stared, frozen in disbelief.

He had worked alongside Wei for seven years. Trusted him. But there was no mistaking what he'd just seen.

For a moment, he wondered—was Wei under duress?

Then he realized it didn't matter.

"Traitor..." Lin whispered, the word caught in his throat.

His whole body trembled. As the fleeing vehicle disappeared into the forest, the adrenaline began to fade. The pain returned, much sharper now. He was bleeding out. Fast.

Lin rolled to his side and reached for his phone. His hands shook as he concentrated to type in the phone's passcode. Finally. Now, go to contacts. There it is. One last call.

He hit send.

After a tense pause, Ming Ho's voice came through.

"Lin? Is everything all right?"

Lin gasped. "Sir... we were hit. It was an ambush. They took her. The president. Wei... He was with them. He handed her over."

Silence.

Then a slow, heavy breath on the other end. "Are you certain?"

Lin's voice was faint now, every word costing him. "I saw it. He... he handed her over. They planned it. They knew we were coming."

"Listen to me carefully, Lin. You did well. I'm sending a team to your location. Tell me exactly where you are."

Lin hesitated, breathing heavily. "Yes, sir. Thank you. But... you won't make it in time. I'm sorry. I failed you. I failed her."

The line went quiet.

***

After receiving the call from Officer Lin, Ming Ho entered the command center.

"Chin, I need you to come with me."

"But Uncle, I'm right in the middle of bringing the main grid back online," Chin replied, fingers still tapping the keys.

"That can wait," Uncle Ming said firmly. "I need you for something more important."

He knew Uncle Ming wouldn't interrupt unless the matter was urgent. He followed him into the conference room, where Matt and his team were reviewing building schematics and satellite images of the cybersecurity facility and surrounding terrain.

Two of the wall monitors showed news feeds covering the situation in Taiwan. Another tracked the cascading effects in the United States. The last cycled through *BBC World News* coverage.

As they entered, Matt looked up.

Ming Ho got straight to the point. "President Fang has been kid-napped."

Chin's face went pale. His breath caught in his throat as he gripped the edge of the table.

"I received a call from Officer Lin. He was in a trailing vehicle during the ambush. He says the head of security, Officer Wei, was col-laborating with the kidnappers. I have to assume he's not acting alone. There may be others, even inside the military."

Ming Ho exhaled. "We don't have time to vet an entire unit, and I can't risk word leaking out. The nearest trustworthy backup is over an hour away. By then, the president could be dead.

"The president's capture isn't just symbolic," Ming Ho continued. "If she's removed, the military chain of command fractures. We've held this fragile unity together with words. Without her, there's no one to rally around when the bombs fall, or when the networks fail."

Ming Ho looked directly at Matt. "Beijing knows this. That's why they moved now to cripple our networks, sever our leadership, and strike before we can respond."

Matt met Ming Ho's gaze. "Then we have to stop them before it's too late. What do you need from us?"

Uncle Ming nodded. "You trust Commander Harris and his team?"

"Absolutely."

"Good. A covert rescue is our best chance. I need you and Commander Harris to execute it."

Matt gave a sharp nod. "We're on it."

As the team turned back to the maps, Chin's heart pounded. The president, his aunt, Fang Wei-sheng, was in enemy hands. Six months ago, that might've broken him. But not now. He had changed. Fear still gripped him, but so did something else: determination.

"Matt," Chin said, stepping forward. "I want to be part of this. I want to go with you. I can help."

Matt looked over at him. Chin could see the hesitation in his eyes.

"Chin, the work you're doing here is critical. Maybe you should stay and finish it."

Chin shook his head. "The technicians here are capable. I trained them. They know how the antivirus works. My place is with you, helping to bring her back. She's family."

There was no wavering in his voice.

Matt held his gaze for a long moment, then nodded. "Okay, Chin. You're with us."

***

After the briefing from Ming Ho and agreeing to let Chin go with them, Matt walked out of the room down the hallway to a vacant office. He pulled out a satellite phone and dialed a number from memory.

"Harris," said a familiar voice.

"It's Scales," he said, as he glanced back toward the conference room. "Situation just escalated. President Fang was kidnapped. We think she's being held somewhere in the Yangmingshan National Forest. The reason the kidnapping was successful was because the head of her security team betrayed her. Ming Ho says we're the only people he can trust."

Harris's voice hardened. "Understood. What do you need?"

"We need to start an aerial search of the forest."

"Roger that. I'll mobilize a couple of UAVs for thermal surveillance over the forested areas. Your team can meet us at our safe house location. We're just outside the forest. Will plan our search and assault from there."

"Appreciate it, Harris. We're on our way."

***

Commander Harris lowered the sat phone and turned to his men.

"Alright, listen up. The president's been taken. We've got a wide search zone and no guarantees. When we find her, we move fast, stay silent, and don't stop until she's back."

Spade unfolded a map across the hood of a Humvee. "If I were them, I'd head east towards the part of the forest that has steep ridges, thick canopy, and only one road in. Easy to control. It's hard terrain, perfect for hiding."

An hour later, Matt's team arrived. Dust swirled around their vehicle as it skidded to a stop.

Harris stepped forward as Matt climbed out of the SUV.

"Scales. Your reputation proceeds you..."

"I'll survive without the compliments," Matt said, brushing past the handshake and stepping closer to the map. His tone was not hostile. Just focused. "Let me introduce my team. St. Bernard, Skip, April Knight, and our tech lead, Chin Ho."

Harris nodded as his eyes moved to Chin. "You related to the guy running Taiwan's intel?"

Chin hesitated. "Yeah. He's my uncle."

Harris whistled. "Damn. Keeping it in the family." He crossed his arms. "Rumor is, you and Scales are practically brothers, but I don't see the resemblance."

Chin grinned. "That's because he's uglier."

Matt shook his head. "That's rich coming from a guy whose high-school yearbook labeled him 'Most Likely to Stay Indoors.'"

The banter settled as Chin exhaled. "One other thing you don't know. President Fang... she's my aunt."

The room went silent. Even the drone operator turned his head.

Harris let out a breath. "Well, shit. All the more reason to get her back."

Matt gave a slow nod. The mission was no longer just tactical. It was personal, and for more than one of them. But there was no time to dwell.

Chapter 27

Day 96 - Yangmingshan National Forest, Taiwan

The buzzing of the fluorescent lights overhead was the only sound in the room.

Lebedev surveyed the space. His eyes moved over bare concrete walls and empty corners. The air was thick and stale. There were no windows to cause distractions for anyone inside. The reinforced steel door behind him was the only way out. Something nagged at him, but he ignored it. He turned his focus to the woman in the chair in the middle of the otherwise empty room.

President Fang sat quietly and stared at him. A thin line of dried blood cut across her temple, a stark contrast against the white of her blouse. Her bound wrists showed deep red marks.

She wasn't broken. Not yet.

Time always worked in his favor. Lebedev let the moment stretch, expecting the silence to unsettle her.

"Madam President, I've followed your career. You have a reputation for being a brilliant strategist." He watched her, waiting for a reaction. Her expression didn't waver. "Yet despite all your diplomacy, despite your powerful allies, your empire falls tomorrow."

President Fang didn't blink. "You mistake discipline for weakness, Mr. Lebedev. Yamamoto made the same mistake when he spoke of the United States after Pearl Harbor. He feared he had awakened a sleeping giant." She straightened as much as her restraints allowed. "You've miscalculated."

Lebedev chuckled. "Your allies are scrambling. Your country is barely holding on." He took a step closer. "Infrastructure is in collapse. The military and airports are inoperable. By this time tomorrow, Taiwan will be under the control of the People's Republic of China."

"Fear and brute force won't hold power forever. You underestimate the resilience of the Taiwanese people."

"Resilience?" He waved a hand. "By morning, your nation will kneel. Wars aren't won with spirit. They're won with power and control."

Satisfied, he turned and stepped into the hallway. An operative approached him holding out a tablet.

Lebedev took it.

"What am I looking at?"

"Sir, the virus we designed is being neutralized across the US and Taiwan. Their systems are coming back online. We still have control over military and airport networks, but..."

Lebedev waved off the operative as his grip tightened on the tablet.

This wasn't possible.

The virus, the invasion, the kidnapping, they were all part of their grand plan, a plan designed to deliver a devastating blow to the arrogance of the West and their allies.

As he stood in the doorway, Lebedev composed himself. He turned and looked at President Fang. "I suggest you get comfortable. This may take some time, but the end result is inevitable."

He slammed the door behind him as he stepped out of room.

***

Matt and Commander Harris sat waiting for an update from Spade McGraw. Harris suggested splitting his eight-man unit into two four-man teams, giving them three operational teams in total. Everyone in the room understood a skilled four-man team could accomplish destruction and devastation at an unmatched scale.

After reviewing tactics and finalizing key details of the mission, the conversation drifted to the old days.

"So, April," Commander Harris said, a teasing glint in his eye, "how'd you end up running with this band of merry men?"

"Well, Matt and I go way back, and St. Bernard and I go somewhat back. As for Skip, he just trails along behind St. Bernard to keep him in line."

Commander Harris paused, his gaze lingering on her for a long moment. "There's a banner back in the squad bay, mounted in an area dedicated to Black Squadron members. It has a quote, in bold letters, attributed to 'AK.' Half the guys are convinced it's a myth, but..."

April raised an eyebrow. "A myth, huh? And what does this banner say?"

"It says, 'You can't fake grit when it's time to bleed.' The initials are AK. Now, I don't believe in coincidences..."

She laughed. "Guilty as charged. Though in my defense, we'd been up for forty-eight hours, caffeine was low, and patience was even lower."

"I thought so. I've always found you Black Squadron types to have a way with words. Now I can tell the guys I met the legend herself."

Matt watched the exchange, catching the bit of amusement in April's eyes.

Spade strode into the room. "I've got eyes on 'em. Looks like they're holed up in an old mining operation on the northeast side of the forest. I've spotted three vehicles with warm engines. The site has two buildings, one large warehouse that looks like an operations center and a smaller one, probably an office building."

"Outstanding work," Commander Harris replied. "What's the distance?"

"Line of sight, about six miles. We can get within two miles using the back roads, but after that, we'll need to go in on foot to keep our presence under wraps."

"Nice work," Matt said. "Print out the overhead maps and meet us in the conference room for the final briefing."

"On it," Spade replied as he bolted down the hallway to grab the maps.

As Matt finished packing his gear, St. Bernard and Skip were also checking their weapons with the same meticulous care as always.

The DEVGRU operators were also testing radios and checking mags and optics. As April checked the action on her sidearm, one of the younger guys, tall, fit, and in his late twenties, gave her a once-over from across the bench.

"You rolling with us on this one?" he asked, not unkindly, but with a raised eyebrow.

April didn't respond. She looked at the table and saw a knife sitting next to a suppressed Noveske rifle. She reached over and grabbed the knife. Without a word, she turned and flung it at a distant support beam near the armory lockers.

The blade struck with a clean thwack, dead center on a sticker target someone had taped up days ago.

The room went quiet. Commander Harris let out a soft chuckle.

The younger operator nodded once. April didn't bother looking back.

St. Bernard gave a low whistle. "Damn, Knight, remind me not to mouth off when you're holding silverware."

April got a serious look on her face as she holstered her Sig Sauer 226. "Takes more than attitude to walk back into this."

"Why did you come back?"

Without looking up, she said, "Unfinished business."

She paused, just long enough to leave a gap, and then added, quieter, "Some answers don't come unless you go looking for them."

"Fair enough," St. Bernard said. "Glad you're here."

She nodded. "So am I."

Across the room, Chin sat watching the action. His eyes darted back and forth between April and the DEVGRU operator. Matt caught the subtle change in his expression, something between disbelief and admiration.

"Chin, double-check your gear. You'll be fourth in the stack behind me and right in front of April."

The group stepped outside and climbed into their vehicles. They drove blacked out, using night-vision goggles. Spade kept the drone overhead, looking for any surprises along the way. Once they reached the two-mile mark, they dismounted.

Matt's team positioned themselves between the two four-man DEVGRU units. He knew his edge in navigating this type of terrain had dulled over time. He always preferred to lead, but this time, he let them take point.

As they advanced, Spade adjusted the UAV's position, shifting its focus from overhead surveillance to scanning the mining operation for heat signatures. The two-mile trek took them forty-five minutes. Matt thought about how, under normal circumstances, it would take longer for a leisurely stroll along the beach. These guys weren't just good, they were damn near perfect.

***

Matt could smell the heavy aroma of pine. The mountain air was dense and cool, a result of the earth beneath him absorbing the remnants of the day's fading warmth. The canopy above swallowed sound, softened the crunch of boots, and dampened the hiss of distant movement. Matt had fought in terrain like this before. The thick air and heavy cover was perfect for staying hidden, or getting killed if you weren't sharp.

He adjusted the range on his night-vision binoculars to scan the tree line for any movement.

Commander Harris crouched beside Matt, his gloved fingers tapping the side of a Panasonic Toughbook. The screen displayed the live infrared feed from the drone circling above.

"The drone is picking up heat signatures twenty meters northeast of the larger building," Harris whispered. He angled the monitor so Matt could see. The structures were outlined in grainy contrast, and small white dots moved in slow, precise patterns.

Matt studied the layout. The heat signatures moved in a way that marked them as sentries. He noted their spacing and movement. It was disciplined but not overly aggressive. They weren't expecting an imminent assault.

"Those faint heat signals out front are the vehicle engines," Chin murmured. "They've cooled."

Matt adjusted his binoculars, fine-tuning the infrared contrast for a clear read on the terrain. The dirt road leading to the structures showed the fresh disturbances from the vehicles' tires. A scan of the nearby foliage showed no unnatural movement.

"Looks like the larger building is well covered," Harris remarked. "Based on satellite imagery and our intel analysis, it's a warehouse. We matched the dimensions against commercial blueprints in the region. The front entrance has two sliding doors." He pointed to a highlighted section on the map overlay. "There are also side doors. No heat signatures near them."

Matt gave a sharp nod as Spade toggled the drone's feed between thermal and night vision, studying the smaller structure. Its compact shape and partitioned roofline confirmed his suspicion.

"It's an office building," he concluded. "Looks like a main entrance out front. There's an access point in the back, a loading door or secondary entrance. We'll recon the rear before we commit. Call it fifteen minutes to breach."

"Roger that," Commander Harris replied.

"Chin," Matt said, catching his friend's eye. "Keep an eye on those heat signatures. The drone sweep should give us a better idea of guard rotation. I'm particularly interested in any guards paying attention to the smaller building and movement close to our entry points."

"Got it," Chin replied as Matt watched Spade hand over his tablet with the drone feed to Chin.

"Movement at the main building. Looks like a guard rotation," Chin murmured. "The secondary building is still clear. No signs of movement."

Matt saw Harris walk over to Chin and glance over his shoulder at the drone footage. Harris studied the screen for a long moment before turning to Matt. "We're good to go. Once we breach, stay in contact until the area is secure. Let's get the president out of there."

Matt gave him a firm nod. "We're all set. Let's move. St. Bernard, lead us out."

***

Commander Harris brought his team into a tight circle. "Two groups," he whispered. "Alpha takes the primary entrance. Bravo hits the side. Stagger your approach by thirty seconds. Matt's team needs time to get into position and recon before the assault. Execution in fifteen. Ready, mark."

Harris's team advanced like shadows, gliding through the underbrush. A guard near the vehicle didn't even get the chance to flinch before Spade's blade slid between his ribs, the operator lowering him silently to the ground. Another barely turned his head before a suppressor's whisper ended him.

Silencers coughed softly in the night as the shots dropped the remaining sentries. The shots were clean, and efficient. Harris caught Spade signaling back with sharp hand gestures indicating the sentries were down. Within moments, the rest of the perimeter was clear. The bodies were swallowed by the undergrowth.

"Alpha team, in position. Side door," Chief Silva whispered.

The team moved up, placing two breaching charges on the massive sliding doors. Their timing was perfect, ten seconds to execution.

"Bravo team, in position. Main door," came Spade's voice.

"Three... two..."

***

St. Bernard led the team through the undergrowth, moving along a narrow game trail toward the smaller of the two buildings. The damp air carried the scent of rain-soaked earth and decaying leaves, a reminder of the recent storm.

They stacked at the door, weapons ready. St. Bernard crouched, lifting his infrared scanner. A faint red glow reflected off the window edges as he swept for movement.

"No heat signatures in the first room," he whispered.

Matt gave a nod. April readied her lockpicks as the first option. Skip had an explosive charge as a last resort.

St. Bernard reached for the handle. It moved too easily.

He froze. Cracking the door open an inch, he pulled a small flashlight from his vest and ran the beam along the inside handle, the molding, then the frame.

"This is too easy..." St. Bernard murmured.

Matt exhaled, his gut tightening. "Yeah. I expected it to be locked."

St. Bernard handed the scanner to Skip, who kept sweeping the building for heat signatures.

"All clear," Skip confirmed.

St. Bernard pulled out a length of parachute cord, tied it to the door handle, and motioned for the team to back up.

Matt checked the time. Sixty seconds left. St. Bernard raised a fist, signaling them to hold. No movement. No sound except the wind shifting the treetops.

When the timer hit zero, St. Bernard yanked the parachute cord, and the door swung open.

Silence.

Then, a thunderous explosion from the main warehouse echoed through the night.

So much for the element of surprise.

"Okay, let's go. Heads on a swivel," Matt ordered. His gut told him this building was a dead end. The real action was with Harris's team, but splitting forces had been the right call.

***

The explosion blew the heavy doors of the main warehouse inward with a metallic screech. The concussion sent dust and shrapnel into the air. Harris pushed forward before the echoes died. Weapon up, eyes scanning. The concussive force hit his chest, rattling overhead beams and swaying loose chains in the rafters. Acrid smoke curled through the entrance.

The mission was clear: move fast, clear threats, and secure the objective. He and Spade McGraw peeled right, sweeping through the shadows along the stacked crates.

Three guards were too slow. The first blinked, fumbling with his rifle. The snap of Spade's suppressed shot cut through the haze. One down. As the second one turned to look at the first guard falling to the ground, Harris's rounds hit him center mass. Then he took one to his head. The third spun to run, but a burst of gunfire from the left shredded him mid-step. No wasted movement. Only the whisper of suppressed gunfire and the dull thud of bodies hitting the floor.

A secondary explosion rocked the side door. Chief Silva's element flowed in, sweeping an adjoining room before folding into position with the rest of the unit. The warehouse belonged to them now.

But Harris knew better than to assume it was over. His focus snapped to the massive sliding door with a heavy steel frame at the far wall.

"Looks reinforced," McGraw muttered, motioning toward the overhead track. "They use this regularly."

Harris signaled a halt. If the hostage was inside, there was no telling what waited beyond that door. His team spread out, covering angles, rifles locked on the entrance.

The steel door jerked open.

Four figures rushed through, rifles firing wild, muzzle flashes strobing through the dark. Harris squeezed the trigger. One shot, first man down. McGraw fired twice. Panic showed in the target's eyes as he crumpled. Silva's suppressed round dropped the third mid-step.

The last man charged. Rounds from three directions hit him. He twisted, staggered, then collapsed.

Then, silence, with thick with the acrid stench of gunpowder in the air. Spent casings littered the concrete floor. Bodies were sprawled motionless in the dust. Harris held the grip on his rifle, eyes locked on the open doorway at the far end of the room.

****

After pulling open the door with the parachute cord, Matt, St. Bernard, Skip, and April stalked into the secondary building. Matt and April went left. St. Bernard and Skip went right. The main office was lit by a dim light over in the corner. The faint hum of a fan over by the dim light was the only sound.

Just after they entered the room, a figure stepped out of the doorway on their right side.

Surprise flashed across the man's face before he spun and bolted through another exit to his right. "That's Lebedev!" Matt's voice cut through the silence. "On me, let's go!"

April followed close behind Matt as he sprinted toward the door Lebedev had vanished through. They were halfway there when another door, where Matt had first spotted Lebedev, burst open. A six-man team of armed operators stormed in, weapons up.

Gunfire erupted as they entered, rounds ripping through the air toward April and Matt.

"Down!" Matt barked, diving for cover behind a steel cabinet. April followed him to the cover of the cabinet.

St. Bernard and Skip flanked right. St. Bernard fired two quick shots, dropping the lead operative, then pivoted and took out the second, while Skip started at the rear of the line and worked his way forward, taking down four in total. The whole firefight was over in less than ten seconds.

As the last echoes of gunfire faded, a sharp, desperate scream cut through the room from somewhere beyond the door the attackers had come through.

"That's got to be the president!" Matt shouted.

April turned toward him. He caught her intense look.

"I'm going after Lebedev."

"Negative," Matt snapped, eyes locked on the opened armored door. "Our objective is the president."

April shook her head. "I'm stopping Lebedev."

She sprinted through the exit Lebedev had used, disappearing without a glance back.

Matt watched her go. Dammit. She knew better. Breaking formation now risked everything. Team integrity, timing, the extraction, and rescuing the president.

He felt a pulse of frustration, and something else he didn't want to name.

A firm hand clamped down on his shoulder. St. Bernard. "We've got a mission, boss."

Matt exhaled. "Right."

He turned toward the scream. "Skip, cover the rear. Let's move."

***

Matt led the team to the stairwell and descended into the basement. The air was thick with the scent of damp cement and mold. Every one of his senses was heightened. He was focused, in his element, leading from the front, exactly where he should be. St. Bernard and Skip trailed closely behind him.

As Matt rounded a tight corner, a lone operative launched at him with brutal speed. The man hit Matt like a linebacker, driving his shoulder into Matt's chest. A glint of steel flashed in the operative's hand. Matt brushed the blade to the side with a swift block, but the momentum of the charge forced Matt against the concrete wall, and Matt lost his grip on his rifle.

The attacker roared as he swung the blade in a vicious arc toward Matt's torso. Matt twisted away. The knife's edge grazed his right shoulder. Blood oozed from the cut through his shirt. There was no time to register the pain. Another swing came at Matt, this time aimed low.

Matt lunged forward, grabbing the man's knife hand and wrenching it upward. With a burst of strength, he slammed the man into the wall. The operative's face hit the rough cement.

With his right hand, Matt reached for the sidearm at his hip. His fingers wrapped around the familiar grip, and with one fluid movement, he pulled the Glock 19 from its holster and pressed the barrel under the operative's right armpit. He fired three rapid shots. The man shuddered, then went slack. Matt released him, and the body crumpled like a puppet collapsing as if the strings holding him up had been sliced away.

Matt stepped back as his eyes scanned for the next threat. He heard the faint scuffle of boots on concrete from behind the door. A split second later, the door flew open.

"Contact, door!" Matt shouted, but St. Bernard and Skip were already moving.

The second guard rushed through the door with his weapon raised. St. Bernard sidestepped, bringing his carbine to his shoulder in one fluid motion. Three sharp pops echoed through the corridor as he fired a tight burst. The guard's head snapped back. Blood misted in the air as he crumpled to the floor.

"Clear," St. Bernard said coolly. Skip stepped forward to cover the doorway.

Matt flexed his fingers around his weapon. Blood dripped off his right hand onto the floor. He took a deep breath.

He glanced at St. Bernard, who nodded. Matt then tapped Skip's shoulder, who was in front of them. Without another word, they pressed towards the sound of the president's faint whimpering.

They advanced down the hallway in a tight formation, muzzles sweeping each corner. The basement was dimly lit, a maze of narrow corridors and cluttered storage rooms. Dust hung in the air. Every door they passed was a potential ambush.

As they moved, two cleared each room while the third covered the hall. The rhythm was steady. Check, clear, move. Each step building tension as they moved down the hall.

At the final door, they paused.

Inside, they saw her.

The president of Taiwan sat slumped in a metal chair, her hands bound behind her back. Her hair was matted, face bruised, clothes torn, but she was alive.

Standing behind her was Officer Wei, the head of her security detail. He gripped her shoulder with one hand, a pistol pressed to her temple with the other.

Matt took a single step into the doorway. He pointed his weapon at Wei.

"Drop it!" he shouted in Mandarin.

Wei's hand shook, his eyes darting between Matt and his men. "I swear, I'll kill her," Wei replied in Mandarin.

"You kill her, and you're dead. You let her go, I can guarantee you that you will not die tonight."

Wei stared at the three men with weapons pointed at him.

"Drop it or die," Matt said.

Wei's weapon clattered to the floor. St. Bernard surged forward, restraining Wei while Skip moved in to untie the president.

***

After their initial encounters, Harris and his team met minimal resistance. The smell of gunpowder still hung in the air. An eerie silence filled the room as his team searched the bodies of the downed operatives. Two of his men combed the building for computers or intelligence.

Harris keyed his comms. "Scales, all clear here. No joy, I repeat, no joy."

Matt's voice crackled through his earpiece. "Copy that. We have the president. She's alive. Start planning for extraction. We also need medics on standby."

Harris acknowledged the order and turned back to his team, already moving to secure their exit.

Meanwhile, across the warehouse, Matt scanned the room, ensuring everything was under control. Only then did he allow himself to think about April. She was chasing Lebedev, alone.

Chapter 28

Day 96 - Yangmingshan National Forest, Taiwan

Lebedev's footsteps echoed off the concrete walls as he sprinted through the dusky basement. He was gasping for air, his heart pounding in his chest. He heard the relentless steps behind him. Someone was closing in, and fast. He glimpsed down the tunnel up ahead, barely visible in the dull light. Freedom was within reach.

As he approached the tunnel's entrance and looked into the darkness, he hesitated. It seemed like the tunnel dared him to enter. Memories of suffocating spaces penetrated his thoughts. Anxiety was coursing through his body. He imagined the tunnel closing in on him. He could smell the stale air. The very thought of going any further made his pulse spike.

A footfall close behind jolted him back to the present. He turned. His pursuer came into view. It was the woman, and she was alone. A small, wicked grin tugged at his lips. He could still escape, but first, he'd take care of this persistent mosquito that refused to leave him alone.

***

April's heart pounded as she sprinted down the dark hallway. She kept her breath deep and controlled. The dim lights cast jagged shadows along the damp concrete walls. The air was thick with the scent of metal and mildew.

She was gaining on him. His silhouette shifted in and out of the darkness ahead.

She pushed, tapping into the rhythm that had propelled her through six-minute miles along the Santa Barbara coast. He wasn't getting away.

He paused at the mouth of a tunnel. Under the light of a murky bulb, she got her first clear look at him. His massive figure dominated the hallway. He turned around, no longer just fleeing, but evaluating the situation. Making a choice.

April skidded to a stop, pulling out her Sig Sauer 226. She gripped the pistol firmly, her index finger hovering near the trigger. His face remained in the shadows.

"Not so fast," she barked.

Lebedev's voice was low, mocking. "I'm unarmed. You Americans don't shoot unarmed people."

Her grip tightened. Her finger brushed the trigger.

He's a killer. He deserves a bullet.

His hands weren't raised. Were they empty? Or just hidden in the dark?

Years of law enforcement training pressed against her instinct to pull the trigger. Lethal force only if necessary.

She hesitated.

He moved.

Fast.

A shift in the shadows, a blur of motion, then he was on her.

She dodged his first strike, deflecting his forearm with a brush block. The impact sent her stumbling. The second punch came blind from the darkness. She barely saw it before it crashed into her raised arm, sending a numbing jolt up to her shoulder.

Her pistol hit the ground.

His fists hammered toward her midsection with quick, brutal strikes. Her vest absorbed most of it, but the force still stunned her. The low light made it hard to track him. Another punch came from the side. She barely got her arm up in time.

He was faster than he looked. And stronger.

She pivoted, dodging his attempt to pin her. A quick step left. Then she struck, driving her knee into his side, following with a sharp kick to his ribs.

He grunted, stumbling back.

Then he grabbed her left arm.

The pressure was instant, crushing. A viselike twist caused pain to shoot through her shoulder. She couldn't see his expression, just the outline of his massive form.

She wrenched free and drove an elbow into his ribs, then another elbow into his head.

Most men would have dropped.

But Lebedev didn't.

He came back swinging.

A fist smashed into her ribs. Pain exploded through her side, stealing her breath.

Breathe.

She barely stayed on her feet. *Don't stop.*

She lunged, sweeping his legs. He stumbled but didn't fall.

They circled each other, both breathing hard, both waiting.

Then without warning he lunged forward and shoved her backward.

April stumbled as she spun sideways. Her arms flailed in front of her. She barely caught herself. She turned back towards him and braced for the next attack.

But it didn't come.

Instead, he turned and bolted into the darkness.

She took off after him. The hallway narrowed into shadows. She was closing in, her eyes adjusting to the dim light, tracking his movements.

Then came a hesitation in his stride. A shift in weight.

The ground gave way under her feet. She felt herself falling. She hit the bottom hard. Her fingers clawed at the rough concrete, trying to pull herself up.

Her left knee screamed out in pain. White-hot. Blinding. Her right shoulder followed close behind.

***

Lebedev heard the scream. The sound reverberated through the tunnels, sharp and gratifying. Initially, he kept running. He was well aware of the trap's location. Earlier, when he had inspected the basement, he took note of the three X's etched into the wall. A sign from his team who had set the trap. He'd jumped over it. After a few more strides, he skidded to a stop.

A slow grin spread across his face.

She was down.

He turned back, taking his time, dragging his boots along the concrete so she would hear him coming. *Let her sit in the moment. Let her feel it.*

When he reached the pit's edge, he saw her struggling.

The woman lay twisted at an awkward angle. Her left knee was jammed deep into the hole. Her right arm sagged uselessly.

She reached toward her left side.

A backup gun?

Lebedev drove his boot into her shoulder.

A metallic clatter echoed from the depths of the pit.

He chuckled. "Oh, that's unfortunate."

Her breath came in ragged gasps. She pressed a hand against the ground, pushing herself up.

Still fighting. He admired that.

Lebedev stepped closer, drawing his OTs-23 Drotik from his holster.

He raised it slowly, letting the moment stretch.

Then he leveled it at her head.

"End of the line," he murmured.

The woman stared down the barrel.

Then she took a breath.

***

Matt ran harder.

April's scream had been raw.

Wounded. Dying!

Matt didn't think. He just moved. His boots slammed against the concrete, his lungs burning, his gun raised as he ran.

Then, April on the ground. Lebedev standing over her, gun aimed.

Matt took it all in. Position. Angles. Risk.

He fired.

Three rapid shots punched through the air. Lebedev jerked back, a single wild shot coming from his gun, missing April by inches. His left hand clutched his shoulder, blood darkening his sleeve.

His eyes snapped to Matt.

"Scales," he spat.

***

April had always wondered if she would hear the gunshot that killed her.

But she had heard four.

How was that possible?

The world felt off-balance. Her ears rang. The cold concrete pressed into her back, anchoring her to the moment.

She turned her head, every movement sending a bolt of pain down through her body.

Matt was running toward her.

She knew that look. Unmistakable anger. But beneath the anger, she saw fear.

She had never seen Matt afraid before.

"April," he said, his voice cracking. He dropped beside her, scanning the blood and torn gear. "Talk to me."

She forced her eyes open. "He's getting away."

Matt hesitated, rage and panic on his face. "I'm not leaving you like this."

"Get him," she gasped.

Matt just stared at her.

She swallowed against the pain and glared at him. "Go."

He hesitated. Just for a second.

Then he sprang to his feet.

April slumped back, exhaling.

She listened to the fading rhythm of his boots against the concrete. The sound stretched longer than she expected. Or time had just slowed.

Pain pulsed in waves, radiating from her shoulder, curling through her ribs, down her left knee. The pain meant she was still alive.

Fighting it took too much energy. She let it settle in.

The room felt incredibly still. She closed her eyes and focused on her breathing, steadying herself, waiting for help.

However long it took.

***

Lebedev stumbled as he ran deeper into the tunnel. His right hand clutched his wounded left shoulder. Each step sent a jolt of pain through his body, and the tunnel walls seemed to press closer. The stale air grew thicker, His throat burned, and he could feel the dust as it entered his nostrils.

His flashlight cast jagged shadows against otherwise absolute darkness. His boots scraped against loose gravel on the uneven floor. He slipped, falling down on the slick patches of mud. The air smelled of rust and decay and the faint metallic tang of old water. Every sound seemed amplified. The scuff of his boots. The ragged wheeze of his breath. The echo of footsteps behind him.

The space around him got smaller with every step. His chest tightened. His breathing quickened. He stumbled, falling to one knee. Sweat dripped into his eyes. He forced himself upright and put his hand against the rough wall. He pointed his flashlight down the tunnel. The tunnel stretched endlessly ahead as his light faded into darkness. The walls closed in like a predator ready to pounce.

Behind him, the sound of Scales's pursuit grew louder. Lebedev paused. He could keep running, but the panic inside him was already clouding his judgment. The footsteps grew louder as they echoed off the walls. He forced himself to breathe. *I can survive the tunnel. I've survived worse.* But he could feel the claustrophobia creeping in, sharpening every fear and dulling every instinct.

If he failed here, everything would unravel. Russia's plans, Beijing's trust. His redemption. Scales would chase him to the end of the earth. And in this tunnel, Lebedev knew he'd already lost the advantage.

He steadied himself with his hand on the cold wall, then turned towards Scales. *Time to fight. I'll face him on my terms.*

***

Matt had a hard time differentiating between the sound of his pounding heart and his boots hitting the concrete. Occasionally, he heard Lebedev in front of him. In the close confines of the tunnel, it was hard to determine exactly how far ahead Lebedev had gotten.

The walls narrowed.

Matt slung the MPX behind him and let it hang across his back. Too tight in here.

The pistol would give him control, speed, and clean angles in the dark.

He drew his Glock 19 with his right hand. The grip felt like shaking hands with an old friend.

He kept one hand on the wall to guide his path, his fingertips skimming across the rough concrete surface while he kept the Glock raised in front of him. As the darkness grew, he forced himself to creep forward. He didn't use his light. No sense in broadcasting his position. He concentrated on the sound of Lebedev's footsteps. The walls glistened with moisture, and the uneven floor kept him on edge. Every step felt deliberate, every sound exaggerated by the echoing space.

Then silence. Lebedev had stopped.

Matt heard a loud guttural groan of frustration coming from thirty feet in front of him. He slowed, creeping forward.

Then he spotted Lebedev's silhouetted figure. He turned on the flashlight mounted under the barrel of the Glock.

"You're cornered," Matt called out, his voice reverberating off the walls.

Lebedev coughed and straightened. He held his weapon at his side in his right hand, pointed at the ground. Blood soaked the left sleeve of his shirt. His chest heaved as he met Matt's gaze with a mocking grin.

"Scales. We finally meet." Lebedev's voice was sharp, but the exhaustion bled through. He stepped forward into the beam of Matt's flashlight.

Matt advanced another step. "It's over. Drop the weapon."

Lebedev glared at Matt. "You and I, Scales, we're not so different. In fact, we're the same. Both patriots, fighting for our countries and what we believe. You kill me now, and nothing changes. The war continues, with or without me."

Matt's grip tightened on his weapon. He had thought about this moment for a long time. The thought of putting a bullet in Lebedev's head to exact revenge for the death of Jimmy Dugan.

But something in Lebedev's words gave Matt pause. For a split second, he hesitated. His pistol lowered a fraction of an inch.

Matt saw the shift in Lebedev's eyes, resignation hardening into determination.

Lebedev's gun started to rise.

Matt fired.

The rounds slammed into Lebedev's chest, driving him backward. He hit the wall with a groan. His gun slipped from his fingers and clattered to the ground. His body slid downward, leaving a smear of blood on the concrete.

Matt lowered his weapon. He edged closer, watching the life drain from Lebedev's eyes.

Lebedev coughed, blood bubbling at his lips. He slumped against the wall. His voice was hoarse but smug.

"You think this ends with me, Scales? You don't even know what this really is. Taiwan was just the first move. Africa, the Arctic, South America, they're already in play. This is just the beginning..."

Matt raised his gun and pointed it at Lebedev. For a fraction of a second, he saw One- Shot's smiling face. Then he saw blood oozing out the back of One-Shot's head, spreading across the floor.

He fired. One shot. Right between the eyes.

You don't get to walk away from what you did.

The silence that followed was deeper than before. Like the air had been holding its breath.

He stood there a second longer, then holstered the weapon and turned.

He felt no emotion. But he did feel closure.

I guess Skip was right.

***

Matt snapped back into focus. April.

He turned and ran.

By the time he reached her, St. Bernard and Skip had already pulled her from the hole. They'd splinted her left leg. Put her right arm in a sling and wrapped a pressure bandage around a long laceration on her left bicep. Blood seeped through the gauze.

"She okay?" Matt asked.

"Nothing life-threatening," Skip said. "She's tough as hell. I offered her morphine to take the edge off. She said no, but I gave it to her anyway."

Matt glanced at April. Her eyes were heavy, her breathing steadier. The morphine had done its job.

"What's the status?"

"Building's clear," St. Bernard said. "We found a cache of computers and documents in what looked like the main office. Harris's team ran into minimal resistance. There were no casualties. The warehouse looks like they were prepping it as a staging area."

Matt looked over at April.

"Let's get her topside and get the hell out of here," he said.

By the time they got April outside, Harris's team had secured vehicles for the trip back to the cyber command center.

***

Once they got to the cyber command center, they turned April over to the medics. The teams then gathered to perform a quick debrief.

After the debrief, Matt went to the medical clinic to check on April. She was sleeping under heavy sedation.

Her doctor walked in and stood behind him.

"She's banged up, but she's tough. The biggest issue is her knee. She's got a third-degree MCL tear. That means the inside ligament of her knee is completely torn, leaving no structural support. The joint is unstable, swollen like hell, and she won't be able to put full weight on it for a while. She'll need a hinged brace, and at least six to eight weeks of rehab. Walking will be slow and painful. Stairs will be damn near impossible for a while.

"She also dislocated her shoulder. Looks like she put it back in herself before she got here. That takes grit. It's going to be sore for a few weeks, but nothing's torn. Compared to the knee, it's the lesser of two evils."

The doctor turned and walked out, leaving Matt in the room alone with April.

He stayed at the head of April's bed, watching the slow rise and fall of her chest. She was breathing. That was enough, for now.

Back on that first mission, he'd thought he was shielding her by holding back intel, protecting the team, and protecting her. But she'd saved his life without hesitation. Moved under fire. Held the line.

He owed her. But he couldn't decide whether he owed her an explanation, an apology, or just a quiet acknowledgment of the debt.

He could leave a note. Could try to explain.

But no words would've matched what she'd done, or what she had come to mean to him now.

There would be time later. Right now, the mission wasn't over.

Matt turned away from the bedside and walked out.

Chapter 29

Day 97 - Taipei, Taiwan

The operations room of the cybersecurity headquarters hummed with low voices and the soft whine of aging air conditioners as a subtitled Taiwanese news broadcast flashed in the corner.

A real-time map of Taiwan showed red markers blinking out one by one and being replaced by green markers as critical infrastructure roared back to life. Power grids surged back online, and air traffic control announced they were ready to handle incoming and outgoing flights. Emergency responders, still cut off from each other, could now communicate, coordinating efforts across the island.

"We're making headway against the virus," Chin said, pointing to the nearest monitor. The display scrolled with data from the electrical grid, water systems, and transportation infrastructure. More indicators were green than red. He could feel the tide shifting.

He glanced at another data stream feeding in from across the Pacific.

"Early reports from the US show the antivirus is taking hold there too. Several major sectors have already stabilized."

Then, the monitor running the *Global Television Network* caught his attention. The image sharpened, revealing a stark, government-branded backdrop. The room quieted as a spokesperson, stiff and expressionless, took his place behind a podium.

"The People's Republic of China has successfully concluded its scheduled military exercises and training operations in the strait between the mainland and the islands. Having achieved all strategic objectives, our forces will now return to their homeland with the honor of a successful operation."

Ming Ho, stood up near the back of the room. "That's their English-language channel. They're speaking directly to the United States."

The screen cut to black. The tension in the room held for a second longer, then Skip broke it with a chuckle.

"When you're getting your butt kicked, you just put on a brave face and pretend it was your plan all along."

Chin allowed himself to smile a brief smile.

He scanned the room. The celebration was rising in volume, and the was tension slowly bleeding away. For now, that was enough.

He saw Matt looking at him and smiling, almost with a sense of pride.

Chin nodded slightly, acknowledging the look. Then he turned back to the monitors. Almost all of them were green,

He stepped back from the console and removed his glasses, rubbing the bridge of his nose. The grid was holding. The antivirus had worked. Taiwan had held.

For the first time in days, he allowed himself to exhale. Not with triumph, but with a quiet sense of relief.

Chapter 30

Day 100 - Taipei, Taiwan - Presidential Office Building

It had been three days since China announced its withdrawal from the Taiwanese strait. The morning sun cast a golden light across the courtyard of the Presidential Office Building in Taipei. A soft breeze stirred the blooming jasmine lining the garden walls. The scent mingled with the faint aroma of oolong tea drifting from somewhere nearby. In the distance, the low hum of scooters signaled the city was coming back to life.

Inside, a television in the main conference room replayed a speech from the night before. The monitor showed President Fang walking past a military honor guard. She spoke in a resolute tone in Mandarin, subtitled in English. "The attempt to silence Taiwan has failed. We are still here."

Outside on a shaded veranda, Chin stood with Matt, Uncle Ming, and President Fang. For the first time in days, there was no urgency, only stillness occasionally interrupted by the soft rustle of leaves.

President Fang turned to Chin. "You've done more for Taiwan than anyone could've asked. I'm proud of you as your president, and I'm even more as your aunt. You've brought great honor to our family."

Chin dipped his head, hiding a small grin.

"I understand you're considering staying?" President Fang continued.

Chin looked back at his aunt and uncle. "There's a lot to do here, and I want to be part of it. This feels like home. I can make a real difference."

Uncle Ming looked at Chin. "Then you're exactly where you need to be."

"We're proud of you, Chin," Matt chipped in. "You earned this. Every bit of it."

He clapped a hand on Chin's shoulder, then added with a wry smile, "Just one question. Who's going to keep an eye on my investments now that you are thirteen time zones away from Wall Street?"

Chin chuckled, shaking his head. "Still worried about that, huh? I'll make it work. But if I make you rich, and you're sipping coffee on a beach somewhere..."

"You'll know where to find me."

For the first time in years, Chin laughed freely and deeply with sincerity. Not out of obligation, not out of politeness. Just happiness.

For so long, he'd carried the weight alone. But here, in this place, among these people, he had found something else. Connection. Trust. Family.

Chapter 31

Day 102 – Taipei, Taiwan

The cyber command center was quiet. Most of the staff had taken a much-deserved break in the other wing. Matt sat alone at an empty desk, the quiet humming of screens filling the stillness.

Matt's tablet buzzed. A new message popped up on screen. An email from Decker.

Matt, you were right. They didn't fire me. But exile comes in many forms. I'm headed to Montana. Still in the fight.

Matt let out a slow breath. He stared at the message for a moment, then archived it.

He went to the next message as a blinking notification caught his eye.

Level III - Sentinel Asset Follow-Up

The first image showed an Asian male in a black windbreaker entering the international terminal at LAX. Rolling suitcase. Face turned just enough to be recognizable: Cho Jianshu. The same man from the Paso Robles traffic stop. The one Mr. Ho had seen in the store.

The second file showed him moving through TSA security. Passport name: Eric Zhao. Real identity: Unk. Mid-level MSS operative, People's Republic of China.

Matt scrolled to the bottom. A note from Reiner.

Showed picture to Mr. Ho. Confirmed ID. Zhao left the US within two hours of China's withdrawal.

Matt tapped the screen to archive the message, then closed the tablet.

This mission was over.

***

Somewhere deep in the Zhongnanhai compound, China's central seat of power, hidden behind government walls and secrecy, Chen Da sat across from a senior party official in a quiet, sparsely lit room. Between them, a Go board stretched across a lacquered table, a slow and deliberate game already in motion.

Rain tapped gently against the windows as Chen placed a white stone along the edge.

"You always favor the slow encirclement," the older man said, setting down his tea.

"Because that's how you win," Chen replied. "The middle of the board is where the bold go to die. The corners decide the outcome."

The official raised an eyebrow. "And the island?"

Chen's lips barely moved. "One stone. Necessary, but not the prize."

His opponent placed a black stone near the center, sacrificing a small group to gain shape elsewhere.

"And what is the prize?"

"Control," Chen said. "Of supply chains. Of data streams. Of how the world moves and remembers. The island province was just a distraction."

He motioned toward a quiet grouping of white stones near the bottom edge. "These looked like nothing ten moves ago. Now they anchor the entire board."

The other man studied the pattern and nodded. "And the Americans?"

Chen smiled faintly. "They still think it's a game of battles. But battles are noise. Strategy is the game."

His gaze drifted to the edge of the board, where a single white stone rested alone. "We've just placed our first stone in the Arctic."

Chapter 32

Three Weeks Later, Santa Barbara, CA

The first light touched the edge of the horizon, soft, low, and gold. The sea was still, just rippling. A flight of gulls soared overhead, but the city hadn't woken yet. Santa Barbara was silent. Just the way Matt liked it.

It had been three weeks since the last Chinese ships pulled back from Taiwanese waters. Long enough for the media storm to die down. Not long enough for everything to feel normal.

He sat on the fourth bench at the breakwater, leaning back with coffee cooling in his hands. Same bench where he'd first seen Lebedev all those weeks ago.

The mission was over. The threat stopped. At least for now.

He'd seen April once in Taiwan, unconscious and bruised, pale under the meds.

He didn't stay long. Just long enough to realize he wasn't ready to say what he needed to.

She'd been medevacked out under her former military status. Dave Johnson had pulled some strings and transferred her to Balboa Naval Hospital while Matt was still buried shutting down the virus and wrapping up the mission.

He'd driven past Balboa Hospital more than once. Sat across the street one morning, looking at the fourth-floor window of her room.

He told himself he wasn't ready. Not to feel the guilt surge back in. Not after everything.

The truth was simpler: he still didn't know what to say.

Limping footsteps approached behind him.

'Do you know what time it is?"

Matt heard the voice and didn't have to turn. He took a breath before saying, "It's the best time of the day."

April sat beside him, careful with her left leg, still in a brace. She handed him a fresh cup of coffee.

They watched the harbor. The water shifted around them like the fog often did at this hour. But today, the mountains were clear and sharp, picture-perfect.

After a moment, she spoke again, her voice softer. "I know you came in Taiwan. I was out cold, but I remember hearing your voice when I woke up."

She hesitated. "But after... at Balboa... I kept hoping you'd walk in."

Matt glanced at her. "I wanted to. I just didn't know what to say. And I didn't want it to feel like I was just... repaying a debt."

She studied him for a moment. "You think that's what this is?"

"No," he said. "Not anymore."

He looked down at the coffee in his hands. "Thank you. For saving me."

"You saved me," she said. "We're even."

Matt shook his head. "Friends don't keep score."

She gave a small nod. Said nothing.

April glanced down at her coffee. Her fingers tightened around the cup, then relaxed. She stood and stretched. Her silhouette cut across the rising sun.

"I'll see you around, Scales."

He glanced up. "You better."

She paused as her eyes swept the shoreline. Then she looked back at him with a faint smile.

"I'll keep your table warm if you promise to visit between deployments."

Matt didn't answer right away. He just smiled with a slight nod. "You can count on it."

She gave him a look, half challenge, half something softer, then turned and ambled down the breakwater with a slight limp.

He watched her go, the sound of her boots growing fainter with each step. When she disappeared around the bend, he stayed there, letting the silence settle in around him.

The waves rolled in slow and steady, the early light finally warming his face. The harbor was quiet. A flight of pelicans soared overhead in a classic V, then dipped low to skim the surface.

Matt exhaled slowly. He thought about Dugan. About April and what they'd been through. About the rest of the team and everything they'd pulled off. For a brief moment, the tension in his shoulders eased. It wasn't peace, but it was enough to let the world feel still.

His phone buzzed.

Unknown number. One line of text:

The Dragon will return.

He turned and looked west, out across the calm morning waters of the Pacific. Behind him, the sky had brightened, casting long shadows across the breakwater. His own shadow stretched westward, reaching toward the sea, like it was chasing something he couldn't see.

He didn't know who had sent the message.

But he knew what it meant.

It wasn't over. Not even close.

EPILOGUE

Chukchi Sea - Arctic Ocean

A heavy fog blanketed the Chukchi Sea, draping the brutal Arctic waters in an eerie calm. Ten miles offshore, far from any trace of land, the silence was unnatural, almost oppressive. In a place where wind, ice, and ocean usually battled for dominance, the stillness felt like a warning. Not peace. Not calm. Something else.

Now and then, the ice groaned and cracked, sharp and sudden, like bones breaking under unseen weight.

Chester "Saint" Bernard double-checked the seal on his dry suit, then the MK-16 rebreather. Oxygen and inert gas mix, good to 200 feet. He was going to 175.

The twenty-eight-foot Custom Arctic Utility Boat was state-of-the-art. Sonar, tracking, thermal gear. Everything was cutting-edge.

On the bridge, Don "Skip" McCoy studied the sonar screen. DCS techs had traced the data cable break to this spot. They guaranteed that the margin of error was twenty yards.

"Gear's good," said Skip after checking St. Bernard's setup. Double-check. Always double-check. Skip's breath hung in the air. "Let's get you down there, see what we're dealing with."

Five minutes later, St. Bernard slipped into the blackness of the Artic Ocean. Cold pressed in immediately. But as a former SEAL, he barely felt it.

He descended fast, equalizing pressure every few meters. At 160 feet, the cable came into view. Algae clung to the casing. His light cut through the dark, revealing the damage. A clean, surgical cut.

"Looks deliberate," he said into his comms. "Thermal cutter."

"Who the hell slices an Arctic cable and expects no one to come looking?" Skip's voice crackled back.

St. Bernard swam closer, brushing his glove along the exposed edge. Whoever did this knew exactly what they were doing.

"Get pictures and get topside," Skip instructed. "Radar just pinged a contact coming from the north. Heading straight for us. ETA forty minutes."

St. Bernard snapped photos, grabbed a section of the severed cable, and began his ascent.

He checked the time. Ten minutes on the bottom, twenty-five to surface safely, if he didn't screw up. That meant no margin. Not for a second.

He started up, slow and steady, pausing just long enough at each stop to keep his blood from bubbling like soda. At twenty feet, he switched to pure O2, buying back seconds he didn't have.

Twenty-five minutes after he'd left the cut cable, he climbed onto the boat. The Arctic air slapped him in his face as he pulled off his mask.

He handed the sample to Skip in a sealed bag. "Yep, you're right. Thermal cutter. High-grade," said Skip. "But who?"

St. Bernard turned north towards the mist. "Russia. China. Iran. Take your pick. The real question is, why here? And why now?"

The radar painted a steady track. A vessel heading their way. Straight line. No drift. No hesitation.

This wasn't sabotage. It was preparation.

St. Bernard exhaled. His breath hung in the air, thin and ghostlike.

He shoved the throttle forward. The twin engines roared to life and the boat surged into the Arctic chop. Ice-laced wind clawed at his face. But his eyes stayed fixed ahead as they gazed into the gray void beyond the mist.

Were they outrunning danger?

Or racing straight into it?

GLOSSARY OF ACRONYMS

AI: Artificial Intelligence – The simulation of human intelligence in machines that are programmed to think, learn, and make decisions.

ALPHA 42 : A fictional elite operational team in *Bear in the Dragon's Shadow*, composed of highly trained specialists conducting classified missions.

ATF: Bureau of Alcohol, Tobacco, Firearms and Explosives. A federal law enforcement agency under the U.S. Department of Justice responsible for investigating and preventing offenses involving firearms, explosives, arson, alcohol, and tobacco, as well as regulating the firearms and explosives industries.

Black Squadron: An ultrasecret unit believed to operate within or alongside DEVGRU, specializing in deniable recon missions requiring total blackout protocols and deep-cover operations.

CIA: Central Intelligence Agency: A civilian foreign intelligence service of the US government, tasked with gathering, processing, and analyzing national security information from around the world.

CONUS: Continental United States. The forty-eight contiguous states, plus Washington, DC, and excluding Alaska and Hawaii.

CPO: Chief Petty Officer: A senior non-commissioned officer rank in the US Navy and Coast Guard, responsible for leading enlisted personnel, providing technical expertise, and serving as a critical link between the enlisted ranks and commissioned officers.

DCS: Defense Clandestine Services. A branch of the US Defense Intelligence Agency (DIA) responsible for human intelligence (HUMINT) collection, often operating overseas in support of military and national security objectives.

DEVGRU: Naval Special Warfare Development Group, also known as SEAL Team Six. An elite US Navy special missions unit specializing in counterterrorism, hostage rescue, and covert operations.

DHS: Department of Homeland Security. A US federal agency responsible for public security, broadly defined to include counterterrorism, border security, immigration, and disaster prevention and management.

DOD: Department of Defense. The executive-branch department responsible for coordinating and supervising all agencies and functions related to the armed forces and national security.

FBI: Federal Bureau of Investigation. The principal federal law enforcement agency in the US, responsible for investigating and enforcing federal laws, including counterterrorism, cybercrime, and espionage.

FISA Warrant: Foreign Intelligence Surveillance Act Warrant. A court order from the Foreign Intelligence Surveillance Court (FISC) that allows the US government to surveil individuals suspected of espionage or terrorism, often in sensitive national security cases.

FLIR: Forward-Looking Infrared. A thermal imaging system that detects heat signatures, often used in military aircraft, drones, and vehicles for surveillance and targeting.

GPS: Global Positioning System. A satellite-based navigation system used for determining a precise location anywhere on Earth.

HALO: High Altitude Low Opening. A military parachuting technique used to insert special forces stealthily behind enemy lines by jumping from high altitude and deploying the parachute at low altitude.

HUMINT: Human Intelligence. Intelligence collected through interpersonal contact, often involving spies, informants, or field agents.

JSOC: Joint Special Operations Command. A component of US Special Operations Command (SOCOM) that oversees elite units such as DEVGRU and Delta Force for highly sensitive and classified operations.

JTF: Joint Task Force. A structure composed of units from two or more branches of the US Armed Forces or other federal agencies organized for a specific mission or operation. JTFs are often formed to respond rapidly to crises and can include elements from allied nations or interagency partners.

LZ: Landing Zone. A designated location for aircraft to land, often used for helicopter insertions or extractions in military operations.

MPX SIG Sauer MPX: A compact, modular submachine gun used by elite units like DEVGRU for close-quarters combat. Chambered in 9mm, the MPX features a short-stroke gas piston system for improved reliability and reduced recoil, and it supports multiple barrel lengths, suppressors, and custom configurations.

NSA: National Security Agency. The US government agency responsible for the global monitoring, collection, and processing of information and data for foreign and domestic intelligence and counterintelligence.

PNNL: Pacific Northwest National Laboratory. A US Department of Energy national lab conducting advanced scientific research in areas including cybersecurity, nuclear technology, and energy infrastructure.

POST: Peace Officers Standards and Training. The state agency in California that certifies peace officers and their required training.

Red Notice: An alert issued by Interpol to locate and provisionally arrest a person pending extradition.

SAC: Special Agent in Charge. The senior FBI official overseeing a field office or major case operation, responsible for all personnel and investigations under their command.

SCIF: Sensitive Compartmented Information Facility. A secure facility used for discussing or handling classified information without risk of surveillance or unauthorized access.

SIG: Short for SIG SAUER, a premier firearms manufacturer renowned for precision engineering and reliability. One of their most iconic models is the P226, a full-sized service pistol known for its balance, accuracy, and durability. Favored by elite military and law enforcement units worldwide.

SIGINT: Signals Intelligence. Intelligence-gathering through the interception of signals, including communications (COMINT) and electronic signals (ELINT).

SPR (Special Purpose Rifle)**:** A highly accurate semiautomatic rifle used by DEVGRU for medium-range precision fire. Typically chambered in 5.56mm and equipped with suppressors and advanced optics.

SITREP: Situation Report. A brief structured update used in military and intelligence operations to convey current conditions, threats, or mission progress.

Sentinel Program: A fictional or classified initiative in *Bear in the Dragon's Shadow* involving surveillance, threat detection, or national security coordination.

Spec Ops: Special Operations. Military operations carried out by specially trained and equipped forces, often involving unconventional tactics in high-risk environments.

The 101: Locals' shorthand for US Highway 101, the main freeway running through Santa Barbara. It hugs the coast, links the city to LA and the Central Coast, and is as much a part of daily life as the beach and the fog.

UAV: Unmanned Aerial Vehicle. An aircraft, also known as a drone, without a human pilot on board, used for reconnaissance, surveillance, or combat missions.

VA: Department of Veterans Affairs. A US federal agency providing healthcare, benefits, and other services to eligible military veterans.

Wagner Group: A Russian paramilitary organization with close ties to the Kremlin, often employed as mercenaries to carry out operations abroad, including in conflict zones where plausible deniability is required.

www.ingramcontent.com/pod-product-compliance
Lightning Source LLC
Chambersburg PA
CBHW050524110726
47899CB00005B/1579